The Winter Family

THE

CLIFFORD
JACKMAN

DOUBLEDAY
New York
London Toronto
Sydney Auckland

Copyright © 2015 by Clifford Jackman

All rights reserved. Published in the United States by Doubleday, a division of Random House LLC, New York, and in Canada by Random House of Canada Limited, Toronto, Penguin Random House companies.

www.doubleday.com

DOUBLEDAY and the portrayal of an anchor with a dolphin are registered trademarks of Random House, Inc.

Library of Congress Cataloging-in-Publication Data
Jackman, Clifford.
The Winter family / Clifford Jackman. — First edition.
        pages cm.
1. Outlaws—Fiction. I. Title.
PR9199.4.J32W56 2015
813'.6—dc23
2014020971

Book design by Maria Carella
Jacket design by Michael J. Windsor
Jacket illustrations © Shutterstock

ISBN 978-0-385-53948-7

MANUFACTURED IN THE UNITED STATES OF AMERICA

10 9 8 7 6 5 4 3 2 1

First Edition

For James Thompson and Joan Jackman,
my literary antecedents.
Death is swallowed up in victory.

Without justice, what are kingdoms but bands of robbers? Indeed, what are bands of robbers, but little kingdoms? Such bands are made of men, ruled by the authority of a prince, knit together by the pact of the confederacy, and share their plunder according to their own law. If a band grows strong enough to take possession of cities and subdue peoples, it will assume the name and form of a kingdom, not because of any reduction of greed, but because of the addition of impunity. And this is why when Alexander asked a pirate upon what authority the pirate took hostile possession of the sea, the pirate answered with bold pride: "The same authority by which you have seized the whole earth; but because I do it with a petty ship, I am called a robber, while you do it with a great fleet and are called an emperor."

SAINT AUGUSTINE

If it were not for the prophetic character, the philosophic and experimental would soon be at the ratio of all things, and stand still unable to do other than repeat the same dull round over again. The same dull round even of a universe would soon become a mill with complicated wheels. Reason, or the ratio of all we have already known, is not the same that it shall be when we know more. He who sees the Infinite in all things sees God. He who sees the Ratio only sees himself only. Therefore God becomes as we are, that we may be as he is.

WILLIAM BLAKE

I tremble for my country when I reflect that God is just.

THOMAS JEFFERSON

CONTENTS

The
Winter Family

Prologue:
Oklahoma 1889

1

High summer night in Oklahoma. Warm winds that smelled of apple blossoms. Now and then a lightning bug winked on and drifted through the air. Quentin Ross caught one in his fist and held it there, with its radiance leaking between his fingers and reflecting in his shallow eyes. For a moment he rolled the lightning bug between his thumb and forefinger, and then he crushed it, smearing himself with its luminescence, and he smiled, wide and empty.

The Winter Family was camped in a stand of blackjack oaks. There was no fire but the moon was up, pushing the stars back into the darkness of the sky. Charlie and Johnny Empire lay on their sides, playing cards and bickering. Fred Johnson wrote in his little book and drank whiskey from a cup not much bigger than a thimble. Quentin wandered from tree to tree, humming to himself, soft and tuneless. The others tried to sleep, tucked between tree roots or curled in bedrolls like pill bugs. All of them, except for Augustus Winter.

He sat astride a pale horse, like Death, leaning back in his heavy saddle and smoking a cigarette in an ivory holder. The suit he wore was well tailored but growing threadbare. His straw-white hair was cropped short and he had an extravagantly waxed mustache. His eyes were very light amber, almost yellow, the eyes of an eagle or a cat. Occasionally he would remove a watch from his pocket and turn it in the pale moonlight, watching as the second hand marched around, and around, and around.

It is often observed that murderers do not look like murderers. No one said that of Augustus Winter.

A little after midnight Winter cocked his head. "They're coming."

"I don't hear anything," Quentin said.

But soon they all did. The sleepers were kicked into wakefulness, the lantern shuttered, weapons drawn, instructions whispered.

O'Shea and two of his hands came around the bend and rode up to the camp. Everyone relaxed. O'Shea pulled up his horse, unstrapped a bag tied to his saddle, and tossed it to Quentin.

"I'd be grateful if you count it now," O'Shea said.

Quentin knelt down, opened the sack, and rifled through the bills quickly. Then he stood, his knees creaking.

"Yes, it's all there, as we agreed."

"Good," O'Shea said and began to wheel his horse around.

"Now just a moment, Mister O'Shea," Quentin called out. "Please, just a moment more." Quentin's voice was very deep, melodious. He spoke slowly, as if he were thinking very carefully, or reciting poetry.

O'Shea turned back to him, reluctantly. Both men were around fifty, but O'Shea was a tall man with a healthy mane of gray hair, while Quentin was small and fine boned.

"We've run into some unexpected expenses . . . ," Quentin began.

"Oh god damn you," O'Shea said.

Quentin continued as if O'Shea had not spoken.

". . . which were not included in the initial estimate of our—"

"Estimate?" O'Shea shouted. "We had a deal, you thieves."

"Yeah," Winter said. He did not speak loudly but all the men fell silent, and the bugs too, and the wind seemed to die down to nothing. "Yeah. Thieves, Mister O'Shea. And worse."

O'Shea looked at Winter and bore his gaze. That was something not every man could do. O'Shea was not like every man. Willpower radiated from him. And he was angry now. He looked at the dirty mob of killers under the trees, white trash and blacks and Mexicans, in their muddy boots and sweat-stiff dusters, thin and poor and dumb as nails. One of them was using baler twine as a rifle strap. He thought: Am I to let these men get the better of me? But then, it was only money.

"How much?" O'Shea asked. Quentin told him. O'Shea nodded and said, "The money will be ready when you get back. I trust that is all." Not a question.

But Quentin said, "Just one more thing, Mister O'Shea! Please! One more thing. A member of our band has taken ill. He needs a doctor. We would be grateful if you could bring him back to town."

"Oh for heaven's sake," O'Shea snapped, but they were already bringing the sick man forward, surprisingly small, wrapped up tightly in a stinking bedroll. O'Shea stood up in his stirrups and looked down. He frowned. The man was an Indian, but his skin had gone gray and seemed thin, as if his bones were likely to poke through at any moment. Greasy foam flecked around his lips and nose and the whites of his eyes were jaundiced, the color of egg yolk.

The little Indian regarded O'Shea with piteous weakness. O'Shea frowned in disgust.

"His name is Bill Bread," Quentin said.

"One of you take him," O'Shea said to his hands.

"Farewell, Mister O'Shea," Quentin called, and tipped his hat. "Take good care of Mister Bread!"

The Winter Family laughed as the hands threw Bill Bread over the neck of one of their sturdy ponies and rode off, holding their noses. They all laughed, except for Augustus Winter, who watched O'Shea's horse in the dim moonlight, until it was lost in the trees.

2

The next morning, Bill Bread was awoken by a strange, high laugh like the call of an asthmatic loon. When he opened his eyes he did not know where he was. A small, clean room with a glass window and wallpaper printed with rocking horses and flowers. The bed was high off the ground and soft.

A crippled boy stood in the doorframe, wearing short pants and suspenders and a shirt with a collar. Large, thick spectacles were strapped to his face with a black cord. When Bill looked at the boy, the boy averted his gaze to the ground, then the window, the foot of the bed, anywhere but Bill.

"Where am I?" Bill tried to say, but his throat was dry.

The boy let out that distinctive laugh again then limped away, leaning on a pair of canes.

"He's awake! Yes! He's awake now. Awake!" the boy said.

Heavy footsteps. A tall man appeared in the door, bald, with shaggy white sideburns.

"Mister Bread, was it?" the man said.

Bill nodded.

"I'm Doctor Simpson. Do you pretend not to know what has made you ill?"

Bill closed his eyes.

"If it is a lecture you fear, let me set your mind at ease. I don't waste them on men like you. I will only urge you to stay away from the Keeley Institute. Their 'gold cure' for drunkenness is fraudulent. You will be dead in six months anyway; in the meantime, stay away from them."

"Six months?"

"If you want to live, you know what to do."

"Yeah," Bill said. "I just don't know how."

"Oh, you know how," the doctor said. "If you'll pardon me for saying so, there is nothing complicated about how to stop pouring whiskey down your throat. You know how, of course you do, but you don't know why. Do you, Mister Bread?" The doctor regarded Bill as if he did not entirely consider the question to be rhetorical, or perhaps simply to admire the effect of his own words. Either way he was disappointed. Bill said nothing.

"Sleep and water," the doctor said. "Mister Bread, good morning."

The doctor tromped out of the room. Bill heard that queer laugh one more time, and then the house was quiet.

He lay still but he could not sleep. Despite the pounding in his head and the terrible painful nausea radiating through his stomach, a strange energy, a lightness, was swimming through his limbs. He swung his feet around and pulled himself out of bed. At first he thought he might be sick, but it passed.

It was darker in the hallway without the dim light from the window. Bill made his way down the corridor, taking small steps and leaning against the wall. The rug felt good on his stocking-clad feet. Small bedrooms lined each side of the corridor; he was in the servants' wing.

When he reached the end of the hall he went down the stairs through the foyer to the parlor, where he sat down in a rocking chair. He rocked back and forth and watched the early morning light come in through the window.

Perhaps it was only light-headedness from the walk down the stairs, or dehydration. Perhaps he was still drunk, but it seemed to him that everything was beautiful here. How long had it been since he had slept in a grand house like this? As a guest? Instead of in dirty hotels, hasty camps, dark sheds. Life on the run, as an outlaw, hunted by the army and the police and, worst of all, the Pinkerton National Detective Agency. Now here he was, in a nice house, with lace on the tables and family portraits on the walls, the smell of furniture polish and warm wood. It was nice. It felt right.

Six months, he thought. It wasn't so long.

3

The Winter Family crouched on the top of a hill about two hundred yards to the west of the Indian camp. They were all low to the ground, their dirty greatcoats pooled around them like skirts, speaking in whispered tones.

A fine mist hung in the morning air. The rising sun was poking through the trees, dimly illuminating the little lean-tos and sheds. One skinny mule paced restlessly back and forth. Otherwise the camp was still.

"They are a ragged bunch, aren't they?" Hugh said, pushing his spectacles higher on the bridge of his nose. "I kind of thought old O'Shea might have been laying it on a bit thick, but they look more like the Sioux or Cheyenne rather than a civilized tribe."

"What do you think, Augustus?" Quentin said. "If we come up on them with knives, we could kill some without awakening the others. Perhaps Charlie and Johnny could—"

"We're not going to do this," Winter said.

Quentin blinked. "Pardon me?"

"We're going to go back to town," Winter said. "And kill them instead."

Johnny Empire laughed, honking, and his brother shushed him. The other men simply stared. It sounded like a joke, but everyone knew Winter never joked.

"Did you lose your damn mind?" Fred Johnson said. He was tall and broad across the shoulders, a fifty-year-old ex-slave with silver streaks running through his dark, curly beard.

"When Quentin asked for more money O'Shea didn't even blink," Winter said. "That means he don't have to go to no bank for it. He's got it in his house somewhere. And that shitsplat of a town don't got any more people in it than that little Indian camp. Why should we kill Indians when we can kill white men for twice the price?"

The men were silent. They tried to think of something to say. None of them had the courage, except for Fred Johnson.

"Winter," Johnson said. "You done lost your goddamn mind. We can't just go kill a whole town full of white folks. It's—"

Winter exhaled, sharply, and his eyes caught fire and turned to gold in the dawn light. Johnson's words all dried up.

"You've come with me this far," Winter said. "You've come all this way, and now you're going to start to tell me there's some things that just ain't done? That what you're telling me, Freddy?"

"They'll hunt us down," Johnson said.

"In case you ain't noticed, they're already hunting us," Winter said. "We got a whole fucking army of Pinkertons combing the woods for us, led by the same son of a whore that killed Dusty and Chris Neville and Manny and the Old Battle Ax. And he's not going to quit till he kills us too."

"You think that's as bad as it can get?" Johnson asked.

At this, Winter smiled, hard and tight.

"You're the one that don't get it, Freddy. This ain't nothing compared to how bad it's gonna get. Ten years ago if the law was on you, why, you'd just run into the woods. There was always more country. Wasn't there, Freddy? You remember that feeling right after the war? Like you could just keep moving forever? Now it's just Oklahoma.

And after the big land run in April, Oklahoma's not even Oklahoma anymore. Nothing but towns and railways and asshole Sooners like O'Shea. We're fucking done. We need to cash out. And this is it. Right now."

Winter stood up. A woman, a girl really, had come out of one of the shanties. She looked up and saw Winter silhouetted against the bruised sky. They looked at each other. She was unafraid.

Winter turned his head and spat.

"Do what you like," he said to them. "I'm going with or without you."

As he always would. But as always, they did not put him to the test.

4

O'Shea's household stirred into activity. First the servants rose. Despite the ambitious size of the servant wing, there appeared to only be two: an elderly black man and his wife. The man sniffed at Bill Bread in his rocking chair, but his wife smiled and asked Bill if he wanted coffee. Bill accepted.

Not much later O'Shea plodded downstairs, coughing and snorting like an angry bull. He went straight out into the fields and Bill could hear him through the windows shouting at his hired hands. After an hour he clomped back inside to the kitchen. The high-pitched laugh of the boy. O'Shea's gruff responses.

Bill held the mug of coffee in his thin fingers. He could not drink it—even the smell of it made him sick—but he liked its warmth. By now, Bill thought, the little Indian village had been wiped out. The Family would be miles away. Perhaps they were drinking; perhaps they were sleeping it off. Tonight he would ride to the rendezvous point with O'Shea or his men. Bill wouldn't receive a share of the night's profits, but they wouldn't leave him behind. Of that much he was sure. For now he could enjoy this interlude of domesticity.

One of the hired hands came in the front door, went into the kitchen, and spoke to O'Shea. Bill did not hear what the hand said, but he heard O'Shea's reply.

"What do you meant it's been cut? Where?"

The hand spoke.

"Well, those telegrams need to go out today. Someone will have to carry them to a different telegraph office."

Bill dropped his mug of coffee on the carpet. He felt like his entire body had turned into glass. Hard, inflexible, transparent. And as if the room around him was not real, but instead a painting or photograph. The moment stretched on, and to his surprise, he found that he knew exactly what he had to do.

Both O'Shea and the boy were having porridge. The boy was not eating much, just stirring it with his spoon and laughing and staring at his feet. But then he looked up abruptly and fixed his eyes on something behind O'Shea. O'Shea turned in his chair. Bill Bread stood in the doorway.

"If you're hungry—" O'Shea began.

"They're coming," Bill said.

"I'm sorry?"

Bill's eyes were almost orange with jaundice and broken blood vessels.

"They're coming," Bill said. "That's why they cut the telegraph line."

It only took O'Shea a moment to understand.

"Coming to attack us?" O'Shea said.

"Yes sir," Bill said.

"Was that your plan?" O'Shea asked.

"No, it wasn't the plan," Bill said. "But I've been with Augustus Winter for twenty-five years, and I'm telling you the plan done changed. I can feel it."

The weight of the years seemed to hit Bill.

"Twenty-five years this November. They cut the telegraph line and they're coming. You got to get ready."

O'Shea stared at Bill, unblinking, then bellowed: "Nathan!"

The black servant appeared.

"I'm going to Pryor Creek," O'Shea said, standing up. "Take my rifle out of the study and keep an eye on Mister Bread here. If he tries to move, shoot him."

Nathan nodded.

"You ain't got time to go to Pryor Creek," Bill said. "How many men you got here?"

"There aren't thirty real fighting men in the whole fucking town," O'Shea snarled. "And they won't last five minutes against the Winter Family."

"Hooah hon hon!" the boy laughed.

The boy's bright blue eyes were fixed on the floor as always, but the expression on his face was almost sly.

"Why are you telling us this?" the boy asked Bill. "Hmm? Won't they kill you if they find out you told? Find out you told? Yes!"

"Hush, Lyndon," O'Shea said to the boy. His voice was rough but not unaffectionate. "Nathan, tell Macy to bring the boy up to his room. And to keep him away from the windows." Then O'Shea turned back to Bill. "Why are you telling us this?" he asked.

"I don't know," Bill said. "I honestly don't."

5

Winter had prepared himself for his visit to town. He was clean shaven, save for his mustache, with his hair neatly combed and parted, and he guided his horse with his knees while he held his Winchester rifle with both hands. The green corn crumpled and snapped beneath the hooves of his galloping horse, and of the horses of the riders who followed him.

The Winter Family emerged from the cornfield behind a farmhouse near the edge of town. A woman drawing water saw them. She let the bucket she was holding tumble into the well and she ran, shrieking, into the house. A few seconds later a man emerged with a shotgun. Winter shot him down.

"Yee haw!" Johnny Empire cawed.

"Winter!" Fred Johnson called. "Winter!"

Winter did not respond; instead, he dismounted on the fly, stalked up to the back door of the house, and kicked it open.

"Jesus," Johnson said.

The Empire brothers and a few of the rowdier ones followed Winter inside. Charlie Empire was already unbuckling his pants as he hopped through the back door.

Johnson turned to face the men still on their horses. "Where's O'Shea's house at?"

"I don't know," Quentin said. "I've never been there."

"We got to get that money quick," Johnson said.

"Oh, there will be no help with the telegraph line cut," Quentin said, his eyes twinkling. "The closest town is twenty miles from here."

"If someone gets out of town, there'll be men in here in an hour."

"Well then," Quentin said, smiling, while his horse nervously danced back and forth beneath him. "I suppose we had better make sure that they don't."

A woman screamed, and Johnson looked back to the house just as Winter marched outside. The expression in Winter's eyes was terrifying. It was as if his irises were slowly turning, rotating like wheels around the hard, dark, tiny pupils. He looked at Johnson briefly, then headed toward town, on foot, his rifle resting against his shoulder and a can of kerosene dangling from his left hand.

"Winter!" Johnson called. "What the hell are you doing?"

Flames flickering up by the windows. The house was on fire.

"Holy hell," Hugh said.

Johnson forced himself to unclench his jaw. "There's only two roads in this goddamn town," he said. "We need to cover every exit. North, south, east, and west. Nothing gets out. Then we need to hit the biggest house and we find the money. The whole goddamn state is going to be up in arms in just a few hours. If we ain't halfway to Texas by sundown we're all dead men."

They nodded at him, nervous, then watched as the pantless Empire brothers staggered confused out of the flaming house.

"What the hell?" Charlie said.

"Exactly," Johnson said.

Quentin laughed, and they spurred their horses around the house and into town.

6

Bill Bread waited in O'Shea's parlor, rocking back and forth. The shakes had settled into his hands, and a dry agony was crawling around in his chest.

The black servant, Nathan, stood by the bay window. He kept the gun pointed at Bill, but every now and then he glanced outside.

"Did you hear a shot?" Nathan asked.

"I'm not sure," Bill Bread said. "I don't suppose I could have a drink of whiskey?" He had intertwined his fingers and was twisting them, like a rag he was trying to squeeze dry.

"No," Nathan said.

"Anything?" Bill asked.

"How can you think about drinking at a time like this?" Nathan said.

Bill made a small, sad noise and looked down at his hands.

A shot rang out.

"Did you hear that?" Nathan said.

"I did," Bill replied. "They're here. Like I told you."

Nathan looked outside, then stiffened.

"Do you see one of them?" Bill asked.

Nathan stepped back and pulled the rifle up to his shoulder.

"I think you'd better get away from the—" Bill started. The window shattered, and Nathan fell to the ground.

Bill Bread stopped rocking. He sat in his chair and waited until the door broke open.

It was Hugh Mantel, big and soft and peering over his spectacles, along with a tall Mexican named Enrique and a bald Swede with a wicked countenance who had only ever identified himself as Foxglove.

"Bill!" Hugh said. "So this is O'Shea's house?"

"Yes," Bill said.

"Where's O'Shea?"

"Gone," Bill said. "There's only a Negress and a boy here."

Foxglove shot Nathan in the head.

"Where's the money?" Hugh asked.

"What money?" Bill said.

Hugh cursed and said, "Enrique, check the cellar, Fox, upstairs. Me and Bill will take the ground floor."

Foxglove tromped up the stairs. He started in the servants' wing, but he did not waste much time there, instead progressing to O'Shea's expansive bedroom, where he pulled the drawers out of the dresser and hacked the mattress with his bowie knife.

From outside, the screams and gunshots grew more frequent.

After O'Shea's bedroom, Foxglove moved farther down the hall and came to a locked door. One short kick with his boot and it broke inward.

A black woman screamed and lunged at Foxglove with something in her hands. Foxglove caught her arm and stabbed her in the stomach. She gave a dismayed and abrupt cry and fell to the floor.

"No!" the boy cried, as he tried to crawl under his bed. "No! No!"

Foxglove looked around the little room, at the books and the toys and the lions and tigers dancing on the wallpaper, then he jerked his knife out of the dying woman and stepped toward the hyperventilating boy.

"No! No! No! No!" the boy cried, weeping and crawling and for some reason bumping into the leg of his bed over and over again, like a blind dog. "No! No!"

"Yes, yes, yes—" Foxglove began, smiling, but then a gun barked behind him. A fist-sized chunk of skull and brain popped out of his forehead and flew across the room. His body tripped forward and hit the floor.

"Eeee!" the boy shouted. "Eeee!"

Bill lowered Hugh's revolver, then bent to retrieve Foxglove's weapons and hurried from the room.

As he was heading for the front door he met Enrique coming in.

"I heard a gunshot," Enrique said.

"Did you," Bill said.

Enrique had only the briefest instant to observe Hugh's body sprawled next to the rocking chair, smeared with blood.

There was another gunshot then, and Enrique fell backward into the yard. Bill followed him out and shot him again, though he was not moving. The sun hit Bill in the eyes and he sneezed. His hands had stopped shaking. He felt as if a tremendous weight had been lifted from his shoulders as he picked up Enrique's gun and walked away from O'Shea's house, toward town.

7

The little nameless town was burning. Smoke rose into the sky and ash drifted down like gray snow. Bodies lay in front of the houses. The wounded rolled and gasped and bled into the mud.

As Fred Johnson had said, there were only two roads in town. He sat upon his horse in the middle of the one heading west, toward Oklahoma City, and looked back to the intersection at Winter's handiwork. One building after another caught fire.

"Son of a bitch," he said.

Everything was going to hell. They ought to be terrifying everyone into staying in their homes, but instead the fires were driving people into the streets, whereupon they tried to flee, forcing Johnson and the other men to gun them down. Johnson had seen massacres like this dozens of times during the Indian Wars but nothing like it in a white town since Sherman's army marched through the Carolinas in the last few months of the Civil War.

He could see members of the Family kicking open doors, dragging men and women outside, filling their bags with loot. But no sign of the money. Where was the money?

Behind Johnson, Quentin was galloping in a tight circle and waving his hat, leaning back in his saddle and singing "The Battle Hymn of the Republic":

I have read a fiery gospel writ in burnished rows of steel:
"As ye deal with my contemners, so with you my grace shall deal";
Let the Hero, born of woman, crush the serpent with his heel,
Since God is marching on.

"Where is the fucking money?" Johnson said.

A rifle fired. That in itself was hardly surprising, but Johnson saw Quentin's horse stumble sideways with a terrible shriek, cutting off Quentin's mad cries of "Glory, glory, hallelujah!"

Someone was shooting at them for a change.

Johnson leaned down onto his horse's neck and spurred it back toward the intersection. He saw a little man coming down the laneway of a great house with a rifle in his hand. The man was walking bowlegged, crouched close to the earth, in a half shuffle, half waddle that was very familiar. It was Bill Bread. Johnson relaxed and looked elsewhere for the shooter, and that was when his horse was shot as well, tripping and screaming and pitching him to the earth before limping away in terror.

Quentin had scrambled away from his dying horse and now he caught Johnson's arm and dragged him down into a ditch.

"One of these wretches has a spine after all," Quentin said as he cocked his revolver. "Did you see where the shot came from? I think it was from the other side of the——"

"Bill," Johnson said, although even as he spoke, he could scarcely believe the words coming out of his mouth. "Bill's shooting at us."

"What?" Quentin said. "No!"

He stuck his head out of the ditch and a bullet kicked up the gravel next to his face, knocking him back down.

"Bill Bread!" Quentin cried. "Bill Bread!"

"Bill Bread," Johnson said. He dropped to his knees and crawled through the ditch toward the center of town. Wet grass and mud scooped into his sleeves and smeared down his pants. The wounded horse was still screaming. Quentin followed.

"Bill Bread!" Quentin said again. It sounded to Johnson like he might be laughing. "Will wonders never cease?"

Johnson stopped, propped his rifle on its side to keep it dry, drew a pistol and cocked it, then popped his head above the ditch. Bill Bread had made his way into the center of town, taking the Winter Family unawares and driving them out of the intersection. He saw Johnson and quickly retreated back behind the post office.

"Cover me, Quentin," Johnson snarled.

"Very well," Quentin said and leapt up and began to fire.

Johnson bolted out of the ditch with the rifle in his left hand and the pistol in his right. He kicked open the door to the saloon and ducked inside. The Empire brothers were crouched underneath the window facing the street.

"Is Bill fucking Bread shooting at us?" Charlie asked, bewildered.

"He done lost his mind," Johnson said. "Quentin's got us covered. Johnny, you shoot out the window. Charlie and me will——"

Quentin ran past, heading east as fast as he could.

"They're coming!" he shouted. "They're coming!"

"Who's coming?" Johnny asked, and his confusion was mirrored in Charlie's heavy, stupid face.

Johnson felt like a dark, deep mine shaft had opened up in his chest and his heart was falling, falling, falling.

The first of the riders galloped past the saloon, hours and hours earlier than should have been possible.

"Oh god no," Johnson said. "Oh Bill, what've you done to me?"

"What the hell, Freddy?" Charlie cried. "How are they here?"

Johnson did not reply. He barged out the door and was immediately confronted by the sight of the posse coming up the road from the west, so many of them, so goddamn many! Like a fucking parade, and before eight in the morning. All of them standing high in their stirrups, horses coated in foam, gasping for breath. The rain of bullets began, but Fred Johnson, hardened in a thousand firefights, stood his ground for a moment. He knew they would not hit him, not with their blood up and from moving horses, and so he took the opportunity to reflect on the end.

8

By all rights it should have been a massacre when the posse rode into town, but the Winter Family had an improbably large amount of experience with such situations. Those who survived long enough to get to their horses managed a somewhat organized retreat.

For his part, when the riders came into town, Bill dropped his smoking weapons into the mud and sat on his heels with his palms on his knees and just watched. It was in this position that he caught a glimpse of Augustus Winter, the last time he would see him for more than eighteen months.

Winter came out of a burning house, his trim, light-colored suit stained with stripes of blood and ash. A rider spotted him and tried to wheel his horse around but Winter raised the revolver in his left hand, thumbed the hammer back, and fired. The rider dropped. Then Winter raised the gun in his right hand and killed another young man, green and inexperienced, who had rushed to this place when he heard that his neighbors needed him. The bullet caught him full in the chest and knocked him down to the earth where he bled out his last.

Winter fired his weapons twice more and drove the riders back. As he turned to flee into the woods he looked over his shoulder and his eyes, wide and yellow, locked with Bill's. Until the day he died Bill would remember their lack of expression. No betrayal, anger, fear, surprise. Nothing. Just bright, alert, and empty. Like the eyes of a mountain lion that glances with magnificent disinterest at the hunter before it plunges away into the underbrush, back into the profound wilderness, unaffected by a brief intercession with the world of men.

9

What was left of the Family waited for Winter in the stand of blackjack oaks on the small hill where they had spent the night before. Now the sun blazed down on them from the east and the smoke rose from the burning town from the west and they could hear, faintly, the cries of their pursuers: the horses, the hounds, the men.

They waited as long as they dared, then fell to quarreling. Some men wanted to flee, others wanted stay out of loyalty to Winter, or fear of what he would do if they broke faith with him. But eventually it dawned on them, all of them, that Winter had broken faith with *them*. That he was gone. That he was not coming. That he had left them to their fate. And so they scattered and fled.

Winter was not far, but far enough. He had dug a hole at the foot of a tall tree and into this hole he dropped his meager possessions: his suit, his belt, his guns, his razor, his watch. Then he covered them with earth and left them behind, walking with purpose, as if he knew exactly where he was going and why. Like he always did.

*Quentin Ross came from a good family in Chicago and he had a
mind like quicksilver, light and lively. But he enjoyed pulling the wings
off flies, he lit fires and wet the bed, and he lied, lied all of the time:
constant, endless, profitless, senseless lies.*

*After the Battle of Fort Sumter, at the outset of the War of the
Rebellion, Quentin's family sought to rid themselves of him by using
their money and influence to obtain him a commission in the Twenty-
Sixth Illinois Volunteer Infantry Regiment. A thousand men served
in the Twenty-Sixth Illinois, a hundred in Company A, and fifty in
Lieutenant Quentin Ross's platoon. After only a few days Quentin
knew each by name and enough about them to carry on a few minutes
of conversation with any of them. It seemed to him that the men would
like him for it, and they did. Every night, before he slept, he ran
through their names in his mind, feeling a secret covetous joy.*

*In the fall of 1861 Quentin's platoon marched to war with the Army
of the Tennessee, creeping down the Tennessee River and capturing
Fort Henry. Quentin distinguished himself during the Battle of Shiloh.
His courage and ferocity, his almost unnatural coolness in the terrible
slaughterhouse of modern war, were subsequently confirmed during the
Siege of Vicksburg, where the Union gained access to the Mississippi
River and split the Confederacy in two, and the Chattanooga
Campaign, which drove the Confederacy from Tennessee.*

*And yet despite the high attrition among the officers, the deaths from
battle, suicide, and disease, and all the sudden and irreversible descents
into madness, Quentin Ross never rose above the rank of lieutenant. For
all of his courage his superiors lacked faith in him. He had not forsaken
his old habit of mendacity, and certain stories were whispered about
his habits, proclivities, appetites. None of these things, on their own,
should have prevented the rise of such a brave and competent officer,
considering the times. The greatest hindrance, perhaps, was that he was
too well adapted to war, too free and easy with it, like a fish darting*

through clear water. There was something vaguely disquieting about his sense of humor and the way he looked when he smiled.

In 1864 the Army of the Tennessee marched southeast from Chattanooga under General William Tecumseh Sherman, toward Atlanta. Quentin Ross and his men were with them. The Union forces pushed the Confederates to the gates of the city and then smashed them in the Battle of Atlanta. The city fell during the first week of September.

The Confederate general entrusted with the defense of Atlanta regrouped and circled north, threatening the Union supply lines. General Sherman faced a difficult decision. He could chase after the Confederates, back the way he'd come, or he could stay in Atlanta and risk running out of supplies. He decided upon a third option: to put Atlanta to the torch, feint south toward the city of Macon to misdirect the Confederates, and then march east across the state of Georgia, living off the country until his army reached the sea. To do so, however, he would need many scouts and foragers. Word circulated, and Quentin Ross volunteered.

After minimal discussion, he was selected. It somehow seemed a natural fit.

Quentin immediately set to work assembling a group of fifteen men. He began by replacing an obstreperous sergeant with a trusting and pliant German named Jan Müller. Quentin would have replaced his other sergeant, Gordon Service, if he thought he could have gotten away with it. But trading two sergeants would surely have raised suspicions, and raising suspicions was something Quentin was careful to avoid.

Next Quentin reached outside of the military. A marching army picks up many followers, including the wives and children of the men, prostitutes, traders, peddlers, preachers, and adventurers of all sorts. The Empire brothers—Duncan, Charlie, and Johnny—had been trailing after the Twenty-Sixth Illinois since Missouri. Quentin had found uses for them before, and he thought they would fit in nicely.

That left the enlisted men. Quentin selected them almost at random, since they did not need to be particularly vicious; Quentin had learned early on that gentle pressure from figures in authority could compel ordinary men to evil as easily as those of depraved character. He simply needed to ensure that he did not bring any remarkable individuals with him. It did not occur to him, even for the briefest instant, that young Augustus Winter (awkward, withdrawn, and silent) was remarkable for anything other than the unusual color of his eyes.

Georgia 1864

10

They rode east through the autumn woods with the sky rumbling above their heads and the air thick with the threat of rain. No one spoke. They were perhaps two or three days ahead of the main army, taking the winding back roads to avoid being seen and wearing ragged overalls instead of uniforms. Still, anyone would have known they were Union soldiers by their Spencer rifles and horses. Young men were a rarity in this part of the world; their movements could not avoid scrutiny.

Around noon they reached a fork in the road and Quentin called a halt. He gave the enlisted men permission to light a fire, despite the frowning disapproval of Sergeant Gordon Service, and jauntily announced that it would be the last time they ate hardtack for a fortnight.

"It'll be roast pork and corn bread from now on for us, boys," he said, and the men cheered. "Service, Müller, a word please."

The men dismounted and set the horses grazing and started a fire where the two little roads diverged. Quentin headed a few steps into the woods with his two sergeants.

"I'm going to divide the unit in three," Quentin said.

"Divide the unit?" Gordon Service asked, confused.

"Yes," Quentin said. "Each of us shall strike out on his own."

Gordon was tall and a little paunchy despite the rigors of military life, with a large bushy mustache and a receding hairline. Before the war he had owned and operated a dry goods store along with his wife. They had not prospered, and he had joined the army early, having decided they could use the money and that the whole thing was likely to be over by Christmas. That was three long years ago. He had served under Quentin Ross the whole time. He had always found Quentin a competent enough officer, though somewhat odd. Now, though, something seemed a little off about the lieutenant. As if he were drunk.

"Aren't we more likely to be captured if we split up?" Gordon asked.

"No, not at all," Quentin said. "Smaller groups are less likely to be detected. And three groups can scout three times as fast as one."

"Yah," Sergeant Jan Müller said. "That is true. Also, it is less likely we will all be captured."

Quentin smiled. It gave him a faintly predatory air. "True enough, Sergeant Müller," he said.

Jan Müller was carefully unfolding his map. His hands were hard and callused but he handled the tattered map gracefully. He was a German immigrant who had been conscripted by corrupt Democratic officials the moment he stepped off the boat, before he had learned to speak a word of English. His fastidious attention to detail and prompt obedience had helped him rise to his current rank. He had never served under Quentin Ross before.

"Well, all right, sir," Gordon said. "Who shall we take?"

"I'll take the Empire brothers," Quentin said. "Divide the rest of the men between you."

"The Empire brothers?" Gordon asked.

Even Jan looked a little surprised at this. He had a long face and when, as now, he was not entirely comfortable with something, he had a sensitive air, like a poet.

"Certainly," Quentin said. "I wouldn't want either of you to have to trouble with them; they can be a little rough. But they've more experience with this sort of thing than our boys."

Gordon looked past Quentin to where the Empire brothers were resting. Johnny, the youngest, was a mountain of a man, well over six feet tall, with a shock of red hair and a dumb malicious laugh. Charlie, the middle brother, was already balding and turning to fat, with close-set, suspicious eyes. Duncan, the eldest, was not much taller than Quentin and had a long cruel face that was pitted with smallpox scars. His eyes were bright with unrefined intelligence and his hair was prematurely gray. The three of them were spitting and muttering together and looking around at the undefended countryside with a kind of suppressed glee.

This sort of thing? Gordon thought.

"Very well, sir," Jan said, dubiously, and then rustled his map. "Where shall we rendezvous?"

When they were finished Quentin strolled over toward the two youngest soldiers in the group, Reginald Keller and Augustus Winter. They were sitting together at the fire, heating hardtack and desiccated vegetables in a cast-iron frying pan. It looked like something that might have been raked out of a gutter, all brown and full of dead leaves.

Reggie was fair-haired and blue eyed with an easy laugh and a generous nature. The other men, Quentin knew, called him "Babe." Winter was even younger and fairer than Babe Keller: his skin was as pale as moonlight, his hair was the color of dried straw, and his eyes were a shade of amber as light as champagne. In strong sunlight they turned gold and gave pale young Winter the look of a corpse with golden coins over his eyes. He was closed off, quiet, almost sullen. The men ironically called him "Old Man Winter."

"Reggie," Quentin said. "Augustus."

"Hello sir," Reggie said, smiling.

"I'll bet you're ready for some real food soon," Quentin said.

"Hardtack's better than nothing at all, sir," Reggie said.

"Truer words were never spoken," Quentin said.

Winter did not speak.

"Do you think there will be any soldiers in the town, sir?" Reggie asked.

"I doubt it," Quentin said. "They'll all be in Macon or Augusta by now."

"We fooled 'em good," Reggie said. "And now we're going to lick these dirty rebs. Right where they live."

For some reason, Quentin found this exceedingly amusing. He chortled. "You think so?" he said. "What about you, Augustus?"

For a while Winter did not say anything. So long, in fact, that

Quentin began to wonder how to handle the situation gracefully. Finally the boy spoke.

"The Confederates have sinned against the Lord. Numbered, numbered, weighed, divided."

"What's that mean?" Reggie asked.

"Don't you know anything, Reggie?" Winter said. "That's from the Book of Daniel."

"Yes," Quentin said. "The Lord's hand wrote those words on the wall of the king's palace in Babylon. Numbered, because God had numbered the days of their kingdom and finished it. Weighed, because they had been weighed in the balance and found wanting. And divided, because their kingdom was divided and given over to foreign soldiers."

Quentin regarded Winter curiously. Winter looked at the fire.

"So you think God's going to punish the Confederates?" Reggie asked.

"I don't know," Winter said. "I guess we'll see."

"Do you think we might see Him?" Reggie asked.

"I don't think we'll see Him directly," Winter said. "It ain't like that. It's more like how you can see the wind because the leaves move on the trees, or the clouds go by the moon."

As Winter spoke, Reggie looked up at the trees and laughed. They were waving with the wind.

"Well, this has been a most illuminating conversation," Quentin said.

After their hasty meal, they remounted their horses and split into three groups. Gordon took the bulk of the men, including Winter and Reggie, on the main road to the town, while Quentin and Jan took the rest along the smaller road to the north.

"Good hunting, Sergeant Service!" Quentin cried. "I'll see you in the morning."

"Yes sir," Gordon said.

Augustus Winter watched Quentin unnoticed, the light of knowledge illuminating his golden eyes.

11

A few hours later, and a few miles to the east, the sun was setting on the small village of Planter's Factory. The factory that gave the town its name was at the north end of the main street. It was three stories high, built of bright red brick. A gristmill and a sawmill were just south of the factory, on the west bank of the slow, brown Ocmulgee River.

As the evening light was fading, three ragged Indians emerged from the forest north of the factory. One of them was a small half-breed with skin the color of dark clay and long, frizzy black hair. His teeth were yellow and widely spaced and sprouted from his prominent gums at canted angles. One of his eyes was gray and the other brown. He wore the blue jacket of a Union soldier and an officer's saber hung from his belt, and he carried a heavy box on his back.

The other two were full-blooded Cherokee, tired and hungry. The elder was a tall man with a big nose and ears like the handles of a jug. The younger man was small and walked in a demoralized shuffle, his hands tied together.

The three traveled south until they arrived at the inn. Warm yellow lamplight spilled through its windows onto their drawn and pinched faces. The eldest Indian stepped forward and knocked on the front door.

The innkeeper, a short, stout, purposeful sort of woman, opened the door a crack.

"Are you Yankees?" she asked.

"No ma'am," the eldest Indian said. "I'm Lieutenant Timothy Stoga, of the Sixty-Ninth North Carolina Regiment. Thomas's Legion. This is my nephew, Private Bill Bread."

The innkeeper peered past them to the half-breed.

"Hidey, hidey!" the half-breed sang out.

"Don't pay him no nevermind," Stoga said. "He's my slave. His name is Navan Sevenkiller."

"Your slave?" the innkeeper said. "What's he doing dressed like that?"

"Bill and I were taken prisoner during the Battle of Atlanta," Stoga said. "He's the one that got us free. Our regiment's gone,

ma'am. They're all dead. We want to get back to North Carolina and
see if we can't get mustered up again. We were hoping we could stay
here tonight."

The innkeeper seemed encouraged by Stoga's manners but a little
put off by the slave's attire.

"He can wait outside if you like," Stoga said. "But he did spring
us loose."

"Well, all right," the innkeeper said. "He's better off where you
can keep an eye on him anyway, I reckon."

Stoga and Bread tromped into the cramped room and sat down
at the table. Sevenkiller wandered around, giggling softly, taking it
all in: the old, heavy furniture, the stuffed stag's head, the stone fireplace, the cheap painting hanging on the wall.

"Salt pork and sweet potatoes," the innkeeper said.

It was not a question, but Stoga said, "Yessum, please." And then:
"Sit down, Navan."

Sevenkiller did. The innkeeper returned with a big bowl of
mashed yams, and Sevenkiller and Stoga began to eat. Bill Bread
did not touch his food. He stared at the floor between his feet and
sweated and looked as if he might be sick.

"I'll get y'all some cider," the innkeeper said.

"No," Stoga said immediately. "No intoxicating drinks at the
table. Thank you, ma'am."

The innkeeper looked surprised but did not comment.

"I'm thirsty," Bill said, flicking his eyes over to the corner of
the room, where the keg of cider rested on its side, and his pupils
expanded with interest, absorption, love. But his mouth tightened.
As if with hatred. At himself or the drink or both, no one could say.

Bill looked down again. "I'm thirsty," he repeated.

"You can have water," Stoga said.

"Well, you're welcome to whatever you want," the innkeeper said.
"I'd rather give it to you than the Yankees. They'll be here tomorrow,
I expect."

"Hrmm," Stoga said. "I don't think so. They're marching from
Atlanta to Macon. They won't make it this far east."

"Don't you know?" the innkeeper said. "The word's all over
town. The skirmishers are already here."

Stoga frowned and put down his fork. "I don't see how they can be this far east. Perhaps they're deserters."

"No," the innkeeper said. "One of them's a German, going door-to-door. Writing things down in a little book. They'll be in town tomorrow. The slaves have even started running off. Over a hundred at the Johnson plantation. Just run right off."

"Hrmm," Stoga said. He looked at Sevenkiller, who grinned and stood up.

"Where is the Johnson plantation?" Sevenkiller asked.

"Why Lieutenant Stoga," the innkeeper said. "You can't send your slave out there."

"He'll come back," Stoga said. "Don't take any risks, Navan. We're leaving tomorrow morning, with or without you."

Sevenkiller wiped his mouth.

"Can I borrow a horse?" he asked.

Soon he was riding on the road to the Johnson plantation, singing a wild and tuneless song: "Hey-a, hey-a, hey-a-ho, hey-a-ho, hey-a-ho-ho-ho!"

His pony's mane was unpulled, and it walked with its mouth a few inches above the dusty road, as if searching for a mouthful of grass.

Cotton fields stretched out to either side. All of the plants had been harvested, stripped of the bolls of cotton and left standing withered and finished. Past the fields were the trees, yellow-gold and red in the autumn.

"Hidey, hidey, hidey, ho," Sevenkiller sang, as he leaned back in his saddle.

The fields appeared to be totally deserted. The barn that contained the cotton gins was dark and silent.

After Sevenkiller passed the barn he could see the big old house at the end of the road, right in the middle of the plantation. Sundown had been some time ago, but Sevenkiller's eyes were sharp, even at night, and he could tell that the shoddy longhouses where the slaves slept were empty.

"Hmm, hmm, hmm-hmm!"

The front door to the house burst open and a black woman came out screaming, a long wordless wail of despair and horror.

Sevenkiller kicked his pony. It lifted its head and broke into a brisk canter, its hooves beating a quick rhythm on the road.

He cut the woman off. She screamed when she saw him and threw her hands up in the air.

"Mercy, sir! Oh please have mercy on me!"

"What happened here?" Sevenkiller said. "Where are the other slaves?"

"They run off to join you, sir," the woman said. "When they heard you was coming."

Sevenkiller laughed. "I'm not with the Union," he said. "I took this jacket off a dead Yankee."

The woman was understandably taken aback by this. But she came to grips with it quickly enough, and said, "Oh sir! Then you got to go help Master Johnson! Freddy came back with an ax! He's going to kill my master!"

The woman sobbed.

"You've got to help him, sir!"

Sevenkiller neatly steered his pony around the woman and gave it another kick. Once again it leapt forward and cantered the last few yards to the porch, where Sevenkiller pulled up and slid off. His feet hit the ground without a sound.

The house was lit with oil lamps in defiance of the darkness outside. Someone very big was moving around, knocking things over, sounding like a panicked bull.

Sevenkiller drew an enormous Colt Walker revolver from inside his jacket; it was over a foot long and weighed almost five pounds. Then he slipped through the front door, which had been kicked in and was hanging on its hinges.

Muddy footprints, of large bare feet, tracked through the foyer, past the staircase to the second floor, and into the living room. That door had also been opened and warm air was leaking out.

A tremendously fat black man sat in an armchair with a small hatchet planted in his forehead. Rolls of flesh hung loosely from his neck and arms, as if his body had surrendered to gravity when the animating force left him. Blood was everywhere. The other furniture in the room had been overturned and smashed.

A man's leg poked through the door to the dining room.

Sevenkiller went over quietly, crouched low to the ground.

The leg belonged to a sturdy, ancient man with a shock of white hair, thick lips, big teeth, angry eyebrows. His head had been smashed and his eyes were starting out of his head. Dark red lines ringed his neck.

"Hmm, hmm, ho," Sevenkiller whispered.

The dining room table had been shoved across the room. It was made of solid wood and weighed three hundred pounds if it weighed an ounce, but it looked to have been almost tossed aside. The chairs were scattered as if someone had lifted the room and shaken it.

The noise was coming from the next room, the kitchen. Sevenkiller crept in that direction, his leather moccasins silent on the floor, the revolver pointed in the air, a look of strange delight on his face.

A huge black man was washing himself in the kitchen, using a large pot of water. Vegetables and a chicken were laid out on the counter, ready to be cooked, but the man had ignored them in favor of his bath.

Sevenkiller briefly admired the escaped slave, for he was a tremendous specimen: young and beardless and handsome with short, messily cropped hair. Something about the way that he moved and washed himself indicated a natural intelligence.

He was dignified, Sevenkiller decided. That was it. It might be strange to call an illiterate slave dignified, when he was shoeless and dressed in rags and covered in his master's blood and washing himself out of a soup pot. But so he was.

The slave's back was covered with scars; as a slave himself, Sevenkiller knew well that such marks were the price of dignity.

Sevenkiller raised his revolver and took a step forward with one moccasined foot, and it was only the sound of a stray piece of china splintering beneath his heel that saved Fred Johnson's life.

Johnson did not turn; he merely heaved the iron pot behind him with all his strength. Sevenkiller pulled the trigger, but the bullet hit the pot and ricocheted through a window. The pot slammed into Sevenkiller, knocking him over, soaking him with water and sending the gun flying.

Fred Johnson was on him instantly, pinning him to the ground.

In one hand he held a heavy meat cleaver and with the other he pressed Sevenkiller's face into the floor.

"Hee hee hee!" Sevenkiller cried.

One of his little crazy eyes, the gray one, was carefully fixed on the cleaver. When it descended with monstrous speed toward his neck, Sevenkiller twisted his hips and brought one of his legs up so that it wrapped around the arm holding his face. The blade missed and sank deeply into the wood. It cut off six inches of Sevenkiller's hair, and the wind of its passing was cool on the side of his head.

No more laughing. Sevenkiller worked on isolating the arm, which was big and strong as a healthy tree, so that his legs were wrapped around it near the shoulder and his pelvis was positioned next to Johnson's elbow.

Johnson was uselessly trying to pull the cleaver out of the floor, so he only realized what Sevenkiller was doing when Sevenkiller pried Johnson's other arm straight and thrust his pelvis against the elbow, hyperextending it.

"No!" Johnson cried, flexing his biceps. So strong was his arm that Sevenkiller could not quite manage to break it even when he used the leverage of his entire body. Johnson rolled desperately, like a gator with its prey in its mouth, and it was all Sevenkiller could do to hang on. Eventually, as the floor and the ceiling changed places again and again, Sevenkiller saw the revolver and let go of the arm to snatch it.

Fred Johnson did not waste any time. As soon as he got his arm loose he sprang to his feet and spared only one wild and frightened look for Sevenkiller, his bright eyes as wide as saucers, before leaping out through the open window.

"Ah ha ha ha hee hee!" Sevenkiller laughed, staggering to his feet. The whole room seemed to be spinning. He looked out the window at Johnson's retreating back and raised the revolver, thumbed the hammer, and let the percussion cap tumble out. Then he smoothly lowered the weapon, aimed, and shot.

There was a flat clicking noise as the weapon misfired.

Johnson disappeared into the trees.

Sevenkiller laughed again, so hard that he had to sit down. He looked at his weapon and saw that it was wet, and that only made him laugh harder.

"Ha ha ha ha ha! Ah, hee hee hee!"

He had a powerful feeling that he would soon die.

Sevenkiller left the house and mounted his horse. He visited a few more plantations on his way back to the inn. When he knocked, Stoga opened the front door. The innkeeper was asleep, but Bill Bread was awake, sitting and shivering at the table, his hands still tied together.

"Hidey," Sevenkiller said.

He tossed his saber and revolver onto an empty chair and shrugged out of his blue jacket.

"I need a drink," Sevenkiller said.

"We aren't drinking," Stoga said. "What did you see? Is it true? Have the slaves run off?"

Sevenkiller ignored him and took a cup off the counter and filled it with cider from the keg. He drank it down, then let out an exaggerated sigh and belched. He looked challengingly, not at Stoga but at Bill Bread. Bill never lifted his head, but the muscles around his jaw clenched. Sevenkiller tittered.

"What did you see, Navan?" Stoga asked.

"The slaves are all gone," Sevenkiller said. "Word got out that the Yankee foragers were just a few miles to the west, with the whole army behind them. So all the slaves ran off. At the big plantation, Mister Johnson is dead, and the overseer. They were killed by a slave named Fred."

"You only heard rumors?" Stoga said.

"Yes," Sevenkiller said. "But I spoke to others who had seen them."

"Hrmm," Stoga said, the noise deep in his throat. "The innkeeper said there are no soldiers in this town. They all went to Macon. The only soldier here is a man named Captain Jackson. She said he was in the cavalry, but he was wounded near Atlanta. He just came back to town last week. His family has a farm and a distillery on the other side of the river."

"Well?" Sevenkiller asked.

"Hrmm," Stoga repeated, drumming his fingers on the table, his face concerned. "Well, let's go see the captain tomorrow morning. It is on our way, in any case."

They went upstairs and slept in a real bed for the first time in weeks. But first, Stoga tied Bill to the headboard. Bill slept, eventually, but his dreams were grasping, muddled, and dark.

12

For his part, the escaped Fred Johnson spent his first night as a free man sleeping under a tree. He'd blundered blindly through the dark woods, nettles and thorns tearing his clothes and poking his flesh, branches slapping into his face, the muddy earth sucking at his feet. It had not taken him long to realize that the little dark Indian had not followed him, but he had kept running anyway. To put more space between himself and the scene of the crime. The farther he went, the less real it seemed to him. Like a dream. He saw the overseer's head absorb the ax that had been meant for Massa Johnson. He heard Bertha screaming. Saw the old white man's eyes rolling with fury (no fear, not even at the end). But he couldn't remember how he'd felt. Had he been angry? Satisfied? Happy? Now he only felt shaken.

Eventually he found a tall willow tree and slept between its massive roots, until he was awoken by the soft touch of fingers on his shoulder.

Johnson jerked and thrashed, and stumbled quickly to his feet. His skin was slick with cold dew and his muscles were stiff and unresponsive. It was very early dawn, very dark.

"Whoa, easy."

The young man, a boy really, who had touched him had taken a step back. He was tall and thin and the whitest man Johnson had ever seen, with skin like snow and hair like straw, and eyes of pure gold. In the dawn light the boy looked as if he were made of silver, or mist.

"I ain't going to hurt you," the boy said. A Spencer repeating rifle was slung across the boy's shoulders. His hands were empty. He was wearing ragged overalls and worn boots. Johnson could tell by the boy's accent that he was not from around here.

"Are you from the North?" Johnson asked.

"That's right," the boy said. "What you sleeping out here for? You run off?"

"Yessir," Johnson said.

"Well, you can come back with me," the boy said. "Our unit split up, but most of us are staying at a big farmhouse not far from here. The Williams place. You know it?"

"Yessir," Johnson said.

"There's loads of run-off colored folk there, just waiting outside. Most of them are from the Johnson place."

To this, Fred Johnson said nothing.

Eventually, the boy spoke again. "You're the most busted-up Negro I've ever seen. Your back, I mean."

After a pause, Johnson said, "That's the life of a slave."

"I seen plenty of slaves without a mark on them," the boy said. "What'd you do to get beat up like that?"

"Run off," Johnson said. "Plenty of times."

"Well, you're loose now," the boy said.

"Yessir," Johnson said, then added, "ain't no one going to hit me no more."

The boy smiled, very thin, very sour.

"I wouldn't be so sure about that," he said.

"No one's gonna whip me now that I'm a free man," Johnson said. His tone was a warning.

The boy did not reply. Instead, he turned around and unstrapped his overalls. Johnson felt as if the breath had been sucked from his body. The boy's back was twisted and crisscrossed with a thousand scars, looping in and around one another like a pile of rope or a ball of rattlesnakes.

"Who did that to you?" Johnson asked.

"My daddy," the boy said. "He was trying to beat the devil out of me. He never stopped till I ran away. So I suppose he never did get the devil all the way out. I reckon it's the same way with you."

Johnson could not think of anything to say.

The boy shrugged his way back into his clothing.

"My name is Winter," he said. "Come on. Follow me."

13

A few miles off, Quentin Ross was woken by the sound of the birds singing. For few minutes he lay in bed, smiling without opening his eyes. The birdsong was remarkable. It was impossible to predict what the next note would be, but as soon as that note was sounded it seemed inevitable. As if the birds were singing according to a pattern that Quentin knew without knowing he knew it.

Finally he sat up and looked around the simple bedchamber, yawning. Then he walked to the kitchen, feeling as if nothing he was seeing could be quite real.

In the kitchen he picked up a copper teakettle, turning it around and around in his hands, smiling and looking at his reflection. For some reason he was convinced that if he turned it at just the right speed, at just the right angle, he would see something miraculous. And then it occurred to him that everything was miraculous, everything, and he started to chuckle; he couldn't help himself.

A voice spoke.

"Lieutenant?"

Quentin tried to focus on the person standing at the back door.

"Are you all right, sir?" the voice said.

Quentin strained his eyes. It felt as if the person were very far away, even though he was standing right in front of him. His mind would not descend to the present moment, like a bird that kept circling in the sky.

"Are you all right, Lieutenant?"

Quentin rubbed his face and looked again. Aha! It was Duncan Empire.

"Never better," Quentin said. "Never better."

"You're not hurt, sir?" Duncan asked.

"Of course not," Quentin said. "Why do you ask?"

Duncan did not respond immediately. He seemed to be performing some sort of quiet calculation. Finally he spoke. "Well sir, you're covered with blood."

It took a moment for Quentin's mind to understand what these words meant. Then he looked down and saw that he was completely naked and that, indeed, there was blood all over him. As if he had bathed in it.

"Oh my," he said.

He looked up at Duncan as if for an explanation. Duncan didn't move. Quentin put his hand to his mouth and thought. Then he started toward the door, heading for the pump out back. Then he remembered he was naked and stopped and turned back for his clothes. Then he realized that he couldn't put his clothes on, because they would get stained with blood. And so he turned back to Duncan, smiling warmly but emptily.

"Wait just a minute, sir," Duncan said.

Duncan stepped outside and motioned to his brothers waiting at the road. Charlie and Johnny looked a bit puzzled but wandered away, dragging their sacks of loot behind them. When they passed out of sight, Quentin went out and Duncan went in.

The kitchen table was set for four. Half-eaten food on the plates. A carved chicken on a platter. Flies jumping off and on, rubbing their little hands together. The sound of them buzzing was very loud.

Duncan made his way through the living room, the two bedrooms. He found nothing and no one. But the sheets in the master bedroom were so heavily stained with blood that they were crusty and stiff. A quick search through the dresser drawers produced a handful of fine gold jewelry and a stack of CSA dollars. Duncan pocketed them both. He also gathered up Quentin's clothes, which were folded neatly at the foot of the bed.

A beautiful painting hung on the wall in the dining room, but of course it was too large to carry.

Back in the kitchen Duncan noticed some bloody footprints around the trapdoor to the cellar. He set Quentin's clothes down, opened the trapdoor, and descended carefully into the cool darkness. The buzzing of flies grew louder. He waited for his eyes to adjust to the dark so he could better see the shelves of preserves and the tools hanging on the walls. Eventually he noticed the bodies in a far corner, only very dimly illuminated by the light streaming down through the trapdoor.

Duncan's mouth twitched.

He walked over slowly. Two women, one old and one middle-aged, and two young children. All of them had been hog-tied and carved up in much the same manner as the chicken on the table upstairs.

One of the children turned her head toward him and opened her mouth. Blood came out, but no sound.

"Jesus," Duncan whispered.

He climbed the stairs and shut the trapdoor and went outside. Quentin was crouching next to the pump, working the handle like a madman and keeping his head under the spout. Duncan loaded up his arms with wood from the pile next to the house, brought it back inside, and stacked it on the kitchen floor. He stuffed some ripped-up newspaper under the wood and lit it with a match. Then he took up Quentin's clothes and walked back out into the Georgia sunshine.

Quentin was still pumping water on his head. Duncan gave him a gentle nudge. Quentin spluttered and brought his head up.

"Duncan," Quentin said. "There you are."

"Hello, sir," Duncan said. "I brought you your clothes."

Quentin was breathing shallowly, blinking and trying to look everywhere at once.

"We should regroup with the others," Quentin said.

"Yes sir," Duncan said.

Quentin unfolded his pants and started putting them on. "Those people had valuable intelligence," he said.

Duncan remembered the mute look of horror on the child's face and smiled without humor. "And they wouldn't give it up?" he asked.

"No," Quentin said.

"What'd you ask them?"

Quentin was buttoning his shirt.

"Have you ever thought, Duncan, about the nature of infinity?"

Duncan only cocked his head.

"Well," Quentin said, his voice high and odd, "imagine a line made up of discrete points. One, two, three, all the way on. All the numbers that exist. All right?"

"Yes sir," Duncan said.

"Now that line would stretch on forever, wouldn't it? Because there's no final number. No matter how big the number you can always add one. Do you understand?"

"Well, all right, sir."

"That's most men's idea of infinity. Everything. The whole universe. Going on forever. But there is another kind of infinity as well. Imagine the distance between two points. Between zero and one. Can you imagine it?"

"I think so, sir."

"That distance is infinitely divisible. Do you see what I mean? It can be divided in half. Than that half can be divided in half, so that we are left with one-fourth. And then the fourth can be divided in half. And so on. No matter how small the distance between two points, there is always another point somewhere between those points. Do you understand? Do you?"

Duncan was smiling now, jingling the gold jewelry in his pocket. Smoke was beginning to pour out of the windows of the little cottage.

"What that means is it is not merely the universe that is infinite," Quentin said, "but that infinity is contained in every single thing. The universe contains everything, and everything contains a universe. Do you see? To know one thing, in its entirety, is to know everything. Everything! Do you see?"

"Oh yes sir," Duncan said, smiling, as the fire steadily grew behind him. "I think I'm beginning to understand just fine."

14

The Confederates, exhausted by their long march and their late night, slept until well after nine o'clock. Sevenkiller was the last to awake, and then they all had a small breakfast of dried apples and hard biscuits.

When they were finished at the inn they crossed the bridge to the east bank of the Ocmulgee River and took a little dirt track north from the main road. After a fifteen-minute walk they arrived at Captain Thomas Jackson's property.

The cornfield was desolate, shorn of its crop, the stalks rustling in the gentle wind. The house was tall and painted white, with an expansive porch and wide pillars, but as they drew closer they could see the paint was flaking, the steps were green with moss, and grass was growing up between the boards.

Stoga knocked. Eventually the door opened inward, revealing a bald man, shorter than average, brutally thin. The man coughed, and it sounded tearing and nasty.

"Captain Jackson?" Stoga asked.

"Nah," the man said. "My name's Early. Who are you all?"

Stoga introduced them. Upon hearing that Stoga was a lieutenant, Early stood a little straighter.

"You'll have to excuse me, sir," Early said. "I been out of the army since February of sixty-three. The cold got into me in the mountains and it never seemed to get out."

"That's all right," Stoga said. "We're all doing what we can."

"Why don't you come in?" Early said. "I'll get the captain. Your boy can't come in this way, though. He can wait outside or come round the back."

Sevenkiller tittered, while he sweated under the wooden box on his back.

"Captain's a stickler for that sort of thing," Early said. "He said it's easy to let it slide during the war but we have to keep up our standards."

"Of course," Stoga said.

Stoga and Bill followed Early into Captain Thomas Jackson's parlor and sat down on the couch. The dark wooden floors were covered by an intricate carpet and the furniture was all very solid and serious. Solemn portraits of Captain Jackson's ancestors hung on the walls. The bay windows were open and the morning breeze ruffled the papers on the writing desk.

Early had a particularly violent coughing fit and the handkerchief he held to his mouth came away stained with blood.

"Are you all right?" Stoga said.

"Oh, you know," Early said. "You fellows want anything to drink?"

"No," Stoga said. "No alcohol, please."

"Your loss," Early said. "The captain's daddy made some mighty fine whiskey in this place, and there's still plenty of it down in the cellar."

"Thank you, but no," Stoga said.

"All right," Early said, sitting down in a wooden armchair.

After a few minutes Captain Thomas Jackson came into the room. He was young and blond and powerful across the chest, but he was leaning on a crutch and walked with a marked limp.

"Don't get up," Tom said. "I just want to sit down as quickly as I can anyway."

He collapsed into an armchair across from the Cherokee, then introduced himself.

"Pleased to meet you, Captain," Stoga said. "I'm Lieutenant Timothy Stoga. This is Private Bill Bread."

"And the Negro outside?" Tom asked. "Who's he?"

"My slave," Stoga said.

"What brings you gentlemen to Planter's Factory?" Tom asked.

"We were in Thomas's Legion," Stoga said.

"That right?" Tom said. "I heard you boys fought well. You had some rough going in the Shenandoah."

"Hrmm," Stoga said.

"I thought you'd been transferred back to North Carolina."

"Well, they took the two Cherokee companies, what was left of them, under seventy men, and put them together. They sent us down here from North Carolina, just in time for the Battle of Atlanta."

"It'd be a shame to have missed that," Tom said.

"We were taken prisoner."

"How'd you get loose?"

"My slave," Stoga said.

"Your slave?" Tom said incredulously.

"Yes," Stoga said. "He slipped into the Yankee camp and cut us loose."

"Well, goddamn," Tom said. "Early, perhaps you'd be so good as to take him out a dram."

Early glanced inquisitively at Stoga, who shrugged.

Bill watched, hungrily, as Early left the room, and listened carefully to the sound of the lock and Early's footsteps on the stairs down into the cellar.

Tom noticed Bill's expression.

"He's a quiet one," Tom said.

"Hrmm," Stoga said. "He is a good soldier."

Bill's gaze flicked to Tom briefly, then returned to the floor.

"Didn't want to come with you, did he?" Tom asked.

"He acquitted himself well in many battles," Stoga said.

"Yeah," Tom said. "But from what I heard, eleven hundred men left North Carolina with Thomas's Legion. And only a hundred made it back. Maybe your boy figured he'd acquitted himself well enough for one war."

His tone was gentle, and nothing in Bill's face indicated he took offense. But Stoga raised his voice, and shouted, "It's not that! It's drink, drink, drink. He has been ruined by drink. Corrupted by drink. Demon drink. It has unmanned him. I will take him home; I will dry him out. He will right himself."

"Well, all right," Tom said. "No offense intended."

"Hee hee hee!" came Sevenkiller's laughter through the window. The sound startled Tom; he glanced over at the window, then back at his guests.

"I'm sorry, Captain," Stoga said. "Let me explain to you why we are here. Almost all of the slaves in town have run off. They say that Union foragers are near and that the army is behind them."

"Why would the army be coming here?" Tom said. "I thought they were going to Macon."

"Still, the slaves are gone," Stoga said.

Tom cocked his head, then motioned to the writing desk.

"Lieutenant, there's a map of Georgia on that table," he said. "Could you get it for me?"

Stoga got the map and laid it out.

"Sherman took Atlanta," Tom said. "Now, he could go south to Macon or east to Augusta. We're right here."

His pointed at a tiny dot southeast of Atlanta, halfway between Macon and Augusta.

"There's nothing in this town," he said. "There's nothing past here either. Milledgeville, I suppose, but other than that nothing but forests and hamlets all the way to the sea. And where would he get his supplies from? How would he run his cracker line? He couldn't bring his supplies all the way from Tennessee, not with raiders from Macon and Augusta picking off his wagons."

"I do not understand," Stoga said.

Tom leaned back in his chair.

"Well then, how about this," Tom said. "I know you all are just passing through. And I know you don't want to run the chance of getting taken prisoner again. I appreciate all that. But how about your boy Sevenkiller and Early head back to town and see if they can't grab one of these bummers. If we learn anything, you can share it with the good folks in Milledgeville or Augusta on your way back to North Carolina. And even if we don't, maybe we can let some of these sons of bitches know that this is my neighborhood and these are my neighbors, and if they want to tear this place up, they're going to have to pay."

"All right," Stoga said.

"Your whiskey is very fine," Sevenkiller called through the window. "Very fine indeed!"

Early and Sevenkiller left within a few minutes, Early coughing wretchedly. Tom excused himself and retired to his bedroom, explaining that he felt much better with his leg propped up. Stoga took a book off the shelf and began to read, with difficulty, his lips moving as his eyes moved over the page.

Bill Bread waited. He could feel the drops of sweat forming on his brow and sliding, one by one, down the side of his face. His stomach had steadied and his head was clear. The sunlight from the window didn't threaten to cut through to his brain any longer. He felt better. He was mostly dried out. His mind turned to the corn whiskey in the cellar. He stood up.

"I want to get some water," he said. "From the pantry."

Stoga watched him go out of the room and gave him a few minutes. Then he walked quietly to the pantry door and threw it open. Sure enough, Bill was crouched up against the door to the cellar, trying to jimmy the lock.

"Look at yourself," Stoga said, his voice heavy with disgust. "Just look. You lied to me. I can't trust you, my own nephew."

Bill looked down at the floor.

"Doesn't that mean anything to you?"

Stoga waited, but Bill remained silent.

"Don't you care about anything except getting another drink?" Stoga asked.

No response.

"Don't you have anything to say for yourself?" Stoga asked.

Bill looked up but did not speak. There was nothing to say.

Except this:

That he had gone to war as a boy. That he had tasted whiskey after the legion's first victory. That the roaring feeling of goodwill, of invincibility, of happiness, had marked him forever. That he had struggled to find that feeling again. That even as his pleasure in drink evaporated his compulsion to drink escalated exponentially, as if he could drink enough he would find the joy he had lost. That the rest of his life became a dull gray exercise he had to pass through in order to get a drink. That it had become crucial to assert that his drinking caused no harm. That such assertions had been easily made in the army because Bill, drunk or sober, had always managed to be at least an average soldier, even on the days when he woke up drunk and his breakfast was whiskey in a tin cup he could not hold without shaking. That the war had concealed his sins, as it had for so many others. That he could never go back to the peace. Never.

Other than that there was nothing to say. And so Bill looked back down at the floor and said nothing.

"Get back in the parlor," Stoga said.

"I need to use the privy," Bill said.

Stoga frowned.

"All right," he said.

They walked out together. Bill shut the door behind him and sat down on the toilet. From underneath his shirt he removed a pint bottle of vanilla extract.

Shame stayed Bill's hand as he raised the bottle to his lips. The shame of lying again, the shame of being unable to control himself, the shame of stealing. But it was his shame also that whispered to him that he would never be able to quit, that he was too weak, that his life was not worth saving in any case. He stared at the bottle, and each moment he did not drink was a kind of triumph. But a thousand triumphs could be undone by a single defeat.

He drank.

15

Sergeant Gordon Service and his men, including Reginald Keller and Augustus Winter, had spent the night in a farmhouse owned by an old woman named Mrs. Williams. In the morning, she treated them to a breakfast of eggs, bacon, coffee, and grits and did everything in her power to be amicable. She told Gordon that she had always viewed secession as a disastrous enterprise and remained loyal to the Union in her heart, although she had kept those feelings to herself, for fear of her neighbors.

It did not matter to him whether Mrs. Williams was lying or not. If she was willing to give him bacon for breakfast, he was willing to see that her house was spared. At least until the main body of troops came through; after that, the fate of Mrs. Williams and her property would be anybody's guess.

They were making quite a pleasant morning of it when the back door banged open and Winter came in.

"Private Winter," Gordon said, barely glancing up from the bread he was buttering. "So nice of you to join us."

"You been outside yet, Sarge?" Winter asked. "There's something out there you might want to see."

Sighing, Gordon followed Winter out the door onto the back porch then came to a sudden stop.

"Goodness gracious me," he said.

More than a hundred slaves were camped behind the house, crammed in the little space between the vegetable gardens and the pigpens. Men, women, little children. Not making much noise, just waiting.

At the sight of Sergeant Service, one of the older men stepped up.

"Are you a Union soldier?" he asked

"Yes," Gordon said, "I'm Sergeant Gordon Service."

All of the blacks leapt to their feet and began to applaud and cheer. Gordon raised his hands and started to try to quiet the crowd, but they would have none of it and instead broke into song. Many of them were weeping openly.

"All right," Gordon said as he walked forward. "All right, quiet, quiet now! That's enough."

After the song was finished and the cheering and whistling finally stopped, Gordon addressed the old man who had spoken. "What's your name?"

"My name is Croesus, sir," the elderly slave said.

"Well, all right," Gordon said. "As I said, I'm Sergeant Service of the Union Army, the Twenty-Sixth Illinois. We're pleased to tell you that you're free and that you've rightfully been free since January of 1863. You are free to come and go and do anything you wish."

Another tremendous cheer, and the slaves rushed him, gathered around, and started hugging him, the children grabbing his legs and the women kissing him and the men just tugging on his clothes and laughing and dancing on the spot.

"However," he shouted, "however, please, however, you should know that the Union Army is not coming this way. We are merely a foraging party. So you should know that we cannot guarantee your safety."

"Oh sir," Croesus said, with a trace of contempt. "We ain't worried about that. We're ready to die for our freedom, sir. Ain't no rebel soldiers around here anyhow. They all down in Macon, waiting for General Sherman."

"Well, my lieutenant will soon be here and I trust he will know what you should do," Gordon said. "Until then, take care of yourselves, and please, don't hurt your former masters—we don't want that."

The slaves quieted a bit at this and glanced at one another. Toward the back of the crowd, Gordon saw one particularly large ex-slave squatting on his heels. The other slaves seemed to be keeping their distance from him.

But before Gordon could think of anything to say, there was another great burst of applause. Quentin Ross and the three Empire brothers came around the side of the house on horseback. Johnny Empire was waving the Stars and Stripes in the air. Quentin dismounted and walked up to Gordon on the porch.

"Lieutenant," Gordon said. "I'm glad to see you."

"Sergeant Service," Quentin said, warmly acknowledging his salute.

"As you can see, the Negroes have heard of our arrival," Gordon said.

"Quite right, quite right," Quentin said. "Let me have a word with them."

Quentin turned and faced the crowd. There was another cheer as Johnny madly galloped back and forth, swinging the flag in the air.

"Ladies and gentlemen, ladies and gentlemen," Quentin called out. "Please! Please! Your attention, please!"

The crowd quieted.

"Ladies and gentlemen, this country was founded on the belief that liberty is the inalienable right of every man. On the other hand, the cornerstone of the Confederacy is that the Negro is inherently inferior to the white man, and that slavery is his natural condition. They believe that it was so ordained by the Creator. They are wrong!"

More cheering.

"Ladies and gentlemen, the Confederates have set their faces against the natural and moral laws of the universe. They have split the country in two. They have driven us to war. And now their armies have been beaten and scattered and our troops are marching through the heart of their false republic. And still they will not surrender. Well, ladies and gentlemen, we have only one task left ahead of us. We must show them they are beaten."

Gordon's mouth turned down a little, as if he had seen a small child take a nasty fall and was expecting a wail.

The ex-slaves made a satisfied sound that was not quite a cheer.

"They made this war," Quentin said, "and only they can end it. We must show them the folly of their actions. We must teach them that their government cannot protect them. For that I will be enlisting your help. If you'll excuse me, I must speak with my sergeant."

Quentin turned around, smiling. Gordon looked as if he'd swallowed a handful of porcupine quills. If anyone had looked at Augustus Winter he would have seen a flicker of knowledge in his eyes again, before they darkened as if someone had drawn a shutter.

"Lieutenant Ross, I'm not sure about what you just said," Gordon said.

"Why?" Quentin said. "I thought those truths were self-evident."

"I mean the ending part, sir."

"I thought that part most self-evident of all," Quentin said. "The laws of war are as true as the principles of the multiplication tables."

"But sir," Gordon said. "The field orders were pretty clear. We're not to enter dwellings or commit trespass and only the corps commanders can give the order to destroy buildings, and we're to refrain from abusing or threatening the—"

"Yes, yes," Quentin interrupted. "I am as familiar with the field orders as you, Sergeant. But have you not been listening to what Sherman has actually been saying these past few weeks?"

"Well . . . ," Gordon began.

"Sherman said that we are fighting a war against anarchy, for the highest stakes. To avoid the fate of Mexico! He told the mayor of Atlanta that to reason with us was like appealing against a thunderstorm! He said that war, like the thunderbolt, follows its laws and turns not aside even if the virtuous stands in its path."

"Well, yes sir," Gordon said.

"Did he not say that war is cruelty and you cannot refine it?"

"Yes sir."

"That the people of the South were barred from appealing to our constitution and laws for protection? That they had instead appealed to war and would have to abide by its principles? That he would impress upon the citizens of the Confederacy that their government was unable to protect them? That he would, in short, make Georgia howl? Are those declarations not inconsistent with these field orders?"

"Well, even if they are, sir, I don't know if I'm comfortable disregarding them."

"Indeed," Quentin said. "Quite sensible, except for this. Once General Sherman cut us loose from the main column and sent us ahead, he specifically told me that his field orders were only for show."

"For show?" Gordon said.

"Yes," Quentin said. "He told me the whole army would have to improvise and live off the land. Proper intelligence and adequate supplies are vital, and so is our mission to break the spirit of the South. This has two components. First, we must do great damage to the foundation of the Confederacy. The fields and farms that feed and clothe their armies are legitimate military targets, as are the factories and railroads. Second, we must convince them of the hopelessness of their cause. We shall do this by bringing to their very hearth and homes the horror of war. I know it seems harsh, Sergeant, but you have fought with me in great battles. What right have these people, having brought this war upon us, to escape the consequences of their actions?"

"Well . . . ," Gordon said.

"Those are my orders, Sergeant," Quentin said. "Straight from General Sherman himself. Now please, assemble your men, then meet me and Sergeant Müller so we can plan our next move."

"Yes sir."

Gordon glanced into the crowd of blacks before he went back

inside. His gaze fell upon the big loner in the back. The freedman's expression was cold and satisfied.

Once inside, he attempted to assemble his men. But he found that Augustus Winter was gone.

16

After Winter left the Williams property he made his way northeast until he came out of the woods into a large hayfield. The grass grew a little higher than his hip, and as he walked he ran his hands over the tops of the plants. Sometimes he would tighten his fingers and come away with handfuls of seeds, which he inspected before letting them trickle away.

The wind was cold and the sky was gray and the air seemed pregnant with rain.

Eventually he reached a wall, only a couple of feet high, made with flat stones fitted together without cement. On the other side of the wall was a shallow muddy creek, smooth and silent. Winter climbed on top of the wall and stretched his arms to balance himself. Mindful of the unfixed stones, he walked along the wall. When he gained confidence, he looked up at the horizon and felt the wind on his face as he made his way between the field and the creek toward a dark line of trees.

"Auggie! Hey! Auggie!"

Reggie was coming toward him through the field.

"There you are!" Reggie said.

Winter hopped off the wall and walked over.

"Sergeant Service sent me looking for you," Reggie said. "Why'd you run off?"

Winter had his usual air when someone asked him a question—as if he was mentally considering whether giving an answer would compromise his position.

"I didn't like all the talk," Winter said.

"You didn't like the lieutenant's speech?" Reggie asked.

"I just don't like that kind of talk," Winter said. "Fancy talk. In the mouth of the foolish is a rod of pride. Proverbs fourteen, verse three."

"Boy," Reggie said, "you got a Bible saying for all occasions."

Reggie plucked a strand of grass from the ground, cleaned it carefully, and put it in his mouth to chew. He then prepared another one for Winter, who took it. They walked back toward the Williams property.

Winter chewed the grass, taking it out of his mouth only to spit. He always seemed to be looking at something very far away on the horizon.

"I thought it was a pretty good speech," Reggie said. "It sure did get the niggers all riled up. Did you hear 'em hollering? Why didn't you like it?"

Winter gave Reggie another one of his searching looks. In Reggie's friendly countenance he saw nothing to fear.

"I've spent a lot of years listening to a lot of fancy talk. One day I realized there wasn't anything to it. A man can say anything. It's as easy as breathing. I can say the sky's green or that fish can talk. It's just air. That's all. A man gets tired of it."

After this speech, Winter retreated into himself like a hermit crab.

"Lieutenant Ross does love the sound of his own voice," Reggie said. "But who don't? I guess you. You treat your words like they cost you a dollar each. You got a Bible saying for that?"

Now there was a rare occurrence: a thin smile from Winter. "A fool uttereth all his mind: but a wise man keepeth it in till afterwards."

"There you go, Auggie," Reggie said. "That's how you do it."

There was the barest rustling in the hay behind them, and Sevenkiller stood up, pointing his enormous revolver straight at Winter. "Well," he said, "hidey-ho there, young fellows. Hidey, hidey, hidey ho."

Early came up out of the grass in front of them holding a rifle. "Don't try nothing funny," he said.

Reggie whimpered and put up his hands. Winter did the same.

Early walked toward Winter, while Sevenkiller approached Reggie. When Early got within striking distance Winter made a queer sound, like a small rodent that had gone mad with fear, and whipped his rifle off his back and swung it at Early like a club. Early's shoulder absorbed most of the blow. He grunted and lunged at Winter and wrestled him to the ground.

"You little pecker," Early snarled, then Winter bit his hand.

"Oh Jesus fuck!" Early shrieked, ripping his hand away. Winter scratched at Early's cheek and screamed, a high sound filled with fear and fury.

Early punched Winter's face, over and over again. After a few solid shots on the chin, Winter went limp. Early gasped for breath, and relaxed, and looked up at Sevenkiller. Before he could speak, Winter, his face a bloody wreck, smashed Early across the ear with a rock.

Early was knocked clean off Winter, who staggered to his feet, then stumbled like a drunk back to his knees, and finally keeled over on his side and lay still.

Reggie had not moved. He stood stock-still, his hands in the air and his eyes wide.

Sevenkiller had his gun trained on Reggie's head. He had watched the battle between Early and Winter with amazement. Now his gaze turned back to Reggie.

"Don't get any ideas," Sevenkiller said.

17

When Winter regained consciousness, he was tied to a chair in a dark barn. Dirt floor, thin gray wooden walls. The only light what leaked through the cracks between the boards. It smelled dank, like a place where things had died, and it was silent, except for Reggie whimpering and the intermittent spatter of rain against the wood.

"Auggie?" Reggie whispered.

Winter lifted his head and felt pain, as if there was a fork in his brain and someone had twisted it. He lowered his head and threw up between his feet.

"Auggie, be quiet!" Reggie said, his voice so high it was a wonder it didn't break. "Auggie, please!"

Winter forced himself to lift his head in spite of the pain and looked at Reggie, who was tied to another chair about five feet away.

"You have to be quiet," Reggie whispered.

"Why?" Winter said. "I don't reckon they forgot they put us in here."

"Shh!"

"Where are we?"

"I don't know," Reggie whispered. "They took us over a bridge. Then we left the road and I got lost on the paths. I'm afraid they're going to kill us."

Winter didn't say anything to this.

"Auggie, do you think they'll kill us?"

"I don't know."

"We're prisoners of war, aren't we?" Reggie said. "They can't just kill us."

"They can do anything they like to us," Winter said.

"No they can't," Reggie said. "There's rules to war."

"Yeah," Winter replied. "And a lot of time they get broken."

Reggie gave Winter a reproachful look, a beseeching look. But Winter turned away. There was no real comfort he could give.

Winter flared his nostrils. "Why does it smell like ice cream in here?"

Something stirred at the other side of the barn. Reggie let out a little cry.

"Who's there?" Winter said.

"It's Bill," a voice said, sounding unsteady. "Who are you?"

Winter did not say anything.

A man came out of the darkness. A small Indian, young, shaking as if with fever, his shirt stained with vomit and reeking of vanilla.

"Who are you?" Bill said. "Are you Yankees?"

"Don't say nothing," Winter said to Reggie.

"It's not me you have to worry about," Bill said, wiping his mouth with the back of his sleeve. "What is the matter with your eyes?"

The barn door swung inward. The sky was gray and the light was relatively dim but it was still blinding, and both Reggie and Winter squirmed in their chairs. Bill held up his hands to shield his eyes and stumbled, groaning, back into the darkness.

"Well fucking well," Early said as he came inside. "Look who's woken up."

Captain Jackson followed behind, limping on his crutch.

"Thought you were real tough, didn't you? Don't feel so tough now, though, I'll reckon."

Reggie's eyes were leaking, and he was making a lot of noise breathing, like he'd been running. Winter was not in much better shape. But there was something defiant in his manner, too, as if he had been in this barn before, and he was used to it, and he was bracing himself for something terrible but not unfamiliar.

"I asked you a question, boy!" Early shouted.

Both Reggie and Winter flinched but neither of them spoke.

Early's belt slithered out from around his waist and the buckle snapped against Winter's face. He gave a cry and turned away.

"You feel like biting me now, boy?"

Winter looked back at Early and his eyes were wide with fear but burning with hatred.

"Fuck you," Winter said.

"You weren't kidding," Tom said. "You got yourself a kicker."

"He's a fucking baby," Early said. "You think you're tough 'cause you don't know how bad it can get."

At this, Winter actually smiled. It was not for show, but a real smile, a reflex. His lip had been smashed and his teeth were bloody. "Try me."

Early stepped forward, went down on one knee, windmilled his arm, and punched Winter in the stomach. Winter released an explosion of air then retched.

"You're sickening," Early said. "You make me sick."

"All right," Tom said. "That's enough for now."

He came forward as Early reluctantly stepped back.

"I'm Captain Tom Jackson. I guess you boys are bummers with Sherman's army. Is that right?"

Winter was still whooping and retching, so Tom looked at Reggie.

Reggie nodded.

"What are you doing all the way out here?" Tom asked.

"We're foraging for the army," Reggie said. "It's allowed, according to the rules of war."

"You fucking thieves," Early said. "Looting and burning our

homes! Whyn't you fight our soldiers if you're so concerned about the rules of war?"

Reggie started to cry.

"I was just following orders," he said.

"All right," Tom said. "Where's the army headed?"

Reggie hesitated and looked at Winter, who was only now recovering. Then he said, "Macon."

"Bullshit," Early said.

Tom put his hand to his sandy beard.

"You're going to tell us the truth," Early said, jabbing his finger at Reggie.

"That is the truth!" Reggie cried. "I swear."

"It's a fucking lie," Early said. "You're too far east."

Reggie glanced at Winter.

"Don't you say nothing, Reggie," Winter said.

Early smacked Winter, hard, with the back of his hand, and Winter's chair fell to the side and he hit his head. Winter let out another high cry of pain. When Early loomed over him he shrank in fear.

"All right," Early said, "let's get this over with."

He trooped off to the far corner of the room and came back with a bucket sloshing full of water. Winter looked at the bucket, uncomprehending, until Early seized him by the hair, lifted him up together with the chair, and dunked his head into it. Winter struggled and made desperate noises. After about forty seconds Early pulled his head back out.

"Still don't have anything to say?" Early demanded.

Winter gasped for air. Fear was clearly written on his face. But he said nothing, so Early jammed his head back into the bucket.

Tom stood with his arms folded across his chest.

Reggie was crying with his mouth open.

The dunking continued until it was interrupted by a voice:

"You're doing it wrong."

Tom and Early started.

Sevenkiller had come into the barn without making a sound. He was smiling and gripping a scarf between his hands.

"He'll break," Early said.

"No he won't," Sevenkiller replied. "You're just taking away his air. He knows you'll give it back. You need to put him on his back, so you make his gorge rise. Go on. Put him on his back. I'll show you."

Early frowned but tilted Winter's chair so it lay on its back. Winter stared at the ceiling and breathed, breathed, breathed while he still could.

"Put this over his face," Sevenkiller said and handed Early the scarf.

Early pressed the scarf down on Winter's nose and mouth.

"Now watch this," Sevenkiller said. "It's such a very little thing."

A stream of water splashed down over Winter's nose and mouth. Almost immediately his whole body went into convulsions. It was a sensation totally unlike being able to breathe. He had never felt anything like it.

"Oh my god," Tom said.

"Hidee-lee, hidee-lee," Sevenkiller hummed.

Winter strained against the ropes. It was like there was a pulsing, writhing thing inside his chest, like he was being turned inside out. He started to weep but he couldn't breathe. His face turned brick red and his eyes popped out and everything else jerked and twitched. It went on and on.

From the darkness, forgotten by everyone, Bill watched without much emotion. He had seen worse: men blown apart and screaming for their mothers in absurd, high-pitched voices. Men weeping as their limbs were sawn off by doctors. Men turning waxy and yellow as they bled out through their guts. That was all much worse than this. It would not go on long. The boy would break. Everyone did. It was the hardest lesson of war: that men were their bodies, not their spirits, and there was much that the body could not bear, no matter how strong the spirit.

The flow of water stopped and the scarf was removed.

"You want to talk now, young man?" Sevenkiller said.

It was a narrow thing. It could have gone either way. Winter almost surrendered. Tears trickling down his cheeks, and he was scared. But he'd been prepared for this moment, this pain, this darkness. He was ready. All they were doing was baptizing him. Pushing him further and further into the man he was going to be.

"All right," Sevenkiller said.

The rag pressed down over Winter's mouth and the water came.

Winter made a howling noise of agony and thrashed from side to side, trying to escape. But his eyes locked onto Sevenkiller's, and they were not growing more desperate. As the strain, the stress, the pain grew, those eyes became harder and harder, like coals being transformed into diamonds by pressure.

Sevenkiller, in spite of himself, felt uneasy.

The water stopped. The rag came off. Winter inhaled in a scream and let out a choked sob.

"Tell us!" Sevenkiller barked. "It's never going to stop!"

Here it comes, thought Bill.

"Kill you," Winter gasped.

The scarf came down again.

Winter bucked in the chair so desperately, with all of his muscles firing blindly, his limbs flailing in a reflexive attempt to escape, that his forearm snapped like a twig. The sound of it was clearly audible.

"Aw, fuck," Tom said in disgust.

"Stop, stop!" Reggie sobbed. "Stop it! We're going to Savannah! We're going to Savannah!"

Early lifted the scarf and stood up. Reluctantly, Sevenkiller set the bucket down.

"Savannah?" Tom said.

Reggie wept unreservedly.

"Savannah?" Tom said again. "Not Macon? Or Augusta?"

"No," Reggie said, still sniffling. "We're going between 'em. All the way to the sea."

"What kind of strategy is that?" Tom said. "You're going to just bypass every military target in Georgia? Where are you going to get your supplies?"

Reggie didn't say anything.

"Oh fuck," Early said. "Captain."

But now Jackson saw it. The Union troops were not going to bring their supplies with them. They were going to live off the land. An army of sixty thousand men cutting a path across Georgia, all the way from Atlanta to the sea. Confiscating food and supplies, burning towns, twisting up the railroads. A ribbon of destruction cutting the state in two.

"All our troops are down in Macon," Early said, his voice panicked. "Sherman fooled us. There ain't no one to stop him."

"All right," Tom said. "Let's go make a plan."

"Should we kill them?" Sevenkiller said.

Tom gave Sevenkiller a strange look.

"No, leave 'em."

"What about just this one?" Sevenkiller said, motioning to Winter and drawing his revolver. "I'll just shoot him now."

"No," Tom said. "Let him alone. That's an order." And then, seeing Bill, who had crept out of the shadows: "You too. Come on."

Sevenkiller looked into Winter's eyes. Pure hatred burned back at him. Sevenkiller felt briefly alarmed. But then he laughed and hummed "Hi-diddly-ho" and holstered his revolver and turned away.

Bill walked past the two Union soldiers. Slowly. He too looked into Winter's eyes. He too saw the hatred burning out of them and an electric sensation ran up and down his spine. The boy had not broken. How was that possible? Bill could feel the strength of will, the sense of purpose, radiating off him like heat. Who was this boy? How could he be only a lowly private? Wouldn't that kind of strength carve its own path in the world? What could contain it? It was so diametrically opposed to Bill's perception of his own character that he could not help but pause, fascinated, before he headed out of the barn.

The door to the barn closed behind Bill. The only sound was Reggie weeping and Winter coughing up water and blood on the floor.

18

The Confederates assembled in Captain Jackson's parlor. Sevenkiller entered through the back door. Bill's hands were tied again and he sat a little apart from the others.

Tom told Stoga what Reggie had said, and after a pause, Stoga replied.

"I don't think it can be true. I don't think they can go so far without a cracker line. I don't see how Sherman can leave his wagon trains exposed to raiders from Macon."

"He don't need no goddamn wagon train," Early said. "He's going to eat up the goddamn country till he gets to the sea. Then he's going to get his supplies over the water."

"Hrmm," Stoga said. "But our men are in Macon and Augusta."

"That's the point," Tom said. "They don't want to fight our soldiers. The Union forces are deliberately targeting our civilians. Do you understand?"

"I don't think so," Stoga said. "I don't think that can be happening."

Sevenkiller laughed. "Of course it can!" he said. "It happened before. Don't you remember? It wasn't so long ago."

"What are you babbling about?" Early said.

"The Cherokee used to live here," Sevenkiller said. "Not even thirty years ago. Their lands had been promised to them by the government, in treaty after treaty after treaty. But in 1838 they were sent west, to the Indian Territory, and four thousand of them died along the way. That's how the good people who live here now got their land."

"That ain't the same thing at all," Early said. "We're civilized people."

"Ah," Sevenkiller said. "But so were they! They lived on farms and they had their own constitution and newspaper and a Bible in their own language and nice white-man names like John and Richard. And everything was stolen from them, except for a lucky few like my master."

"It ain't the same thing!" Early shouted. "What would a goddamn nigger Indian like you know about it?"

"Everything." Sevenkiller giggled. "I would know all about it. Wouldn't I?"

"Enough," Tom said. "This is happening, whether we like it or not. So we need to get the word to Milledgeville, and to Macon too. But first we have something to do."

Tom gestured to the map on the table.

"If we can take out that bridge," Tom said, "the whole Union

Army will be stuck on the west bank of the Ocmulgee. They'll be exposed to raiders from Macon and they'll have to eat up their supplies. And it might just buy us enough time to move our army around."

"Hrmm," Stoga said.

"They've got no cracker line and no lines of communication to Washington," Tom continued. "We can still make the state of Georgia their graveyard. Lieutenant Stoga, I know this is a lot to ask. You and your men have only been free a few days, and I know you want to get back home."

"We'll help," Stoga said. "We'll stay with you till the bridge is destroyed."

Sevenkiller tittered and said, "It's a good chance to try out my new toy!"

No one paid him any mind.

"All right," Tom said. With an effort he hauled himself out of his chair.

"Lieutenant, with all due respect, I think we'll leave Private Bread here on the farm," Tom said. "I think he could use a little time to recover."

"Hrmm," Stoga said. "I do not like to leave him alone in a distillery."

"Well then," Tom said, "I suppose we'll have to tie him up in the barn with the bummers. I hate to do it, but if I can't trust him in the pantry, I can't trust him on an errand like this."

"All right," Stoga said.

Bill looked at the floor and said nothing.

19

Meanwhile, at the Williams farm, Mrs. Williams was preparing porridge for a hundred ex-slaves. While she was distracted, Duncan Empire swiped a dozen spoons. They felt cold and hard in his hands as he slipped them into his bag and walked back outside.

Quentin sat on a chair on the back porch. He was examining a map and speaking with the ex-slaves, including the old man Croesus.

None of the ex-slaves had seen a map or knew how to read, so Quentin was asking them questions and writing the answers in a little leather-bound book, stopping frequently to lick the tip of his pen.

In the distance, plumes of smoke were rising into the air as the railway ties and cotton gins burned. Upon Lieutenant Ross's orders, Sergeant Service and Sergeant Müller were leading the ex-slaves in the general destruction of the countryside. The lit up anything to do with the cotton industry, flipped over railway tracks and burned the ties, and wrapped white-hot iron rails around the trees. The railway and the cotton fields were legitimate targets of warfare. Still, Sergeant Service had been concerned, particularly with the decision to employ the former slaves, a move guaranteed to inflame local sensibilities.

Duncan squinted and saw that selfsame Sergeant Service coming up the path from the woods. Duncan's face gave nothing away, save for a slight contraction around his eyes.

"How wide is the river?" Quentin asked.

"Oh," Croesus said. "Real wide. Say from here all the way to the woods."

"Deep? Swift?"

"Yes sir, and yes sir," Croesus said. "Can't get across it with no wagons, that's for sure."

"Many bridges?"

"No sir," Croesus replied. "Only one for miles."

"How far?" Quentin said.

"Oh, many many miles, sir," Croesus replied. "Lord! Many miles. Got to go many miles before you find another bridge."

"Sounds like an important bridge," Quentin said. "Now, none of you have seen any soldiers for days. Is that right?"

"No sir," Croesus said. "They walked through three days ago. They's going south, to Macon."

"Excellent," Quentin said.

"There's some troops still here," one of the blacks said. A tall, powerful young man.

Croesus pressed his lips into a thin line and shook his head without turning around.

"Really?" Quentin said. "Where?"

"Saw one back at the plantation. He had a blue uniform on,

though, and he was a black man. But he had straight hair like an Indian."

Croesus arched his eyebrows skeptically. The other ex-slaves let out incredulous noises. But Quentin made eye contact with Gordon Service, who was just arriving.

"Indeed," Quentin said. "Where did you see this man?"

Now the black man who had spoken paused.

"I went back to the plantation."

"After you escaped?" Quentin said.

"What's your name, boy?" Gordon said.

The big black did not reply.

"His name's Freddy," Croesus said.

"That's just about what I figured," Gordon said, slinging his rifle off his back.

"Is there a problem, Sergeant?" Quentin asked.

"Yeah," Gordon replied. "This one killed his owner. The word's all over town."

"Is that true?" Quentin asked Johnson.

For a very long time, Fred Johnson stared at Quentin, his expression desperate, pleading, and wrathful.

Quentin saw something there he liked.

"I don't doubt he had it coming," Gordon said. "But sensibilities on that particular issue down here are a little touchy. We don't want to give them the idea that they've got to fight till the last man."

"It's all right, Sergeant," Quentin said.

"What do you mean?" Gordon said.

"We'll deal with it later."

"Lieutenant, don't you think we better deal with it now? The whole town's talking about it."

"We're here to bring freedom to these people, Sergeant."

"Like hell we are!" Gordon said. "Lieutenant! I am sorry, our orders are clear."

"I told you, Sergeant," Quentin said, annoyance creeping into his voice. "The liberation of the slaves is of prime importance to General Sherman."

Gordon's expression hardened.

"Can I talk to you for a minute, Lieutenant?"

Anger darted across Quentin's face, there and gone, like a rabbit crossing a narrow path.

"Very well," Quentin said. He stood up and motioned with his head to Duncan Empire, and the three of them walked over to the edge of the porch.

Gordon looked oddly calm. He didn't even acknowledge Duncan; he only said, "Sherman doesn't give a straw for niggers. And you know it."

"Are you calling me a liar?"

"Whatever you like," Gordon said. "Because there's no fucking way Sherman told you to let it slide if slaves started killing their masters. No way."

"Maybe you should watch what you say to your commanding officer," Duncan said.

"You aren't even in the fucking army!" Gordon snapped. "Quentin, you want to turn this nigger loose, then you go right ahead. I'll follow your goddamn orders. But the general will hear about it."

Quentin was unruffled. "Sergeant, that's quite enough. You'll follow my orders."

"Yes sir."

"Now, take your men and go and secure this bridge that Croesus was telling us about."

At this, Gordon lost some of his confidence.

"Well sir, that's why I came here. I can't find Winter and Keller."

"You can't find them?" Quentin asked.

"They ran off and now they're gone."

"Sergeant!" Quentin said.

"I know, sir. I'm sorry, but I can't watch them every moment."

"At any rate, we need to secure the bridge," Quentin said. "Take Duncan and his brothers. And bring that Freddy along with you. I'm sure I needn't explain to you the importance of that bridge."

"Yes sir," Gordon said.

Gordon slung his rifle onto his back, stomped off the porch, and shouted at Fred Johnson: "Hey boy! Come with me. Today's your lucky day."

Duncan walked to the other side of the porch, where Charlie and

Johnny were rocking back and forth in their chairs and cackling. He had to step around Mrs. Williams.

"Mrs. Williams!" Quentin said. "Do you have the porridge for our guests?"

"Lieutenant Ross," she said, "someone has made off with my spoons!"

At these words Quentin's eyes flew wide open. He grinned. And then he started to laugh. He laughed so hard he stumbled back into his chair. He laughed so hard he wept. A couple of the blacks started to laugh as well.

"Your spoons!" Quentin said. "Your spoons!"

And he laughed some more.

20

Fred Johnson led Gordon and the three Empire brothers into Planter's Factory. All of the houses were locked and shuttered and the streets were deserted. Charlie began to whistle "Dixie" loudly, and Johnny guffawed. They reached the foot of the bridge without incident. The only sound was of rushing water. Not a soul in sight.

Gordon felt good when he set his feet upon the bridge. Here was a real object of strategic worth, straightforward and clean, without any of the ambiguity of their mission.

"All right, boys," Gordon said. "We'll stay close to this bank, but we want to get a clean line of fire on anyone sneaking up at us."

"Okay sir," Duncan said. "How about we send my brothers up to the factory for a minute? That's another important objective."

"All right," Gordon said. "If you hear a shot, come running."

Charlie and Johnny winked at Duncan and headed north along the riverbank. Johnson, Gordon, and Duncan walked about one-third of the way across the bridge.

"Can I be honest with you, Sergeant?" Duncan said.

"Certainly," Gordon replied.

"I'm a little worried you and me are getting off on the wrong foot. That you've got the wrong idea about me."

"Mister Empire, I don't have the wrong idea about you," Gordon said. "To you, this war is nothing more than a license for criminality. I know that, and so does the lieutenant."

Duncan stopped walking and so did Gordon.

"Well now," Duncan said. "What else is war but the suspension of the regular rules? And why wouldn't a man seek to profit from that little holiday, if he could?"

"There are rules of war," Gordon said.

"Rules?" Duncan said. "To this here? What we're doing?"

"It is not as difficult as you make it seem."

"Let me tell you something, sir," Duncan said. "You think the rules are vague by accident? Uncle Billy knows we're out here breaking the rules. He sets our quotas too high to fill by following the rules. So he makes sure the army's fed and the people here feel the pain of war, but if the country gets too riled up, he'll have us hung. The rules are for his protection, not yours. The rules will not save you, not on this campaign."

"I will tell our commanding officers what Lieutenant Ross has got up to," Gordon said. "It will be up to them to decide."

"About what?" Duncan said. "This nigger?" Duncan pointed his rifle at Johnson. "Say the word, sir."

Johnson's whole body tensed.

"Lower your gun," Gordon said.

"You think it will save you if you tattle on Quentin?" Duncan said. "They'll either ignore you or hang you with him. No, Sergeant Service. We need a lighter touch. You trust me. We're all in this together. I'll get us through this. I don't want to get hung any more than you do."

"Trust you?" Gordon said. "I don't think so. Mister Empire, I've heard quite enough. You and your brothers will obey the lieutenant. When he tells you to obey me, you'll do that too. And in my company, you will follow the field orders. Understood?"

Duncan smiled. The lines around his eyes were very hard.

"Duly noted," he said, and raised his rifle and shot Gordon in the face. The back of the sergeant's head blew off and he crumpled to the earth without a sound.

"Lord!" Johnson exclaimed, raising his hands to his face.

"He won't help you, sonny," Duncan said. "Either He doesn't care or He's dead."

Duncan pointed his rifle at Johnson, but before he could pull the trigger, a bullet struck the wood at his feet. Startled, he swung his rifle toward the west end of the bridge, and in an instant, Johnson was moving. He was up and over the bridge's rail before Duncan could turn back.

"Limber son of a bitch, aren't you?" Duncan said.

Two more shots cracked into the wood around him, and he felt one whistle past his head. The muzzle flashes were coming from the woods on the far side of the bridge. Duncan had no cover, so he too jumped into the water.

Spluttering, Duncan broke the surface and swam to the shore, where he climbed up the bank and took shelter behind the stone mill. Very briefly, he peeked around the edge of the building and saw four men sprinting onto the bridge. One of them, a small black, was carrying a box on his back.

"Looks like we're in for some action after all," Duncan said.

He made his way up the gentle slope to the main street of the town, where he met with Johnny and Charlie Empire. Both of them were carrying large sacks that made clanking noises as they moved.

"What happened?" Charlie said.

"What do you think happened, you motherless bastard?" Duncan said. "The rebs took us by surprise. The sergeant is dead. Now run! We've got to get to Quentin before those rebel whores chop that bridge down."

When Johnny made as if to drop his sack, Duncan shouted, "You drop that and I'll kick your teeth in, you dumb ox! It's worth more to me than you are."

They sprinted out of town, into the fields, where the fires were raging.

The largest pillar of smoke, so thick and massive it might have been supporting the sky, was also the closest. Quentin was directing a company of Negroes in burning a field of cotton. Sparks leapt up into the air, glittering to life and winking out into darkness a moment later. Great sheets of ash wafted high on the hot wind and drifted across the horizon.

Duncan arrived first, well ahead of his brothers and only slightly out of breath.

"The rebels have taken the bridge," Duncan said. "Sergeant Service is dead."

Quentin, who had been grinning at the holocaust before him, started at this sudden arrival. His eyes looked very large and white in his soot-stained face.

"Pardon me?" he said.

"Lieutenant Ross, the rebs have taken the bridge and it's a safe bet they're going to try to burn it down. We got to get over there just as soon as we can."

Quentin turned to the old man Croesus, who was watching the cotton burn with sad satisfaction.

"Croesus, my good man," he said. "Spread the word! The rebels are here! They've killed one of my men, and they're destroying a critical bridge! We need every able-bodied Negro to rally to the Union's banner! Go quickly now! There isn't much time!"

Croesus ran off, shouting across the fields.

The other Empire brothers arrived. Their sacks clanked when they hit the ground.

"Where is big Freddy?" Quentin asked.

"Ran off," Duncan said, his eyes glinting.

Quentin arched an eyebrow. "Strange of him to do that in hostile territory," he said.

Duncan turned and motioned to Charlie and Johnny, and they backed off. When they were gone, he said, "You had two problems before, and now you have none."

"Sergeant Service wasn't a problem," Quentin said.

"Sure he was," Duncan said. "He would have found out about your little games sooner or later. Like in the cottage."

To this, Quentin said nothing, but his face drained of any human emotion, so that it looked as if it were carved out of wax.

Duncan laughed. "Did you forget about that already? Well, I won't forget anytime soon. But you can trust me. You and I both know what this is. We're both having our fun. You in your way, and me in mine. So live and let live, I say, and we'll both get through this all right, when things go back to normal."

Only then did Quentin react. A short spasm flashed across his features. A look, for an instant, of dismay.

Duncan raised his eyebrows.

"Something the matter, sir?" he said.

"I thought . . . ," Quentin started.

"You thought what, Lieutenant?"

"I thought you would be different," he said.

"Than who?"

"You sound so eager for the war to be over," Quentin said.

Duncan threw back his head and laughed. "Of course!" he said. He kicked one of the sacks and it clanked. "What would I do with all this if the war never ended?" he asked. "Who'd buy it from me if they knew I could break down his door an hour later and take it back? Who'd buy anything from anyone, for that matter?"

Quentin did not reply.

"You enjoy your little holiday," Duncan said. "And after the war what you do is your own business. But I'm going to set myself up as a gentleman of leisure once this is all over. And you're not going to stand in my way any more than Service did. Do you follow me?"

Just then Sergeant Müller arrived with the rest of the soldiers, and Croesus returned at the head of a crowd of ex-slaves. Quentin's face reassembled into an expression of relaxed confidence. He turned to address them, raising his hands.

"Gentlemen!" he called. "The rebels are seeking to destroy a bridge of enormous strategic value! We shall need your help to dislodge them. My men will take up positions along the riverbank and fire upon their flanks, while you, newly liberated slaves, will charge the bridge. We must act quickly, before they damage it beyond repair!"

"Three cheers for the Union and President Lincoln!" Croesus cried.

They cheered and began marching toward the town.

21

Winter and Reggie remained tied to their chairs in the barn. Bill Bread had been tied to a beam. He watched Winter lying on his back. Winter's eyes were closed, so Bill could not see those strange golden irises. The boy's face was lean and angular and drawn with pain, but it seemed to suit him somehow. Made him look like something strong and feral, like a bird of prey.

Finally, Reggie spoke.

"Auggie?"

". . ."

"Auggie? Auggie?"

"What?"

"Do you believe in heaven?"

Reggie had been weeping a long time, and his handsome baby face was puffy and bloated and streaked with dirt.

"Well, do you?" Reggie said. "Your daddy was a preacher, wasn't he?"

"Yeah."

"Well, do you think we're going to heaven?"

"I don't know."

"We gotta," Reggie said, his voice crumbling under the weight of his fear, more tears leaking from his eyes. "This can't be all there is."

Winter opened his eyes and breathed in the dirty air. He looked at Bill for a moment, then closed his eyes again. "I don't know about heaven," he said. "I just can't see how He'd make heaven after He made all this."

"Auggie, please. Please."

"A lot of things are just talk, Reggie," Winter said. "I don't know what's what anymore. God made the world. He made all of it, the good and the bad. So what's He like? That He could let all this happen? What's He want us to be?"

Reggie shook, literally trembled, in his bonds.

"Before my people were Christians," Bill said, "we believed that when people died, they went to the darkening land in the west. Animals too."

"Well, that strikes me as likely as anything else," Winter said.

After that, no one said anything for a long time. Eventually they heard footsteps outside the barn.

"Who is that?" Bill called. "Uncle? Is that you? I want a drink of water."

There was a tremendous noise of iron striking iron. Reggie screamed. Winter did not even flinch. His eyes narrowed to slits. The noise was repeated and the door burst inward.

Fred Johnson stepped into the barn, his drenched overalls plastered to his muscular body. He carried a tremendous metal bar in his hand, and Winter's rifle was slung across his shoulders.

"Well, ain't you a sight for sore eyes," Winter said.

Johnson cocked his head as if he didn't understand.

"Cut me loose," Winter said.

Johnson freed Winter first, and he stood, clutching his broken arm close to his chest.

"Who's he?" Johnson asked, nodding toward Bill Bread as he untied Reggie.

"I don't rightly know," Winter said. "Who are you, anyway?"

"Bill Bread," Bill said. "Take me with you."

"I don't know about that," Winter said.

"Please!" Bill cried. "I don't want to go back to North Carolina. I don't want to go back to the Confederacy! I was going to fight for the Union after I was taken prisoner. Sevenkiller and my uncle kidnapped me. Don't leave me here!"

Reggie had already bolted out into the sunlight. "Come on!" he shrieked over his shoulder.

Johnson slapped the metal bar against his palm. It made a heavy, meaty sound.

"Please," Bill said. "Don't leave me!"

Johnson and Winter looked into each other's eyes.

Winter shrugged. "Why not?"

They cut Bill loose, snatched their rifles from the house, then fled into the forest, heading west, not stopping until they were about twenty feet from the rushing river. It had begun to rain, cold and flat through the red and gold leaves, which were muted against the colorless sky. Winter shivered like a newborn puppy.

"Let me look at your arm," Johnson said.

He took Winter's broken left forearm in his big black hands. His palms and the underside of his fingers were surprisingly white, hard, and callused.

Winter screamed.

"Shhh!" Reggie hissed. "Shhh!"

"It ain't set yet," Johnson said. "But you can't yell like that."

"Gimme your belt," Winter said to Bill.

Bill Bread undid his belt and handed it over.

Winter took it with his good right hand, folded it a few times, and bit down. His swollen yellow eyes rolled toward Johnson and he nodded.

The motion of Johnson's wrists was gentle but unyielding. The manipulation of the broken bones went on for some time. Winter's screaming was considerably muzzled.

Reggie retreated to the water's edge.

"There," Johnson said. "It's done."

He pressed a sturdy branch against Winter's arm and strapped it on with cloth.

"I'm gonna faint," Winter said.

"You all right now, boy," Johnson said. "You gonna be all right."

Winter threw up between his legs, a thin yellowish stream. Reggie came back up from the river.

"Is it over?" he said, his voice small.

"Yeah," Winter said.

Reggie sat down on a rock next to Winter.

"Where'd you learn to do that?" Reggie asked Johnson.

"Lotta broken bones on Massa Johnson's plantation."

Winter looked at the river and, light-headed, was suddenly reminded of the Illinois River back home.

"Help me up, Johnson," Winter said.

Johnson lifted Winter, who swayed on his feet.

"We should cross the river now," Bill said. "I'm a good swimmer. I can help him."

"You go on and swim 'cross the river," Johnson said. "I can't go with you."

"Why not?" Bill asked.

"I killed my master," Johnson said.

"Was he very cruel?" Bill said.

"He was to me," Johnson said, adding, "I didn't make it easy on either one of us. I wasn't born to be a slave."

"No," Winter said. "I see that."

"He could have had me sold or killed or crippled," Johnson said. "But he thought he would break me. He was making a big point about it. But he never did."

Winter nodded slowly. "Okay," he said. "Reggie, you take our friend Bill back to the lieutenant. I'm going to stay here with Freddy."

"What?" Reggie said, glancing nervously at Bill Bread.

"Go on," Winter said. "Go on now."

Despite his fear and to his credit, Reggie was reluctant to leave Winter. But in the end he walked up to Winter and embraced him, like a boy, and like a boy, Winter embraced him back. Then Reggie ran down to the bank and plunged into the cold water up to his knees and splashed forward, swimming hard across the river. The current swept him south, toward the bridge.

"What are you going to do?" Bill asked. "Why are you staying?"

"Why don't you get out of here?" Winter said. "Before we change our minds about you."

Bill shrank back and made his way to the water. Winter stood on the bank watching until Bill was halfway across. Then he walked with Johnson into the woods.

22

Stoga and Tom hacked holes into the bridge and stuffed them with kindling and wood chips to set alight. It was very slow going because the wood was thick and strong and showed no more inclination to burn than stone.

Early and Sevenkiller set up a rough barricade made from beams they'd pried loose. When they were done, Early walked to the edge of the bridge and looked down into the town. A small white man standing on top of a crate was haranguing a crowd of Negroes.

"Well, he's sure stirring them up all right," Early said and then began to cough wretchedly into his fist. "Come right in this little village where there's no soldiers and turning all the slaves against their masters. That's their idea of war."

Sevenkiller laughed. "Don't worry," he said. "We'll show them what modern war is all about, very soon."

Sevenkiller was fiddling with something inside his box and humming even more quickly and tunelessly than usual.

The little white man threw his hands in the air and pointed at the bridge. The Negroes gave a tremendous cheer and ran toward them.

"Shit," Early said. "Here they come."

Tom hobbled over. He saw the crowd of blacks surging forward. He thought, Slaves were attacking, slaves who had never questioned their lot, who would never have dared to participate in such an act of rebellion. Despair rose up in him. Even if they won, how could things ever go back to the way they were before?

Early, coughing, tugged on Tom's sleeve. "Captain, watch the river."

A few of the bummers waded into the water and aimed their rifles up at the Confederates, trying to flank them while the ex-slaves charged with nothing but picks and shovels. Tom fired his pistol twice. One of the bummers, a young one, dropped into the water. The others scattered back. But the blacks were at the foot of the bridge, only fifty feet away.

Early fired his rifle. One of the blacks dropped; the rest kept coming.

Tom pumped his remaining shots into the crowd then dropped behind the barricade.

"Now Sevenkiller, now!" he shouted.

Sevenkiller tossed the box away, revealing a cylindrical metal device set up on a tripod: a pepper-box gun, designed by Orison Blunt, stolen from the Union Army, capable of being operated by one man and of firing seventy shots a minute.

"Ha ha ha ha ha!" Sevenkiller laughed as the Negroes closed to within twenty feet. He began madly spinning the crank.

The sheer momentum of the crowd carried them all the way to the barricade even in the face of the bullets. Perhaps they could still have overwhelmed the Confederates. But so many were killed so quickly, and the noise of the gun was so startling, that the mob trembled, then broke and rushed back down the bridge, screaming, one corpse dropping after another while Sevenkiller blasted away at their retreating backs, laughing.

23

Quentin and Duncan crouched against the stone wall of the mill and watched as the ex-slaves were carved up by the machine gun.

"My goodness," Quentin said. "What manner of weapon do they have there?"

"Sir, perhaps we'd better take cover," Duncan said.

"Did you see the kind of gun they were using?"

"No sir."

Most of the Negroes were running straight into the woods, but some were staggering back into town. A few were screaming and tearing their hair.

"I don't think we can drive them off the bridge," Quentin said.

"What do we do now, sir?" Duncan asked.

"Well, if we cannot dislodge them from where they are, perhaps we can force them to come to us."

Duncan understood. He wasn't sure whether to laugh. He thought that Quentin was both more and less mad than at first he appeared.

Quentin gathered the Union foragers and the remaining ex-slaves in the town's main intersection, just in front of the inn, and gave his instructions. Sergeant Müller alone looked troubled. His eyes quickly fell upon Duncan and his sniggering brothers.

"You three," Jan said. "Come with me."

And so it was that the Empire brothers followed Jan into the factory, where they methodically wrecked everything that could be wrecked. Duncan thought that it was typical for the German to start in the only building of actual military significance in the town and the only one without anything of value to steal.

The massive industrial looms looked imposing and powerful, but they were made of wood and fragile because of their complex interlocking design. They burned for only a short time before collapsing in on themselves like dried twigs.

While the others watched the looms burn, Duncan darted out of the factory. Out on the street he looked around for Quentin but did not find him. He had readjusted the bag on his shoulder and started toward one of the fancier houses when Reginald Keller staggered into the main street, his soaked clothes clinging to his body. Trailing behind Reggie was a little Indian who Duncan did not recognize.

"Hey!" Duncan called. "Babe! Where have you been?"

"Winter and I were captured, but we got loose," Reggie said. He was shivering and his lips were blue. "We were held by some Confederate Indians."

"Who the hell is this?" Duncan said.

"His name is Bill Bread," Reginald said. "He says that he wants to join us."

"He does, does he?" Duncan said. "Well, where's Winter?"

"On the other side of the river."

"What the hell is he doing there?"

"He's with the nigger who sprung us loose," Reggie said.

After hearing these words, Duncan felt as a mouse must when the shadow of a hawk passes by.

"Nigger?" Duncan said.

"Sorry, Mister Empire," Reggie said. "I meant colored fellow."

"What colored fellow?"

"His name was Freddy," Duncan said.

"What did he say to you?" Duncan said, coming close to Reggie and putting his hand on the knife on his belt.

Bill stiffened. But Reggie was oblivious.

"He didn't say nothing. He just turned us loose. Winter's arm is busted and he couldn't swim."

"He didn't say anything about how he came over there?" Duncan demanded.

"No," Reggie said. "I don't know where he came from."

This one was too dumb to be lying, Duncan decided. Reggie didn't know about what happened on the bridge. But there was no telling what Johnson had told Winter by now.

Duncan let go of his knife.

"Perhaps I'll go look for him," Duncan said. "You go on and find the lieutenant. Take this Indian with you."

"Yes sir," Reggie said. He walked down the street, hugging himself and shivering. Bill hesitated.

"Well, go on," Duncan said. "Do you need a kick in the ass to get you moving, you reb turncoat?"

Duncan loped down to the edge of the water while Bill made his way back to the inn. The front door had been kicked in, the furniture knocked about. The innkeeper was nowhere to be found.

The keg of cider was gone, but after a frantic search, Bill found a bottle of brandy hidden away in the kitchen. The first swallow hit his nerves with soothing fire. He sighed, closed his eyes, and pressed his forehead against the wallpaper. Then he walked back into the common room and sat by the window, where he had a fine view of the burning bridge.

He could see his uncle and Sevenkiller working with the other men to destroy the bridge. For three long years, he had done everything the Confederacy asked of him. Those days were over. He was free of the army, and free of his uncle. Free to drink, finally, drink the way he really wanted to. Without restraint. It was liberating and terrifying at the same time. Where would he go? What place was there for him in the peace?

His mind turned to Winter. He remembered the sound of the arm snapping in the barn. He saw the golden eyes looking at him, the pupils narrowed to black pinpricks, focused and drawn inward with hatred. That force of will. What could you do with will like that? Where would it take you? What could stop you? How would it all end?

Now Winter was waiting on the other side of the river. For what? Revenge against Sevenkiller? And the other man, the one who had asked Reggie *What colored fellow* and *What did he say to you* with his hand on his knife. Why was he crossing the river?

Bill took another drink. Strangely, he was not in as much of a hurry to get drunk as he would have expected. His mind kept drifting away from the drink, across the water, to what was happening there.

24

The Confederates made steady progress hacking up and burning the bridge, despite the rain splattering down from the slate-colored sky.

It was Early who first saw the slender strand of smoke rising from the mill. He walked to the edge of the bridge for a closer look and noticed that the mill's wheel was no longer turning a moment before it toppled over into the water, bobbed under the surface, and began to drift toward the bridge.

"Oh my god," Early said.

He ran back to Tom and Stoga.

"Captain!" Early cried. "Captain!"

"Careful," Tom said. Early had come perilously close to stepping through a hole chopped in the bridge.

"Look at the town!" Early said, as he began to cough. "Look what they're doing to the town!"

"What?" Tom said.

"They're looting the town," Early said.

"What?" Tom said. He hobbled carefully around the damaged sections of the bridge to get a better view. "Why?"

"They want you to come down off the bridge," Sevenkiller said. "To save the town."

"But there are no soldiers in the town," Tom shouted. "There aren't hardly any men, even."

"Hee hee hee!" Sevenkiller giggled. "Tell them that, sir! You should tell them that!"

Tom balled his hands into fists and felt something hot and sharp rise in the back of his throat. He hated these invaders, who had come to a land where they were not wanted or needed and shattered every notion of what was good and just in the universe.

"This is their idea of war?" Tom said. "Don't they have any notion of decency?"

"What do we do, Captain?" Early said.

"Yes, Captain," Sevenkiller said. "What do we do?"

Tears welled up in Tom's eyes as he saw the church catch fire. "If we lose this war," he said, "it will be because we refused to stoop to the depths like them."

"Eee hee hee!" Sevenkiller squealed. "Unless when we get to heaven, it turns out niggers are human beings. Then we're in for it, eh, Captain?"

Tom ignored the slave and continued. "There's a lot more towns on the other side of this river, and if we leave this bridge here they're all going to meet the same fate. Don't let anyone on this bridge. We only need a little longer."

"Yes, Captain," Early said.

Sevenkiller delivered a mock salute and returned to his work destroying the bridge. So did Tom and Stoga.

Early, too sick to be much help, watched the Union soldiers move through the town. Fires sprang up and houses collapsed. He heard the screaming, the shots, the shouts. Now and then he blinked the tears away, but they returned so quickly there scarcely seemed any point.

Sevenkiller's callused hand fell on his shoulder.

"Time to go," he said.

Early stood up, coughing, while Sevenkiller put the machine gun in its box. They made their way back across the bridge, which had been entirely shattered except for a narrow path. The posts and pillars had been hollowed and stuffed with straw and set alight.

Just as they stepped on solid ground the bridge gave way with a suddenness that was astonishing and sublime. There was a trembling, a cracking noise, and then the whole thing was gone, breaking up and drifting south with the current.

Tom said, "It's done. Let's head back. We'll pick up Bill and our prisoners and head to Milledgeville and spread the word about what's going on."

They had only taken about five paces toward the woods when a light flashed in the trees. Tom fell backward, grunting in surprise. A moment later, they heard the gunshot.

"Get down!" Early shouted.

Sevenkiller was already on his belly, slithering toward the woods like a snake.

Tom felt a terrible pain in his chest, right around his collarbone. It was difficult to breathe.

"Captain!" Early shouted, and he cradled Tom in his arms.

Tom looked at him but was unable to speak.

The rifle cracked again. Sevenkiller raised his rifle, and returned fire.

"He's by the oak tree," Sevenkiller cried. "The pale one!"

Early laid Jackson down on the ground, and then he and Stoga charged toward the source of the shots, past Sevenkiller, who was approaching cautiously and giving them covering fire. Early sprinted ahead and burst into the trees. He saw Winter reloading his rifle, and he sprang forward, but Fred Johnson came out of the bushes and struck him hard with an iron bar.

Sevenkiller tried to take aim at Johnson, but there was too much movement as the big ex-slave fought the two men, and no clear target. Another flash of light came from the woods and Sevenkiller felt a bullet whiz past. He saw Winter dive back behind the oak tree.

"Hee hee hee!" Sevenkiller said. He circled around with his rifle at his shoulder, hoping to catch Winter fleeing into the woods. Instead Winter leapt out and tackled him, making a sound like a saw biting into hard wood.

"You little black fucker!" Winter shouted.

They landed with Winter on top, pressing his splinted left forearm into Sevenkiller's neck while his raising a broad knife with his right hand.

Sevenkiller dug his fingers into Winter's arm, which he well remembered was broken, and Winter almost buckled. Sevenkiller dodged the knife easily by moving his head and then swept Winter off with a quick, strong movement of his hips, ending up on top of him, straddling his chest.

"Goodbye," Sevenkiller whispered.

He kept squeezing Winter's broken arm with one hand while he struggled for the knife with the other. Winter tried to buck him off, but it was impossible; the little man stuck close to him.

Finally Sevenkiller pinned the knife arm to the ground with his knee and smashed Winter's face with his free hand, hissing, "You see? You see?"

Sevenkiller yanked the knife away. But Winter used his every ounce of strength to lift his legs and twist his whole body and pitch Sevenkiller off, howling as he did.

Sevenkiller scrambled to gain his feet, but this time it was Winter who was a little quicker, and his shin connected violently with Sevenkiller's face. Sevenkiller stumbled back.

"You little—" Sevenkiller said, laughing, and then stopped. He was looking at something behind Winter. Winter turned around. It was Fred Johnson, breathing deeply, flexing his big hands. He was covered in blood, but very little of it seemed to be his own.

Sevenkiller's eyes flicked between them and then he ran.

Winter stooped and picked up the rifle Sevenkiller had dropped.

"Forget it," Johnson gasped. "He gone."

And indeed Sevenkiller had made it into the trees and was darting from side to side, crouched low to the earth, using every bit of cover he could find.

Winter lifted the rifle to his shoulder and held it there for a long couple of seconds. Finally he fired. From the woods there came a surprised shout of pain. And then laughter.

Winter gave Johnson a brief look, then lowered the weapon and walked into the forest.

"Hee hee hee hee!" Sevenkiller giggled. "Hee hee hee!"

They found him nimbly worming his way over the ground, his black hair plastered to his head and a big red stain blossoming on his shirt. The bullet had struck him in the lower back and he was crawling away over the mud and the leaves and the tree roots as quickly as he could. Surprisingly fast, but not nearly fast enough.

"Hidey ho! Hidey ho!"

Winter jammed the barrel into the back of Sevenkiller's head.

"I'm free at last!" Sevenkiller screamed. "Free! Free!"

The words struck a peculiar chord with Johnson, so that as the gun fired, he flinched.

25

Duncan was halfway across the river when the bridge collapsed into the water, the flaming beams cracking and snapping and lighting up the gray autumn afternoon. For a brief time he stopped swimming, kicking against the current and holding his rifle above his head. Then he resumed swimming until his feet were on solid ground.

When he came over the top of the bank he saw the bodies lying at the edge of the woods, and he made his way over there as quickly as he could. There were two: an older Indian and a white man. Both of them looked to have been beaten to death with a blunt object.

The sound of voices came through the trees. Duncan turned his head and saw Johnson and Winter. They did not notice him. He lifted his rifle to his shoulder, lined up Johnson, and pulled the trigger.

Click.

Nothing.

Fuck, Duncan thought.

In all the excitement, he had forgotten to dry his weapon after he fell in the river the first time. He quickly fixed his bayonet to the end of his rifle and stepped into view.

"Don't move!" he barked.

Johnson froze. Winter stepped in front of him.

"Get out of the way," Duncan said.

"No," Winter said.

"He killed Sergeant Service," Duncan said.

"No," Johnson said. "You did."

"That's a lie," Duncan said. "Get out of the way, Winter."

Duncan took a few steps forward, but Winter held his ground. Johnson tensed and looked as if he would bolt.

"Drop your rifle!" Duncan said. "Do it now!"

Winter hesitated, then let go. The rifle clattered into the dirt. Winter put his hand on his hips and watched Duncan.

"Now get out of the way!" Duncan said, inching forward.

"No," Winter said.

"You're taking this nigger's word over mine?"

"Sergeant Service ain't got nothing to do with this," Winter said. "He saved my life, Duncan. I ain't going to let you hurt him."

Duncan laughed. "Well, you're right about one thing," he said. "Sergeant Service don't matter. But your new friend here killed his master. The story's all over the county. And that means he's going to hang, whether he killed Service or not, whether he saved you or not. You can't be stupid enough to think they'll let that go. You know they won't. So get out of the way."

Duncan stepped forward again, so that the bayonet was only a few feet from Winter's chest. Winter didn't say anything.

"Last chance, boy," Duncan said. But a hand clapped over his mouth from behind and jerked his head back, and an instant later a knife pierced his chest. Duncan let out an abrupt, surprised noise as he was pulled onto his back.

Bill Bread sat on top of him and jabbed the knife into his chest again. Duncan tried to struggle free, but then Johnson was on top of him too, and the iron bar smashed into his head. Duncan let out a hopeless, agonized wail and then was silent. Bill stood up and wiped the knife on his pants. Winter had not moved, except to pick up his rifle. The three young men eyed one another. Johnson and Bill were breathing hard.

Duncan suddenly laughed. They looked down at him. His breathing was hitched, as if every breath caused him great pain. But his eyes were still clear and focused, lit up with malevolent intelligence.

"Caught . . . me . . . there," Duncan said. "Stupid . . . gun. Didn't . . . think . . ."

He coughed three times, each seeming to cause him more pain, his face going red and the cords of his neck standing out, a thin stream of blood coming from his nose.

Bill flinched. Duncan stared at him again, a smile on his lips.

"What's . . . the . . . matter? Can't . . . look . . . at . . . me?"

The sound of his breathing, so truncated and harsh and unnatural.

"He's . . . mad . . . Quentin . . . mad . . . I was . . . the only . . . one."

Duncan closed his eyes and relaxed, and they all thought he was dead. But no such luck. He opened his eyes again and looked at Winter. When he spoke next it was all in a rush.

"I was the only one who could have saved you all."

Duncan's face screwed up in pain and he let out that terrible cough.

"You . . . remember. You . . . remember. You . . . remember . . . me."

Bill was trembling, and Johnson's eyes were wide. But Winter was calm. He looked at Duncan very closely, as if he were attempting to engrave Duncan's appearance on his memory for all time. Eventually, Winter nodded.

"You remember," Duncan whispered. "Where . . . where . . . do you think . . . it's going to . . . end? What . . . do you think . . . going to . . . happen. So stupid. So . . . stupid."

Duncan shook his head a little. Then he said, "Go . . . on. Do . . . it."

"All right," Winter said.

Winter lifted his rifle. Duncan grinned, his teeth stained with blood, his eyes so lively. And it struck Winter that Duncan was alive, even now. His hair and fingernails growing, his stomach digesting its last meal, heart beating, lungs working. Alive. But not for long. It was the end. And each time in this war that someone had died, this same thing had happened. This same unimaginable finality. How many times the universe had been destroyed.

Winter began to cry then, and he looked very much like a little boy.

"You . . . coward."

The shot rang out and Duncan's head skipped in the dirt.

Winter lowered the rifle and wiped his streaming eyes with his broken forearm.

"What the hell are we going to do now?" Johnson asked. "They going to hang us all."

"It's all right," Winter said. "We'll say that half-breed did it."

"Where is Sevenkiller?" Bill asked.

"He's dead," Winter said. "Him and your uncle."

"You killed them?" Bill asked.

"Sure did," Winter said, and as he spoke the weakness began to evaporate from his face.

Bill shivered; he was still soaked from swimming across the river and back. He was hit with a sudden heavy blow of guilt. His uncle, who had tried to save him, was dead. All the men in his regiment were dead. The war was lost. His family's humble lands would be forfeited, or destroyed, just like the town of Planter's Factory. He was alone in the world.

"I didn't . . . ," Bill started. Then he stopped and looked down, momentarily overcome.

"You didn't what?" Winter asked. When Bill didn't reply, Winter said, "Why'd you come back here anyway?"

"I knew he was coming to kill you," Bill said.

"Yeah? What was that to you?"

"I don't know."

"You don't know," Winter said, tilting his head back, his strange golden eyes pinning Bill in place.

"I don't know," Bill repeated. He thought of his uncle, dead, and another wave of guilt washed over him, but this time commingled with another sensation. Of freedom. Of relief. When he lifted his head he looked into Winter's eyes and again he felt that thrill of excitement in his spine. The feeling that anything was possible. And then more guilt, the payment for this feeling, and he looked down.

Finally, Winter said, "Well. You saved our lives. You can go where you want."

"Where am I supposed to go?" Bill asked.

Winter shrugged and turned to Johnson.

"Same goes for you, I suppose," Winter said. "And before you ask, I don't know where you should go neither. That's what freedom is all about. There's nowhere in particular you're supposed to be."

"They'll kill me no matter what," Johnson said.

"Then it doesn't matter much where you go," Winter said.

Johnson remembered how the lieutenant had stopped Sergeant Service from killing him. If he had protected him before, perhaps he would protect him again. What other choice did he have?

"If you're coming with me," Winter said, "then let's move."

26

Captain Jackson lay on his back and struggled to breathe. Where was everyone? He felt as if he'd been lying in his own blood for hours. His neck and shoulder pulsed with pain every time he took a breath, and his leg had flared up as well. The thought of trying to move was terrifying.

And then Bill Bread was looming over him.

Bill, he tried to say.

But blood just bubbled up in his mouth.

The Indian looked at him sorrowfully.

"Hello, Captain," Bill said.

Bill, Tom tried to say again.

Another shadow fell over him. Tom's heart froze in his chest. It was a Negro, tall and powerful.

"What do we do?" the Negro asked.

Bill, Tom tried to say.

But Bill only shrugged.

"Ask Winter," he said.

27

Jan Müller led his men from the mill out into the fresh air, feeling physically and morally tired, wiping sweat and soot out of his eyes. They had thoroughly wrecked both the mill and the factory. Then he saw the blackened skeleton jutting out of the water. It took him a moment to realize that it was all that remained of the bridge.

They made their way to the center of the village, where they found Quentin and the rest of the Union foragers crouched on their heels in the town square. Many houses burned, while others had been smashed and looted. Angry blacks ran back and forth, hurling flaming torches and shouting in triumph.

"Lieutenant Ross, what is happening?" Jan asked.

"Why hello, Sergeant Müller," Quentin replied.

"Why didn't you tell us the bridge was gone?"

"Well, Sergeant," Quentin said, "I made the decision that it was necessary to inflict some punitive damages on this village. After all, General Sherman made it perfectly clear that the Union Army's right to forage was clear and uncontroversial and attacks on his foragers would not be tolerated. The level of resistance we have encountered in this village has been nothing short of astonishing. Therefore, it was necessary, in the good general's own words, 'to order and enforce a devastation more or less relentless.'"

Jan looked concerned, but he didn't say anything more.

"Look!" Reggie cried.

Winter, Johnson, and Bread were coming up from the riverbank. Bread and Johnson were carrying a wounded man between them.

"Lieutenant," Winter said.

"Where have you been?" Quentin asked.

"We took on the Confederates," Winter said. "This here is their captain. He's still alive."

Bread and Johnson dropped Captain Tom Jackson onto the ground, and the Union soldiers gathered around him and gawked.

Tom closed his eyes and turned his head away from them.

"Well done, Winter," Quentin cried. "I'll see you commended for this!"

"Who is this Negro?" Jan said.

"He saved my life," Winter said.

"Well then, he deserves our thanks," Quentin said.

"No," Jan said. "He is the one who killed his master. He is the slave Freddy."

"I didn't do nothing," Johnson said.

"I know you," Jan said.

"He saved my life," Winter repeated flatly.

"Sergeant Müller, a word, please," Quentin said.

Quentin took Jan by the elbow and led him a little away.

"But sir," Jan said.

"Now, Sergeant, those rebels took Reggie and Winter and this Negro saved them both. His only crime is the killing of his cruel master. Surely you don't expect me to kill him, or to turn him over to the army."

"We have to, sir," Jan said.

"You trust me, don't you?"

"Yes sir."

"Well then, leave it in my hands for now," Quentin said. "We can discuss it later. Perhaps we will be able to apply for clemency on his behalf."

"Very well, sir," Jan said. His sensitive eyes, disapproving, met Johnson's defiant gaze. For a while neither of them looked away.

"Well, we should be moving out soon," Quentin said. "Are we all here? Where's Duncan?"

"He's dead," Winter said.

"Dead?" Charlie Empire cried.

"The Confederates killed him too," Winter said. "Duncan crossed the river and a little half-breed jumped him. He's dead."

Winter's tone was unemotional.

"What do you mean he's dead?" Charlie cried again, starting to his feet. "How could he be dead? Why would he have gone to the other side of the river, away from the town?"

Charlie's voice was shocked and wildly angry. Johnny was on his feet too. But Winter only shrugged.

"I don't know, Charlie," Winter said. "I don't know why people do the things they do."

"Sergeant Müller," Quentin said. "Take them across the river and secure their brother's remains. Take a boat if you can find one; there must be one around here somewhere. The rest of you, we are to finish our duties in this town and continue moving east."

"Shouldn't we wait here?" Jan asked. "And make our report?"

"Not yet," Quentin said. His eyes were lit up and dancing. "Not yet. I want to keep moving. Not yet. I . . . perhaps at Milledgeville. Yes. Perhaps then. Just not yet."

28

When the body of the Union Army arrived at the ruins of Planter's Factory they marveled at the destruction. They were astonished to hear that Union foragers had incited the slaves to violent rebellion. Astonished, and skeptical. It was exactly the sort of story most likely to inflame southern sensibilities, and nothing similar had happened elsewhere during the entire war.

One thing that did not worry them was the destruction of the bridge. Less than an hour after their arrival, the engineers were hard at work, unloading flat, light pontoon frames off the wagons and dragging them to the water. The frames were then attached to one another with canvas sides and anchored six feet apart, all the way across the river. Next the men laid beams across the pontoons, then planks across the beams. The new bridge was ready by dawn, and the right flank of Sherman's army marched across it that very same day, chasing Quentin Ross and his men across Georgia.

For a time, Quentin's lies to his superiors were believed because he told them with such impassioned conviction, and because they were more plausible than the truth. The Confederates had every reason to exaggerate the crimes of Union foragers; Quentin had no reason at all to do the things he did. But by the time they reached the sea in mid-December, it was over. Quentin had begged off two appointments with the brigade commander, claiming exigent circumstances. He was informed that if he missed a third he would be shot as a deserter.

Very few of Quentin's men had seen the sea. It made an impression upon them, all that endless blue, so vast beyond imagination. Perhaps it affected their behavior; perhaps it showed them that none of them had been the men they had believed themselves to be. For when Quentin told them they were outlaws because they had sheltered a slave who had killed his master, and that if they did not wish to surrender him then they would have to desert, they all deserted as one.

Sergeant Müller had advocated strongly in favor of abandoning Fred Johnson, but Quentin was loyal to Johnson, as were Winter and many of the other men. Some were concerned that having aided and abetted Johnson for so long, a pardon was not certain. But there was also something more. Something that had stirred in them, gestating, feeding and growing and coiling over itself, waiting to spill out, to be born. A swath of smoke and carnage and destruction had followed them to the sea, to the blue edge of infinity, to the end of the world. To turn back then? To surrender themselves to hypocrites who claimed rules governed what they'd seen? What they'd done? To have come this far, only to be hanged?

They turned north instead, staying well ahead of the army, passing themselves off as foragers. In the chaos and destruction visited upon the Carolinas, ten times as furious as the march through Georgia, their depredations were scarcely noticed. When the army turned east toward Wilmington, Quentin and his band headed west. In the disorder of the new peace, with the roads choked and flooded with the dispossessed, it was easy for them to travel to the City of Kansas. Sleeping in barns during the day and riding at night, they took a savage part in the endless skirmishes and settling of scores that marked that ill-named peace. A lesson in human brutality taught to a people and to a land that could not have needed it less.

They lived well enough, paid in coin by vengeful Unionists. Their group attracted Union veterans, former slaves, and young troublemakers. Their central meeting place in the City of Kansas was the home of one Molly Shakespeare, a whore with three young sons who fancied herself a thespian.

But it was a directionless life, without hope and purpose, the men always looking out for vengeful Confederates and the forces of the law. There did not seem, at first, to be any sort of path forward. However, events were in motion in the South, where the antebellum way of life had been destroyed. The blacks were free and they sought to better themselves, to learn and to lead. Former Confederates had been stripped of the vote and barred from public life, so blacks and Republicans were elected to many southern offices. Northerners purchased land for pennies. And in December of 1865, something happened that changed their lives forever. In Pulaski, Tennessee, six well-educated Confederate veterans founded the Ku Klux Klan.

Robed and hooded men riding at night by torchlight. They burned churches and schools, they tarred and feathered carpetbaggers and scalawags, but above all, they murdered black leaders: schoolteachers and politicians and any who sought to vote.

Word of the talents of Quentin and his men made their way south. Union veterans were already forming unofficial bands to fight the Klan, and the newly wealthy Unionist landlords sought to protect their power and holdings from vigilantes. By then, the landowners of Kansas were only too happy to see Quentin depart; despite his effectiveness, he had worn out his welcome.

So they rode south, to continue the war they had left behind them only a year ago. With the South in rebellion, they could work out in the open, their past misdeeds public knowledge. For years they hired themselves out as mercenaries to one carpetbagger after another, but despite every victory, the violence only accelerated. Captain Tom Jackson, recovered from his injuries and burning for vengeance, now led a group of Klansmen who hid in swampy forests and conducted midnight raids on the freedmen and northern blacks who were felling the timber in the Mississippi Delta.

Quentin and his men were powerless to stop them until Augustus Winter learned the location of Jackson's next attack. Jackson's men were butchered from behind and Quentin's men were celebrated as heroes. Until photographs circulated, in newspapers all over the country, of the men, women, and children killed in a barn in Aberdeen, and it became clear how, precisely, Augustus Winter had learned where Jackson was planning to strike.

Quentin and his men had always had problems with their superiors and employers. In Georgia, Kansas, the Deep South. Orders slightly exceeded. Unnecessary force. Petty, profitless crime. Now it was all remembered and they became despised across the nation. The men fell out, disbanded, and spread across the country.

But then, in 1871, a fire burned in Chicago for two days and destroyed three square miles of the city. In the wake of the destruction, the Democrats (who had been banished from politics since the end of the War Between the States) were included in a unity government and grew rich by skimming city contracts and powerful by appointing flunkies to the judiciary and the police. A mayoral election was scheduled for the fall of 1872, and in Washington fears grew of a Democratic political machine in Illinois to match the one in New York. It was whispered that the fate of not only the state, but the country, hung in the balance. And with the stakes so high anything became possible.

Chicago 1872

29

A train began to move in Rome, Georgia. Thick black plumes pumped out of the smokestack and the whistle trilled. The wheels accelerated infinitesimally but inevitably, and soon the train was out of the station, heading west toward Alabama.

The train came upon the barricade ten miles out of town. At first, to the engineer, it looked as if a group of men were trying to move something across the tracks. It was broad daylight, and a robbery was the furthest thing from his mind. He pulled on the whistle, and the piercing shriek of it rang out through the trees, over the hills, and across the narrow river. The men by the tracks did not move. As the train drew closer the engineer saw the white sheets draped over the men's heads, the rifles they were holding, and the heavy trees and boulders blocking the track.

"God damn it," the engineer swore.

The fireman looked up from his dime novel.

The engineer considered attempting to barrel through the barricade. But the thought prompted a horrible vision of the train derailing and the passengers being hurled against the ceiling or through the windows, glass breaking, screaming. So he cursed again and yanked on the brakes, hard, so the fireman was thrown forward off his chair.

"What's happening?" the fireman cried.

Shouts came from the passenger car behind the locomotive.

The engineer lifted a shotgun from the rack above the window.

"Robbers?" the fireman said. "How many of them?"

"Looks like they're from the Klan," the engineer said. He was a little man, missing his left leg below the knee, neat in his dress, with a bushy mustache. "I'll be goddamned if I let them get into the express car."

"You really want to die for the Brink's Company?" the fireman asked, but he lifted his shovel, ready to use it as a weapon.

The train had stopped and the Klansmen were running at them. The engineer leaned out of the window to take a shot, but someone jumped up from the ground and grabbed the barrel of the shotgun with one hand and the collar of his jacket with the other. The man braced his legs against the steel side of the train and hauled the engineer through the window.

"Jesus!" the fireman cried.

He dropped his shovel and held his hands in the air.

"Open the door!" someone barked.

Down on the ground, the acrobatic Klansman was kneeling on the engineer's back and jamming a pistol against his head. The other Klansmen, dressed in everyday clothes except for the white hoods, clambered up the ladder into the locomotive and pushed into the passenger cars.

"Hands up!" they barked. "Get them up where we can see them!"

Gunshots barked in quick succession. Screams from the passengers.

"That'll be the conductor," the Klansman said as he bound the engineer's wrists behind his back with wire. "You're a salty bunch, ain't you?"

"What's your accent?" the engineer said. "You ain't from around here."

The Klansman jerked the engineer to his feet.

"Are you boys even in the Klan?" the engineer demanded.

The Klansman let out a low chuckle and said, "As far as you're concerned, I'm the grand wizard."

The engineer clenched his teeth and allowed the Klansman to propel him up the ladder into the train.

Inside the Klansmen were moving through the first passenger car, pointing their weapons at the passengers, collecting wallets, watches, and jewelry. A smear of blood was on the rear wall. Underneath it the conductor sat in a crumpled heap, not moving.

"You goddamn murderers," the engineer said.

"You all want to act like heroes," the grand wizard said. "Well, in my experience, this is what heroes get."

"We can't get into the express car," a Klansman said to the grand wizard.

"Yes we can," the grand wizard replied.

"The door's made of iron," the Klansman said, "and they bolted it from the other side."

"Well then," the grand wizard said. "We're gonna have to get them to open it."

The engineer let out a short laugh.

"Think that's funny, do you?" the grand wizard asked.

"I think you're all a joke," the engineer said as he limped through the passenger car. "I think you're all a disgrace to southern manhood. I think you're a disgrace to the Confederate States of America, which I gave my leg fighting for. The Klan's supposed to fight for white rights. Here you are robbing honest southern folk trying to make an honest living."

"You're full of opinions," the grand wizard said, leading the engineer through another car filled with passengers, all of their hands in the air, no one moving. At the end of the car was the promised steel door, locked shut. As they approached it, the grand wizard ducked behind the engineer to avoid being shot through the eye slot.

"Don't listen to anything they say!" the engineer shouted.

"Who'd they shoot?" an expressman called through the door.

"They got Bedford," the engineer said. "They snuck up on me and Ronnie. Don't worry about us none, we deserve whatever we get."

The grand wizard struck the engineer in the back of the head, hard but not too hard, just to shut him up.

"I'll make this short," the grand wizard said. "This is a robbery. You open that door, you open the safe, and we will be on our way. If you don't do what I say, so help me God, I will personally kill every man, woman, and child on this train. I'll save you for last, and what I do to you won't take long, but I'll fit a goddamn eternity into it."

"You're bluffing," an expressman said.

"No," the grand wizard said. "I ain't. And I'll prove it to you."

"You can't prove something like that."

"Sure I can. This little old engineer has got plenty of salt and pepper, don't he?"

"If you lay one hand on him . . ."

The grand wizard grabbed the engineer's shoulder and spun him around. The engineer braced for a blow, or a shot, but nothing came. He noticed that the other Klansmen had fallen quiet. They were looking at their shoes. They seemed almost abashed.

"Look into my eyes," the grand wizard said.

The engineer did, and what he saw took his breath away. He opened his mouth but no words came out.

"Donald?" the expressman said through the door. His voice was unsure. "Donald, what's he doing to you?"

"My god," the engineer said.

His bladder released. The sound of urine hitting the floor was unmistakable.

"Donald?" the expressman said. "Donald?"

"Open the door," the engineer said. "Open the door."

And the magic word was being whispered back and forth, moving through the passenger cars like waves chopping across the surface of an unruly sea: Winter, Winter, Winter.

30

A few days later, another train rocked from side to side, sending up showers of sparks from the tracks, as it made its cacophonous way through the southern slums of Chicago. Men and women caked in filth and wrapped in rags leapt out of its way as it crashed through one ground level intersection after another, never slowing.

The terrain was perfectly flat, marked only by an endless stretch of dirty, flimsy two-story wood cottages that had been hastily thrown up after the Great Fire.

When the train left the congestion, the smoke, and the squalor of the city and emerged into a darker and muddier place, it was invaded by a smell like the den of an ancient and insane animal: rich, full, expansive. It seemed to have a texture; it was almost generous. And it only grew stronger as the train picked up speed.

The whistle shrieked and the brakes howled as the train came to an unsteady halt. The doors opened and the few men aboard stepped down into the yards. The last one to disembark was the only man not holding a handkerchief to his face. His hair was combed and he was wearing an expensive suit, but there was nevertheless something careless about his appearance. As if he knew how he ought to dress but was only willing to go through the motions. A little stubble was on his cheeks and his cuffs were wrinkled and the bottoms of his trousers were muddy. Only his spectacles were perfectly clean.

He made his way over the crisscrossing railroad tracks until he came to the gates of the Union Stock Yards. A crowd of men were gathered there, waiting to be called for work. They sat on the ground or crouched on their heels, blowing on their hands and pulling their collars up against the cold.

"Hello, Mister Ross," one of the guards said.

Two of the other guards began to push open the gates. While he was waiting, Noah Ross spared a glance to the slum crouched between the walls of the stockyards and its dump. The vile, stained houses were built next to gutters filled with blood so thoroughly congealed that cats could scamper across them. Children ran and laughed in the gloom of the smoke and the rising sun.

When the gates opened the smell redoubled and Noah's ears were assaulted by the screaming of the pigs. Thousands of them were crammed in square pens divided by wooden walkways, packed so tight they stood in shit up to their knees and could scarcely turn around. All of them raised as much din as they could, as if they were sending an appeal up to heaven.

Buyers and sellers paced the walkways and leaned over the railings to inspect the animals. More than one buyer raised his hat to Noah, who passed them all with a curt nod, on his way toward the huge, windowless pork plant.

The plant manager, a man named Dennis Addy, was waiting outside the front door, dressed in a long faded coat that was stained with shit and blood. As they shook hands, Addy gestured to a group of workers in one of the pigpens. Whips cracked and the workers shouted, driving the pigs up the "Bridge of Sighs," a chute that ran up the wall of the plant.

"Come on in, Mister Ross," Addy said. "I trust you'll find everything to your specifications."

Inside the stench was so overpowering it was like having a foul rag pushed in your mouth. They had entered an enormous room where the floor was tacky with blood. Dirty men with heavy knives and cleavers waited at various tables. Addy ushered Noah to a staircase in the far corner that led up several flights to an observation deck.

Noah Ross took out a small, leather-bound notebook from his pocket and handed it to Dennis along with a pen.

"I'd be very obliged if you'd take some notes, Addy," Noah said.

"Certainly, sir," he replied.

Across from the observation deck was the catching pen where the Bridge of Sighs ended. As Noah watched it rapidly filled with pigs driven up from the yards. Five men waited next to a solid metal wheel with chains attached to its edge. The wheel was turning slowly.

Noah removed a heavy silver watch from his pocket. At the click of a button it sprang open.

Behind him, Addy raised his hand, and the five men in the catching pen leapt to work. Three of them drove the pigs toward the wheel by striking them with wooden sticks while two took turns grabbing the pigs and using the chains to attach them to the wheel.

The pigs tried to scamper free and shook their legs to get loose but the wheel kept turning inexorably and they were lifted, one after another, squealing and kicking, into the air.

Noah looked at his watch.

"Ten seconds," he said. "Seven seconds. Eight. Eight. Seven. Ten. Eight."

Addy wrote the numbers in the book.

When the pigs reached the top of the wheel they were transferred to a metal rail that slid them down toward a tall, burly man bearing an enormous knife. He caught the first pig, and while it was still struggling and shrieking, jabbed his knife into its throat and then did his best to dodge the massive stream of blood that exploded from the wound.

"Eleven seconds," Noah said. "Thirteen seconds. Fourteen seconds. Thirteen. Twelve. Sixteen. Hmm. See how the blood is pooling in the gutters?"

"Yes, Mister Ross."

"Make a note of that," Noah said. "Does it often do so?"

"Oh, yes sir."

"Make a note to hire someone to sweep those gutters," Noah said. "A child perhaps. We could have a boy or girl for fifteen cents a day. There's fifteen cents of blood hardening right there. I can see it."

Once the pigs had been mostly drained of blood, they slid farther down the rail and were dropped, in some cases still wriggling and bleating, into a huge vat of boiling water. A steam-driven rake dragged through the water and tumbled the pigs, pink and clean and scalded, onto another table where a group of workers attached a chain through each pig's nose so it could be dragged through another machine.

"Ten seconds. Ten seconds. Ten seconds. Good. The machine is very reliable."

When the pig emerged it had been shaved nearly bald. Two workers quickly removed any remaining hairs. Powerful butchers stepped forward and chopped at the pigs' necks, almost severing their heads. Then they lifted the carcass back up and hitched it to the overhead rail, sending it to another butcher to be disemboweled and split in two, then whisked into the cold room for storage.

After a few more observations, Dennis and Noah made their way through the chilling room. Big blocks of ice rested in front of fans, and the dripping hog carcasses dangled in row after row like stalactites in a cavern far below the earth.

And then they ended the tour where they began, on the ground floor, in the chopping room, where the real magic took place. On broad tables surrounded by butchers, the hogs underwent a final transformation from something that was still recognizably the remnants of a living creature—something that had, after its fashion, thought and felt—into products. Items of practical utility and economic worth. The pig was transformed from a grunting, useless thing into a number of items that, collectively, were worth more than the whole had been.

To Noah, it was like magic, this creation of monetary value, this alchemy, this conversion of dross into gold. It was the harnessing of a force greater than man. It was this force that had brought these men to this place and organized them in this fashion. The previous order, with its useless middlemen and wasted time and sinews, was dead. Though in one sense the Union Stock Yards was an innovation, in another it was a return to nature. Everything had been stripped away but the bare and fundamental laws of economics, as if some sort of undergod whose shackles had been loosened was shaping all before it in its own image, man and beast alike, with Noah Ross as its priest.

He did not speak, he only bathed in the hum of activity around him.

The hogs were transformed in thirty-five seconds from carcasses into various cuts of meat. Hams, ribs, pork chops were sent to be pickled, salted, smoked, and frozen.

"I trust you find everything to your satisfaction?" Addy said.

Noah smiled thinly. "Never."

Noah spent the ride back to Chicago performing calculations in his notebook, conducting a mathematical search for bottlenecks, for things that were slowing them down. The trick was to remember that nothing truly lay outside the system; nothing was really separate from anything else. How many pigs could be produced within shipping distance of the plant? How could that distance be increased? How many pigs could be delivered to the plant in one day? How long did it take to process each pig? Which stage of the transformation could be shortened? How many carcasses could be sent out of the plant? How much time did they spend being rerouted in Chicago? How far could they go?

There were a thousand such questions, and they hummed through Noah's mind like a swarm of locusts.

When he disembarked in Chicago, he spotted his personal secretary waving a telegram from Washington. Noah read it, then tucked it away in his pocket.

"I need you to send two telegrams immediately," he said. "One to Molly Shakespeare in the City of Kansas, and the other to General Philip Sheridan. I believe he is in town, but he may have left for the Dakota Territory."

"Yes sir," the secretary said.

There in the bustle, with passengers coming and going and pickpockets and porters shouting and shoving and the black smoke pouring down from the trains, Noah scrawled a fateful message in his notebook:

POTUS CONSENTS TO TERMS FOR ELECTION ASSISTANCE FOR ALL BUT WINTER STOP HELPERS SHOULD PROCEED TO MICHIGAN AVENUE HOTEL IN CHICAGO WITH HASTE AND DISCRETION STOP CONTACT PULLMAN COMPANY TO ARRANGE PASSAGE STOP REPEAT WINTER NOT INCLUDED

Noah tore the page out of his notebook, handed it over to the secretary, and said, *"Alea iacta est."*

"Sir?" the secretary said.

"Julius Caesar said it," Noah said. "It means the die has been cast. You can do all the preparation you like. In the end you always must take a chance."

31

In the Dakota Territory, the sky was blue and distant against the fall colors of the trees. A carpet of leaves covered the rocky ground. It was warm for October, but Bill Bread still felt chilled under his coat. His flask of whiskey was drained, though it was not yet midmorning, and he had reacted with impatience when Jan Müller ordered a halt to their march so that he could wash the blood off his hands and face in the creek. But one look at Jan's strained face and the glint in his eyes, like a panicked horse, told Bill that Jan had been pushed to the very edge by the massacre they had perpetrated in the hills. So Bill consented. It was while he, along with Dusty Kingsley, waited for Jan to get himself cleaned off that the little Indian boy sneezed. They looked up and saw him hiding in a tree.

"Shit," Bill said.

"Hey there," Dusty called up to the boy. "Come on down! We won't hurt you."

Dusty took some dried meat out of a pouch on his hip. Surprisingly this was enough to entice the boy out of the tree. He took the meat like a thing half tamed and bit into it and then smiled.

"There you are," Dusty said. "Here, have another."

The boy took it and laughed: a free, high, relieved sound, like a baby's laugh. It made Dusty laugh too. Not Bill, though. He leaned on his rifle and trembled a little and watched Dusty and the boy with his wise, bloodshot eyes.

Jan came back from the creek. When he saw the boy he jerked as if he had been stung by a scorpion.

"What are you doing?" Jan said, his German accent stronger with his emotion.

Dusty looked at Jan as if he had just remembered his existence. His face fell.

"Uh," Dusty said. "Well, we found this boy hiding in a tree, Sarge. He's hungry as get all."

Jan's blue eyes narrowed in contempt. "He is hungry?"

Dusty did not respond.

"I see. What are you going to do with him after you feed him, I wonder?"

"Well, maybe we could take him back to the fort and drop him off with someone," Dusty said.

"With someone?" Jan spoke like his breath was being taken away. "With someone? We should come back to the fort with an Indian boy? Hmm?"

Dusty could not meet Jan's gaze.

Jan looked at Bill. The boy looked at Jan, then Bill. Bill sighed. Then Bill spoke to the boy, in Cheyenne.

"Come here boy. Come here with me."

The boy walked over to Bill.

No one watched.

Bill knelt and smiled at the boy. He was not yet thirty, but he looked old. Still, the lines around his eyes were kind. Bill gave the boy some dried fruit. The boy ate it and laughed that baby's laugh for one last time. Bill led him away in the woods.

When they stopped, Bill put his hands on the boy's shoulder. *"Close your eyes, and I will give you some more."*

The boy did as he was told and the shot rang out, rustling through the leaves like an animal burrowing for cover. When Bill returned, none of them looked at one another. They just started walking home.

After an hour's silent march they arrived at the wooden fort, which stood in the center of a waving ocean of golden grass. The hotel bar was crowded in the early evening with soldiers and travelers and Indians who had come to do their trading. Jan immediately went to his room, but Bill and Dusty went to the bar.

"You Bill Bread?" the bartender asked.

"What does that matter?" Bill asked.

"Someone here already got your first round," the bartender replied.

"Who?" Bill said, turning to scan the crowd. A man sitting in the back corner tipped his hat. Bill's eyes widened in surprise.

"Is that who I think it is?" Dusty said.

"Get me a whiskey," Bill said. "I'm going to go get the sergeant."

Bill returned a few minutes later with a visibly irritated Müller. When Bill brought Jan to the table in the back, Jan stopped short with shock.

"You!" Jan said.

"Me," General Philip Sheridan said.

The general wore civilian clothes, a dark suit, and held his hat in his hands.

"Good work out there today, Müller," Sheridan said, smiling. He had a receding hairline, a domed forehead, and a neat mustache. His easy manner was belied by the intensity about his eyes and his angular face, which gave him the air of a man of firm, even fanatical convictions.

"I am surprised to see you here in person," Jan said. "Now how will you say you don't know who we are?"

"It's important. Won't you sit down?"

Bill and Jan sat down with Sheridan and Dusty. Bill poured himself a drink from the bottle sitting on the table.

"I came to tell you about an opportunity for more work," Sheridan said. "In Chicago."

"Chicago?"

"Yes," Sheridan replied. "As you may know, your former lieutenant, Quentin Ross, came from a good family in Chicago and he has a twin brother, name of Noah. Noah started out wealthy enough, of course, but he got even wealthier through speculation and some timely investments. He sits on the board of almost every major corporation in the city. He's also high up in the Republican Party in Illinois, and I've just learned, by telegram, that he's managed to convince the president to pardon his brother and his associates, including you, if you help out during the upcoming election."

"Full pardon?" Dusty said.

"So they say."

"God damn it!" Dusty swore. "Full pardon! Ross came through for us after all!"

"How are we supposed to help out?" Jan said.

"I am simply a messenger," Sheridan said.

Dusty immediately lifted his glass in an enthusiastic toast. He had left a young wife behind when they had deserted, and the life of a fugitive had never agreed with him. Jan seemed almost dazed. The only one who did not react was Bill.

"See," Sheridan said. "I told you it was important. Give me a drink, Bill."

Bill passed the bottle. Sheridan refilled his glass.

"Anyway, I know this is an important chance for you boys," Sheridan said. "Still, I almost feel bad bringing it to you. I somehow don't think you'll profit by it in the end. Noah Ross is a clever man, but he's missed the mark this time. Quentin Ross can't be trusted. There were always problems with him, all through the war and after, right up until that ghastly debacle in Mississippi."

"That wasn't Quentin," Jan said. "It was Augustus Winter."

"So the papers all say," Sheridan said. "Sherman doesn't believe it. He told me he knew it was Ross somehow. He said he couldn't understand before why Quentin would throw so many opportunities away. How he could lie to us so blatantly. How he could be so cruel and stupid when he didn't stand to gain anything by it. You know what Sherman thinks now? He thinks Quentin Ross is a madman. His methods are rational, but his aims are insane. He told me that it haunted him to have enabled a man like that for so long. To perhaps even have created him."

"That's a good story!" Jan barked. "It's fine for you to tell me not to trust my comrade in arms who so many times saved my life! Why should I trust you? You send us out in Georgia to burn it down and then you denied it. You sent us to fight the Klan and then you denied it. Today you sent us out to kill Indians and you deny it. Tomorrow you send us to rig an election. And you tell me it is Quentin I cannot trust?"

"I was always straight with you, Jan," Sheridan said. "You know we made peace with the Sioux in '68, and I told you that if you got caught shooting those Indians I'd deny I sent you there. I can assure you I meant it."

Jan waved his hands in front of his face as if he were swatting a mosquito.

"In Georgia!" Jan said. "In Georgia Sherman told Quentin his field orders were only for show. He told us to make Georgia howl. When we did? When we got to the sea? We were court-martialed. We had to go into hiding. My life was ruined!"

Sheridan leaned back in his chair. An ironic smile was playing on his lips. "Well, there was the matter of that murderous slave you had with you."

"I could have convinced them on the slave," Jan said. "If only . . .'"

"But, perhaps more to the point," Sheridan said, "is that Sherman never told anyone that his field orders were just for show. They weren't just for show. They were important to prevent the South from hating us, as far as possible. Quentin Ross lied to you."

"What reason would he have to lie?" Jan said.

Sheridan's smile broadened. "What reason, indeed?"

"You expect me to believe that?" Jan said, his voice tight with emotion. "The hypocrisy makes me sick. Generals make a war that kills thousands, but common soldiers must be hanged if a few houses are set on fire."

"Well," Sheridan said, "ethics aren't rational, they're emotional. You kill a thousand Indians by depriving them of the buffalo, you're a great leader. But if you shoot one little Indian boy, you're a murderer."

Dusty found something interesting to look at on the floor.

"Of course, you were quite right, from a strictly rational point of view," Sheridan said. "But irrational feelings are rather powerful forces. I hope you, and your former lieutenant, keep that in mind. In Chicago."

32

That very same evening, in the city of Chicago, the Democratic alderman Mickey Burns jogged up the stairs of the Store, a four-story brick gambling hall located within a stone's throw of city hall. He climbed the steps two at a time, but he paused to warmly shake the hands of both guards, slipping each one a dollar.

Burns was a handsome man, a little shorter than average, but broad across the chest, powerful, with dark, tightly curled hair and a sensual mouth. The pinstripe suit he wore fit him like a glove, though his tie was rather too short. A diamond pin the size of a grape sparkled on his lapel.

Inside he weaved a practiced path through the card tables and the spinning roulette wheels, winking at the cigarette girls, until he came to another guarded door on the far side of the room. He shook the hands of those guards as well, was ushered inside, and was greeted by the sound of a hundred men shouting his name.

A wide variety of kegs, casks, and bottles, calculated to cater to the diverse tastes of the men assembled there, were stacked on the card tables, along with sacks of oysters packed in ice. A thin fog of blue tobacco smoke hung in the air.

Burns's ears picked up at least half a dozen languages. English, of course, spoken with a distinctly Hibernian twang, but also German, Italian, Polish, Greek, Norwegian, and Bohemian. Each ethnic group clustered together, easily identifiable by their dress, their hair, the drinks in their hands. Half of the aldermen in the city were in the room, and virtually all the leaders of the vice trade. Newly appointed police officers were shucking oysters for union leaders. Everyone seemed to be getting on well enough.

"Mickey!" Honest Jim Plunkett bellowed from across the room, waving his hands with their missing fingers. Honest Jim towered over every man around him, and his face was knotted and shiny with scars. "Mickey, come over here!"

Burns made his way through the bristling hedge of glowing cigars and glasses of whiskey, slapping every man's back along the way. He grabbed an oyster from one of the sacks, pried it open with his knife, and sucked it clean before he arrived at his destination.

"Now isn't this a lovely sight," Burns said, grinning.

"Fucking Mickey Burns," Honest Jim said, "come to visit us at last. What kept you? Might I venture a guess? Making arrangements for a funeral?"

"Indeed," Burns said. "I am sorry to say. Another little angel sent to the Lord before his time." Burns shook his head sadly, but soon enough he was smiling again. He said, "You really did it, Jimmy."

"Well, of course I did, didn't I? Never doubted it for a second."

Honest Jim turned to the man standing on his left, portly and mustached, looking dissatisfied and holding a pewter stein. Clearly German.

"Mickey didn't think I'd get nobody but Irishmen here tonight," Honest Jim said to the German.

"Hello, Ollie," Burns said.

Ollie Reiman raised his mug and smiled.

"And this one," Honest Jim said, "is complaining about my man for mayor."

"What are you worried about?" Burns said. "This Harrison's likely enough, isn't he?"

"Likely?" Honest Jim cried. "Likely? Likely doesn't do it by half. Mickey, that man, he's a visitation. That's what he is. I never met a man like him. Can't stop smiling to save his soul. Can't hold a grudge if you paid him. Loves to give a speech."

"Yes," Reiman said. "Yes, he does love to give a speech."

"Loves everyone in the city," Honest Jim said. "Kisses every baby he sees. You can't stop this man from kissing babies. I defy you to stop him. I defy you, sir. I tell you, I've never seen the like. I've got him marching with a Negro militia tomorrow."

"Yes," Reiman said. "He will say anything to anyone. How do we know he will stay our friend? Of course I trust you, Mister Plunkett. We all do. But Harrison does not seem to be principled!"

"Principled!" Honest Jim said. "Well now, that depends on how you reckon your principles, I suppose. He'll look out for his friends, I warrant. And ain't that the most important principle of them all? Principled! Mister Reiman. Politics ain't beanbag, after all. Harrison's our boy, you'll see. He'll come through for us, and I'll be damned if he don't remember those who put him there."

Reiman shrugged and drank. Somewhat morosely, he said, "I suppose," but Honest Jim was already turning to the crowd.

"Gentlemen!" he shouted, waving his hands for attention. "Gentlemen, please! I just have a few short words for you all."

The Irish were whistling and stamping their feet, and the other ethnic groups were drunk enough to applaud warmly.

"First of all," Honest Jim bellowed, "I want to thank you all for being here today. I know I don't always make it easy to like me."

Cries of "No, no" from the Irish and laughter from the rest.

"I know, I know, I know. We've had our disagreements in the past. And that's just how they've lorded it over us all this time. Playing us against one another like dogs in a pit while they sit in their mansions and cheat on their taxes. And we've all suffered, haven't we? Whether they're picking on the Irish or telling our Teutonic friends when they can and can't have a glass of beer. They even blamed the Fire on the shacks our people live in!"

An angry roar went up from the crowd.

"Oh, and they've got their money and they've got their newspapers," Honest Jim shouted, spitting out the last word as if it were a particularly vile epithet. "But what's that to us? What's that to us? This is still a democracy, after all. And there's more of us than there is of them. Yes sir. We'll show them. It don't matter how many stories they put in their newspapers. It don't matter how many Pinkerton provocateurs and spies and thugs they hire. Money ain't nothing to the greatest currency of them all, gentlemen, the currency of votes."

Another cheer.

"Now gentlemen, gentlemen," Honest Jim said, "we've got our differences. Don't we? Who's to say we don't? That's why here in the Democratic Party, we say, Why, who am I to tell my neighbor what's good for him? A Republican is a man who wants you to go to church every Sunday. A Democrat is a man who says you can have a drink if you want. That's all. You don't have to like me, you just have to know I'm an honest man. The newspapers might tell you different. But what's their idea of honesty, I ask you? I say an honest man is one who does right to you when you do right to him. That's me, gentlemen. That's me to the bone. You just put your faith in old Honest Jim. I never forget a favor."

"Honest Jim!" an Irish voice cried out, and everyone lifted his glass and cheered.

"Now gentlemen," Honest Jim said, "you just see King Conor there about your money on your way out. You just see about it. He's got your names in his little book, and if he don't, why, you come and talk to me. You take what you need and don't you worry, I won't be asking you for no receipts as long as you get the votes out on Election Day. I won't be asking for no accounting, as long as you do right by me."

Honest Jim gestured toward the door, where the owner of the Store, "King" Conor McDonald, stood with a leather-bound book and an enormous iron cashbox.

"Just remember," King Conor snarled. "If we lose, this is a fucking loan."

Laughter.

"Votes, gentlemen!" Honest Jim cried. "A toast! To votes!"

Everyone drank. Afterward, some took more drinks, some took oysters, and some returned to their conversations. But most lined up before King Conor for their money.

Mickey Burns took Honest Jim by the shoulder and nodded to a far corner of the room where they could separate themselves from the crowd. Everyone knew not to approach them while they spoke.

"I've got some news," Burns said.

"Do you now?"

"Well, you know this fellow Noah Ross? The speculator? Professional investor?"

"Oh yes, I know of him. Queer fish! Tough to tell whether he's a friend or foe of the workingman."

Burns smiled and said, "He's what our Mister Reiman might call a principled individual."

"Is he!" Honest Jim exclaimed. "Well, what about this Ross, then?"

"Apparently he's the brother of Quentin Ross, the Republican hatchet man who got himself into trouble a few months back in Mississippi."

"What trouble?"

"You must have read about it. Talk about stories in the papers. All those horrible pictures of the women and children strung up by their heels? In that barn?"

"Oh yes! What was that madman's name? Autumn Winter?"

"Close enough. Anyway, this man Winter was part of a little band led by Quentin Ross. They were all bummers in the War of the Rebellion. The whole lot of them were court-martialed at the end of the war for a long list of misdeeds, including sheltering a slave who'd killed his master. But it didn't take long for them to find work fighting the Klan and the Red Shirts. Aiding with the Reconstruction, you see. All on the behalf of the Republicans, although they deny it. Especially after the massacre in Mississippi."

"And what have they got to do with us?" Honest Jim asked, but he looked as if he knew.

"Well, the word is that Grant's agreed to give Quentin Ross and his men pardons for their murders if they come to Chicago to help out in the election."

"Help out?" Honest Jim cried. "They're going to use the same lackeys against us as they do against the rebels? They're going to treat Chicago like a defeated secessionist city? Like we lost the war? Like we'd never given our blood for the Union?"

"So they say," Burns said.

"Well fucking let 'em," Honest Jim said, calming instantly. "Let 'em. I like my chances in a street fight. It'll take more than a few soldiers of fortune to tip the balance in their favor. Wouldn't you say?"

"Oh, for sure, boss," Burns said. "Just keeping you in the know."

"And for that, my dear Mister Burns," Honest Jim said, "I'm much obliged."

33

The next morning, Quentin Ross awoke in a soft bed. He blinked a few times and then, remembering where he was, grinned. He threw off the sheets and sank his feet into the thick carpet and flicked the switch on the wall. Electric light illuminated the green and gold wallpaper, the gilded mirrors, and the frescoed ceiling.

He stood, steadying himself against the gentle rocking of the train, and pulled back the velvet curtains from the window. The sun had already risen and it was beaming down directly ahead of them, as the train chugged east, toward Chicago.

First he washed his face in the bathroom, filling the pink marble sink with steaming hot water. Then he dressed himself (his suit had been vigorously brushed and his boots had been polished while he slept) and made his way into the dining car.

A crystal chandelier hung from the ceiling, making a tinkling noise as it vibrated. The tables were covered with white cloths and laden with fine china and silverware. Quentin drank coffee and ate an omelet and read a copy of *Harper's Weekly* magazine, enjoying as usual the engravings by Thomas Nast. Then he stood up, thanked the waiter, and apologized for his inability to offer a tip.

"My dear friend, I must confess that despite all appearances I have rather been down on my luck as of late."

Turning from the dour waiter, he entered the smoking car, with its reclining chairs, its writing, card, and billiards tables, its stocked bar and cabinets loaded with cigars and cigarettes, and its little library. It was this latter feature that had attracted Quentin's companion.

"Improving your mind as always, I see."

Fred Johnson looked up. He was dressed roughly, except for his boots, which had been polished to a dull glow. He had no beard and his hair was cropped very short. A book was in his hand and a cigar smoldered in an ashtray next to him.

"It does you credit," Quentin said. "I don't suppose I might be of any assistance?"

Fred flipped back a few pages and offered his book to Quentin. Quentin took it and read:

Why leave we not the fatal Trojan shore,
And measure back the seas we cross'd before?
The plague destroying whom the sword would spare,
'Tis time to save the few remains of war.
But let some prophet, or some sacred sage,
Explore the cause of great Apollo's rage;
Or learn the wasteful vengeance to remove
By mystic dreams, for dreams descend from Jove.

If broken vows this heavy curse have laid,
Let altars smoke, and hecatombs be paid.
So Heaven, atoned, shall dying Greece restore,
And Phoebus dart his burning shafts no more.

"Well now, this is ambitious," Quentin said. "What's the problem?"

"What's a hecatomb?" Fred asked.

"A hecatomb, my dear Frederick," Quentin said, "was, in ancient Greece, a sacrifice to the gods of a hundred cattle."

Fred held out his hand for the book.

"But surely that isn't your only question?" Quentin said, as he handed it back. "My good Fred! You're the brightest pupil I've ever taught. Not, I suppose, that I have taught many other men. Perhaps I am simply an exceptional teacher. In any case, I'm not sure you ought to be wasting your time with Pope. That really is a dreadful translation."

Quentin took a cigar from one of the cedar cabinets behind the bar and walked out onto a balcony on the tail end of the train, where he could smoke and watch the terrain whip past.

Eventually the pastoral scenery gave way to the urban expanse of Chicago and Quentin reentered the car and sat with Fred. The train came to a halt at around ten in the morning. "Chicago!" the porter shouted as he threw open the sliding door. Immediately a cloud of black smoke billowed into the railway car, followed by the din of a thousand machines and the cry of a million voices.

"Fagh!" Quentin cried, waving his hand in front of his face. "What an abominable stench!"

They stepped down and were immediately assaulted by an army of shouting touts, grimy men waving their hands looking around, in vain, for their luggage.

"The Michigan Avenue Hotel," Quentin said to a filthy man with his head sunk deeply between his shoulders, who nodded and beat the others away and led them to his carriage. Quentin and Johnson climbed into the back while their guide cracked his whip and got his vehicle moving.

The Michigan Avenue Hotel was made of wood, not brick, with

bright red and white awnings. The front door was locked and a sign in the window read CLOSED FOR RENOVATIONS.

Quentin knocked and waited for about sixty seconds until the door opened. A young bellhop led them through an empty lobby where their footsteps echoed on the stone floor. In the restaurant, they gorged themselves on carrot soup, beet salad, cold lobster casserole, potatoes, and then baked Alaska. Their waiter was a slender man around thirty with short hair and skin as black as midnight. He kept winking at them. Quentin winked right back.

Afterward they reclined in their chairs and picked their teeth and drank coffee until Noah came into the room.

"My dear, dear brother," Quentin said, apparently overcome with emotion.

"Quentin," Noah said, taking his twin brother's hand.

The Ross brothers looked very similar and shared many little mannerisms and movements. Still, it was easy to tell them apart. Although Quentin's clothes were shabby, they seemed to fit him more naturally than Noah's clothes fit him. Quentin had a sharp, handsome, feral look about his face, while Noah had a more puritanical, almost snobbish air. Yet Noah was more entirely present than Quentin, really seeing what was in front of his face, whereas Quentin was always preoccupied with private amusements.

The winking waiter quickly brought over a cup of tea for Noah.

"Can I interest you in a cigar?" Quentin said.

He produced two handfuls, stolen from the train.

Johnson looked nervous. Noah noticed Johnson's discomfort and smiled.

"Don't worry," he said. "I would not have put my brother on that train if there was anything on it I didn't want him to steal."

Quentin laughed heartily.

Fred Johnson took a book out of his jacket.

"I took this," he said.

Noah took it from his hand.

"You're reading this?"

"Indeed," Quentin said, between puffs of his cigar. "He's come a long way. Putting the boots to all the theories of Negro intellectual inferiority."

"That's not what I mean," Noah said. "It's a dreadful translation."

"I told him so!" Quentin cried.

"If you want to read the *Iliad* I'll send you something better. I'll send you all the books you want. You'll have plenty of time to read, and plenty of quiet too. You'll have the hotel entirely to yourself."

"You own this hotel?" Quentin said. "Remarkable place. How much did you pay for it?"

Noah sipped his tea and said, "A thousand dollars."

"A thousand dollars?" Quentin cried.

"I bought it during the Fire," Noah said. "It was quite something, the Fire. At first the wind was feeding it, but after a while it made its own wind. This great hot, dry whooshing up and down the streets. And it was coming south toward this hotel. I walked in on impulse and offered the owner a thousand dollars for it. He accepted and called me a fool. The transaction was witnessed. And the Fire was stopped one building to the north."

"What a story!" Quentin said. "That's my brother for you. A gambler at heart. Oh, I grant you, he is a most meticulous gambler, unafraid of research and hard work. But a gambler nonetheless."

"I'm certainly gambling on you," Noah said.

"My dear Noah," Quentin said. "You can count on me, I assure you. What you've done for us, I simply can't . . ."

Quentin seemed to tear up. Noah looked unimpressed.

"I can't put it into words," Quentin continued. "A second chance! We'd have to be mad to let it slip away. Don't worry, my brother. I can't control how the good people of Chicago will vote but I can promise you that we'll do everything in our power to sway them."

"For now, you must simply stay here until I tell you to leave," Noah said.

"Now, Noah," Quentin said. "It will be just as you say, of course, but is that really necessary?"

In answer, Noah opened his briefcase, removed a newspaper, and tossed it toward Quentin. The headline was in an enormous font. Quentin picked it up and read it.

"Goodness me," Quentin said. "I certainly wouldn't describe us as carpetbagger mercenaries."

"It seems a rather apt designation to me," Noah said.

Quentin put the paper down. "How could they already know we are here? This paper must have been printed before we arrived."

"Obviously," Noah said, "they have a spy. One of our first tasks will be to return the favor. I rather think the German sergeant in your unit would be a fine candidate."

"Sergeant Müller? Unfortunately, we've fallen out of touch recently."

"I've found him," Noah said, "and he's coming here."

"Wonderful!" Quentin cried, his eyes dancing. "That's wonderful news."

"He has two men with him. I thought you had another five or six?"

"Well," Quentin said. "We had dispersed, you understand. I left your telegram with the lovely Madame Shakespeare. I expect that both Empire brothers will arrive shortly."

"But not Augustus Winter," Noah said.

"No, no, of course not," Quentin said. "Although, you should realize that what transpired in Mississippi was not entirely his fault."

"Then was it yours?" Noah said. "Because I have been operating on the assumption that he, and not you, was responsible for that atrocity. If I was wrong, I'd thank you to tell me now."

"I merely meant that it was a very difficult situation," Quentin said. "Very, very complicated."

"It is not nearly as complicated as the situation here," Noah said. "The election will take place in a matter of days, and we know what we will face because we have already seen it in New York. There will be ballot-box stuffing. There will be repeat voting. There will be intimidation at the polls. There will be bribery. There will be trumped-up arrests of Republican election officials. There will be violence directed toward anyone with a clean collar, or who looks likely to vote Republican. Votes will be lost, miscounted. Hundreds of immigrants will be transformed into citizens by corrupt judges. If the Democrats win the mayoral election they will become entrenched in this city. They will build a political machine and grow powerful by stacking the police and the bench with their allies and rich by taking a percentage of city contracts. Fortunately for you, that possibility has made certain men in Washington very nervous. Grant has no worries about his own reelection next month, but in four years? In 1876? The former Confederate states will likely have their electoral votes restored to them, and it is very unlikely they will vote Republican. A Democratic political machine in Chicago could tip the balance in that presidential election."

Noah stopped his speech. Quentin was reading the newspaper. Suddenly he laughed.

"Did you read this? The Democratic candidate for mayor marched with a Negro militia yesterday? The gall of it! A Democrat courting the Negro vote!"

"The Democrats don't care about the Negro vote," Noah said, sipping his tea. "There's barely a thousand Negroes in Chicago, and we can rely on them, at least, to vote Republican. He is merely trying to distance himself from the rebellion."

"Ha ha ha! The gall! Listen to this, Brother: he told them he had nursed at the breast of a colored mammy. The cheek!"

"It's one of his tricks, these constant appeals to race. Harrison is from Kentucky. He claims to be an opponent of slavery but it was the sale of his slaves that set up his fortune here, and he voted for Davis in 1860. You see what we're up against. I need to stress to you, Quentin, that we are dealing with very cunning and manipulative men. They know how to twist words and win the hearts of the common people. This has to be handled very delicately."

"Of course, of course," Quentin said.

"You aren't down south any longer," Noah said. "This isn't the war. Your pardon is conditional upon how you handle this matter. Do you understand?"

"Of course, Brother!" Quentin said. "I understand."

Noah did not look satisfied. He leaned forward in the chair.

"That means you must stay in the hotel until I tell you to leave. And it means you must keep the men under your command on a tight leash. Do you understand? They don't trust you in Washington. I was only able to get you this chance because the Republicans have no other choice. They can hardly send in the army, and the Pinkertons and other mercenaries don't want to take sides."

Quentin cried, "I understand! Brother, I understand. This is our last chance, and we must behave ourselves."

Noah looked at his watch and said, "I have another appointment."

"Well," Quentin said, "don't let us keep you."

"I don't mean to be hard on you, Quentin," Noah said. "I've taken a great risk to get you this second chance."

"And don't think I'm not grateful."

"Only, it's not your second chance, is it? Or your third or your fourth. It is your last, Quentin. Your absolute last. I can assure you of that. Please, please. Just do as I say."

"Of course!" Quentin said. "Of course!"

Noah stood up.

"Gentlemen, I take my leave."

After the sound of his footfalls receded, Quentin smiled at Johnson and shrugged.

"He ain't like you," Johnson said.

"Oh now," Quentin said, "we're like two sides of the same coin. We really are. Gamblers, but men of the world. We're both concerned with natural law and we don't give a damn what anyone thinks of us. And he's successful. Just look around! This all belongs to him! My brother. I've never been so close to anyone. He's saved my bacon more times than I can count and he can be a little short with me. And he's right of course. He's always right. Still, sometimes I wish . . ."

Here Quentin trailed off and the expression on his face became oddly blank. Like the unnatural placidity of a statue half effaced by erosion and time.

"I wish he would listen. I wish I could just make him see."

As Quentin shook his head, a smile slipped back onto his face. He puffed on his cigar. The black waiter materialized at his side and winked at him again.

"I don't suppose I could trouble you for another cup of coffee," Quentin said.

"Oh, yes sir," the waiter said. And then he added in a lower voice: "You gentlemen looking for a little action?"

"What kind?" Quentin asked.

"Oh," the waiter said, smiling, "any old kind you like."

"What's your name, my friend?"

"Archibald, sir," the waiter replied.

"Well," Quentin said, "I do believe you may be of some assistance to us. However, I warn you that we've yet to be paid by my brother for the services we are shortly to render to him, and we'll need a brief extension of credit."

The waiter's smile disappeared and was replaced by a sober, reproachful look. He looked like a man who was about to say that he was not angry, but only terribly disappointed. The look was so comical that Quentin threw back his head and howled with laughter that echoed around the empty dining room.

Then he reached into his pocket and fished out a thick roll of golden coins and tossed it on the table. It landed with a heavy thud.

"How much action can that get me?" Quentin asked.

The waiter's impish smile had returned.

"As much as you like, sir," he said. "In Chicago? You can get into as much trouble as you like."

34

After the completion of the Hannibal Bridge in 1869, the railway pumped the City of Kansas full of humanity that spread and spilled outward across the unresisting plains. The stockyards sprang up on the Kansas side of the Kansas River, where the two railways met, and the slums came with them: row upon row of little houses, identical in their squalor.

In one of those little houses, Austin Shakespeare let out a youthful shriek, awakening his older brother Lukas. Lukas moaned, slid underneath the pillow, and clutched his head in his hands. He had been drinking cheap gin the night before, and his head was thrumming with pain, while his stomach was turning over and over, like an eel trying to squirm loose from a sack.

After the shriek the boys were quiet. Presumably, Matt had reminded Austin, in a whisper, not to wake their dangerous older brother. But a few minutes later, their feet were thumping on the floor again, then Matt giggled, then Austin shrieked again, and a dish broke.

Luke sat up in their mother's small bedroom, glared angrily around at the frilly curtains and the jars and bottles of makeup and perfume on the side table, and then got up and smacked the door with his palms, knocking it wide open. The sunlight in his eyes did not improve his mood. Matt and Austin froze, their faces fixed in expressions of terror and dismay. They had been wrestling near the kitchen table. Now they released each other and stood back.

"What in the goddamn nine hells are you two nancies doing?" Luke hissed.

The boys looked down. Matt was eleven years old. Austin was eight. Both were tall for their age, bony, with light orange hair. Of the two, Austin was noticeably more delicate, with a shy manner and an overbite. Matt was more spirited, and all of his movements had a kind of clumsy elegance, like a spider hurriedly making its way across its web. Awkward, but precise.

Lukas himself was only fifteen years old. Although he was not much taller than Matt (they had different fathers) he nevertheless seemed, through his violent temperament and force of will, to tower over him. Even their mother had become afraid of Lukas; it was probably no accident that she had left the house early that morning.

"Buggering each other? Is that it? Is that why you've been giggling like girls?"

"I'm sorry, Lukie," Austin said, and Lukas lunged at him.

"No!" Matt said, stepping in front of Lukas.

Lukas hurled Matt to the floor. Austin screamed and ran.

"You prancing little sodomite!" Lukas screeched. "You slack-titted poxy whore!"

Matt raised his hands to protect his face, but Lukas knocked them away and started slapping. Matt cried out. It went on for a while, and then there came a knock on the door. A jaunty, musical knock. Seven notes in total.

Shave and a haircut, two bits.

The rage fled Lukas's youthful face, replaced with shock.

Again: Shave and a haircut, two bits.

"What is it?" Matt said. Tears were still gleaming in his eyes, but he had stopped crying the instant he had seen the terror in his brother's face.

"Shut your fool mouth," Lukas said. "Get in the bedroom! Both of you!"

"Who is it?" Matt said, confused. "Who is it, Lukie?"

"Shut the fuck up!" Lukas shrilled. "Get in Mom's room! Close the door."

A sigh came through the thin wood. Quiet, and impatient. Only barely audible, but Lukas heard it and jerked as if he'd been stung.

"Hurry, hurry!" he hissed, and it was the fear in his voice, so strange to their ears, that got them moving. Lukas saw them under the bed and then he shut the bedroom door and walked to the front of the house.

The young man outside wore a long duster and had his hat pulled down low over his forehead to hide his famous face.

"Well, howdy there, Master Shakespeare," the young man said. "Well met."

Luke's tongue clicked in his throat. He said nothing.

"Charlie around?"

Lukas shook his head.

"I thought Charlie and Johnny were coming up to hide out with you for a while."

Lukas shook his head again.

"No?" The young man lifted his head a little. Beneath his hat his yellow eyes flashed a warning.

"No," Lukas said. "I mean yes. They did come here, but now they're gone."

"Is that right?" Winter said, lowering his head again. "Whyn't you come with me down the road to the gin joint? I'd like to talk a bit."

Lukas nodded. Winter took his arm and they strolled down the row of shanties, crowded close together, with their dirt gardens and broken fences and piles of garbage lying in the brown rainwater in the gutters.

"How's the family?" Winter said.

"All right." Lukas's voice was returning to normal. "They got to get used to having a man in the house."

"I don't see why," Winter said.

The gin joint, as Winter called it, was just another house that happened to be situated at the intersection of two fairly prominent laneways of the slum. Drunks lay stretched out in the muddy yard, coated in puke and dirt.

"Go get yourself a drink from the lady, Lukie," Winter said.

He dropped a heavy gold coin in the boy's hand. Lukas gawked at it.

"Winter, they ain't going to be able to take this. We could buy the whole block for it."

"Then take her upstairs after you're done drinking," Winter said. "Find a way to get your money's worth."

Lukas held the coin nervously. He did not want to buy five cents' worth of moonshine with a double eagle. But neither did he want to displease Augustus Winter. And so he went over to the shack and handed the coin to the crone through the broken living room window. The coin disappeared.

"You'll be wanting a party for this!" she said. "I'll send for the girls."

Lukas took the clear whiskey back to Winter, who was staring up and down the alley with his alien eyes. He looked like a visitor from the moon, or the depths of the sea.

"Look at this place," Winter said. "You spread some money around a place like this, and they'll die before they give you up."

"Yes sir," Lukas said.

"Jesse James has been hiding in places like this for years."

"That's what they say," Lukas said.

Winter lifted his pint bottle, and Lukas lifted his. They clinked.

"Your health," Lukas said politely.

Winter drank, coughed, and wiped his mouth with the back of his hand. Lukas pressed his tongue up against the neck of the bottle and did not swallow.

"So I guess it's true about the train," Lukas said. "I didn't credit it. You riding with the Klan."

"Where are the Empire brothers?" Winter asked.

"Chicago," Lukas said, without hesitation.

"Chicago?"

"Yes sir," Lukas said. He had been sworn to silence on this point but he would not lie to Augustus Winter. "Quentin Ross hid out here for a little while, along with big Freddy. Mother didn't like it. Didn't they fight! It was like a sackful of cats lit on fire. My mom read about what happened in Mississippi in the papers and she didn't want nothing to do with them. Then a telegram came, and Quentin left with Freddy for Chicago. Charlie and Johnny came later, and they went on after him."

"Did they say where?" Winter asked.

"You mean where in Chicago?" Lukas said. "I don't know. Something about Quentin's brother? I didn't even know he had a brother."

Winter took another drink of whiskey.

Word had circulated about the double eagle, and men started coming up to the front of the house. All of them tipped their hats to Winter as they passed. One of them let out a little cheer. The women were tracking in as well. Anything above the age of sixteen looked impossibly dirty, finished, and old. All of them winked at Winter. He paid them no mind.

Twenty dollars. Winter could have had any man, woman, or child on this street for two bits. Lukas felt suddenly cold inside, and ashamed, though he could not say why.

"He said something about getting a pardon," Lukas said. "Quentin's brother was going to get them a pardon."

At this Winter smiled thinly.

"Well, I guess we better head on up there and see what it's all about," he said.

At the word "we," Lukas stiffened.

"I don't know, Mister Winter," Lukas said. "I was thinking of lying low for a while."

Winter lifted his hat, looked at Lukas, and said nothing.

"You know, let the dust settle," Lukas continued.

Winter's pupils began to contract, down to little dark points.

"My family . . . ," Lukas began.

"If you gave one good goddamn about your family," Winter said, his voice conversational, "if you gave one little shit, which you don't, you'd stay the fuck away from them. You ain't no good for your fucking family, Lukas Shakespeare. If you cared about those two fatherless bastards back in your hovel, hiding under the goddamn bed, because you brought the meanest son of a bitch in this country to their doorstep, you'd leave them a hundred dollars in gold and then come with me. Where you belong."

Winter drank his whiskey. Eventually, Lukas did the same.

"But you don't care about them," Winter said. "Not except for how they make you feel about yourself. I know your type, Lukas. So have a drink and enjoy the party. And go or stay. I ain't your goddamn keeper, thank Christ. But don't be giving me any bullshit. I'm sick to death of it."

35

Jan, Dusty, and Bill arrived at the Michigan Avenue Hotel well after ten o'clock. The door opened immediately after their knock, to almost pitch darkness. They fumbled their way inside and the door was shut behind them. Only then did the man who had opened the door raise the shutter on his lantern.

"Gentlemen," Noah Ross said.

Jan Müller started. "You look just like your brother," he said.

"The likeness is remarkable," Dusty said.

"You must be hungry," Noah said. "Please come with me."

He let them into the dining room. Cold meats, cheese, and bread were waiting for them. While they ate, the waiter Archie pumped out foaming mugs of beer and set them down at the table.

"Is Quentin here?" Dusty asked.

"Yes, and Fred Johnson," Noah said. "The Empire brothers arrived earlier today. They are both upstairs. You will be staying in this hotel. My brother will give you your instructions. All except for you, Mister Müller. Because of your German heritage we have picked you to attempt to infiltrate the Democratic Party. You will begin tomorrow. I recommend you attend the saloon of Ollie Reiman around noon and pass yourself off as a new immigrant looking for assistance. If you earn their confidence they may let you in on their other plans."

"How shall I earn their confidence?" Jan asked around a large mouthful of bread and cheese.

"I will leave the details to you," Noah said. He looked at his large silver pocket watch and then nodded at the three of them. "I must be off. I have a busy day tomorrow. Have a good evening, gentlemen."

"Yes sir," Dusty said.

Bill had already finished his beer, and he motioned to Archie for another. When Archie appeared to be moving slowly, Bill put a silver dollar on the table, and the waiter made it disappear and then increased his pace.

They ate and spoke by candlelight. Bill moved from beer to Scotch. A pleasant haziness enveloped his mind: the liquor, the dark, the quiet night. They heard footsteps approaching their table and turned to see Fred Johnson, dressed in only a union suit and carrying a candle.

"Freddy!" Dusty cried.

"Well look at you sorry sons of bitches," Johnson said, shaking his head in disapproval.

Dusty stood up and clapped Johnson on the back. Jan only nodded, without making eye contact. Johnson did not acknowledge Jan at all. Shortly afterward, Jan excused himself and, taking Johnson's candle, went to his room.

After he was gone, Dusty said, "Shit. How long are you two going to keep that up?"

"Ain't no reason to quit," Johnson said.

"It was eight years ago now," Dusty said.

"It don't matter," Johnson said.

"How are you going to like being locked up in a hotel with him?" Dusty asked.

"Oh, it'll be fine," Johnson said with a smile, and his eyes caught the candlelight.

Dusty laughed.

"Is Quentin upstairs?" Bill asked as he took another swallow of whiskey.

"Nah," Johnson said. He jerked his thumb in the direction of Archibald. "This whoreson's been letting him out on the sly. He's at some cathouse with the Empire brothers."

Archie's bright white smile was very noticeable in the dark.

"Are you sure that's a good idea?" Dusty said. "What if someone sees them?"

"Hell no, it's not a good idea," Johnson said. "But what are you going to do?"

When Bill became drunk he gained a sad and knowing air, and he had it now.

They chatted more, and then Dusty went up to bed. Bill and Johnson were quiet for a while. Then Johnson turned to the waiter and said, "That'll do, Archie."

Archie left, and other than the candle at their table the darkness was complete in the shuttered dining room.

Johnson leaned back in his chair, so his face was out of the light. Bill sipped the last of his drink.

"They don't lock up the bottles here at night or nothing like that?" Bill said.

"I thought you were going to quit," Johnson said.

"I'm always going to quit," Bill said. "You know how it is. You say you won't have a drink, then you say that one can't hurt you. Then you think, Well, hell, the first one didn't hurt me, it's not like one more will make a difference. Things proceed. Eventually you're drunk. You can't deny it. You're drunk. Then you think, What a weak-willed son of a gun I am. I did it. I went and did it. I got drunk again. No self-control, no self-respect. What should you do then? Well, since you're so worthless, why not get drunk? Perhaps tomorrow will be different."

Johnson made an amused noise from the darkness. Eventually he said, "It couldn't have helped. What happened in Mississippi."

"There's always an excuse," Bill said. But then: "No, of course it didn't help."

After a pause, Johnson said, "We never got to talk too much after."

"No."

"I thought you were going to North Carolina."

"I was."

"How'd you end up with Müller?"

"There wasn't nothing for me in North Carolina," Bill said. "All my family's land was gone. First it went to carpetbaggers. Then the Klan ran them off, and it was white folks. My family were sharecroppers, they had nothing for me, and no use for me. By then I was already drinking again. I kept thinking of my uncle. You know?"

Johnson's eyes were flat. Bill continued.

"I knew Reggie had family in West Virginia so I went there. I met up with him. He was going to head out to Minnesota to meet with Müller. As it turned out, I went to Minnesota, and he went to Kansas instead. Those were tough days. I had some close calls with the law."

"Why didn't you come to Kansas?"

Bill shrugged.

"Müller had work. I could trust him."

Johnson spat on the floor. "You can trust him," he said.

"More than some," Bill said.

"I know Quentin is no saint," Johnson said. "But it wasn't his fault what Winter did."

"I know it," Bill said. "I was there."

"It can't be true that the Empire brothers didn't know anything about it."

"I don't believe it myself," Bill said. "But I don't know for sure. Winter sent me away, you know."

"What do you mean?"

"Well, we were in Aberdeen," Bill said, toying with the crystal glass in his hand. "Me, Reggie, Johnny, and Charlie. And Winter. Some men from the town were missing and the people were telling us different stories of where they were at. Winter got the idea that they were with Captain Jackson, planning some raid. To be honest, I couldn't disagree, but of course no one in that town would talk. And Winter, he just looks at me. Gives me this long, appraising look. Like he's figuring how much I'm worth. So I said to him, What are you looking at? And he said, Bill, whyn't you go search the Rodney place? It was about fifteen miles away."

"I know it," Johnson said.

"I took Reggie with me," Bill said. "I had the strangest feeling riding out of that town. It was so quiet in the streets. Such a poor town, houses so run-down. No money there at all. I felt like there was a cold wind at my back. I felt like I was running, like I was being a coward, but I didn't know what I was running from. Or I didn't want to admit it."

Bill shook his head, tossed the heavy crystal glass in his hand,

and caught it. Then he held it up to the candle, so that it broke apart the light and scattered it over the soiled tablecloth.

"I don't see how he could have killed all those folks just on his own," Bill said. "But that's what he said. And no one who survived remembered Charlie or Johnny doing anything. Just Augustus Winter with his white hair and golden eyes."

"Don't think they don't know it," Johnson said. "Charlie and Johnny don't suffer anyone to talk ill of Winter. It's like he cast a damn spell on them or something. I think they've been looking for someone to boss them around since Duncan died."

"Well, whatever anyone says," Bill said, "Winter got rid of the Klan in that town."

"Yeah," Johnson said.

"Did you read about Winter in the papers? About how he was riding with the Klan?"

"I read it," Johnson said. "I don't believe it."

"No?" Bill asked.

"Of course not. The Klan?" Johnson shook his head.

"Why not?" Bill asked.

"I can't see how they'd have him. And he wouldn't do that. Winter's been fighting those sons of bitches for years."

"Hmm," Bill said. And then he whispered, so quietly that Johnson had to strain to hear him. "You didn't see him. When Sevenkiller and Captain Jackson were torturing him. You didn't see him then. I knew right away."

"I think I know Augustus Winter by now," Johnson said.

"You ought to," Bill said. "There ain't much to know."

36

The next day found Ollie Reiman standing behind the bar in his saloon. It was just before the lunch rush and Ollie was polishing one mug after another and stacking them on the shelf. The door opened and a stranger came inside.

"Hello there," Ollie said.

"*Guten Tag,*" the man said.

"Do you speak English?" Ollie asked in German.

"No," the man said. *"I've just come from New York. My cousin told me to come here."*

"Oh, welcome," Ollie said. *"Sit down, sit down!"*

The man took off his cap and approached the bar. Ollie drew him a mug of beer and set it down on the bar.

"Ten cents," Ollie said. *"And it comes with free lunch."*

Ollie nodded toward the table at the other end of the room and said, *"Why don't you get something to eat before the regulars show up."*

The man put his dime down on the bar and walked over to the food. A heaping mound of loaves of rye bread, hard white cheeses, cold meats, and pickled vegetables was laid out in a buffet. The man loaded up a plate and sat back down at the bar, lifting his mug.

"Your health," he said.

Ollie nodded as he polished the mugs.

The saloon was very large, perhaps twenty feet by eighty, and filled with solid wooden furniture, mostly benches and long tables. Stout waitresses were sweeping the floors and wiping the tables. German accoutrements, flags and maps and art and photographs, hung on every wall, alongside long mirrors.

The man smacked his lips.

"Good, isn't it?" Ollie said. *"I bet that's the first real beer you've had in a long time."*

"Yes," the man said.

"What's your name?"

"Jan Müller," the man said.

"And your cousin told you to come here? What's his name?"

"Hans," Jan said.

"I know many Hans Müllers," Ollie said. *"What does he look like?"*

Jan looked uncomfortable.

"I have not seen him in more than twenty years. I do not know. I know he works at the reaper factory. He said he would leave a message for me."

"The reaper factory?" Ollie said. *"I don't think . . . I don't know. Well, I don't have a message for you."*

"Oh," Jan said. He looked down at his free lunch and picked up a pickle and ate it.

"Well, don't worry!" Ollie said. "Your cousin steered you to the right place. I have cared for hundreds of men like you who are new to the country! What's your profession?"

"Woodcutter."

"That's good! They're rebuilding the whole city. I can get you on a work gang in the morning. If you have no place to stay, I can find you lodgings for tonight. Just stay here till after the lunch rush. And tomorrow we'll have you made a citizen."

"Tomorrow?" Jan said. "I thought it took much longer than that."

Ollie winked. "I'll take care of it. Don't worry. I have many friends."

"I don't want to get in trouble," Jan said.

"You won't. We have friends even on the police now. You're lucky you came here. Do you know anything about American politics?"

"No."

"Well, the Democratic Party are our friends. The Republicans are our enemies. They're always working to keep the little fellow down. They try to close our saloons on Sundays. They even complain that we give men a free lunch here. Imagine that! They complain we give working-men a free lunch. We need to make you a citizen so you can vote for the Democratic man. His name is Harrison. He's gone to the beer gardens with us on Sunday many times. He's practically a German himself. He even said so."

Jan was making a crude sandwich and stuffing it in his face.

"Anything you say," he said around a mouthful of food.

The sound of high-pitched, excited voices came from outside.

"Here they come!" Ollie cried, his voice rising in a little squeak. "I'll be back!"

The door banged open and children poured in, most of them carrying two or three metal lunch pails. They rushed straight to the bar and lined up, yelling and laughing, and Ollie filled their buckets with beer, one after another, writing down names in his little book. One of the boys, a tall one, had a staff across his shoulder with which he could carry four pails at once. Once they had the beer they came for, they turned and hurried, carefully, out of the saloon.

Soon after the men came in and grabbed food and beer and rushed to the wooden tables to save a spot. They were stained with sweat and grease and their clothes were poor but they were all laughing and talking. None of them looked run-down or defeated. Many of them took a newspaper off the rack to read. They shook salt and pepper on boiled eggs and smeared mustard on salami and clanked their heavy mugs together and drank.

How they did drink. One beer after another, as if it were a race, as if they were trying to get as much down as they could before the whistle blew, calling them back to work. Before long men were weaving, barely standing on their feet.

Someone who was clearly not a workingman came into the saloon. He was short and broad and dressed in a fine suit that was as sharp as the autumn air. His hair was slicked back and there was a diamond pin in his lapel. The men gave a great cheer when they saw him and he waved his cane in the air and grinned and motioned at the bartender. The gesture was unmistakable: a round for the house.

The remaining children crowded around the man in the suit and he dropped hard candies in their hands.

Ollie scurried around the bar and soon he was pumping the hand of the new arrival and they were speaking quietly to each other, their words lost in the din.

Jan turned toward the men on the benches and made an almost imperceptible movement with his head. Immediately, someone bellowed, "Thief! Thief! That man's a fucking thief!"

The conversations cut out.

A man stood up on the other side of the room. He was young but balding and inclined to fat and he had a stupid, mean face. "He's paying for your beer with your own money. He stole it from you!"

"Shut up!" someone cried.

"You stupid fucking krauts," the man shouted. "The Irish have been running the Democratic Party like a private club for twenty years! You think it's going to be different when you put their man in the top spot! They're not going to need you once they've got what they want! Workers' rights, I say! Hurrah for socialism!"

Someone lunged at the shouting man but he struck his assailant in the neck and knocked him to the ground. Next a few tried at once, but the man had a club and he beat them off.

"Come on then, you fuckers!" the socialist said. "Come on you stupid . . ."

Jan launched himself at the man, knocking him back into the wall, wrapping one of his scarred and powerful hands around his neck.

"Fuck you," the socialist said, clubbing Jan across the face with his wooden baton. Blood splattered the wall. Jan threw punches wildly, and although he took a savage beating, he seemed to be getting the better of it.

Finally the socialist drew a knife and stabbed it into Jan's side. Jan cried out in pain but didn't let go. He drove the socialist's head into the wall until he slumped and went limp, and then he dragged him to the door and threw him outside for the kids to kick.

When Jan turned around to face the crowd everyone applauded, and whistled, and shouted their approval. Jan pulled the knife out and felt the blood rush down his side in a sticky flood, momentarily unstable on his feet.

A buxom waitress with thick blond pigtails steadied him and brought him around the bar to the back room.

"It's okay," she said. *"You'll be fine."*

It was a cold room, with barrels of beer stacked up along the walls and cuts of meat hanging from hooks. The light came in from a little window near the ceiling. Jan sat down, a little more heavily than he'd intended, on a box of pickle jars. They made a clinking noise.

He lifted up his shirt and the girl pressed a rag into his wound. The cut on his face was dripping blood onto the dirt floor.

Ollie and the man with the diamond pin in his lapel came into the back room.

"Nice work, boyo," the man said in a thick Irish accent.

"He doesn't speak English," Ollie said.

"Really? That's grand. I actually came here looking for a tough man who doesn't speak English."

"Why?" Ollie asked.

"A few problems with one of me fellow aldermen."

"Who?"

"Terry Sullivan."

"But he's a Democrat."

"Ollie, you know I trust you," the Irishman said. "But trust everyone and cut the cards, as I always say. You don't need to know these things. Just let me know if this man is one of us."

"I've never met him before today."

Jan looked up at both Ollie and the new man.

"Introduce me," the Irishman said.

"Jan, this is Mickey Burns. He's one of my friends who I was telling you about."

"All right," Jan said, as the blood trickled down from his scalp to his chin.

"Ask him if he wants to come work for me tomorrow," Burns said.

"Are you sure?" Ollie asked.

"Sure I'm sure. He's fresh off the boat, isn't he?"

"We don't know a thing about him."

"And he doesn't know a thing about us. It's perfect."

Ollie shook his head.

"Jan, Mickey has some work to do tomorrow, but he's worried about his safety. The Republicans have brought in some very dangerous men from out of town to try to intimidate us before the election. Do you think you could stay with Mickey to keep him safe? He would pay you very well. And it would be good to have him as a friend."

Jan looked down at the floor and wiped his brow. Then he looked back up again.

"Do you know where my cousin is?"

"No, I don't. I can try to find him for you."

"I don't know who to trust."

"What is he saying?"

"He says he doesn't know who to trust."

Burns grinned and took his billfold out of his pocket.

"Tell him I've got something he can trust right here."

37

That afternoon, Charlie Empire returned to the Michigan Avenue Hotel to find Quentin Ross and Johnny drinking in the dining room. Bill Bread was at the bar. Everyone took a turn laughing at Charlie's face, which was mottled with blue and yellow bruises. One of his eyes was almost swollen shut.

They ate peanuts and threw the shells on the ground, laughing

and talking, and smoked one cigar after another. Archibald came for
them a little after sunset.

"Well, you're all just having a grand old time, ain't you?"
Archibald said.

"Archibald, my good friend," Quentin cried. "Please tell me
you've come to release us!"

"I surely have," Archibald said. "But you best keep your voice
down. Mister Bread, you coming?"

Bill did not even look up from his tumbler of whiskey.

"He's at home right where he is," Quentin said. "Archibald, time's
a-wasting."

"All right," Archibald said. "Let's go!"

They went through the kitchen and out the service door. A carriage was waiting right outside, and they were only exposed to the
street for a second. Johnny Empire was last in line, and by the time
Quentin and Charlie were seated there was barely any room.

"Johnny," Charlie said, "go up on the fucking roof!"

"No, no," Quentin said.

"Yes, yes," Charlie cried. "The roof, Johnny!"

Johnny hesitated, with one foot in the door.

Quentin said, "We must make room. We'll make room." Quentin crammed himself into the side of the carriage. "Come on, John!
Get in before someone sees you!"

Johnny wedged himself through the door with difficulty, then
balanced uneasily between them all.

"Don't fall on me!" Charlie cried. "Fall on him!"

Johnny laughed and then collapsed into the empty corner of the
carriage. He had to bend his head almost all the way down to his
knees.

They passed the bottle back and forth and shouted and laughed
until the carriage came to a stop. The door opened and Archibald
herded them out into an alley. The buildings had windows with lacy,
frilly curtains that blocked any view of what was going on inside but
allowed reddish light to shine through.

"Not very subtle, is it?" Quentin remarked.

"Oh, they're all paid up with the police here," Archibald said.

"These are all King Conor's places, and he just about owns the police these days."

"Remarkable!" Quentin said. "What a town! It truly does embody the American spirit, just as my brother said."

The men made their way down the narrow alley to a side door to one of the brothels. Within an hour they ran back out, disheveled, half undressed, the women screeching and launching chamber pots at them from the windows.

"What the fuck, Johnny?" Charlie said, drunk, angry, hopping on one leg as he tried to pull his pants on.

"Ha ha ha ha!" Johnny bellowed, loud enough to wake the dead. He was shirtless and what little hair he had was gummy and tangled and standing straight up.

The three men charged down the alleyway. Archibald was waiting by the carriage.

"How'd you get kicked out of that one?" Archie asked. "I don't know where I'm gonna find somewhere low class enough for you sorry beggars to spend more'n an hour."

"It was all a misunderstanding," Quentin said. "Johnny means well but he does not know his own strength. Please, we must hurry."

They piled into the carriage. The coachman struck the horses and they were off at a brisk trot.

"Ha ha ha!" Johnny laughed, rocking back in his seat. His hands were bloody.

"I'm going to cut your fucking peter off," Charlie said.

The carriage clattered down the road for a time before it came to a stop. The door opened to reveal the Michigan Avenue Hotel.

"Why are we back at the hotel?" Quentin said. "The night is young."

"You boys need to lay low for a time," Archibald said.

"Like hell we do!" Charlie said. "We're paying you well enough."

"You paid me to take you to a cathouse," Archie said. "I took you to the cathouse. It ain't my fault you didn't last an hour."

Charlie's bruised and battered face contorted with rage and he made as if to lunge out of the carriage. Quentin caught his shoulder and whispered in his ear. Charlie struggled once but Quentin dug in his fingers and kept his mouth pressed up against Charlie's ear. Eventually Charlie relaxed.

"Very well," Quentin said. "Tomorrow night?"

"That's too soon," Archibald protested.

"Tomorrow," Quentin said again. "We shall make it worth your while. And we will be on our very best behavior."

"I don't know, Mister Ross," Archibald said.

"Double."

"Double?" Archie said.

"Indeed," Quentin replied.

"All right," Archie said. "Tomorrow."

"You see what happens?" Charlie snapped at Johnny, slapping him across the face.

The three of them staggered back into the hotel. Quentin called for Bill to get their drinks ready, but when they arrived at the bar they saw someone who surprised them.

"Herr Müller!" Quentin cried.

Jan smiled at them from the shadows, where he was sitting with Bill.

"Sergeant," Charlie said. "How'd it go after you threw me out of that kraut saloon? Did they buy it?"

"Better than we hoped," Jan said. "I've gotten very deep very quickly."

"How's the little scratch?" Charlie said, his eyes narrowed to slits with malevolent humor.

Jan made a face.

"I suppose I got carried away," Charlie said. "Made it look authentic, though."

"I suppose," Jan said.

"Time to celebrate!" Quentin said. "Have a drink with us."

"No," Jan said. "I will need all of my wits about me tomorrow. But I need to speak with you."

"Oh, all right," Quentin said. "Charlie, Johnny, give us a minute, will you?"

The Empire brothers made their way to the bar, while Quentin sat down with Jan. "What's troubling you, my friend?" Quentin asked.

"It's not easy for me to say," Jan said.

"Is it about what happened in Mississippi?" Quentin said. "We didn't have much chance to speak about it."

Jan looked so upset that he might cry.

"It wasn't our fault," Quentin said. "We all knew Winter was a bit wild, but I don't think any of us believed he was capable of that. Did you?"

"I don't know."

"Well, a certain amount of responsibility rests with me," Quentin said. "I should have kept a tighter rein on him. Still, Jan, how could I have known? You don't believe I had anything to do with it?"

"No," Jan said. "But why do these things keep happening? All the way back to the war. These things keep happening again and again. And every time we are getting in so much trouble. So that now if I'm caught here in this city, this city I fought for, I'll be hung."

"Well, Jan," Quentin said. "What were we to do? Execute Johnson? Would that be justice?"

"It wasn't just about Johnson," Jan muttered. He glanced into Quentin's eyes, which were wide, honest, and earnest. But something was in them, or something missing from them, that made them hard to look at for too long.

"My brother is far more trustworthy than Sherman," Quentin said. "If he says he will stand behind us, then he means it. He won't say one thing to us in private and then leave us hanging out to dry."

Jan forced himself to look Quentin in the eye. "Quentin," Jan said, "I spoke with Phil Sheridan before I came here."

"Yes?"

"He swore to me that Sherman told you that it was important to respect his field orders. He said you'd been warned again and again."

"Of course he'd say that," Quentin said. "They wanted us raising hell, but also to be able to deny that they had anything to do with it. They'd reap the rewards of our hard methods without having to pay the price. You can't trust anything they'd say."

Jan looked away. Surely Quentin could not be lying. He had no reason to lie. What was the alternative? If Quentin had engaged in butchery merely for the sake of butchery, and transformed himself and his men into outlaws by so doing, and was able to lie about it with such a perfectly calm and reasonable expression on his face, as if he believed his own words, then he was mad and Jan had never really known him at all.

"Well," Jan said. "I suppose that's true."

"Good," Quentin said. "We'll put this behind us."

"All right," Jan said.

He did not have the heart to ask Quentin where he had been with the Empire brothers. The sound of laughter and breaking glass followed him as he walked up the stairs to his bedroom.

38

In the little town of Morris, sixty miles southwest of Chicago on the Illinois River, Louis Parker was in the barn behind his home, milking a cow, his face pressed up against its side and his hands reaching under, gently and rhythmically squeezing.

The barn door opened and his wife, Dorothy, came in.

"Louis," she said. "I thought I heard gunshots."

Louis leaned back on the stool, away from the cow, and wiped his forehead.

"Pardon me?"

The cow made a low noise.

"I thought I heard gunshots coming from the reverend's old place," Dorothy said.

Dorothy's gray hair was tied back in a tight bun. She had broad arms and an enormous bust. Louis was slight and entirely bald and wore spectacles.

"Well, maybe someone's hunting," Louis said.

"Oh, Louis," Dorothy said. "Couldn't you go have a look? I'm awfully worried. If someone came up to the house when you were down here I don't know what I'd do."

Louis sighed. He looked around the barn at the three other cows waiting in their stalls and then he took the lantern from where it was hanging and walked up the well-worn path to the house.

Dorothy followed behind him speaking nervously. "I can't think who would be down there."

Louis sighed again. He went in through the back door, set the lantern down on the floor, took the shotgun off the rack, cracked it open to make sure it was loaded, picked up the lantern again, and went back outside.

It was a cold morning, without much wind, and the stench coming off the Illinois River was strong. The sun was rising in the east and it cast fingers of light over the murky water, almost black with coal dust and dirt and the blood of hogs. Bits of white cloth, chunks of wood, and animal corpses all bobbed along with the sluggish current.

The Reverend Winter's house was next to the water's edge. No one had moved in since he had died and the windows were shattered and the dock was washed up on the shore like a shipwreck. The gardens were all dead and even the grass struggled to grow.

Louis came up to the house with the lantern, shining its light around. There were two sets of tracks in the soft earth and he heard the sound of someone's boots scraping on the floor inside.

Instead of calling out, Louis tucked his shotgun under his arm and used his free hand to shutter the lantern. Then he set it down on the ground and walked the rest of the distance to the house in the darkness. He came up to the window quietly and peeked inside.

What he saw caused him to jerk his head and tiptoe away as quickly as he could. As he was picking up the lantern, a little figure stepped into his path and shrieked, in the piercing voice of an enraged adolescent.

"Get your hands up you dirty little ratfucker, or I'll blow your head off!"

The boy looked to be about fifteen. He was skinny and dirty, wearing a ragged set of overalls with no shirt underneath, and he had an enormous pistol hanging at each hip, over which his hands were twitching eagerly.

"Hsst," Louis said, scrambling with the shotgun, but the boy drew his pistols with such overwhelming, unnatural speed that Louis was startled and his weapon tumbled through his numb fingers and landed on the depleted earth.

"I said get them hands up, you ugly whoremaster!" the boy screeched.

Louis heard a heavy tread on the ground behind him, and his heart fell. He turned around and saw the man coming out of the house, saw his long hair and his thin scratchy beard, both the color of winter wheat. Saw his yellow eyes, as slick and as hard as chrysoberyl.

"Augustus," Louis whispered. "It's me. Do you remember me?"

Winter gave no sign that he did. He walked up to Louis and stopped a few feet in front of him and stared into his face.

"Auggie," Louis said, "it's me. Louis Parker. I live up the hill. You remember me? My wife, Dorothy? You used to come over to our house when your daddy . . . you used to visit our house sometimes? Remember? She'd give you biscuits and gravy?"

"Shut up!" the boy cried, and Louis felt both pistols dig into his lower back. "Should I shoot him, Auggie?"

Winter never broke eye contact with Louis, who stared right back, hoping to touch something, move something, kindle some spark of the boy he'd once known.

"Louis!" Dorothy cried as she hurried down the hill. "Louis, what's happening?"

Louis wanted to tell her to stay back, but he was not as quick as the boy, who trained one gun on Dorothy while keeping the other on Louis and shouted, "Get back!"

Dorothy took one look at the boy and either failed utterly to understand the danger he represented or else knew instinctively how to handle children, for she simply narrowed her eyes and said, "You point that away right now, young man," and kept hurrying toward her husband.

And either the boy was afraid to fire without instructions from Winter or else there was something in the tone of her voice that stopped him, for he fell quiet.

"Louis?" Dorothy said as she came closer and peered toward them in the dark. And then: "Oh my goodness. Oh my goodness. Auggie? Is that you, Auggie?"

And now Winter's gaze fell upon her, like a weight of merciless stone, but once again Dorothy seemed oblivious.

"Oh my goodness, it is you!" she cried, and she went to him and gave him a hug.

Winter was so surprised that the hardness of his expression cracked. He did not look affectionate or sorrowful, or anything at all, other than momentarily unsure of himself, and unguarded.

Dorothy stepped back and her face was wet with tears but she was smiling. She looked from Winter to Louis to the boy and said, "Well, come on up to the house! I think we still have some pie from last night."

"Pie!" the boy cried, holstering his guns. "Oh boy! I'm fucking starving."

"Young man," Dorothy said, "what's your name?"

"Lukas Shakespeare," the boy said.

"Well, Lukas, if you don't watch your language, you won't get any pie."

"Yes ma'am," Lukas said.

When they walked through the front door, Dorothy said, "Make sure to take your boots off."

Lukas sat down and lifted his feet and pulled his boots off like a monkey. Then he threw them aside and sprinted after Dorothy.

Winter followed Louis, holding the shotgun. He left his boots on and they made little imprints of dirt on the carpet.

"Won't you sit down, Augustus?" Louis said, sweating. "Come sit down in the living room, here."

Winter settled in a large armchair. He laid the shotgun across his knees and kept his eyes on Louis.

Dorothy was in the kitchen with the boy, forcing him to wash his face and his hands. Then she brought cups of coffee for the men. She glanced once at Winter's boots but didn't say anything.

"It's so wonderful to see you again, Augustus," Dorothy chattered. "We haven't heard a word about you since you left for the war. I know how hard that must have been for you. Your father was in a rage about it but we could all see how proud he was of you. The reverend was a good man underneath his temper and he loved you very much. I'm only sorry he didn't live long enough to tell you himself. We have all his things if you want them. Oh! Listen to me prattle on when I'm sure you have plenty of things to tell us."

Dorothy stopped and looked expectantly at Winter. He flicked his eyes to her for a moment and then looked back at Louis.

"Well," Dorothy said, "the little fellow is in there eating all the pie, so perhaps I'll get some breakfast on. I'll let you two catch up."

She bustled out of the room and said something sharp to Lukas, whose reply was lost as the door closed behind her.

Winter gazed off through the window toward the little town of Morris. It had never seemed so far away to Louis as it did now.

"My daddy's dead?" Winter asked.

"Yes," Louis replied.

"It was the river that got him, was it?"

"Yes."

"Why's the river flowing the other way now?"

"They reversed the flow of the Chicago River back into the Illinois," Louis said. "To keep the lake clean for Chicago's drinking water."

Winter's lips twitched a bit.

"So Chicago killed my daddy in the end, did it?"

"I suppose so," Louis said. "It killed a lot of people. But the governor won't do nothing about it."

Winter didn't say anything more.

Louis cleared his throat. He tried to meet Winter's gaze, then looked down again.

"Augustus," Louis said, "I won't tell anyone you came here. I promise."

Winter's face was without expression.

"I promise you. Please. I wouldn't ever tell. Augustus, I swear. We were always good to you. My wife loves you. She don't know about what happened in Mississippi. I kept her away from the papers."

"That why she thought my father was a good man? That he loved me? Did you keep the papers away from her about him too?"

Louis shrank into the sofa.

"Your wife is a goddamn idiot," Winter said.

Louis stared desperately at Winter's face, as if he was trying to catch on to something human, to draw sympathy out with his eyes. To make Winter feel something. But Winter only looked at him as he would the sluggish, polluted Illinois River flowing by. And then Louis did what many men did when they had to spend much time with Augustus Winter. He started to cry.

"Augustus, please."

"The world's a hard fucking place," Winter said. His hand moved just a little on the stock of the shotgun. "A little hard to get by with just please."

"Augustus," Louis said. He wiped his eyes and then spoke almost without thinking. "My lord, Augustus, when you say things like that, you sound just like him."

That got a reaction. Winter stood up so quickly he knocked over the chair. He pointed the shotgun at Louis, and his eyes looked as if some infernal gate had come loose inside them, as if they had become windows to Hell.

Louis was too shocked to be afraid. He had never seen a face so distorted with surprise and hatred and he simply assumed that he was about to die.

And then Winter let the shotgun drop to the floor and walked down the hallway and the front door banged open.

Louis reached for the gun, remembered Lukas drawing the pistols, and then let it lie.

"Where did he go?" Dorothy cried out from behind him.

"Stay in the kitchen," Louis said.

Winter had walked about twenty paces from the house and was standing by the road and looking out over the river. Then his shoulders crumpled forward and he pressed his hands to his eyes and his whole body began to shake.

Louis walked up to him very carefully, conscious that he could not afford a mistake. He circled around Winter a little to the left, keeping a healthy distance, then he said, "Hey now, I didn't mean it like that. You ain't like him. I just meant you reminded me of him when you said how hard the world was. That sounded a lot like your father, Augustus, was all I meant."

And Winter turned and looked at Louis and Louis was startled by what he saw. Because there was no grief or sadness in Winter's eyes. He was weeping; his face was slick with tears that were turning the dust on his face to mud. And his mouth was open and hitching with his unsteady breaths. But he was looking at Louis with a peculiarly calm expression, unconcerned and unembarrassed. It was as if by weeping Winter was purging a part of himself, as if he knew he was crying for the last time.

And the worst part was that Louis thought he knew why. Because the world had been awfully hard to young Augustus Winter, a hard and cruel place, and Louis thought that Winter had decided that he needed to give up certain kinds of feelings in order to survive. And Louis, who could remember Augustus as a boy, felt deeply that this was not so.

Winter raised his hands and wiped his eyes, two or three times, and breathed through his mouth in great gulps of air.

"Augustus," Louis said, "you ain't like him. I don't care what you've done. I know you from when you were a little boy. All right?"

"You don't know anything," Winter said. "You don't know what I've seen."

"Yeah," Louis said, "okay. You've seen some terrible things. I know you have, Augustus. But you're still seeing them. And they're gone now, they're gone. The only bad things here are the ones you've got inside you. And if you just let them go, they'll be gone too. I swear, Augustus. I promise you."

But Winter's expression had become hard and distant.

"You see that?" Winter said.

"What?" Louis asked.

Winter motioned his head toward the river. Sluggish and brown and running against gravity, against the way nature had intended.

"It's not just in me, Louis," Winter said. "It's everywhere. Once you know where to look."

39

That same dawn Jan Müller stood in the fashionable drawing room of Justice Francis Bernard. It was packed so full with immigrants of all nationalities that they sat on the tables and the arms of the chairs and knocked their elbows together. Everyone had taken his boots off at the front door and the smell of feet was overpowering. They had come over straight from the saloon after their eye-openers and many were drunk and singing, including a little man wedged next to Jan.

The judge came in through the large oak double doors that led to the foyer. He was a hefty, cheerful man with a halo of white hair around the back of his head and a hard red face. A faint echo of an Irish accent was in his voice. He stood on a footstool to address the crowd.

"All right, men," he said, "we've got your certificates right here. You've all been taken care of so there's no worry about payment. You just remember who your friends are at the end of the month. Your saloon keepers'll let you know how to vote. Don't be afraid of Republican thugs, we'll take care of them too. After a favor like this one we expect you to vote three or four times, at the barest minimum."

The men cheered.

"Every man put your hand on a Bible," the judge said, and the Bibles were produced and circulated and every man stretched out a hand, right or left, to find one to touch.

The judge administered the oath, although many present could not speak English, and he congratulated them all, for they were now American citizens.

Jan was handed a certificate of citizenship on the way out. It read: JACK MILLER.

The air was damp and pungent outside, earthy. It was cold and steam was rising from the sewers. Mickey Burns waited on the street next to a carriage.

"Come on," Burns said. "Time's a-wastin'. It's election time, and I've a large number of funerals to attend." He threw his cigar into the gutter and entered the carriage. Jan got up on top with the driver, because the seats inside were filled with flowers.

Between the hours of six and nine in the morning, they attended three funeral services. One was for a man killed by a train, one was for an ancient grandmother, and the last for a young child poisoned by swill milk. All three of the families were precisely as poor as dirt; all of the funerals had been paid for by Mickey Burns, the Great Mourner. At each of them he made the rounds, squeezing everyone's hands, a tear in his eye, with Jan staggering behind underneath an enormous floral arrangement.

"God bless you, Mister Burns," they all said, choked with emotion.

After the last funeral they were stopped outside by a small ill-favored man with a cast in one eye and thinning, greasy hair.

"Top of the morning to you, Mister Burns," he said.

"Corky," Burns said affectionately. "Grand to see you."

"I know you're busy with the election and all," Corky said, "so I'll cut to the chase, if you don't mind. I've been the subject of unjust persecution from the police. They've called my saloon a common gaming house."

Burns laughed, but only after a brief hesitation. "Imagine that," Burns said, "calling it common!"

"I was hoping you'd intercede on my behalf," Corky said, drawing an envelope from his jacket.

"My dear Corky," Burns said. "I know you'll believe me when I say it pains me greatly to let down a man of my district, and that it pains me even more to refuse a contribution to my campaign."

"Oh fuck off," Corky said.

"But you'd really better take that envelope to King Conor."

"He'll bleed me dry!" Corky said.

Burns winced. He did look genuinely pained.

"Mickey, come on now," Corky said. "I've been kicking back to you from the very start."

"I'll have a word with him," Burns said. "It's all I can do for you. He's straight up bought the monopoly."

"I know he had to go through one of you to get me shut down."

"That's the thing, Corky," Burns said. "He don't have to do that at all. The coppers sit around in his joint and he tells 'em where to go. I'm sorry, boyo, I really am, but we got less for the streetcar franchise than what he paid for the gaming franchise."

Corky looked angry but resigned.

"And to think of all the money I've kicked you," he said, "and for what?"

"We had some good years, though, didn't we?" Burns said.

Corky shook his head, disgusted, and turned away.

They drove to the courthouse next. Burns jogged up the steps, barged through the front doors, and took a seat at the back of a courtroom crowded with dozens of dirty Irish youths, reeking of cheap whiskey and vomit. Many of them were bruised and bloodied. Burns wrote their names down in a little book. The youths waved at him to get his attention but he paid them little mind.

Between nine in the morning and noon he bailed out each and

every young man from his district, scolded them, gave them a railway pass, and told them to visit his office and speak to his secretary about getting a city job. Some of their mothers were present, and they often burst into tears.

"I'm fecking starving," Burns said afterward to Jan as they jogged back down the steps. "Run and get me a sandwich, will you?"

Jan was a hair, the merest hair, from doing so. It was only the pain in his side that caused him to hesitate and gave him time to think. He kept moving down the stairs, his heart thudding in his chest, and he looked at Burns with what he hoped was an ignorant expression.

Burns was studying him for any sign that he had understood. Eventually he said, "Well, you ain't the liveliest help I ever had, but where we're going next you won't need to do much talking. Hey?"

Burns mimed throwing a few punches and said, more loudly, "Next stop? Fighting? Hmm?"

Jan nodded.

They drove a short distance to a restaurant off one of the main streets. The windows were small and dirty and it was dark inside, but the linen was spotless and neat red candles were on every table. The dining room was deserted save for a table toward the back where an elderly and overweight man was eating a shepherd's pie. Three tall, powerful men loomed around him.

"My fellow alderman!" the old man cried. "Fucking Mickey Burns as I live and breathe. A young lion like you making time for Old Man Sullivan? During an election? And to think everyone calls you an ungrateful cunt."

"Hello, Terry," Burns said.

"I don't recognize your boy there," Sullivan said.

"He's a kraut."

Sullivan laughed, a chortling sound like a whirlpool, as he crammed food into his mouth.

"Don't want any of yer regulars hearing how you sell out your party, do ya?"

"Something like that," Burns said amiably. He was taking his belt off and wrapping it around his fist, so that the buckle dangled down. One of the big boys stepped toward him but Sullivan raised one finger and he stopped.

"I would do the same if I was a traitor like you," Sullivan replied. "Imagine selling out your principles for a Republican."

"Principles?" Burns laughed. "Here are me 'principles': nobody in the ring sells his vote to more than one bidder. You can call that a principle if you like. I call it simple fucking economics. Now we've already sold our votes to widen State Street, and been paid for them, but I hear you've been boodling the other way. That's just short-sighted, Terry. It's just short-term thinking, is what it is. If people can't trust the quality of the goods, the price will fall. It'd do you well to have a little more vision."

"Go fuck yourself," Sullivan said. He leaned back in his chair and smiled. "Sold them you did, to a Republican. And you didn't even get a good price for them."

"Well, now, Terry," Burns said. "I wouldn't be so sure about that, if I were you. As a matter of fact this particular Republican has been very helpful with the election. Alerting us about Noah Ross's plans and such. But even leaving that to one side, Terry, men like you and me shouldn't get caught up in partisan bickering. Ain't our word our bond? Don't our customers count on us to keep our word? And what's it to us whether a man's a Republican or a Democrat? This isn't the South. It ain't even New York. This is Chicago, and politics ain't beanbag. It's money. I trust I can rely on your vote."

"No," Sullivan said. "Get the fuck out of my joint."

"Well, let it never be said that I didn't try to do this the nice way," Burns said.

He dangled the belt buckle as if he would swing it, just enough to catch the eyes of the bodyguards, who moved toward him. And then he produced a knife with his other hand from under his jacket and planted it in the gut of the first man to reach him.

Jan struck out, a hard, quick, straightforward punch, and smashed one of the others right on the tip of his chin, catching him by surprise and knocking him backward. Then he and Burns heaved the lone remaining bodyguard through the table onto the floor. Jan held him down while Burns stomped on his face with the heel of his shiny patent leather shoe.

Sullivan staggered away from the wreckage of his lunch, his face as white as the tablecloth.

"Where the fuck d'you think you're going?" Burns snarled.

"You've lost your mind," Sullivan said.

"No, Terry," Burns said. His voice was very soft now. "You were the one who lost your fucking mind. When you crossed me."

Burns nodded at Jan, who closed the distance to Sullivan in two long strides and pressed him up against the wall.

"You ran this city for years, and what did you ever do with it?" Burns said. "You made a tenth of the money we do now, doing things properly with the ring, instead of every man for himself. And you let the fucking Republicans have the big job for twenty years. In a city full of Irishmen, Polacks, and krauts. Why? No fucking vision. That's why."

Burns cracked the belt like a whip. It struck the wall above Sullivan's head, sending a shower of plaster chips across his face and making him cry out.

"So listen to me now, and remember it's not just me, it's Honest Jim and King Conor and the whole crew speaking. You'll vote straight or you'll go in the river. If not before the election then after. You mind me, Terry. You mind me now."

Burns looked into Sullivan's eyes, and Sullivan looked back. Then Burns nodded again at Jan, and he shoved the fat alderman to the floor.

The bodyguard who had been stabbed was still moaning as they walked into the daylight. Burns's hands were bloody and his clothes and hair were disheveled. His diamond pin was sticking out at a crooked angle. He got into the carriage and Jan followed.

"You're a stout lad," Burns said. "You're a good man to have in a pinch, and if that's not the finest compliment of them all, I don't know what is."

They returned to his office, where Burns met with the men and women of his district for the rest of the day. He gave out money and gifts, but more than that, he put things in their place. If a boy could sing he asked him to join the glee club. If he was an athlete, he was invited to join the baseball club. Disputes were resolved, promises were made. The unemployed were given jobs, the bored amusement, and the hungry food. All this largesse was dispensed with charm and grace.

The late afternoon saw them attend two more funerals, both for children. As the sun set they took one last carriage ride to a cluster of wooden shanties pressed up against the river to the east of the lumberyard. Burns walked up and down the muddy paths in his fine suit, catching the men on their way from work and handing out railway passes, bottles of fine store-bought whiskey, turkey, geese, and scuttles of coal. Jan, weak from his wound, lagged behind. He crouched on his heels in the dust of the slum, watched the crowd of dancing children following Burns, and felt the familiar sensation rise within him. The feeling that he was doing something very, very wrong in the service of some higher ideal that was slipping further away all the time, all the time.

He left Burns then, ostensibly to return to Reiman's saloon, but instead he headed back to the Michigan Avenue Hotel. Archie opened the door for him and ushered him into a small office behind the hotel desk. Noah waited inside along with a lawyer and a stenographer.

"Well?" Noah said. "What happened?"

Jan dutifully related the day's events: the ceremony at the judge's house, the funerals, the meeting with Corky, the courthouse, and the fighting.

"Widening State Street?" Noah cried out, looking over at the lawyer.

"Yes," Jan said. "That is what he said."

"Well," Noah said. "I do believe that will allow us to identify the spy who advised the Democrats of your arrival."

"Amazing," the lawyer rumbled, as he carefully took notes.

"Go on then," Noah said.

But that was all, except for the assorted acts of philanthropy, which interested Noah and the lawyer not at all.

"I should be going," Jan said. "They will be expecting me at the saloon."

"You can't go back to Burns," Noah said. "This won't make the papers tomorrow morning, but I think this is enough to lay charges."

"More than enough!" the lawyer said.

"And then they'll be looking for an informant. Stay here. You've done well."

"It was luck," Jan said. "Only luck."

To his surprise, Jan found that he regretted that he would not be returning to Reiman's saloon. To hear the German language, to have proper beer and food, to be surrounded by honest workingmen, men who did not need to lie about who they were or what they had done, men who could trick themselves into being proud about what they did, even if they worked for a thief.

"There was some luck, but you did well," Noah said. "I'm glad to see that at least some of my brother's men can show a little discretion. I hardly dared hope that they'd have the sense to stay indoors until the election, but I'm a little shocked at the amount of trouble they've managed to stir up."

This snapped Jan from his reverie.

"I am sorry, Mister Ross," Jan said. "Quentin, he has very little patience."

Noah smiled sourly. He motioned for the lawyer and the stenographer to leave, and they did, promising to return with a final version of Jan's statement for him to review before it was notarized.

"You don't have to tell me about Quentin's failings," Noah said as he checked his watch and packed up his bags. "He never changed, not really. I remember him as a boy, what a terror he was. Wetting the bed, torturing the cat, and lying, lying all the time, about trivial things, silly things, without any reason. And yes, always impatient. When he behaves well it only makes me nervous. I always find myself wondering what he's really thinking about."

Jan looked very uncomfortable.

"However," Noah said. "We need only make it a few more days. What you've given us here will win us the election for sure."

Jan furrowed his brow. "Forgive me," he said. "But I am not sure you are correct."

"Hmm?" Noah said.

"I was only with Mister Burns one day, but I do not believe the people who vote for him are concerned that he is corrupt."

"He's stealing from the city," Noah said. "It's their money. That money could be going to help them and make their lives better."

"It could be, yes," Jan said. "But they do not believe it would be. They do not believe that if the Republicans were in power, things would be any better."

"Burns is a common thief," Noah said. "He makes three dollars a session for serving in council but he lives in a house worth fifty thousand and he owns three saloons."

"Of course," Jan said. "It is obvious he is a thief, but he is generous with what he steals. To them, it's better than the alternative."

"We've run this city fairly since its inception. Chicago's made hundreds of men into millionaires. This is the greatest city in the world. Burns is nothing but a leech, sucking the blood from this city. Don't tell me that a day of watching him hand out nickels has turned you into a Democrat."

Jan's face went blank with astonishment, and when he spoke again his voice was high and loud.

"Don't you call me that! Don't you dare! No one knows what these men do more than me! The Democrats sold me into the Union Army when I had just stepped off the boat and could not speak English! If it wasn't for those crooks I would never have—"

"I am sorry," Noah said. "I did not think you would take it so ill to be called a Democrat."

"You don't understand!" Jan said. "You sent me to spy on Burns, but you should study instead the men who voted for him. If you don't know them, you'll never win this election."

"Jan," Noah said. "Thank you for your advice. But here are the facts: the man is a thief and if our institutions mean anything, our democratic institutions, including the courts and our free press, we need only make sure the voters are informed and then keep the election free of outside interference, and we will surely win."

"Well said, my brother! Well said!"

Quentin had appeared in the doorway.

Quentin said, "I trust everything went well?"

"Quite," Noah said. "If you can avoid doing anything dreadful for the next little while, this may work out after all."

"Wonderful," Quentin said. "Simply wonderful."

Noah left, and Quentin disappeared upstairs, after congratulating Jan warmly again. Jan went to the dining room. He found Bill at the bar and sat down next to him for a drink. Archie poured them both stiff glasses of whiskey. Bill was so drunk he could only squint.

"I have been thinking about my uncle, Sarge," he said. "About the days before all of this."

Jan drank.

40

That night, well after midnight, Mickey Burns sat on a wooden crate on the rocky shore of Lake Michigan and admired all the dark water. It smelled better. Not good, precisely. But nothing like it used to in the old days. The stench of the water then had been like nothing on earth. Seemed like progress. Still, where was all that shit? Those hog parts and the human filth? Just washed the other way down the river, that's all. The shit always had to go somewhere. It was nice for it to be somewhere else; there was no doubt about that. But it hadn't vanished just because you didn't see it. That was the truth most men didn't like to think about.

The shore was deserted at this hour and so the footsteps of the approaching police officers were very loud. The man they were dragging cried out as he was hurled to the ground, but he fell silent quickly enough when Mickey Burns turned to face him.

"Mister Burns," Archie said.

"Shut up, you black bastard," Burns said, his Irish accent making the words sound like a song. "When I tell you it's time to talk, we'll talk. Until then, shut up."

"Mister Burns," Archie said, "I can explain. I was gonna see Mister McDonald tomorrow morning. I didn't—"

Burns's hand snapped forward and caught Archie's testicles, and he squeezed and twisted. The air in Archie's lungs exploded out in a noiseless burst and then he could not inhale. Burns's eyes were vibrating, jumping rapidly back and forth. "I said shut up."

He let go of Archie's balls and Archie collapsed to the ground and began to whoop and weep.

Burns looked him over with a critical eye. Archie had been beaten pretty effectively, but nothing on the face or the hands or anywhere it would show. Good. Burns motioned to the towering cops and they took a few steps back. Once they were out of earshot, Burns looked back over the dark, choppy water.

"Luck," Burns said. "You work hard, you struggle. Perhaps God gave you some talent, some brains, some nerve. But everything's just luck, Archie my lad. The men who built this city believed it would be a great city, the greatest in America. And they were right. But do you know why they believed it would be great? Do you?"

Archie said nothing. Burns grinned.

"They said you were a clever lad," Burns said. "You're right. Keep your trap shut."

The water lapped up against the rocky shore.

"They said this city would be great because of the waterways," Burns continued. "The water. You see? Chicago was built here because it's close to a portage between the Great Lakes and the Mississippi River watershed. A few little canals, and boats could travel from the Atlantic Ocean, down the St. Lawrence, through Buffalo and Detroit, and then Chicago, and finally all the way down to New Orleans. Steamships, do you see? Riverboats. My father came here to dig the canal in the thirties. But it wasn't canals that made this city great at all. It was the railways."

Burns laughed.

"You can't predict the future," he said. "The race is not to the swift, nor the battle to the strong, nor bread to the wise, nor riches to men of understanding, nor favor to men of skill. Time and chance happeneth to them all."

He slapped his knees and leaned back.

"Just look at me. I had a productive day, I thought, getting ready for the election, and then my man in the courthouse tells me that the Republicans are getting all set to put me under arrest. Next I hear the newspapers will soon be running lurid stories of how I allegedly stabbed a fellow alderman in a dispute over whose bribes we ought to be taking. As you can imagine, I went to bed a man concerned. But then I was awoken by the police, who had come to tell me that tonight a young lady had been cut up, a young lady who worked in an establishment that operates under what you might call my aegis. Now, I know what you're thinking. You're thinking, What kind of men would do such a thing? Cut up a lady? Well, no one knew who these men were. No one had ever seen these men until quite recently, when they started their late night depredations, which have gradually escalated until this sad point. But they did know the man acting as their tour guide. Oh, yes, they most certainly did."

Archie frantically gestured toward his mouth, but Burns only smiled and continued on.

"Poor old Archie. Archibald Patterson, isn't it? Such a clever boy, they tell me. Doesn't miss a trick, they say. And a brave one, too, distinguishing himself in the war. But what does it profit a man to be too brave and too clever for his station in life? In the end, not much."

Burns's friendly, dangerous eyes flicked back to the dark water.

"But what were we talking about? Luck? How quickly it can turn? No one could identify those men, who were so rough where they ought to have been gentle, but they could certainly describe them. Oh yes. Those big lunkhead brothers who called each other Charlie and Johnny. The little one with the big eyes. They described them very well. And it seems perhaps that my luck has turned. Just as yours might. Because, Archie my lad, you're in need of some luck right now. It's you that King Conor would normally hold responsible for this little contretemps. The world is full of bad men but he expects better from clever, brave boys like you, who know how this city works, who bring clientele to the establishments with which he, and therefore I, am affiliated. We expect you to act as a gatekeeper, and in this regard, you have let us down. I don't normally concern myself with these matters. I'm not what you'd call a details man. But I daresay in ordinary circumstances King Conor would have cut your pecker off and left you here to feed the fish as a warning to every other clever boy out there. But you're in luck, just as I am. That is, of course, if you are willing to assist me."

Archie's expression made it abundantly clear that he was at Burns's service. Still, he did not speak.

"Now is the time for you to talk," Burns said.

41

When Noah Ross arrived at Burns's house the next morning the police and the reporter were already there. It was very cold and their exhalations were clearly visible, like little yellow ghosts in the lamplight.

"You look nervous," Noah said.

Deputy Brown smiled. His face was red and hardened, like the shell of a boiled lobster. He had been a police officer in Chicago for seventeen years. The two officers with him were no more than boys. The newspaper reporter from the *Journal* was smoking a cigarette and his eyeglasses flashed opaque in the cold light.

"It's my only job," Brown said. "I've got a family to feed."

"They know you're a Republican," Noah said. "If they win you'll lose your job anyway."

"Everyone takes care of their own in this city," Brown said.

Noah walked up to the door and seized the brass knocker. Before he could let go the door opened inward, revealing Mickey Burns's thirteen-year-old daughter, smiling at him.

"Are you looking for my father?" she said.

Noah nodded.

"He's expecting you. There's breakfast if you'd like it."

The police officers and the reporter took their shoes off. Noah hesitated and then did the same. They walked over the soft carpet until they came into the dining room, where Mickey Burns, Honest Jim Plunkett, King Conor McDonald, and Burns's lawyer were eating eggs and sausage.

"Noah Ross," Burns said. "How'd you do?"

Deputy Brown stepped forward.

"Good morning, Mister Burns. I've come to tell you that you're under arrest."

"Warrant?" the lawyer asked, his tone friendly.

Deputy Brown took a folded paper out of his pocket and handed it over.

"Two hundred thousand dollars?" the lawyer exclaimed as he read the warrant.

"The man your client stabbed has died," Noah said.

"Who's the judge?" Burns asked, his mouth full.

"Robinson," the lawyer replied, as his eyes flicked back and forth over the warrant.

Burns nodded. "Well, I've got me bail ready, so's we can draw up the papers. Don't think you'll need to stick around, Ross. You're time's rather valuable, after all."

"You think you've finished us, do you?" Honest Jim said to Noah.

"Now Mister Plunkett . . . ," the lawyer said.

"It's all right," Honest Jim said, but there was a dangerous glint in his eyes. "We're just talking."

"I think it will be rather difficult for you to win an election under the circumstances, yes," Noah said.

"Well, that shows how much you know about politics, doesn't it?" Honest Jim said. "Tweed won a seat in the state senate after he was arrested, and they had a lot more on him than you do on Mister Burns."

"So," Noah said, arching an eyebrow, "you're comparing Burns to Tweed, are you?" He turned to the journalist. "I do hope you're getting all this down."

Honest Jim smiled, but it was hard smile, hard indeed.

"You're a funny one, aren't you? You're all about the free markets. You'd think a man like you'd know that everything has its price."

"A free market depends on some things being without price," Noah said. "Such as the rule of law."

"Isn't that something," Honest Jim said. "For someone who don't like regulation, you're awfully keen on rules. I wonder if you have any idea about what life's really like. Maybe you should ask your brother when you go back to your hotel."

Honest Jim looked at the reporter and grinned. "Print that, boyo. Print that I told him to ask his murdering brother."

"Good morning, gentlemen," Noah said.

He left the house with the reporter while the three police officers stayed inside. On the doorstep, Noah said to the reporter, "Make sure you write that King Conor is one of his bondsmen. You can leave out the part about my brother. I'm sure their papers will cover that angle."

42

After the policemen finally left, the Democrats ate in silence.

"That rat-bastard Reiman sold us out," Honest Jim finally said. "He stuck you with a spy."

"I admit that was first my thought," Burns said. "Then I remembered that Reiman told me that he didn't know the man. Tried to get me to take someone else."

"That's just the way he fooled you," Honest Jim said.

King Conor laughed.

"Rather subtle stratagem for a kraut, don't you think?" Burns said. "More likely Ross sent a man to spy on Reiman but I ended up taking him instead. If only I'd stuck with me own boys!"

"Ah," Honest Jim said. "They was bound to get a few licks in. After all, Mister Ross is a sharp one, and we're no angels. Are we, gentlemen?" Honest Jim was smiling broadly and looking from Burns to Conor. You could not have told, by looking at him, that anything was amiss.

Burns was buttering a bun, staring at his plate. Twenty-five years ago he had been as poor as potatoes. Lifting heavy things to earn his living, sleeping in hovels, and fighting at night. It was politics that had brought him here, and luck, but most of all it was shrewdness. It cut Burns to the quick to have been tricked.

King Conor wiped his mouth with a napkin and threw it down on the table, hard enough to make the silverware and china clink.

"If Jim ain't going to say it, I will," King Conor said. "I've put a lot of money in this man Harrison, and I don't want you screwing it up to protect your clients. You don't have nothing to worry about in this election but the fucking main event is as tight as a gnat's asshole. You were worried about your fucking alderman's syndicate. Well, this is my election, because I fucking paid for it."

"I told you, Conor," Burns said. "The man who paid me to widen State Street has been giving us tips on what the Republicans have been planning. That's why I brought someone who didn't speak English, to keep it secret like."

"You think I believe that?" Conor said. He kicked back his chair and towered over them. Suddenly he was shouting. "You think I need you, Burns? You think I can't reach out into the street and—"

"Conor!" Honest Jim thundered.

And King Conor, for all his money and power, for all his policemen and hired thugs, stopped at the sound of that voice. It was a voice that had boomed across crowded party conventions where every man had a knife up his sleeve, that had commanded platoons of volunteer firefighters, and that had carried across open fields during stump speeches. Honest Jim Plunkett had never run for office, but it was only because he'd never needed to.

"You do need him, Conor," Honest Jim said. "Votes ain't like cans on a shelf that you can go up and buy for a set price. You've got to grow them like cabbages. Now all my men, Irish or not, have been working their districts like their gardens. They've been planting and watering and tending all this time. They're the head of every glee club and every firefighting force, they've gone to the weddings and funerals, they've done it all. That's how they got the loyalty of the voting public. And so you do need him, just like he needs you. All right?"

Conor scowled. "He was looking out for his syndicate."

"What if he was?" Honest Jim said. "I ain't saying he was. But what if he was? Everyone's in this for himself, Conor. Everyone stands to profit. I wouldn't ask them to throw in with us elsewise, would I? He's every right to look out for his syndicate."

King Conor's face abruptly shifted into a smile, a little too quickly for Burns's liking. "Well, all right then," he said, sitting back down. "What are we going to do now?"

"Election's in two days," Honest Jim said. "We've just got to keep on. Get them votes out. All the usual tricks."

"The police are ready?" Burns asked.

"When the voting starts, we can count on the support of three-quarters of the constabulary," Honest Jim replied.

"It cost me enough," King Conor said. "It better be worth it."

"What do we do if they turn those fellows loose?" Burns asked. "The ones they've got cooped up in the hotel?"

"They won't dare do it now," Honest Jim said. "But even if they do, our boys have been in scraps before. They're ready."

Burns shook his head.

"What?" Honest Jim said. "You scared?"

"There was something about this German," Burns said. "He wasn't mean. It was more like he was hurt somehow. Damaged. He was a wild one in a scrap."

"Ours are wilder," Honest Jim said. "Plus we've the police."

"I'm worried, Jim," Burns said. "I don't want to spread ourselves

too thin. Maybe we ought to pull out of some of the touchier neigh-
borhoods. The Polish ones . . ."

"Fuck off," King Conor said.

"Mickey," Honest Jim said patiently. "It's those ones as are most
important. We can't just give 'em to the Republicans. Come on now.
Buck up, my son. You just do your part in your district and get the
repeaters out there on the street. Get all your tough boys organized
and ready. It'll be quite a scrap, but you just trust old Honest Jim. It'll
all turn right in the end."

43

When Dusty Kingsley woke up, there was a dull throbbing
behind his eyes and his mouth was dry, but all in all it was one of
the mildest hangovers he'd had since he'd moved into the Michigan
Avenue Hotel. He dressed quickly and made his way down the stairs
to the dining room. What he saw when he arrived made him stop
short in his tracks.

"Jesus, Bill. Didn't you go to bed last night?"

Bill sat at the bar. At the sound of Dusty's voice he turned around,
very slowly, with exaggerated care. The whites of his eyes were orange
and he was slick with sweat. As Dusty approached he caught a whiff
of urine and wrinkled his nose.

"Oh my god," Dusty said.

A half-empty bottle of gin stood at Bill's elbow. Dusty snatched
it away. Bill made no move to stop him. It did not look like Bill could
make any sudden movements at all without toppling from his stool.

"Just hold tight," Dusty said. "I'll be back."

A gilded mirror hung behind the bar. Bill Bread slowly lifted his
eyes and looked into it. You could try to look at other things, sitting
at this bar. The label of the bottle in your hand, the slick zinc surface
of the bar, the flickering light of the gas lamps. But you couldn't hide
from yourself.

At the beginning it had been sort of sadly amusing. He would
wake in the morning, appallingly sick, and the game would start.
Attempting to take a day off. Just one. Part of him knew that he
would lose the game every time he tried to play, and after a while,

Bill didn't see the point in playing. But when the game ended, when the force of his own staring and bloodshot eyes in the mirror stripped away all his illusions, and he stopped pretending that he was not going to get drunk, Bill discovered that his self-delusion had been restraining his behavior far more than he had guessed.

When Dusty returned to the dining room, bringing Johnson with him, they found Bill lying stomach down on the bar, blindly fumbling for another bottle.

"Bill! Quit that!" Dusty said.

Bill surrendered as they took him by his armpits.

"He stinks," Johnson said.

"I'm gonna be sick!" Bill said, and both Dusty and Johnson dropped him. Bill helplessly threw up on the floor.

"Fagh," Dusty said.

Johnson only frowned.

They waited a while after Bill was done, just to be safe, and then they carried him to his room. Dusty went to draw a bath while Johnson carefully laid Bill on his side.

"I'm sorry," Bill said.

"No you ain't," Johnson said.

Johnson brushed the sweaty black hair out of Bill's eyes, a gesture devoid of tenderness. "You don't even know what it means to be sorry, Bread. You ride with a cold bunch, but you're the coldest."

Bill smiled. "I can't help it."

"So it would appear," Johnson said. "I'll say this much for your sorry ass. It ain't good for you to be cooped up like this. If Noah was trying to kill you I don't know if he could have found a surer way to go about it."

Bill said, "I feel guilty about my uncle."

"You were drinking before your uncle died," Johnson said.

"I don't mean it like that," Bill said. "It's not to do with that."

"Hmm," Johnson said.

"He wasn't an imaginative man," Bill said. "I keep wondering what he'd think if he could see all this. I don't reckon he could have even conceived it. Conceived any of it."

Dusty came out of the bathroom with a pint bottle of whiskey in his hand.

"He had it stashed behind the toilet," Dusty explained.

"Let's get him cleaned up," Johnson said.

When they were halfway through undressing him, Bill looked up at Johnson and said, "Men aren't meant to know that everything is possible."

A noise was coming from outside, a kind of murmur, rising above the normal din of the busy streets.

"You're quite the philosopher today," Dusty said.

They got Bill naked and tossed him in the tub and left him there.

"Do you think we should do something about him?" Dusty asked.

"We already did," Johnson said.

"I mean about the drinking in general."

Johnson said, "Let him go to hell in his own way."

The noise from the street was louder. Someone laughed—the sound of it cut through the drapes—and then a knocking came from the ground floor.

"What is that?" Dusty said.

They pulled back the drapes. Johnson had enough sense to be subtle about it. That was when they saw the mob of newspaper reporters, policemen, Democratic agitators, and general miscreants gathered at the front door of the hotel.

44

The tailor's shop in downtown Chicago was well lit by the windows facing the street. Men's clothing hung on the racks and a mirror leaned against the back wall. The bell rang. John Jones, an elderly Negro with bright white hair and a long, smooth mustache, looked up from his sewing. A man and a boy had come into his shop. The man had fine pale hair, milky skin, and golden eyes. The boy had pistols hanging from his hips. They were both raggedly dressed.

"May I help you?" Jones said. His voice was slow, calm, deep.

"We need a suit for the boy," Winter said. "Before the end of the day."

"Well now," Jones said. "I'm not sure I can have something ready for you by then."

Winter dug into his pocket and tossed a cloth bag onto the table in front of the tailor, landing on the jacket on which Jones was working.

"You go on and name your price, old man," Winter said. "And don't you make me ask again."

Jones dumped the contents of the bag over the table. The coins were mostly gold, with some larger silver ones scattered through. Jones carefully separated a number that seemed fair to him and then looked back up at Winter speculatively.

"Don't suppose you want one too?"

"No," Winter said.

"Aw, come on Auggie!" Lukas said. "Think how good we'll look, n'how surprised they'll be! They'll be tickled to see us'n suits! Get yourself one!"

"Those clothes are just about falling off," Jones said. "You'll need some new ones soon anyway."

"Fine," Winter said.

Jones separated a few more coins and dropped them in his pocket. Then he put the rest of the coins in the bag and walked it over to Winter.

"Here you go," he said. "Come into the back with me."

Jones took their measurement with firm, strong hands, taking no notes, repeating the numbers under his breath only once.

"I suppose you gentlemen don't have any particular kind of suit in mind."

"You sure got that right," Winter said.

"Well, all right then," Jones said, glancing at the clock. "It's nine thirty. You get on back here round three o'clock or so. Then I'll make some minor adjustments and try to have you on your way by five. Meantime if you want to get a shave and a haircut, just head on down the street."

The bell rang again as the door shut behind them. Jones drew the curtains and flipped the sign from OPEN to CLOSED.

"What are we going to do, Auggie?" Lukas asked. "Want to get a haircut?"

"All right," Winter said.

They walked down the street to the barbershop in the Palmer

House. As they waited, Winter read the newspaper and paid particular interest to the various exposés concerning Mickey Burns. Lukas, who could not read, kicked his legs back and forth in his chair and whistled with effortless skill.

A stout barber called Lukas to his chair, and a few minutes later Winter was summoned by a tall, thin man with an effeminate manner.

"So what were you thinking?" he said as he gathered Winter's long hair and pulled it behind his neck.

"Wasn't thinking of anything in particular."

"I take it you are accustomed to simpler haircuts?"

"You are correct."

"You don't mind if I try something a little different, perhaps, than what you are used to?"

"Knock yourself out," Winter said. "If I don't like it I'll say so."

"Very well," the barber said grandly, and spun Winter away from the mirror and tilted his head back into the sink. The warm water rose up around his ears and the barber sank his fingers into his scalp.

"You have the most beautiful hair," the barber said. "It's fine, but strong, like silk."

Winter said nothing. He looked at the ceiling and relaxed. I'm in the city, he thought. Sinful old Chicago. Getting my hair done at a two-dollar barbershop. What would he think of that, I wonder.

The barber raised Winter out of the sink, spun the chair around, and began to dry his hair vigorously with a towel. Again he deeply massaged Winter's scalp and the back of his neck with his strong fingers. Then he ran the comb through Winter's hair and snipped away, taking a little bit at a time. Eventually the barber was satisfied. He then applied a hot towel to Winter's cheeks, rubbing gently back and forth, and laid on the lather from a brush.

The razor glided across his flesh again and again. It was strange that an act so close to being deadly could be so soothing.

"No mustache," the barber said. It was not a question and Winter did not demur.

He applied scented aftershave to Winter's face and the back of his neck, and then he used hair cream to shape Winter's shortened hair into ringlets against the side of his face.

"Voilà!" the barber exclaimed.

Lukas, whose haircut was done, brayed with laughter.

Winter came very close to telling the barber to cut it all off. Yet something stopped him, as if he caught a glimpse of something he remembered faintly but could not identify. He ought not to like the haircut—it was pretentious and affected. It made him look ridiculous. And yet. It was not precisely weak looking, so much as wholly different. Alien. He liked that it was tightly controlled, carefully designed, that it was urban, that it was modern, that it was fashionable. He liked that his father would have despised it. He liked that by wearing it he was showing he did not care what men thought of him.

"All right," Winter said.

"All right!" the barber said.

In the hotel's restaurant, Lukas ordered a series of desserts: fruit pies, cakes, and ice cream. Winter had a coffee and bacon and eggs. They drew many stares but no one approached them. At three they returned to the tailor.

"Hello, gentlemen," Jones said. "You're looking mighty fine."

"Auggie's a dandy now!" Lukas giggled.

The boy put his suit on first. It was a little long in the legs, so Jones pinned it up and drew on it with chalk and muttered numbers to himself under his breath, and then took it all off. Lukas stood stark naked in the shop with his hands on his hips while Winter tried his suit on.

"It don't fit right," Winter said.

"It fits you like a glove, son," Jones replied.

"The shoulders are tight," Winter said. "The sleeves are short."

"Excuse me," Jones said, "but I've been a tailor in this city for thirty years and I've put a lot of uncivilized men in their first suits. I'm telling you it's supposed to fit like that and I think I'd know."

Winter seemed momentarily at a loss.

"Put your tie on," Jones said, "and pull your pants up."

"I don't like 'em that high."

"You'll get used to it," Jones said. "Use the suspenders."

Winter did as he was instructed, slowly and reluctantly. His movements were stiff with anger. Jones seemed oblivious, focused entirely on Winter's clothes. For his part, Lukas wasn't laughing any-more. Instead he stood with his mouth gaping open, his eyes wide, like he had fallen into a trance on his feet.

"Go on," Jones said. "Take a look. You look like . . . well. I'm not exactly sure."

Winter walked up to the mirror and stopped in his tracks.

"There it is," he whispered. "There."

The suit, indeed, fit him well. It clung to him tightly but it was still composed of crisp, straight lines. As if it had hardened him, made him into something geometric. Unnaturally clean. An entirely new thing. His appearance now was to his old like what a cut gem is to a rough stone: the ordinary refined through artisanship to a higher form of nature. Extraneous parts removed to catch the light and to set a fire inside.

Winter took a few steps forward and reached out and touched the mirror.

This was it. This was what he had been looking for all his life without realizing it. This look, this studied, practiced, contrived look, was the truest outward expression of his inner being.

"Well?" Jones said.

"Okay," Winter said. "Okay."

45

When Reggie Keller arrived at the Michigan Avenue Hotel, a large crowd of newspaper reporters were standing around the front step in cheap suits, smoking and spitting and laughing. The shutters were fastened and the door was locked.

"Well son of a bitch," Reggie said.

He was now a tall, broad man with good teeth and wavy golden hair. He smiled—handsome and healthy and unconcerned, and of slightly less than average intelligence, and wanted for murder—and strolled up to the reporters.

"What's all the fuss about?" he asked.

"Don't ya read the papers?" one of the reporters said.

"Hell no," Reggie said.

"The Republican Party brought in a pack of criminals from down south for the election."

"Those fuckers," Reggie said.

"No one's allowed in or out," the reporter said. "They say the place is under renovations. The police are going to kick in the door any minute now."

"Well," Reggie said, "we'll just see about that."

He hammered on the front door with both of his muscular arms.

"Hey!" he cried. "Hey! Open up in there!"

There was no answer, and so he drummed harder.

"Let me in, you fucking mercenary sons of bitches!"

When his arms got tired he stopped. Some tittering came from the reporters. But then a bolt shifted on the other side of the door and it cracked open a bit and Reginald slipped inside.

"Why, Dusty Kingsley," he said. "As I live and fucking breathe."

Dusty held a finger to his mouth and bolted the door as the reporters rushed forward, shouting in surprise and amusement. Dusty beckoned and Reggie followed him through the darkened lobby into the dining room.

Most of the crew were lounging around drinking and playing cards. The waitstaff had vanished.

"It is you!" Quentin cried.

Reggie smiled, innocent, open. They crowded around him. Quentin, in the center, banging his spoon against his goblet. Dusty Kingsley with his ironic smile. Charlie Empire, swaying on his feet, holding a bottle of bourbon by its neck, Johnny grinning madly. The only ones who were not smiling were Fred Johnson and Jan Müller. Johnson was leaning up against the bar, drinking soda water and shaking his head in disgust. Jan sat stiffly at a table. He nodded once at Reggie but said nothing.

"Do you have a drink?" Quentin called. "Someone get him a drink. All right. Gentlemen, gentlemen. A toast! I give you Reggie 'Babe' Keller. To the Baby!"

"To the Baby!" everyone called, and they drained their glasses.

When they were done Charlie pivoted and whipped his bottle up at the chandelier, missing it by a good three feet but causing general hilarity. Dusty smashed his glass on the ground and the other men followed suit. Then Charlie ran across the room and flipped over a table, knocking chairs left and right and sending a crash of silverware onto the floor.

Everyone laughed, but when Charlie turned back toward them, his face was twisted with a rage so black it was almost insane.

"You laughing at me?" he shouted, pulling a knife from his belt. He loped toward them but fell down a couple of times on the way and was easily restrained by Johnny.

Reggie chuckled, then said, "So'd you hear the news?"

"About the mercenaries in the Michigan Hotel?" Dusty said. "Yeah, we heard it."

"Naw," Reginald said. "Winter's joined the Klan!"

"Reggie, come now," Quentin said. "You can't believe everything you read in the papers."

"Papers, hell!" Reggie said. "I went to the City of Kansas looking for you all and I showed up at Molly Shakespeare's place right after Winter and Lukas had left. The whole town was talking about it. He'd been buying bathtub gin with twenty-dollar gold coins. He hit that train with the Klan, no doubt."

At the bar, Johnson's eyes went wide. Everyone else fell silent. Reggie's smile faded slowly.

"No, I cannot believe it," Jan said from his table, the first words he'd said. "I do not put anything past young Winter, but I cannot see how they would have him."

"How they'd have him?" Reggie said. "Shit, Sarge. The Klan ain't what it used to be. They're mostly bandits and moonshiners now. They wear the white robes so no one'll prosecute. Winter was with 'em when they hit the post office, banks, trains. That kind of job. He ain't torching schools or shooting senators or nothing. It's just funny, is all."

"It's not fucking funny," Johnson said. His voice was a low rumble.

"Now, Fred," Reggie said. "You know what I mean."

"I know what you mean," Johnson said. "You better know what I mean. Riding with the Klan? The Klan?" Johnson's voice rose dangerously.

"It was just for the money!" Reggie said. "They weren't picking on colored folks."

"In any case, he's not our problem any longer," Quentin said. "Let's all have another drink."

Johnson looked as if he would say more. But then shook his head, glowered at everyone, and turned to the mirror.

At that moment, Noah entered the room.

"Noah!" Quentin cried. "Everyone, it's my brother! Someone get him a drink."

"Well," Reginald said. "I'll be double damned if he ain't your spitting image, Quentin."

"Fuck him," Charlie said, but Johnny clapped a hand over his mouth.

Noah walked over to the men slowly, looking around at the shattered glass and overturned tables. By the time he reached them they had fallen quiet.

"Gentlemen," Noah said. "The police will be here at any minute. You have to get out, and you obviously can't go through the front door. Fortunately, there's a passage under the street that leads to a restaurant I own. Please gather up your things."

"Of course, Brother," Quentin said. "Johnson, go upstairs and get Bread."

Charlie's eyes glittered at Noah from over Johnny's thick fingers.

46

Unlike the hotel, the restaurant was actually being renovated. The walls were unpainted and unpapered, the floor was rough and uneven, and there was no furniture save for a few tables and chairs.

When the men woke the next day they were stiff from sleeping on the floor. There was no food in the pantry and the men did not have much to entertain them other than a deck of cards. They spent the morning sitting around at the tables and staring at the boarded-up windows and making desultory attempts at conversation.

Charlie was badly hungover and his mood was as black as tar. He was the one to finally say it. "Fuck this. I'm going out for some real food."

Jan was sitting at a table by the door. He'd known this moment would come.

"No, Charlie," he said. "You have to stay in."

"Who's going to make me?" Charlie snapped. His eyes were red rimmed and his thin hair was standing up. "You?"

"Yes, Charlie," Jan said. "Me. I will make you stay."

Charlie tramped toward the door, with Johnny hard on his heels. Jan stood up to block their way.

Quentin was sulking in the corner. Every now and then he would press his eyes up against the cracks between the boards on the windows where the thin lines of light were sliding in.

"Charlie, Johnny," Quentin said. "Do what Sergeant Müller says."

Charlie stopped, then Johnny bumped into him from behind. Charlie shoved his brother back and glared at Quentin.

"The fuck are you talking about?" Charlie said.

"You have gone outside enough," Jan said. "I will not let you ruin my pardon like you have ruined everything else."

"Shut the fuck up, kraut," Charlie said, without taking his eyes off Quentin. "Quentin, this is ridiculous. I'm not going to do nothing, but I want my fucking breakfast. Your brother wanted us to stay here, he should have given us our fucking breakfast. It's not our fault his business is in the newspapers."

Quentin's face was lined with shadow from the boarded-up windows. He looked thoroughly demoralized. "Charlie, I understand your frustration," he said. "The election is very soon. We are almost there."

"Quentin," Charlie said. "You can't tell me you're going to let that little popinjay coop us up in here. I don't care if he is your brother. I know you. You won't let him do it."

Quentin made a frustrated motion with his hands and leaned farther back into the shadow.

"Hey, come on, Charlie," Dusty said. "Ease up."

"Don't you tell me what to do!" Charlie said. "Quentin, come on now!"

"Go sit down, Charlie," Jan said.

"Don't push me, kraut," Charlie said.

"Sit down now, you fat bully," Jan said. "It's your last chance."

Charlie's eyes widened and he seemed, with his anger, to grow calmer. He glanced from side to side. Charlie was not a smart man but he had a fair amount of low cunning. He knew that he and his brother were not well liked and without Quentin's support no one would stand up for him. In particular, he saw Fred Johnson looking at him, just looking, his intelligent and expressive countenance as flat and hard as a penny.

And so he did not lunge. He said, "You don't tell me what to do, Müller. This ain't the army. You get that?"

"Fine," Jan said. "Anything you like."

But by lunchtime, still with no food, it became clear that something had to be done. The men decided that Jan would go out for provisions. He was back so quickly that the men feared he had not given himself enough time to shop properly, but to their relief he had come back with enough bacon, bread, and coffee for days. He even had a cheap cigar for Charlie, who accepted it with superficial good grace.

Dusty was in the kitchen frying the bacon while the other men drank coffee and ate bread, friends again, when there came a knock at the front door. The sound of it was sharp and distinct, like it was made with a small and heavy metal object.

The men fell quiet. The knock was repeated, deliberate but jaunty. Seven notes.

Shave and a haircut, two bits.

"It can't be," Jan whispered.

Shave and a haircut.

A clear voice cried out with childish fury, "Let us in, you pack of floppy goat cunnies!"

Charlie's eyes flew open wide. "Well kiss my grits!" he said.

"Lukie!" Johnny cried, barreling toward the front door.

The air seemed to grow colder, and sounds more distinct and clean. The fingers of light coming in from between the cracks were particularly bright and well defined against the darkness.

Stop him, Jan wanted to say, but his throat was frozen.

Johnny threw open the door, and Winter was standing there.

"Auggie!" Johnny howled, throwing his arms around Winter.

"Jesus," Dusty whispered. A cast-iron frying pan he was holding slipped from his fingers and clattered on the floor.

Charlie jogged toward Winter. Reggie glanced at Jan, looking

ashamed and a little confused, like a dog after its owner has pre-
tended to throw a stick and instead hidden it behind his back.

Lukas Shakespeare popped out from behind Winter, shrieking
greetings to everyone he recognized.

"What the fuck are they wearing?" Dusty asked.

Jan still could not speak, could not move. Laughter was building
inside him, trying to get out, but he was afraid that if he started he
wouldn't be able to stop.

Winter was wearing a crisply pressed cream-colored suit. His tie
and handkerchief were pink, his hair was heavily styled into curls,
and even across the room the smell of his aftershave was overpowering. He wore white gloves and shining white leather shoes, and he was
carrying a long cane with an ivory handle.

He has lost his mind, Jan told himself. He has gone insane.

But if he had gone mad he had not done so in pedestrian fashion.
It was a new kind of madness, a kind of alternate sanity, a different
way of reacting and fitting into the world.

Quentin rushed up and shut the door behind the new arrivals.

"Shit, Jan," Dusty said. "What the hell are we going to do?"

"Go back in the kitchen," Jan said.

Jan and Dusty moved into the kitchen and closed the door behind
them. A moment later it opened again and Johnson came in.

"How did he find us?" Jan asked.

"Don't sound like you were too inconspicuous out there," Johnson said. "Acting casual was never your strong suit."

"What's Quentin doing?" Jan asked. "His brother said . . ."

"He's talking to them. Telling him his brother don't want them
here. But he won't make Winter leave."

Jan put his hand on his mouth, then glanced from Dusty back
to Johnson.

"The Empire brothers?"

"They think he walks on water since he took the fall for them in
Mississippi. If they only knew."

"Knew what?" Jan asked.

Johnson just shook his head.

"I know you don't like me," Jan said. "And I know you and Winter went through a lot during the war. But he can't join us."

"Not after he rode with the goddamn Klan, he can't," Johnson said.

"We've got to watch that kid," Dusty said. "He's the fastest draw I've ever seen."

"I am more worried about Winter than a boy," Jan said. "Fred, we can't do it without you."

"I ain't afraid of him," Johnson said.

The door to the kitchen opened again and Jan's hand dropped down to his gun. But it was only Bill Bread.

"Are you with us, Bill?" Jan said.

"What are you going to do?"

"What do you think?" Jan said. "He is going to cost us our pardon."

After a pause, Bill said, "Jan. You know there is never going to be a pardon."

"What are you talking about?"

Bill shook his head. "Nothing."

Johnson looked at Bill very carefully, then said, "You know he's got to go. Riding with the Klan? After all we fought for?"

"What do you think we were fighting for down there, Fred?" Bill asked. His hair stuck up at a funny angle and he smelled, but his eyes were calm. "What do you think we're fighting for here? Really?"

"This isn't the time for your Indian shit," Dusty said.

"We have to move quickly," Jan said.

"I'll take care of Winter," Johnson said. "Jan, you make sure you've got the kid. Dusty, you cover the Empire brothers and the rest. All right?"

"Yes," Jan said. "Certainly."

"Motherfucker riding with the Klan," Johnson said, "and showing his face around here."

They walked back into the main room. Winter was sitting at the head of a large table near the front door. He was smoking a cigarette in an ivory holder and blowing inexpert smoke rings in the air, to the delight of the Empire brothers.

Winter's pale yellow eyes locked on Johnson the minute he stepped into view and tracked him all the way across the room. A dribble of smoke slipped through his lips. The boy Lukas tilted his head back and narrowed his eyes into slits and put his hands on his pistols.

As their group came closer, everyone fell silent.

"Good morning, Freddy," Winter said. "Now how do you do."

"What the fuck are you doing here, Winter?"

Winter paused, and then said, "Excuse me?"

"You heard me," Johnson said. "And you know what I'm talking about."

Johnson grabbed a chair and dragged it toward Winter's table. Jan slipped around behind Lukas and drew his revolver. Winter made a movement with his hand and there was a loud bang. Jan cried out in pain and his weapon hit the floor.

Lukas drew both his pistols and brandished them at Johnson. "Jesus, what was that?"

In Winter's hand there was a two-shot derringer, a palm pistol smaller than a deck of cards, a girl's gun. Its handle was ivory and matched the rest of Winter's outfit. Jan raised his wounded hand to his mouth and sucked the blood.

Johnson didn't move. The derringer was pointed at him now.

"Why don't you sit down, Fred," Winter said, "and we'll talk this over. Do it real slow now."

Johnson stared at Winter with his big brown eyes, unafraid, unyielding. He carefully lowered his powerful body into the chair, settled back, and kept looking at Winter.

"You too, Bill," Winter said.

Bill had crept up with a sawed-off shotgun and had put himself in a position that gave him a clear shot at Winter and the backs of both Empire brothers.

"You first, Auggie," Bill said.

"No," Winter said. "You first, Billy."

Bill braced the weapon against his shoulder.

"Come on now, Billy boy," Winter said. "It'd have been easier for me to put that shot in Jan's belly than his pistol. Ain't no one else going to get shot here. And we both know you're going to back down before I do. Don't we?"

Another second, and Bill lowered the shotgun.

Winter made a quick motion and the derringer disappeared up one of his immaculate sleeves. "Now that's better, isn't it?" he said.

He did not smile. Instead he looked directly into Johnson's eyes and remained silent. Lukas still had his guns out. No one else had moved.

"Why don't you let me know what this is about?" Winter asked.

"You know."

"Go on. Say it."

"You joined the Klan. You went to the other side."

"The other side?" Winter said.

"Yeah," Johnson replied. "And you ain't welcome here no more. A derringer ain't going to stop me from throwing you out."

Winter lifted his cigarette holder to his mouth and inhaled and then leaned back in his chair. He looked at Johnson through a veil of smoke.

"Freddy, you've known me almost ten years now and you know I ain't in the habit of explaining the things I do. I generally let people take me as they like and if there's a problem I sort it out. But you saved my life in Georgia and a few times since then and so this one time, and only this time, I'll explain myself to you."

Johnson didn't move or respond.

"There's a lot of talk about what happened in the South, in Mississippi. The truth is, right now, in the South, the war's still going on. Any civil war is a battle of wills. We won the war because we had the will to do some terrible things, and they didn't have the will to stand them. They gave up the war because of what we done to them in the Shenandoah, in Georgia and the Carolinas."

Winter stopped, and his face crinkled in deep thought, as if he was trying to put some kind of feeling into words. The cigarette smoldered in its holder. His expression cleared and he resumed speaking.

"Well, all right. We saved the Union. But now we're fighting another war, to see what kind of peace we're going to get. There's a war going on right now, about what's going to happen to the freedmen down south. And there's a lot of talk going on about it up here. But the will is gone, Freddy. There ain't no will to win the peace like there was to win the war. That's why they turned on us after Mississippi."

Winter sucked on his cigarette and exhaled two streams of smoke through his nostrils.

"They were women and children. But they knew where Captain Jackson and his Klansmen were riding and they wouldn't have told us if I'd kept the gloves on. Hell, most of them chose to die rather than talk."

"Did you ever think that the ones who didn't talk might not have even known?" Jan barked.

"Well, how many colored lives did we end up saving?" Winter asked. "Two dozen that night alone? But what did that matter to them? After all their talk? You mark my words, Freddy. They'll turn their backs on your kind. They'll give you up. They'll leave you to your fate. Just like some men here wanted to hang you for killing your master."

Johnson's eyes flicked away.

Winter glanced over at Jan, his expression cold, and then turned back to Johnson.

"Did I ride with the Klan? Sure I did. Our little company had disbanded. Some hard words were said. So I met up with these boys who were hitting a train. You ride with the Klan and you rob the federal government, the people won't talk about it. We all learned that the hard way, didn't we? What's more, the courts won't prosecute. I took away a thousand dollars for two days' work. I'd do it again in a fucking heartbeat. And you're giving me shit for it? After all we been through?"

Johnson looked back at Winter, but the force of his will was gone.

"Here's the thing, Freddy. Not everyone in this room is smart, or handsome. Ain't nobody in here a good person. But everyone here has fought together. Everyone here has put his life on the line for everyone else. Everyone here was out in the woods together, out in enemy country, with bushwhackers looking to take our scalps and Klansmen looking to burn us alive. Everyone here put everything he had in the pot. Everybody. Now that's not talk, Freddy. That wasn't just words, wasn't just noise and air. That was real."

Winter shifted his gaze over to Bill.

"Real," Winter repeated. "There's your explanation, Fred. Now I don't ever want to have this talk with you again. Dusty, pour Freddy a drink."

Dusty poured a shot of whiskey in a teacup and passed it to Johnson. Winter already had a glass and he lifted it.

"Pick it up," he ordered Johnson.

Johnson didn't move.

Winter's face seemed to lengthen. He shifted forward in his chair and stared down at the cup and then looked back up at Johnson again.

Slowly, Johnson moved his hand down and took up the whiskey.

Winter smiled a little. His eyes flicked to Jan.

"Get the sergeant a drink too," Winter said.

"I won't drink with you," Jan said.

"Oh, sure you will, Sergeant Müller," Winter said. "You'll go along with everyone else, like you always do. Better to have me in the tent pissing out than outside the tent pissing in. Ain't it?"

Someone pressed a glass into Jan's hand.

"I'm tired of all the talk," Winter said. "I'm going to get down to brass tacks. Any man who sticks with me will never need to watch his back."

"To brass tacks, then!" Quentin said. He looked at Jan and smiled apologetically, but his eyes were dancing.

"Brass tacks," Charlie said, with satisfaction.

They all drank. All of them.

47

The pain was like a needle behind the bridge of his nose. Noah kept seeing little winkles of light in the corners of his eyes, sparkling like gemstones. One of the terrible headaches he remembered from his childhood was coming on. He hadn't had one in years. Not since before he had gone to Harvard with Quentin. It was the loss of control that was doing it. He had not felt this powerless even as a child.

And so, in the tunnel between his hotel and his restaurant, he stopped walking, placed the lantern on the ground, and put his hands to his forehead, pressing his temples.

"Just stop," he whispered. "Just stop."

Eventually he gathered himself and quickly jogged up the creaking wooden stairs and emerged in the kitchen.

Inside the dining room the men were scattered around at various tables.

"Brother," Quentin said. "You don't look well."

Indeed he did not. Noah was pale green, almost waxen. His suit seemed particularly ill fitting and his hair was standing up in clumps.

"They're trying to have me arrested for hiring you," Noah said.

"What's their evidence?" Quentin cried.

"What do you think, Quentin?" Noah said. "Archibald Patterson's affidavit."

That silenced them, to Noah's satisfaction. All of them, except for one.

"Who is this Patterson?" someone wearing an expensive white suit said.

Noah barely glanced at the speaker.

"He was the waiter my brother was bribing to take you out on your visits to the brothel."

"Is that right?" the man in the suit said. "Well, where's he at? I'll take care of him tonight."

Noah looked at the newcomer. Had he been a more sensitive man, he would have noticed the tension in the room. "Are you mad?" he said. "He's already sworn the affidavit. You can't kill him now."

The man in the suit was putting a cigarette into an ivory holder. He was quite a dandy, Noah noticed, with a boutonniere in his lapel.

"Well, you can't say that we can't kill him," the man said. "Because we could. We could do it tonight. If you don't want to, that's all right. It's your dime. You can swear all the affidavits you like. Up to you."

The man lit a match and held it to the cigarette.

"It would destroy us in the election if we were to do such a thing," Noah said.

"The election?" the man said.

There was something about him, Noah thought. What was it about him?

The man exhaled a cloud of smoke and looked Noah straight in the eye.

"The election can go whichever way you like," the man said. "Ain't no reason to leave nothing to chance."

Cat's eyes. The man had the eyes of a cat.

Oh god, Noah thought distantly.

"You're acting like there's some kind of rules after you broke the rules," Winter said. "Well, there ain't. They broke the rules and now you're breaking 'em too. You best stop holding on to them rules. You've gotta let them go now. The one who leaves 'em farther behind will take the prize."

No, Noah thought. No, Quentin, no, this can't be happening.

Here was the terrible thing: the shuttered light of madness was in Winter's eyes, and the deep hollow sound of a bottomless well was in his voice. But in that moment, Noah could not find the fault in Winter's reasoning.

Noah had confronted so many: millionaires, shopkeepers, farmers, commodity traders, unions. To all of them he had been an enfant terrible, a heretic, an antinomianist, a revolutionary. And Noah had seen himself the same way. He had always believed himself concerned with the immutable laws of economics instead of the arbitrary and changeable customs of men.

And now he was perfectly conscious that Winter's words were inspiring in him the feelings that he, Noah, had always inspired in others: That what he had believed to be the iron laws of the universe were merely his own prejudices, a tottering shanty built of questions, a stack of assumptions all the way down. That the marketplace was a deep, dark pool of chaos, and that this man was its true apostle.

But then he shook himself, blinked, and remembered that Winter was just a murderous lunatic, brought here by his brother.

"Quentin," Noah said, his voice low and husky, and he turned back into the kitchen.

Quentin stood up slowly, everyone's eyes on him, and followed his brother. If Noah could see his expression he would not have been reassured. It was the way Quentin had looked as a child after he had been caught in some causeless sadistic mischief: irritated at the interruption, unafraid of consequences, and faintly amused by the squeamishness of the rest of the human race.

48

They were under the earth in the tunnel leading to the hotel. Noah was carrying an oil lantern in one hand, and as he gestured the light splashed and folded around them, making the shadows slide back and forth along the walls.

Noah hissed, "What is he doing here? Was I not clear? Was I not crystal clear at every juncture? Every time we spoke?"

"Brother," Quentin began.

"Are you mad? Are you mad? Quentin! For the love of God! You are a grown man now! A grown man!"

"Brother," Quentin said, "please."

"Why is he here? How could he be here?"

"Molly Shakespeare told him we were in Chicago," Quentin said.

"How did he find you, though?" Noah said.

"Jan went out to get us food!" Quentin said. "Winter must have seen him."

Noah's face was screwed up with rage. Quentin waited for it to relax, but it didn't. Instead Noah put the lantern down and sat on his heels and began to massage his temples.

"Is it one of your headaches?" Quentin asked sympathetically.

"You are mad," Noah said.

"I am not mad," Quentin replied, and now his voice grew a little angry. "Stop calling me that. Why do you insist on calling me mad? I am not mad."

"Oh no?" Noah said. "Then why are you here? Hmm? Why are you here? Why are you here, in a tunnel, underground, wanted for murder, despised by your former employers and benefactors, with only me standing between you and the gallows? And why am I shouting at you? Because you have disappointed me, just as you have disappointed everyone who has ever tried to assist you!"

Quentin's expression was blank, as if he were hearing someone speak in a language he could not understand. But eventually a smile crept across his face.

"The real question, dear brother," Quentin said, "is if you are so wise, and so rational, then what are you doing down here? With me?"

Now Noah's face went blank.

"You know, Noah, we haven't had much time to talk," Quentin said. "How was it, exactly, that you made such an enormous fortune? Trading in wheat? Legal work?"

"Investing," Noah said.

"Investing in what, might I ask?"

Noah rubbed his eyes, and said, "Are you asking me when you already know?"

"Just tell me how you made . . ."

"I shorted all the major insurance companies in the city before the Fire."

"Shorted them?"

"You know what that means."

Quentin shrugged. "I know it means you make money if the price declines. Why did you short insurance companies, Noah?"

"Negligent city construction. Corrupt building-code inspection. Insufficient resources in the fire department. There were a number of smaller fires. It was clear there would be a big one."

"When did you assume this short position?"

"In the spring of 1870."

"So you maintained that short position for a year and a half?"

"Yes."

"During which the price of the securities you had sold short rose?"

"Yes."

Quentin's big round eyes locked with Noah's.

"Were you afraid?"

"Yes."

"Was it expensive?"

"Yes. I had to borrow more and more money to cover my position. I mortgaged everything I had, everything I'd inherited, and more."

"Did you ever doubt yourself?"

"No, never. I knew I just had to last long enough and the fire would come."

"And in the summer of 1871, when there were droughts and dry winds, and the wells ran dry and the cheap pine houses turned to tinder, could you feel it? Could you feel the fire in the air?"

"I'm not sure what you mean."

"What did you do then, Noah? What did you do?"

Noah was trying to look away from his brother but he could not.

"I shorted everything," he said.

"How long could you have lasted?"

"I would have been bankrupt by Christmas. I would have lost everything."

Quentin nodded.

"Well then, Brother. My last question is this. When the fire started. When the wind picked up so huge balls of flame hurled across the sky like thunderbolts cast by an angry god. When the sparks and cinders fell like snow. When the fire raced through the slums like a hungry animal so fast men could scarcely outrun it. When even the river began to burn. When all of the complicated machinery of capitalism, the shopping district, the reaper works, the grain elevators, the lumberyard, when all of them yielded to the beast. When you witnessed all of this devastation. And when you knew that it had made you the richest man in Chicago. What did you feel?"

Noah finally turned away.

"What did you feel when you saw the city, this shrine to the power of free enterprise, burn?"

"I felt vindicated."

"You were happy."

"I wasn't happy. No."

"You were happy," Quentin said. "You've embraced chaos. But it is a peculiar kind of chaos that depends upon a number of assumptions, including that men, and the world, are rational. Those assumptions are flawed. Don't you see how little difference there is between you and me? You only need to take one more step."

"Quentin," Noah said. "What does this have to do with Augustus Winter being in my restaurant?"

"Don't you know what the poet said?" Quentin cried. "William Blake? Reason is only the outward bound of what we know, and it shall not be the same when we know more. Noah! You think the universe is just a dull mill with complicated wheels. But it is infinite, and the infinite is in all things. I have seen things beyond what you could ever know, Brother."

"You are a criminal, Quentin," Noah said. "The men you consort with are sadistic lunatics. The only reason you are a free man is because of me."

"But . . . ," Quentin began.

"No, Quentin," Noah said. "That's enough. Here is the simple truth. You have already, through your actions, greatly harmed our hopes for this election. Now I find that Augustus Winter is with you. The chance of you and your men receiving pardons for what you have done is almost gone. Tell the other men that and they will send Winter on his way. And from this day forth, you must comport yourself in such a way as to be impervious to reproach. Your work in the election will be extremely delicate. Do you understand?"

"Yes, Brother," Quentin said. He was beginning to look rather bored. "I understand."

"Tell your men they have to act with scrupulous care," Noah said. "Tell them to imagine that they are continuously being watched. If they do not, I can do nothing for them. Do you understand?"

"Yes, yes," Quentin said impatiently. "Do you think I am stupid, Brother? I know! I know!"

Noah shook his head.

"You must arrive at city hall a few hours before dawn tomorrow. You'll receive your instructions there. It will be a rough day, Quentin. Please, just this once. Do as I say. When you're a free man I'll never trouble you again."

"Of course, Brother," Quentin said, but he seemed not to be paying attention. "Of course."

49

When Quentin reentered the restaurant, Jan was the first to speak. The anxiety in his voice was painful to hear.

"What happened?" Jan said. "What did he say?"

"Well," Quentin said, "he was surprised to see Mister Winter of course. Augustus, I'm sorry to say, there will be no pardon for you."

Everyone looked at Winter, but he only shrugged.

"I told him that I didn't bring Winter here and he seemed to believe me," Quentin said. "Otherwise, he came to reassure us that everything is going well. The deal still stands firm. At the election tomorrow we must do everything in our power to ensure victory."

"We've had promises before," Charlie said. "How do we know he'll come through?"

"This is my brother, remember," Quentin said.

"I don't care who he is," Charlie said. "If he's fucking lying to us like all the rest, he's going to pay."

"Now now, Charlie," Quentin said. "No need for talk like that."

"Did he say anything about what we're supposed to do?" Dusty asked.

"Well, we're to meet at city hall tomorrow morning," Quentin said. "We're to stop repeat voters, protect Republicans, make sure that the populace can vote freely at the polls. We're also to keep an eye out for fraud and protect election officials."

And now Quentin hesitated, for the briefest moment. Most of the men assembled did not notice it. Jan certainly would not have if he had not, at some level, known that it would be there.

"He also made it perfectly clear," Quentin said, "that we are to do whatever it takes to ensure this election is free and fair. 'Whatever it takes, Quentin.' Those were his words to me. We must be willing to go as far, if not farther, than the other side, if we are to prevail."

"Hell," Charlie said, "that ain't a problem. He's just got to come through for us at the end."

"Oh," Quentin said. "He will. Don't worry. He will."

Suddenly Jan could not bear to look at them. All these fugitives, with nowhere to run, with Quentin Ross their only hope of redemption, and with something wrong, deeply wrong, hanging in the air.

Bill's eyes: so tired. *You know there is never going to be a pardon,* Bill had said.

"Sit back down, Charlie," Johnny said. "I'm dealing you in."

"Hey," Lukas shrilled. "Where's my hand?"

Charlie straddled his chair and drank bourbon from the bottle. He said something and Johnny laughed and Lukas shrieked in protest. Dusty returned to the kitchen. Quentin was smiling benevolently, although no one was paying attention to him any longer.

Jan found himself turning to Winter, almost against his will.

Their eyes met. Jan stood up and walked over. The others stopped and looked at them. But Jan simply sat down across from Winter without saying anything, and everyone returned to what they were doing.

"What good's it do to worry, Sergeant?" Winter said. "Either do something or quit worrying."

"If I don't get my pardon," Jan said, "I will have nothing to live for."

"If you say so," Winter said. "What you live for is up to you."

"I'm not threatening you, but . . ."

"Sure you are," Winter said. "But you heard the lieutenant. Gloves are off tomorrow. If you disagree, you'd better talk to him. He's running the show."

Jan looked at Quentin, who was hovering over the card game, smiling, not saying anything. Could he contact Noah directly? But they were only here because Quentin was Noah's brother. If Noah lost confidence in Quentin, he would cut ties. Without Quentin, there would be no pardon.

"You think there's such a big difference between you and me," Winter said. "But there's no difference that matters. No difference at all."

50

As always, Burns was up early on Election Day. He rose before the sun and kissed his sleeping wife, descended the stairs, and went out into the empty streets. But not quite empty. Already gangs of men were hurrying back and forth, carrying boxes and bundles of papers, riding horses. You could feel the battle coming in the air.

In his youth he had been one of those young men, rushing from one crisis to the next, wielding an iron pipe or short jagged knife. Now that he was the boss he had to stay in one place so men could come to him for directions. But in the early morning, that blackest time that still did not feel like night, he was free to prowl around a little.

His first stop was the church, a tall stone building composed of hard dark angles. The side door was locked but Burns had a key. Inside he dipped his fingers in the font and made the sign of the cross before making his way to a pew. There he knelt facing the altar and pressed his face into the polished wood and whispered a few words, for support, for guidance.

"You're here early, my son," the priest said.

Burns's head jerked up. He had been so focused he had not heard the priest approach.

"Sorry, Father," Burns said.

"Come to ask for the Lord's assistance today?" the priest said. "I wouldn't have thought that would be necessary. The Lord helps those who help themselves, after all."

"We've done everything we could."

"First Democratic mayor in twenty years," the priest said, sounding pleased. "It'll be grand to think next year we'll have parish schools for the children. When I think of the poor boys and girls led astray by the Protestants I can hardly sleep at night."

"We'll see, Father," Burns said, standing.

"If you've done right we'll win," the priest said. "Have faith, my son."

Burns looked up at the altar and the dark stained glass windows high above.

"Well," he said. "We've come a long way, anyway. Do you remember Long John Wentworth?"

The priest smiled. "I do indeed."

Burns shook his head. "Now, I was just a young man in those days. Living in a room in Bridgeport with eight other boys, working for whiskey and a dollar a day. I remember I was assigned the responsibility of escorting some good Democratic voters in 1857. We had some problems with a police officer, and tempers becoming heated, he drew his revolver and I drew mine. We shouted at each other for a while and eventually he backed down. But I wonder sometimes, Father. What if he'd refused? I wasn't about to be pushed around. What if neither one of us had backed down? Why, someone would have been shot, wouldn't he?"

"Men must be allowed to vote," the priest said.

"Ah, but how many times, Father?" Burns said. "That's the point of contention."

"Well, don't you worry," the priest said. "The police are on our side this time."

"And King Conor has paid for fifteen hundred deputies," Burns said.

"Bless his heart," the priest said.

"If he has one," Burns replied. "But that Noah Ross. He wouldn't have put his pistol away. Not if he thought he was in the right. And these men he's brought to the city . . ."

"Never mind them," the priest said. "You're worrying too much, my boy. Come and have a drink with me."

"I was wondering whether I hadn't better give my confession."

The priest laughed and the lines assumed a mischievous pattern. "My boy, in the interests of your immortal soul, don't you think you should save it until after the election? This is Chicago, after all."

51

It was still before dawn. Jan, Dusty, and Bill galloped through the narrow, dirty streets of Chicago's Polish district, standing high in their stirrups and looking for the police.

A shrill woman's voice was screaming: *"Spierdalaj ty glupia pizda!"*

Bill, always a crafty horseman, cut abruptly to the right, across traffic. His horse leapt over a wall of trash cans into a narrow alley between two tenement buildings. The others followed, much more slowly. When they caught up, they found Bill speaking to a middle-aged woman on her front step. Down the street, a covered police carriage was lumbering away.

"Another Republican arrested for disturbing the peace," Bill said, a faint smile on his face. "Before dawn. In bed."

"I told him!" the woman screeched in her thick accent. "This is what comes of angering the Irish! They break my plates, they get mud on my floors! You tell Stanislaw if he wants to stay in politics, he don't come back!"

"Let's go!" Jan said.

All three of them spurred their horses and quickly caught up with the carriage. Four deputies sat on the roof, passing a bottle of whiskey around and singing. They made such a racket they didn't hear the hoofbeats until Dusty was pointing a rifle at them.

"Gentlemen," Dusty said. "I'll thank you to keep your hands where I can see 'em."

The driver, drunk, frightened, whipped his horse harder.

"Why you little fucker!" Dusty cried.

Bill pulled up next to the carriage and stood up in his stirrups and then put one foot on the saddle and jumped up next to the driver, who cried out, drew a knife from under his seat, and stabbed Bill in the arm. Dusty fired his rifle and the front part of the driver's head came off.

"Jesus!" one of the deputies screamed.

"Dusty!" Jan cried from his horse.

"What?" Dusty replied.

Bill jerked hard on the reins and the horse, whinnying in protest, came to a sudden stop. The deputies went flying.

"Murderers!" one of the deputies cried as he staggered to his feet. "Murderers! You've kilt a deputy!"

Dusty dismounted and drew his pistol on the man who had spoken. The man put his hands in the air.

"Kingsley!" Jan shouted. "Stop! Stop! Everyone stop!"

Bill Bread took the corpse from the top of the carriage and wrapped it in a blanket. The bottle of whiskey the deputies had been drinking disappeared into his coat.

The men on both sides were quiet, like children who had played progressively more roughly until someone had been hurt.

"He stabbed Bill, Sarge," Dusty said.

Jan didn't reply.

"Murderers," one of the deputies spat out.

Jan looked at him with a clear, cold hatred.

"One of you open the carriage," he said.

The door opened, revealing four prisoners, all of whom were cowering against the far side.

"Come out," Jan said. "You are free now. Come on."

They hesitated, but all eventually came out. Last was Stanislaw, a Republican election official, who limped into the street and stood in front of Jan.

"I didn't think it was true," Stanislaw said, blinking in the early dawn.

"I said you can go," Jan said, giving him a bit of a shove.

When Stanislaw took one backward glance over his shoulder he saw them forcing the deputies into the carriage and locking it shut.

"Are you Stanislaw?" Bill said, as he took a pull of whiskey. "Your wife thinks you should stay out of politics."

Stanislaw had large, expressive eyes. Right now they were sad.

"Maybe you should," Bill said. "Things'll change. But not really how you want 'em to."

52

Inside Reiman's saloon the polling station was next to the bar, guarded by two German vote watchers. Rows of pewter steins sat on a table, and every man who voted Democrat was handed one as soon as he made his mark, and was given a hearty cheer by the assembled voters, who were well in the bag.

The floor planks were littered with splintered peanut shells. Blond, pigtailed waitresses wandered between the men with plates piled high with sausages. The voters had to shout to be heard over the tumult of voices.

And then the door smashed open and two men came inside. One of them was a tall, muscular Negro, the other young and blond. They made straight for the polling station and before the surprised inspectors could move they had thrown the first punches. Fred Johnson knocked one inspector's head against the wall where it made a horrible sound and left a small red splatter. Reggie was less dramatic but equally effective: the first blow to the chin staggered his man and then he finished him with a knee.

The electorate, their reflexes slowed by drink, were only starting to shout and move to interfere when a small man with an unsettling smile stepped inside, brandishing a rifle.

"Please," Quentin said. "Everyone remain calm."

And then he walked over to the bar, laid his palms flat down on its surface, tilted his head, and grinned.

The door opened one final time and a nervous man entered, holding his hat and looking like he was trying to hide in plain sight.

"Madam," Quentin said to the barmaid. "Would you be so kind as to give me your hand?"

She tucked both her hands up next to her breasts. Quentin snatched one of them. She let out a little scream. Some of the men started forward, but Johnson and Reggie drew their pistols.

Quentin pressed the woman's hand onto the bar and looked her straight in the eyes.

"Now my dear *Fräulein*," Quentin said. "Our friend Max, by the door there, told us that he came in here a half hour ago and his vote was discarded. Apparently, he was also not provided with any refreshments."

The barmaid's eyes widened.

"Why would he come here to vote?" she said. "There are other places to go."

Quentin reached with his free hand behind his back and drew out an enormous knife. The barmaid looked away and made a choking noise. The rest of the room was silent.

"My dear *Fräulein*," Quentin said.

He pressed the knife down onto her fingers like they were carrots he was going to chop.

"No, no," she said.

"Shh, shh," Quentin said. "Just listen. Max is going to stay here and supervise this polling station. To ensure that everyone can vote, and there will be no bribery."

"Ahh!" she cried out as the knife pressed down into her fingers. Blood seeped into the wood. "No! Don't!"

Quentin leaned next to her ear. His voice was no more than a ticklish whisper.

"And I'm going to entrust you with Max's safety. If he should be injured in some accident, if he should fall down and hit his head, or if he should eat some bad food, then we'll have to have a little chat."

"Ahh!" she cried as more blood trickled down.

"Am I making myself perfectly clear?" Quentin asked.

"*Ya! Ya!*"

"*Wunderbar,*" Quentin said, letting her go. She shrank back, clutching her wounded hand, while Quentin smiled and licked his knife. He sauntered out of the bar, followed by his men. Max stood alone and frightened in the room, now silent, the party over.

53

In front of another saloon, Lukas Shakespeare sat on a wooden porch and picked his teeth with a splinter, staring at the little soft beige bits that he managed to dig out from his gums and then wiping them on the bottom of his shoes. From behind he heard the sounds of glass shattering, furniture being overturned, and screaming.

A workingman in dirty overalls came up to the front door carrying a heavy lunch bucket that bounced against his knees. Presumably he wanted to vote.

Lukas drew a pistol in the blink of an eye.

"You just keep on walking, you dirty old fish-fucker," he said. "Go on now. Get."

The man backed away with his free hand in the air.

Lukas narrowed his eyes until they were like windows in a castle through which a defender might safely fire an arrow. Only when the man turned his back to run did Lukas holster his pistol.

A few minutes later a flatbed wagon rounded the corner at a good clip. Eight or nine Irish thugs were on board, dressed in heavy leather aprons and wielding axes and clubs.

"Auggie!" Lukas screamed. "Charlie!"

He sprang to his feet and drew both his pistols and put his thumbs down on the hammers. Just as the wagon began to slow to a stop he fired two shots, one from each gun, into the mass of men standing on the flatbed. There were some screams and one man fell off. The driver snapped the reins sharply and the flatbed took off down the street. The man who had fallen leapt to his feet and ran after them.

"Run, you papist coward!" Lukas hollered, and fired his pistols at the man's feet.

The door behind him opened.

"I scared 'em off!" Lukas turned around, then stopped smiling abruptly.

Winter stood in the doorway. He had taken off his jacket and his tie, and his shirt was undone at the collar. He was splattered with blood and his hair was mussed and his eyes were shimmering with the energy of a wild animal chewing off its own leg to get out of a trap.

Lukas gazed past Winter and saw a man crawling on his hands and knees. Somewhere, out of sight, Johnny was braying laughter.

"Don't you call me out here again," Winter said, "unless you mean it."

Lukas tried to speak but he couldn't. His throat worked uselessly as if he were trying to suck something through a very long straw.

The door shut.

54

"There's always a few who don't make it through Election Day in Chicago," Burns said. "Always a few who get shot or stabbed or just hit a little too hard. Always been that way. Always will. But this is different."

Mickey Burns and Honest Jim Plunkett were in Burns's humble office with the door closed. Burns had sent everyone out. Papers were scattered everywhere. Half-empty cups of coffee sat forgotten around the room. More than one whiskey bottle jutted out of the wastepaper basket. The window was open to the street and the sun was streaming in, along with the voices of the crowd waiting outside, all of them having come from every part of the city to say the same thing.

That there were men fighting for the Republicans, men who were unafraid to kill police officers or sheriff's deputies, men who were remorseless and fearless and dispassionately competent, and that the worst of them all was a tall man, dressed like a dandy, with golden eyes and hair so blond it was almost white.

"It's dangerous out there," Burns said.

"Politics ain't beanbag," Honest Jim said.

"Perhaps we ought not to send the repeaters out," Burns said.

"Not send the repeaters out?" Honest Jim shouted.

"Keep your voice down," Burns said.

"Have you lost your mind, Mickey?"

"I don't want any more of our boys hurt," Burns said. "Christ knows there's been enough already."

"You're going to let Noah Ross push us around?"

"Jim, we've got them licked anyhow. We must have them beat two to one in this thing, fair and square."

"Who's to say?" Honest Jim said. "Who's to say the count'll go our way if we get muscled out?"

"I didn't say we should leave the count to them, did I?" Burns said. "I'm talking about the repeaters."

"I thought you were a fighter," Honest Jim cried. "And yet you're standing here telling me you're going to let them take away our rights."

"Jim, for the love of all that's holy. We don't have the right to repeaters. They're repeaters. Remember?"

"Don't give me lawyer talk," Honest Jim said. "It's war out there, and I ain't going to leave it to chance. Now you stick with me here, Burns. I need you out there talking to your ward. I ain't a man to threaten a friend and you're an important man to the party. But I'm the chief and I'm telling you now how things are going to be. You've got to get out there and do your job when your party needs you. And the party needs those repeaters out there."

Burns rubbed the lower half of his face, raised his eyebrows, and shrugged.

They walked outside to the cheers of the crowd. A few men came forward urgently as if they had something to say.

"We already heard it," Honest Jim said. "We already heard it all. They're treating us no better than the secessionists. That's what happens when you stand up to Republicans. But don't fret, boys! Mickey and I are here for you. We ain't scared! We don't care a whit for those murderers! You watch us and see if we don't vote three times today!"

The crowd cheered again. They were drunk and shoddily dressed. A few police officers in their blue uniforms lurked toward the back.

"You boys all voted at this poll?" Burns said, waving at the voting poll in the alley between his office and the saloon.

"Yes sir," one drunk said. "They won't let us vote no more here."

"All right," Burns said. "You come on up with us to vote again. Don't you have no fear. Me and Honest Jim'll take care of you. Anyone interfering with you patriots'll have the police to answer to."

"Hip hip, hooray!" the crowd shouted.

They set off, a drunken procession with Honest Jim and Mickey Burns at its head and a layer of police officers guarding its flank, marching like an army off to war, or a herd of pigs trudging up the Bridge of Sighs.

The first stop was a voting station in a cheap hotel, and everything went well. The men cast ballots under the names of famous presidents: Thomas Jefferson, James Madison, and Abraham Lincoln. Everyone was drinking. While Honest Jim pumped the hand of the hotel keeper and made jokes and grinned, Mickey Burns had a low and urgent conversation with a group of ward heelers. These precinct captains had each been provided one thousand dollars in walking-around money by King Conor and had at least ten lieutenants each. All of them were telling the same story.

"I been robbed," a dark, intense-looking Italian said. "Mickey, you know I never steal from you! Never! I use the money like-a you told me! I had all-a my boys! But they all had guns! You said the police would protect me!"

"What the hell, Mickey," another said. "You hired all these new cops but they're just getting gunned down. What do you expect us to do?"

"I expect you to tough it out, boys, if you want us to remember you after Election Day," Burns said. "If it was easy work it wouldn't pay so well, now would it?"

"Mickey!" the Italian cried reproachfully.

Burns made a gesture with his head toward Honest Jim, who shouted, "All right, boys? Anyone want to vote again? No? Then on to the next one!"

The men streamed out of the hotel. Burns and Honest Jim stayed behind.

"Who were those grim buggers?" Honest Jim asked. "More ward heelers?"

"Yes," Burns said. "Ross's boys are robbing them. They're going to make a pretty penny out of this."

"They'll need it," Honest Jim said. "Whole city's going to turn against them. Word's spreading fast. Right now people are scared, but we've got 'em outnumbered ten to one. Just can't let 'em intimidate us, Mickey."

Burns didn't reply.

Outside the repeaters were milling around a flatbed wagon with a number of young toughs sitting on it.

"What's going on here?" Honest Jim cried.

"Those dirty bastards are holed up in the Riel Tavern," one of the toughs shouted. "They've taken over the polling station. They shot Jeffrey!"

"Did they now?" Honest Jim said. "Well, we'll see about that, won't we?"

"Jimmy," Burns said. "Hold on to that temper of yours. Let's think about the best way—"

Honest Jim's hand clamped down hard on Burns's shoulder, making Burns wince, and he grinned a terrible grin that had nothing to do with humor or happiness. It was more like a monkey showing its teeth to a rival in a dispute over a coconut.

"Maybe Conor was right about you," Honest Jim said. "But that's a question for another day. For now, if you show weakness before these men, just know I'll tear your fucking arms off."

Honest Jim wheeled to the crowd.

"Whose city is it?" he howled. "Eh? It's ours! We're taking it! We're taking Chicago!"

The men roared. There must have been close to sixty, including the police officers.

"Follow me!" Honest Jim cried.

55

Lukas saw the mob coming up the road toward the saloon. He hesitated, the image of Winter coated in blood still swimming in his mind, but eventually he turned and banged on the door.

"Charlie!" he cried. "Charlie, get out here! Charlie, there's a whole pack—"

The door flew open and Charlie emerged, angry, and then he looked in the direction Lukas was pointing and his face went slack. He said, "Johnny! Auggie! You better get out here."

Johnny came out first, Winter a few seconds after, with his jacket back on and his bow tie hanging around his neck. The crowd of men stopped just short of the wooden sidewalk in front of the saloon, up to their ankles in the mud of the street.

"Yer fucking dead!" someone in the back of the mob shouted.

Winter rested his hand on the pistol strapped to his thigh.

"Good afternoon, gentlemen," Winter said. "How can I help you?"

Honest Jim stepped forward.

"Who are you?" Honest Jim said.

"Augustus Winter," Winter replied.

"I'm surprised to see you admit it, sir," Honest Jim replied. "You're wanted for murder."

"In Mississippi, I am," Winter said. "This is Illinois."

"It certainly is," Honest Jim agreed. He looked Winter up and down and then said, "I never heard it said that you were a dandy."

"It's what you might call a relatively recent development," Winter replied.

"City living agrees with you, does it?" Honest Jim asked. The drunkards behind him were tittering.

"It ain't that," Winter said. "It's like the poet said. The time came, as it always does, when it was harder to stay in the bud than it was to blossom."

The repeat voters laughed scornfully. Honest Jim's worn and scarred face rearranged itself into a contemptuous expression. Lukas and the Empire brothers looked perplexed; Lukas even craned his head around to stare at Winter in bewilderment. Winter just tilted his head back. Although his face was serious there was the slightest gleam of amusement in his eyes.

Burns could feel his stomach sinking, as if he were in an elevator falling down the shaft.

"I have you at a disadvantage," Honest Jim said.

"I wouldn't say that, sir," Winter said.

"I mean you don't know my name."

"All due respect, I'm not sure what your name's got to do with anything."

"I'm Jim Plunkett," Honest Jim said. "Honest Jim they call me. Now I don't have no official position but I'm what you might call a leading citizen. These men with me have come to vote. Step aside."

"Well," Winter said. "Everyone's got the right to vote, don't they? And this is a polling station, ain't it? So that's all right, I suppose."

But he didn't move and his eyes roamed the crowd.

"Oh," Winter said. "Mister Plunkett. I do believe there's been a mistake. That man there, the tall thin one, with the gray hat. He voted already. Didn't he, Lukas?"

"Yep," Lukas said, his eyes shifting from side to side.

"You're mistaken," Honest Jim said.

"No," Winter said. "I ain't."

"Officers," Honest Jim said.

A sheriff's deputy stepped forward.

"Out of the way, Winter," the deputy said. "You're interfering with the election."

"Well," Winter said, "you all interfered with it first."

Many men in the mob were armed. At least a dozen pistols and rifles were pointed at Winter. Lukas and the Empire brothers were shifting on their feet and trying to look everywhere at once. But Winter never moved, never blinked, never acted for an instant like he was not in control of the situation.

"This is your last chance, you goddamn mercenary," the deputy said. "That's the law talking."

"The law," Winter said. "If I live to a hundred years old I'll never understand your type. In case you hadn't noticed, we ain't doing things by law today. That's how you wanted it and now you've got it."

"Get out of the way," Honest Jim said, "or you're dead."

"I'd rather die," Winter said.

He drew his pistol quickly. Someone in the crowd pulled the trigger of a rifle but missed. And then Winter, Charlie, Johnny, Lukas, all of them, began to fire.

The gunfight, such as it was, lasted less than thirty seconds. The two groups stood ten feet apart and blasted away. The mercenaries were outnumbered, but they were hardened killers who'd been under fire before. The repeaters had always stopped short of murder, unless their passions blinded them, and the men they'd battled had fought by the same code. Johnny was shot in the shoulder while Winter took one in the side of the neck. Blood spouted like a little fountain from the wound. But then the repeaters broke and scattered and fell back, shouting and screaming and leaving behind the wounded and the dead.

Winter clapped a hand to his neck and grimaced. He ducked down against the side of the building and struggled out of his jacket.

"Wee-oo!" Charlie shouted. He inhaled deeply and shook his head. "Smell that, boys!" he shouted. "Smells like victory!"

A pall of gun smoke hung in the air.

"Fuck all of you!" Lukas shrieked.

The scattered mob took shelter wherever they could: behind carriages, lampposts, inside buildings, around corners. A few returned fire.

Honest Jim was crouched in an alley.

"Murderers!" he exclaimed. "They can't get away with this!"

Mickey Burns was next to him.

"Mother Mary," Burns said. "How many are dead?"

Honest Jim grabbed a young man next to him.

"Rouse up the neighborhood!" he snarled. "Spread the word! I'll have all their hides! Get everyone into the streets! It's war! It's war!"

56

Jan was kneeling next to a public pump in an alleyway between two rows of shanty houses, working the handle, desperately trying to get a drink. He knew that in this sewer of a neighborhood he stood a fair chance of getting cholera from the water, but he was so desperate he was willing to chance it. His clothes were stuck to him with sweat and his hair was standing up where he'd run his hands through it. No matter how hard he worked the handle nothing came out. It only made a weird choking noise, like a sick infant in its sleep.

"Do you hear that?" Bill asked.

"Yes," Jan said. "I think some water will come out soon."

"No," Bill said. "Stop for a minute."

"It's almost here," Jan said.

He was desperate for the water to wash over his scalp. He felt so dirty.

Bill took Jan's hand away from the handle.

"Listen," he said.

"I don't hear anything," Jan said peevishly.

"Me neither," Bill said.

Jan wondered whether Bill was making a joke. Then he realized how quiet it was. They were in a densely packed neighborhood, a hive of humanity, and yet there were no women in the backyards hanging laundry, no sounds of children, nothing. Except for some sort of hum, growing louder and louder all the time.

"What is it?" Jan said.

Dusty, Bill, and Jan stood around the pump with their heads cocked, like hounds straining to hear a distant bugle.

A single man appeared at the mouth of the alley and pointed toward them. He shouted something, but he was too far for them to hear.

Dusty raised his rifle to his shoulder. "Get back, you little prick," he bellowed.

And then the mob flooded into the alleyway, like a tidal wave rushing into a shallow canal.

"Run!" Jan shouted.

They ran, staring behind them at the stunning horde that had come from nowhere, without warning, but when they turned their eyes forward they saw another mob at the other end of the alley.

"Shit!" Dusty screamed.

He raised his rifle to his shoulder and fired, and a man staggered, and fell, but the mob was surging forward, men and boys, children even, old women, waving clubs in the air, knives, planks of wood. Fingers hooked into claws. Shouting.

"Through here!" Jan shouted.

He leapt over a rickety wooden fence into a muddy yard and ran toward the back door of a shanty. The door splintered underneath his boot. Inside an ancient woman tried to stab him with a knitting needle. A blow from the back of his hand sent her sprawling. He bolted through the little one-room shack, the rags on the floor sticking to his boots, and blundered out into the afternoon sunshine.

"They're everywhere!" Dusty screamed.

And indeed they were. There was nowhere Jan could look where he did not see the mob.

"Go, go!" Jan cried.

They ran across the road and burst through another cheap home and crashed out the back door and sprinted through the tangled, trash-filled garden and hopped another fence and came onto a broader street, only to discover that this road was even more crammed with men than the alleys behind them.

"It's Winter!" Bill said.

"What the fuck are you talking about?" Dusty said.

"Look!" Bill said, and pointed, and sure enough, a couple of blocks down the street, Winter and Lukas and the Empire brothers were leaning out of the window of a faded bungalow, firing their guns on the hordes of men besieging them.

"Go, go!" Jan cried.

They ran down the middle of the street. Men were coming at them from every direction: streaming out of buildings, jogging along the sidewalks and springing out of the alleyways. The threat of getting shot kept the pursuers at bay for a time. Finally Bill pulled the trigger on one of his pistols; the only sound was a little click. The mob pounced.

Jan looked behind him and saw that they were on Dusty, and he drew his knife and cut him loose. He looked forward and saw that they had wrestled Bill halfway to the ground, and he stabbed a man in the neck, a boy really, and Bill wriggled free but then someone hit Jan and he fell and dozens of men pressed down on him.

"Help!" Jan screamed. Someone kicked him in the face. He still had hold of the knife and managed to swing it a few times to generate a little space, but as he was rising up to his knees a powerful man knocked him to his back and wrapped his hands around his throat.

"Fucking kill you," Mickey Burns snarled, "you double-dealing kraut!"

Burns sat on Jan's chest, straddling him, trying to choke the life out of him.

"You did this!" Burns screamed.

Jan saw that Burns was crying.

"Look how many people are dead!" Burns said. "It was you! It was you!"

Jan's vision was turning pink.

Okay, he thought. Okay.

It felt natural and inevitable, like something he didn't need to worry about.

And then Burns was struck on the head, very hard, so hard in fact that his head cracked geometrically like an unripe melon. His grip loosened and Jan gasped for air while a strong arm jerked him back to his feet.

"Come on, Müller," Winter said. "Fucking move!"

Winter swung the rifle in his hands back and forth to clear a space and Jan followed. It felt as if he were climbing over a crowd of people. His fingers were scratching, pulling hair, digging into eye sockets. Eventually they got free and staggered up to the porch of the saloon, where they saw that Bill Bread alone was leaning over the rail to provide them with covering fire, ignoring the bullets smacking into the wood all around him.

They barged into the house and ducked under the windows and then Bill got down as well. Bullets were smashing into the house and glass was shattering.

"God damn," Dusty said.

He was staring at Winter.

"I've never seen nothing like that," Dusty said. "That was true grit, Auggie."

Winter gave Dusty a casual look and put his hand to his bleeding neck.

"All right, boys," he said. "We can't stay here. We ain't got much ammunition and there's plenty more of 'em out there. We need to bust out and split up. We'll all meet up back in Morris, Illinois. We'll let Quentin take care of our wages. I know we done all we could and we've earned them."

"Fucking right," Charlie said.

Jan was coughing.

Winter stood up. When he smiled there was blood on his teeth.

"What you all waiting for?" he said.

57

The enormous grain elevators stood silhouetted against the sky and pressed up against the river. They were the tallest buildings in Chicago, visible for miles. Each one was over a hundred feet high and could store over half a million bushels of wheat. In the Fire they had collapsed one by one, falling in on themselves in showers of sparks and smoke. But they had been built back faster than any other buildings in the city, in a matter of months, reconstructed by the nameless, decentralized force that had compelled their construction in the first place. They were the temples of a new natural order that would remake the world in its image.

The train lumbered westward and crawled up to them, coming to a shrieking halt in front of a massive steam-powered conveyor that stretched up into the dim and smoky rafters.

Two men came up from the riverbank. They jogged past the massive gray walls of the grain house and skipped over the railway lines to the waiting train. A few of the workers glanced at them but went back to their work, thinking they were only the usual beggars, come to pick handfuls of spilled wheat out of the dirt.

Jan Müller and Bill Bread crouched up against the train. They were bruised and bleeding, tired and very hungry. They had no ammunition for their weapons. Separated in the tumult after they burst out of the saloon, they had reunited in the middle of the night on the muddy banks of the river.

The train crawled forward for an hour, so that each car came to the elevator, tipped to the side, and dumped its silky golden cargo into the pit where the screaming elevator scooped it up and carried it aloft. Then the whistle shrieked, and the train backed out. Jan and Bill climbed onto the roof of one of the cars as it left.

"Lie down," Jan said.

And so they did, right on the spine of the serpent winding its way through the heart of the city, but even if they were invisible to the men on the street they still felt dreadfully exposed to the windows of the buildings and to the eye of God above.

It was worst when the train came to a stop, at it often did, at crossings and in rail yards. They would have to wait, knowing that if anyone recognized them they would be as helpless as if they were in a cage. But it was at one of those stops, in a crowded rail yard where half a dozen trains were resting next to one another, that Bill saw Fred Johnson sitting on a train car less than a hundred yards from them.

"Look!" Bill said.

Jan turned and looked. His heart froze, but he quickly came to a decision.

"We have to let him know where to meet," Jan said.

They stood up and leapt across the gap to the next train and ran along the cars for a while. Then leapt to Johnson's train and made their way over to where he was waiting, and watching, with his wise and dangerous brown eyes.

"Are you all right?" Jan asked.

"How do I look?" Johnson said.

Jan heard a strange noise. He realized that the railroad car they were standing on was full of pigs, grunting and rooting around beneath him.

"What about the others?" Jan asked.

"Don't know about Reggie," Johnson said. "Quentin's all right. He went with Winter."

The train shuddered to life and began to roll slowly forward.

"So you know we're meeting in Morris?" Jan said.

"Yeah," Johnson replied. "That's what Winter said."

"We'll go with you," Jan replied, settling back down against the train.

Johnson looked at Jan with what he perceived as hostility.

"What?" Jan said. "You'd rather be by yourself? I know you don't like me, but I came all the way over here to—"

"I ain't going to Morris," Johnson said.

Jan realized that what he had mistaken for hostility was frustration. And it was not directed at him.

"Where are you going?" Jan asked.

"I'm going to the stockyards," Johnson said.

"Why?"

"'Cause that's where Winter is."

"I don't understand," Jan said.

Johnson hesitated, then spoke. "I went with Quentin to go see

Noah. This was midnight, nearabouts. We climbed up a drainpipe and broke a window and we found his office. Noah came in real early the next morning. When he saw us he was mad. Him and Quentin went into another room. I could hear them screaming. Quentin came out. Smiled at me. Said it would be all right. I said, Where are we going? He said we'd be fine."

The train was picking up speed, rocking back and forth on the tracks. The pigs squealed louder, as if they were engaged in a heated debate and had to talk over the noise of the moving vehicle.

"Well, it was fucking morning. We went out in the streets and I didn't know what we were going to do. Everyone was looking for a big colored man. There wasn't no place to hide. We went back to the restaurant and Winter saw us. He was in an alley, hat pulled down over his eyes. Real still, like some animal waiting for dinner to walk up. He said he'd sent everyone to Morris and we should go there. Then he asked about our pardons. Quentin started to give him the runaround. You know how he does. Well, I don't think it's so easy to give the runaround to Winter no more."

Now the pigs sounded as if they were struggling to burst free.

"Quentin admitted that Noah backed out of the deal. Winter said Noah told you the gloves were off. Quentin said yes. Winter said well, we took 'em off. Quentin says it's his brother, he can work it out. Winter said he's sick of Quentin working things out. He's sick of these Republicans turning their backs on us. He said he'll sort it out himself. He said where's your brother? Quentin kind of gives him the runaround again. Then he said he's at the Stock Yards. They went off together. They told me to go to Morris."

The train passed from the city core into that endless field of houses, small and plain and wooden, all alike, all new, the new growth after the cleansing fire. They were picking up speed. One of the pigs began to scream.

"Maybe we should just go to Morris," Bill said.

Johnson and Bill exchanged a look that Jan did not understand. Johnson's eyes were wide and furious. Bill's were weak and blinking. But it was Johnson who turned away.

"I checked a newspaper," Johnson said, through clenched teeth. "There was more in there about me than any of us but Winter. Big black man. How the fuck were we supposed to get a pardon after this anyway? It was in the fucking papers."

Jan could hear Bill's voice: *You know there is never going to be a pardon.*

"Dandy Killer. That's what they called Winter. How are we supposed to get a pardon after this? I need to talk to Noah my own self. This is my life. My life! He fucking dangled that pardon in front of me and I laid it on the line for him. He must have known he couldn't give it to me."

Jan sat up. It seemed safe; they must have been moving at thirty miles an hour. More and more of the pigs were starting to scream.

"I know," Jan said.

"Well," Johnson said, "him and me are going to have a little talk."

"You and Noah?" Jan said.

"That's right."

Jan looked at Bill, only to find that he too could not meet the Indian's sad, blinking gaze.

"What if it was Quentin who lied?" Jan blurted.

"Why would he lie?" Johnson said. "He's in as much trouble as any of us."

"What if he was lying all along?" Jan said. "What if he was always lying, all the time, from the beginning?"

Johnson frowned. "You're crazy," he said.

"What if it was always Quentin?"

"Quentin saved my life when you wanted to give me up," Johnson said.

"Yes," Jan shouted. "I wanted to give you up. Why? Why? Because I didn't want to be a fugitive! Ha! Like I am right now!"

And now the stench. Chicago was not a sweet-smelling city in the fairest of seasons. As they approached the Stock Yards the smell reached the limits of human endurance.

"It didn't bother Quentin, though, did it?" Jan said. "Do you ever wonder why he wouldn't turn you over to the Union troops? Eh? Well do you? The kindness of his heart? You think Quentin is a kind man?"

Johnson hesitated, and then said, "The first time I met Noah he told Quentin we would have to be careful. And we weren't careful yesterday. But Quentin don't have no reason to lie."

Jan started to laugh like a lunatic. "No reason at all!" Jan screamed. "No reason at all!"

When they reached the Stock Yards the train rolled through a side gate of the complex. The swineherds were waiting, leaning on their wooden poles. Almost before the train had stopped rolling the swineherds undid the gates of the railway car and the pigs spilled out, squealing. You couldn't tell Jan that they didn't know what was going to happen to them.

The men jumped down and landed amid the pigs.

"What the fuck are you doing here?" a burly swineherd shouted above the din.

"Mind your own business," Jan said.

The herd of pigs surged forward through the black mixture of mud and pig shit that covered the ground. The only way to go was forward; the universe was constructed to send them in one direction.

Bill, Jan, and Johnson staggered through the muck that sucked at their boots and entered an enormous pen. Far above them were raised platforms where men in suits looked down on them in astonishment.

"Look!" Bill cried.

He was pointing up at the top floor of a building on the other end of the pen. A long ramp led up to a square door cut into the concrete wall. And framed in this door, for just an instant, appeared to be a man in a neat gray suit with a walking stick.

"Was that Winter?" Johnson said.

The three of them moved through the pigs, who grunted and occasionally took little exploring nips, as if they wanted to check how these intruders tasted in case they stopped moving long enough to eat. Eventually they reached the base of the Bridge of Sighs and saw that the pigs were eagerly gathered in a tight circle, rooting at something in the mud. Johnson savagely kicked them and they scattered, honking and chirping indignantly, to reveal a human corpse, which they did not recognize as Dennis Addy, the plant manager.

Johnson was the first to charge up the ramp, but Jan was close behind him.

As they went up the ramp they heard, more and more clearly, the grinding sounds of the machine within, drowning out the terrified cries of the pigs.

And they dropped down into yet another filthy pen filled to bursting with pigs. It was too dark, so for a moment they could only hear Noah's screaming.

"Quentin! You have to tell them! Quentin!"

Their eyes adjusted to the gloom and they saw that Johnny Empire held Noah next to an enormous steam-powered metal wheel that was turning slowly, round and round. The chains attached to the wheel clanked and clattered on top of one another. Winter had Noah's watch in his hand. Just as they came inside, he put it in his pocket. Quentin hovered nearby, hopping from foot to foot, looking like a man who enjoyed being in control and who now decidedly was not.

"Augustus, Augustus," Quentin said. "Please. Please."

"Last chance," Winter said.

"Quentin!" Noah cried. "You have to tell them! I told him, I swear, I told him that if there was trouble you couldn't have a pardon! How could I arrange a pardon after what happened?"

Jan felt his stomach turn over.

"Augustus, please, this is my brother," Quentin cried. "It won't solve anything now."

Winter swung his head around to look at Quentin, and that was when he noticed the new arrivals. His gaze sharpened on them, as if he were trying to read small lettering on a sign far away, and then he relaxed, right into the present moment, as if he had just figured out how the universe had managed to bring exactly the right people together, at exactly the right time, once again.

Quentin followed Winter's gaze and saw them, and then looked back at Winter.

"Augustus . . . ," he began.

"Is it true, Quentin?" Winter said.

"What?"

"Did he tell you what he said he told you?"

"Well, I don't know how to answer that."

"Tell me the fucking truth."

"Quentin!" Noah screamed. Then he looked at Jan. "Müller! Get help! Call the police!"

"The police?" Johnson said, letting out a bitter laugh.

"I don't know what you mean by the truth," Quentin said. "I mean, what I told you was true. It was my understanding of what happened. But reasonable people can disagree. And that's why I think . . ."

"Quentin," Winter said. "Did you fuck us? Or did he fuck us?"

There was a moment of silence.

"Quentin!" Noah cried, weeping, squirming in Johnny's grip.

Quentin looked at his brother. "I warned you," he said sadly, but his face was weirdly lit up, like a lamp.

"Quentin!"

"I did warn you," Quentin said.

"Oh Jesus," Jan said.

Winter nodded and Johnny dropped Noah down among the pigs and the shit and held him there with one hand while he attached a chain to Noah's ankle.

"Still think this world is governed by the laws of reason?" Quentin said to Noah, and smiled. "You still think there's nothing stronger than your institutions?"

It ought to have been his final triumph. But instead, Quentin's words seemed to remind Noah of something that he had forgotten in all the excitement, something that took away his fear. Noah's face grew solemn.

"Oh yes," he said. "Yes. You'll see."

He turned his gaze to Winter.

"You'll see," he said.

The chain jerked and Noah was raised howling into the air. The clasp on his ankle was seamlessly transferred to the rail hanging from the ceiling and Noah rushed down toward the floor, where Charlie was waiting with a tremendous knife. Noah came to a stop and had a chance to scream out one last plea before Charlie plunged the knife in and out of Noah's throat. Blood spurted into the gutter, and then Noah's body plunged farther down the rail to where he dropped, still living, into the boiling water.

"Hoooo-weeee!" Charlie screamed.

"I tried," Quentin said. "My own brother."

Winter looked at Quentin, and in that moment, Jan realized that Winter knew that Quentin had lied. Maybe, just maybe, Winter had known for a long time. And then Jan fell to his knees, among the startled, scampering pigs and began to throw up.

When he looked up, he knew that his face was giving him away. Quentin and the Empire brothers and Winter all looked at him with varying degrees of malice. Johnson had backed up to the ramp leading down to the pens. Only Bill was calm, but he was looking at Jan with the same kind, weary, sad expression with which he had regarded the Indian boy he had shot upon Jan's orders.

Jan stood up and straightened his back. "I have to go."

"Go where?" Quentin asked.

"I have to go my own way. I'm sorry. I can't stay."

No one said anything.

"I can't follow you. You should just kill me now if you won't let me go."

"Jan, Jan, Jan," Quentin said, smiling like the lunatic he'd always been. "My old friend. What kind of talk . . ."

"I am not talking to you," Jan said.

And indeed he was not. Jan was staring right at Winter. So were they all, except for Quentin, oblivious, secure in his egotistical belief that the world revolved around him. A look flashed across Quentin's face like a hot desert wind, powerful but empty and alien. No one saw it, because everyone was looking at Winter.

Winter cocked his head.

"I'm sorry, I can't," Jan said, and now his voice broke up. "I can't do it. I can't go with you. I have to stop."

Winter walked over toward Jan. The sunlight hit his face and his eyes shifted to an inhuman golden hue. How clean and neat Winter's suit was, how little of the pig shit seemed to stick to him, as if it slid right off. Jan stiffened like a deer that couldn't think which way to run. He tried not to close his eyes.

"I didn't mean what I said," Jan said. "About nothing to live for."

"Well I meant everything I said," Winter said. "We are building something here."

"I know you are," Jan said. "But I have to get out. I can't. I can't."

"I ain't going to hurt you if you stay," Winter said. He came all the way up to Jan. His breath smelled like candy.

"I am not afraid you will kill me," Jan said. "I am afraid, one day, I will be like you."

Winter looked at Jan for what seemed like a long, long time.

"I won't ever trouble you," Jan said, tearing up again.

How hard Winter was, how cold, how closely sealed against the outside world.

"Winter, I swear," Jan said.

"Everything out there is a lie," Winter said. "Can't you see it? It was them behind us in Georgia, Kansas, Mississippi. It was them behind us yesterday. And then they just pretend. They just talk. 'Cause they can't face this."

Winter made a gesture that encompassed the blood, the flesh, the clattering steel and steam, the darkness, the herds of terrified pigs.

"Jan," Winter said. "This is what's real. This is how the meat you eat gets on your plate. This is how everything works. Everything they tell you is just a lie to hide it."

"I know." Jan wept. "But I can't bear it. I just can't bear it."

Winter's mouth twitched a little and Jan knew that his mind was made up, but didn't know how.

"Go on then," Winter said. "I better never see you again."

"Thank you," Jan said. "Thank you."

Jan turned his back on the Empire brothers and Quentin and looked at Johnson.

"Fred," he began.

But Johnson looked away.

"Fred, think."

"Fuck you, Müller," Johnson said.

"Fine," Jan said.

Jan turned to Bill. He did not ask Bill to come with him. Instead he said, "I don't know what to say."

"There is nothing to say," Bill said.

"You tell yourself that because you need to believe it," Jan said. "That there's no help for any of this. Because you knew all along. I'm a trusting idiot, and Freddy is a nigger without a friend in the world. We didn't know. But you did. And if you could have done something, then you ought to have done it. So you say you couldn't have. But you are lying to yourself, Bill. You are telling yourself what you need to hear."

Bill smiled. "We all do that," he said. "Every one of us."

Jan descended the ramp back down toward the living pigs.

58

In his life he had attended hundreds of funerals. In his death thousands attended his.

For the funeral of Mickey Burns, the Great Mourner, the streets were lined with stricken men and women and children, wearing black clothes or black armbands, trooping in solidarity behind the procession. The casket was borne in a massive carriage in a series of massive carriages. One corpse seemed like such a small thing to have stirred up such a fuss.

It was the largest funeral in Chicago since Lincoln's, an irony not lost on any of the Democratic luminaries who delivered the eulogies, though they were tactful enough not to mention it.

Honest Jim Plunkett's speech was the best received, especially his stories of how Burns had, when the violence appeared to be growing out of control, favored avoiding further conflict. This story caused raptures of grief even though it was believed by precisely no one. Burns was remembered instead for virtues he had not possessed.

One small part of his legacy:

There was a man in a train on the slow path west, to California, as far from Chicago as possible. The man had a certificate of citizenship in his pocket that read "Jack Miller." After a considerable passing of time and a significant price this man had finally been made into an American.

They rode out of that black abattoir into broad daylight, reeking and smoking with the blood of pigs and men. The whole country was in a fury, like a smashed hive of bees. They hid in Morris for a week and then took the train west, through growing Iowa to Nebraska, only five years a state, and still largely ruled by the Sioux and Pawnee and other warlike Indians who would not submit to the hordes of the east.

Herds of buffalo stampeded over the plains, miles and miles of them, as far as the eye could see, the benefice of an insanely generous elder god. Philadelphia tanners had recently perfected a method to transform buffalo hides into leather, and at the outskirts of civilization they passed mounds of corpses, some skinned, some left to rot with their skins on by inexpert butchers. Farther from the cities the herds still ruled, powerful and stupid and helpless, and Winter and his men were able to feed themselves until spring.

Civilization changes when it abuts the wilderness. When any man might cast it aside and walk off and be out from under its eye. In those days the triumph of civilization seemed an uncertain thing. It seemed weak, impermanent, a novelty, soon to pass and fade. And perhaps it will, but only after it has run its course all the way to the end.

Men were carried by boats across the ocean and then pumped by trains across the country, but for a year the Winter Family (for so it was then called) lived with Indians, trappers, hunters, and traders outside of the grasp of the modern world. They roamed north to Canada and south to Colorado, where a mineral boom caused an explosion in population, saloons, whorehouses, and violence.

The sparsely settled West was lawless and chaotic. Men dueled, drank, poached, grazed their cattle and cut trees on the land of others. They sold whiskey to Indians, raped and whored. Banditry was endemic. Men took what they wanted and disappeared.

The Winter Family entered what might be called its golden age. It ranged in size from ten men to thirty and it committed every crime under the sun. They robbed the mail, the stagecoaches, the railroads, the banks. They murdered the inhabitants of isolated farms and homesteads, letting the blame fall upon Indians. They killed men for their mining claims. They broke strikes and stirred them up, sold protection to successful ranchers and then stole their cattle. They fought in one range war after another.

It was the age of the outlaw, but the Winter Family were not like other bandits, who hit soft targets for money and then hid with those who would hide them. Other bandits carefully crafted a romantic image, courted the newspapers, and dispensed largesse like Robin Hood. The James Gang cast themselves as Confederate partisans, while the Reno Gang started out as bounty jumpers, accepting money to enlist in the Union Army and then deserting. The Winter Family never gave a damn what anyone thought of them, and if men gave them shelter, they did it out of fear.

More than once the Winter Family came under the protection of some powerful local figure. They were useful men to have on retainer in that dangerous age. But it never lasted. However it began, it always ended the same way: screams, fire, robbery, death. And then men disappearing into the night, swallowed up into the endless wilderness of plains, forest, and mountain, subsumed by the great god Pan.

They roamed south across the great salt flats and deserts of Utah and Nevada into Arizona. There Lukas Shakespeare left the group to join his brothers, Matt and Austin, who had moved with their mother to Phoenix. The Winter Family traveled farther south to Mexico. A new trade had opened up in those bloody twilight days of the West, as civilization tightened like a creeping vine, choking the life out of a great oak, and there was work for them to do. There always was, it seemed, no matter where they went, no matter what they did, no matter how many people died. The work never seemed to be done.

But the spread of civilization was exponential, not linear, and as such it hid itself like a crocodile under the surface of muddy water. Ready to explode out after its prey when the moment came.

Phoenix 1881

59

The sun was setting as the two bounty hunters crossed the border into Arizona. The desert glowed with the evening light and the cacti and scrub stood silhouetted against the bruised sky. Colorful flowers stood out from the dull red sand and rocks.

The tracks were easy to follow, as they had been left by well over a hundred Indians: men, women, and children stampeding north into the Arizona Territory, making no attempt to hide their passing. The Mexican bounty hunter pulled the reins of his horse and dismounted. He stooped to pick up a roughly made doll from the dirt and he turned it over in his hands.

"We should go back," he said.

His companion was a handsome blond man with an air of uncon-cern. Though he was no longer young, he was called Babe.

"Winter said to press on till we laid eyes on them," Reggie said. "He ain't going to be satisfied with a doll."

"It's dangerous," the Mexican said. He was a squat, competent man. Unafraid but pragmatic. "Easy for some of them to double back in all this mess." He gestured toward the trail in the sand. "Especially now that it's getting dark. Plenty of places to hide."

"I know it's dangerous," Reggie said. "It's just less dangerous than disappointing Winter. Trust me on that."

The Mexican shrugged and remounted. They loped on for less than a quarter of an hour, and then Reggie was shot clean out of his saddle. He landed hard on his back, spat blood into the air, and looked extremely surprised.

The Mexican did all the right things. He crouched down low in the saddle, turned his horse to shelter his body, and drew his pistol while the sound of the shot was still echoing across the desert. But two more shots rang out and his horse stumbled to its knees and threw him into the rocks and sand.

The Apache weaved their way toward him from all sides, appearing and vanishing around the rocks and cacti. The Mexican fired his pistol a couple of times. He was shot in the back and knocked to his knees. Perhaps the wound was not fatal, but he had no intention of being taken alive. He kept shooting until they killed him.

Reggie had no such opportunity. The breath was knocked out of him, and it was a struggle to roll over onto his side, and then another to get onto his knees. By then they were all around him. He could see their shadows, hear the chatter of their alien language.

"Are you Winter?" someone asked him in a deep and serious voice.

Reggie grinned. Blood was smeared all over his chin and his teeth were slick with it. "When you meet him," Reggie said, "you ain't going to need to ask that."

Reggie pressed his hand to his chest to stem the bleeding but it kept squirting through his fingers.

The Apache all wore white men's clothes and wielded rifles and pistols. They looked dirty and tired.

A younger man was waving what looked like a wet rag in the air. Reggie eventually identified it as the Mexican's scalp.

The Apache parted and an old man with long hair stepped forward. He was small and looked a little like Reggie's grandmother when she was angry. He spoke in Apache, and a tall, earnest-looking Apache translated.

"He said you white men are like soldier ants."

The old man spoke some more.

"Big swarms of you, big streams, like a river, no real home, just eating everything you see," the translator said.

"I don't like where this is heading," Reggie said.

The old man said something else and the Apache laughed. This time, the tall Apache did not translate.

"So you're not going to kill me straight," Reggie said, contempt in his voice. But then he raised his handsome eyebrows and an expression of bemusement wandered onto his face. "What the hell am I talking about? I wouldn't do me straight if I were you neither."

The young man translated this to the others. The Apache did not laugh. Instead, they nodded and looked oddly respectful.

"Let me tell you this, though," Reggie said. "You know what's good for you, you'll surrender to the U.S. Army up here. Don't you go back to Mexico and don't you let Winter catch you neither."

"We know a safe place," the tall Apache said. "We will never surrender."

"There are no safe places for you people no more," Reggie said. "How the hell do you think this is going to end?"

It was a rhetorical question, but the tall Apache dutifully translated it. The old man with the long hair smiled. It was not a nice smile. He made a broad gesture with his hand. Reggie did not know if he meant to encompass the men standing here, the desert, or the whole world.

"He asks you the same thing," the tall Apache said. "He asks you: How do you think this is all going to end?"

60

Something was a little off about the first confectioner to set up shop in the newly incorporated city of Phoenix. His features didn't line up in some subtle way. When he laughed it was either too early or too late or too loud, or just at the wrong thing entirely. He tended to stand too close and his accent was unusual and he smiled too much.

His best feature was his hair, which was long and thick and jet-black and always combed slick back against his head.

His name was Homer De Plessey. He was from New Orleans and he was a man of substance. Principally he traded in dry goods, which he sold from a small and tidy store on Center Street near the outskirts of town, but he had a fairly profitable side business in chocolates and candies. Children could press their faces against a fine glass counter in his store and goggle at peppermint sticks and peanut brittle, ropes of red licorice and tins of marshmallows, fizzy powders in paper packages and clear glass jars. In the evenings the smell of melting sugar drifted through the air.

The good people of Phoenix were accustomed to the terrible violence of the wild frontier. But Phoenix was a small, new town and its citizens were of limited imagination and unprepared for De Plessey's careful and metropolitan brand of evil. So it took three days after his daughter's disappearance before Bobby Proudfoot kicked in the door to De Plessey's home, holding an ax in one hand like a toy and bellowing the name of his baby girl.

61

Sheriff Thomas Favorite was in his office, leaning back in his chair and chatting with the antiquarian who'd come from Boston to study the canals. Tom could feel the commotion slightly before he could hear it, like a hand brushing over the back of his neck an instant before the shouts became audible. He listened, still and patient, and then he stood up and took his Winchester rifle off the gun rack and cracked it to make sure it was loaded.

"Is something wrong?" the antiquarian asked.

"Go back to your hotel," Tom said before stepping outside into the desert sunlight.

It always seemed to him like the devil's own country this time of the day, with the sun setting and everything blood colored and the air hot and dry. You could see a long way in every direction along the straight streets, all built within a few years. Between the houses on every side the desert stretched on and on.

Homer De Plessey was running down Center Street with a mob at his heels. Bobby Proudfoot was leading the pack. Tom made the connection, and then spat on the dry road and lifted his rifle.

Homer saw Tom and skidded to a stop, his ugly and expressive face contorted with some strange emotion (not fear, or not fear alone anyway). But Tom made a brief motion with his head, as if gesturing behind him. Homer saw and bolted forward again, flailing his arms, tilting his head back, and gasping for air, until he collapsed at Tom's feet and scurried around behind his legs. Tom felt a hand touch his ankle and he jerked it free, disgusted.

Bobby was outpacing the rest of the mob by a fair margin. His long hair streamed behind him and he was brandishing the ax over his head in a roughly circular motion. His eyes never moved from Homer's cowering form.

Tom pointed the rifle slightly above Bobby's head and fired it. Then he pumped the lever and pointed the rifle at Bobby and told him that was the only warning he'd get.

Bobby slid to a stop, kicking up a little wave of dirt that skittered over Tom's pants and boots and struck Homer in the face.

"Sheriff," Bobby said, out of breath from the exertion and his emotion. "Step aside."

"I can't do that, Bobby," Tom said.

"Sheriff," Bobby said, "that cocksucking Frenchman killed my Jenny. Now step away. We're a-going to hang him."

"Not without a trial, you won't."

"A trial?" Bobby said. "A fucking trial?"

The rest of the mob had now caught up. Standing next to Bobby was his brother, Hank, who looked like Bobby, only smaller and meaner. Behind them, but in front of the others, was Bobby's hired hand, a freedman named Kendron Parkins, who was lean and had gray streaks in his curly hair and beard.

Sheriff Tom Favorite was average height, but built big and solid all the way through. He was well over forty and he was starting to go to pieces: bags hung under his eyes, his fine yellow hair was thinning and had mostly turned gray, and his wrists, waist, and ankles were thick. More than this he gave the unmistakable impression of having passed over some peak and knowing himself to be on a slow, steady decline that he would never be able to reverse. And yet in spite of this (or because of it) he seemed unyielding and implacable, as if he would never give way, never give ground, never allow himself to be pushed aside while he was still breathing.

"Yes," Tom said. "A trial."

"There's not going to be any fucking trial!" Bobby said. "We don't need a trial."

"Sure we do, Bobby," Tom said. "That's how you make sure he's really the one that done it."

"We know he's the one that done it."

"Then you shouldn't have any problems proving it," Tom said. "Right, Bobby?"

"Get out of the fucking way, Sheriff," Hank shouted. "Get out of the fucking way."

"I would rather die," Tom Favorite said.

"Maybe you will," Parkins rumbled.

"I would rather die," Tom repeated, "and do you know why?"

The members of the mob glanced at one another, not wanting to listen, feeling that by listening they were losing something, but none of them wanting to take the first step and risk being shot.

"Well, I'll tell you. It's because I was in Georgia when Sherman's bummers rolled through, stealing and murdering and ripping up railroads out of plain meanness. I was in Cotton Gin Port in 1871, right after the Ku Klux Klan Act was passed, when the night was lit up with Negro homes on fire and dozens of common thieves and rapists draped in white sheets were out settling their private scores. And I was here in Phoenix to bury my brother after he was shot and killed by John Chenoweth in a duel, and them two both running for sheriff at the time. So what I reckon I'm saying is that I've spent the better part of my adult life watching the bestial things men get up to in the name of higher ideals that don't leave them no time to worry about the law. And I'll be goddamned if I see it going on in this town. And so I won't let you kill this man without a trial. I'd rather die. But you'll die first, Bobby. You take so much as one more fucking step."

"He killed my daughter," Bobby said. "He killed her!"

"Bobby, I'm going to put him in the jailhouse. He's not going anywhere."

"Oh god," Bobby said. "And you'd give him a trial? Let him try and talk his way out of it? Not everything is just talk."

"Why don't you get back to his house and turn it inside out," Tom said. "I'll send Dick Moore to help out. This one ain't going anywhere. I got him. You can trust me, Bobby."

Bobby wiped his eyes with the back of one meaty forearm. A look of dumb despair and betrayal was on his face, like a loyal dog that had been kicked for no good reason. Something had gone out of the crowd, and they didn't seem likely to charge. Tom backed up and pointed his rifle at Homer's crouching body.

"Come on. Get a move on."

Homer hurried toward the sheriff's office, watching the mob over his shoulder. Tom didn't look back. He didn't want to catch Bobby's gaze and wonder whether he was doing the right thing. He'd been down that road and he knew exactly where it went.

62

"I suppose you're it," Tom said.

"You suppose correctly," Matt Shakespeare replied.

Matt Shakespeare and his younger brother, Austin, sat in wooden chairs facing the sheriff's desk. Tom moved around the office closing the shutters, shutting out the red desert light. The darkness grew.

"I'm sorry," Austin said. His hair stuck up in the back and he had an overbite. Now he was chewing on his lip, like he'd been caught cheating on a test. "Benjamin wouldn't answer the door. Patrick told me, well, he said no."

"The judge?" Tom asked.

Matt just laughed. He was young too, they both were, but with his orange beard and the cynical lilt of his laughter, he was like a grizzled old man compared to his brother.

"Jesus," Tom said. "You told him I'd calmed them down?"

"Calmed them down?" Matt said. "Tom. They ain't even started to drink yet."

Tom peeked outside before he fastened the last set of shutters and he saw Kendron Parkins sitting directly across the street, his rifle laid out across his knees. No drinking for old Parkins; his wife was a religious Indian and she didn't hold with it. His body was bent almost double by the labors of freedom and slavery alike, but he was justly renowned for his skill with a rifle, being known to bring down a rabbit on the run at fifty paces. And if Big Bobby Proudfoot told him to train his rifle on Sheriff Favorite, would he do it? Would he.

As Tom walked back to his desk, he passed the cell holding Homer De Plessey. Something deep inside him told him to keep his head straight, but he couldn't help himself. He looked.

Homer was staring at something he was holding in his hands, and a series of grotesque expressions was marching across his face. They seemed to be poor simulacrums of grief and fear, too clumsy and exaggerated to be convincing, like a frown painted on the face of a clown. But more alarming than this procession of masks was the look on Homer's face between each one. It was calm and sly, but mostly it was empty.

Homer glanced up at Tom and their eyes met. Homer's face abruptly produced an unconvincing look of anguish. A wink of light flashed from Homer's hands and Tom thought, A mirror, he's looking into a shaving mirror.

Tom walked over to the Shakespeare brothers. It was not his imagination; he could feel Homer's gaze resting between his shoulder blades.

"Well, all right," Tom said. "What has Bobby got on De Plessey anyway?"

"Jenny Proudfoot told one of her friends she was going to the candy store after school on the day she disappeared," Matt said.

"Anyone see her actually go there?"

Matt shrugged.

"Oh hell," Tom said.

"Sheriff, you know there's something not right about him."

"Well? You can't just hang someone who's got something wrong with him every time something bad happens."

"Well, all right," Matt said. "I'm just curious: Where do you see this one going? How's it going to end? No one wants a goddamn trial here. The judge don't. Bobby and his friends don't. The town don't. Even your French friend in the cell there don't, because you put him up in front of any twelve men living in this town in the morning he's going to be swinging from a tree in the evening. The only one who wants a trial here is you."

"It ain't about what I want," Tom said.

"But it is. Don't you see that? That's exactly what it is."

"No, it ain't. It's about not giving up on what's important the first moment things get a little tough. We don't want to be living in a world where you can get hanged without good cause. Trust me. We don't. Because I've lived in that world. Are you with me, or not?"

Matt grinned. He was very quick to smile. "Shit, Tom, you know you can count on me."

"All right. What about you, Austin? How do you feel about getting deputized?"

Austin looked up at Tom with an awed expression on his face, but Matt cut him off.

"Sheriff, you do me a favor," Matt said. "Hold off on the deputization. All right? It was a little bit against my better judgment even bringing him here."

"Okay, we'll hold the tin star," Tom said. "Matt, go check on Dick. Turn that goddamn store inside and out. Keep an eye on things, and if they start to get hot you get back here and let me know. Austin, you stay with me. I might need you to go run some errands."

"No dangerous errands," Matt said. "You save those for me. All right?"

"Why don't you just let me be a man?" Austin said.

"Well, isn't that adorable," Matt said, pinching his brother's cheek. Austin rolled his shoulder and jerked his face away.

Matt stood up and stretched, all six foot something of him, the two pistols dangling at his hips. A dangerous looseness was about him. Outside he tipped his hat to the patient sentry across the road, who never blinked.

63

Deputy Dick Moore sat on his horse outside of the confectioner's home, watching through the windows as the mob smashed the place up, ripping up the floorboards with pry bars and throwing the furniture around. Every now and then Dick would eject a thin brown stream out of the corner of his mouth. At the sound of hoofbeats he turned his head and saw the middle Shakespeare boy riding up the street. Then he frowned and looked away.

"Evening, Dick," Matt said.

"Sheriff's holed up, huh."

"You always were a sharp one."

"They ain't found shit."

"I don't reckon they will. Do you? Our Mister De Plessey always struck me as the meticulous type."

"You'd better hope they find something."

"Maybe they brought their own evidence. A set of undergarments, perhaps. That's what I'd have done."

"It's a shame not everyone in this town is clever like you, Shakespeare."

"That's what I think to myself," Matt said, "every day."

Matt took a tin out of his pocket. Inside there were a number of small, withered Indian hemp cigarettes. Some had already been smoked into little nubs, and it was one of these he put in his mouth and lit with a wooden match while his horse paced back and forth at the ruckus going on in the house.

"And so," Matt said, once he had the cigarette going. "I don't suppose it crossed your mind to head inside and ensure that they aren't bringing their own evidence. Since you disapprove of the practice."

Dick had been a deputy sheriff in Phoenix for ten years and a lawman in Kansas before that. The lines in his face looked carved in wood, but his chin was fat. His hair was receding and what little he had stood straight up when he took off his hat to wipe his brow.

"Well, I'm here, ain't I?"

"You are indeed."

"That's more than can be said for some of the deputies in this town, ain't it?"

"For two, to be precise."

"And I think that's saying something. Because this is an exercise in damn foolery."

"I don't know why you think you have to tell me."

"Well then maybe you can tell it to the sheriff."

"Why don't you tell him yourself?"

"Maybe he'll listen to you. Because he's your pal, ain't he? Your keeper more like. He thinks he's reformed you. You can try to roll off all your devilry on Lukas, but those of us as have been in this town awhile know a little different. And after the next election you'll be shipped out, I think."

"You're all quick to bring up my brother when you want to take me down a peg or two," Matt said. "Only, where were you all when he was running this town? Hmm? Where were you then, my fat friend?"

Dick spat.

"Election's a long ways off, Dick. You'd do well to keep that in mind."

Matt swung his leg over the cantle of his saddle and dropped to the ground. He looked up at Dick.

"You coming?"

The foyer had been demolished. Coats and boots were scattered everywhere. The furniture had been sliced open and the vases from the mantel smashed. The men who were still searching were sullen and hostile.

Matt and Dick climbed the stairs to the master bedroom. Four-post bed, rich velvet sheets, curtains hanging down. The air was full of feathers, drifting this way and that on the little indoor movements of air, as Hank Proudfoot attacked the mattress and the pillows with an enormous knife.

"The fuck are you doing here?" Hank snarled.

"Just come to see how you boys are coming along, see if we can lend a hand."

"Yeah?" Hank said. He squinted at Shakespeare and threw the mattress down and came over. Matt was hit by the overpowering odor of crème de menthe. Liberated from Mr. De Plessey, no doubt. "Well, how are we coming along, Shakespeare?"

Hank was squat and ugly and he had an enormous head with a nose that curved down sharply like a beak. It was generally agreed that he was smarter than his brother, but that this increased intelligence only served to make him less industrious.

"Looks to me like you're being real thorough," Matt said, taking a drag on his cigarette.

"What do you think we've found?" Hank asked.

"I don't know, Hank."

"Guess, then."

Matt glanced around the shattered room. He saw clothes thrown on the floor, broken bottles of rose water and laudanum, scattered books and papers.

"Nothing."

"We ain't found a goddamn thing," Hank said, as if Matt had not spoken. "Now what do you make of that?"

Matt had the sense not to suggest that Mr. De Plessey might be innocent.

"Look, what do you want, Hank? We'll work something out. Don't lose that temper of yours. That never does anyone any good."

"Work something out?" Hank said. "Work out what? Jesus. This can only go two fucking ways, Shakespeare. You're going to give him to us, or you ain't."

Hank shoved his face up against Matt's, who smiled humorlessly and said, "That's bothering me, Hank."

"Is it now, boy," Hank said. But he pulled his head back all the same.

"Thank you kindly."

"I can't fucking believe you're in here, telling me the law. You of all people, you fucking criminal. There ain't shit in here. Does that mean that murderer gets to go free?"

"Keep on looking," Matt said. "You just keep looking."

Outside, Dick said, "Hell."

"How long do you think we've got?" Matt asked as they retrieved their horses.

"They'll get tired of searching soon. Question is whether they'll head right over or start drinking first. I'd say drinking but Hank is wired tighter than a snare drum. I don't even want to think how Bobby's doing."

"Fuck," Matt said, rubbing the lower half of his face. He looked at Dick questioningly.

"You're the smart one, Shakespeare," Dick said. "You tell me."

"Okay. You run on up and see how Bobby is doing. I reckon he won't want to see me."

"He won't want to see me either."

"He'll want to see you a good deal more than he wants to see me.

See if you can get him drinking instead of charging straight in. I'll work on the sheriff."

"See that you do."

"All right. But I'm curious. How is it that you all think I'm some sort of born criminal but you also think that our sheriff's unyielding principles are all my doing, at the same time?"

"Because you're trouble, Matt Shakespeare," Dick said. "That's all you are."

Matt grinned and pulled himself back up onto his horse.

64

The sun had set and the sheriff's office was almost completely dark. Matt closed the door behind him and waited for his eyes to adjust until he made out the dim forms of two men in De Plessey's cell.

"That you, Matt?" Tom called.

"Yeah," Matt said. "Where's my brother?"

"I sent him for the horses."

"Ah," Matt said, a helpless sound. He walked into the darkness of the cell and saw that Tom had shackled Homer's hands behind his back.

"You shouldn't be in here alone with him," Matt said.

"Where's he gonna go? I'm the only friend he's got."

"I'm reminded of the story of the scorpion and the frog. Things aren't going well out there. They haven't found anything."

"I'm innocent," Homer said suddenly, in his rich, courtroom voice.

"Yeah, okay, sunshine," Matt said. "Sheriff, if Austin brings horses here we're going to get shot."

"He's not bringing them here," Tom said. "I'm going to sneak out the back, get in one of the old canals, and meet your brother south of town. I'm going to make a run for Tucson."

"Tucson," Matt said. "Well, no one will ever say you lack for ambition, Sheriff."

"I need you to stay here and hold them off. See if you can't misdirect them a little too."

"Sheriff, what is this all for?"

"I can't just hand him over to them to be hung," Tom said. "All right? I can't."

"Why not? He killed a little girl."

"I didn't—" Homer started.

Matt moved as quickly as a trap springing shut. He drew the revolver from his right holster and pressed the barrel into Homer's jaw, pushing his face away.

"You just keep your mouth shut," Matt said.

"Leave him alone," Tom said.

Matt holstered his pistol.

"Look, here's the long and the short of it," Tom said. "I would rather die than let them take him out and string him up from a tree. All right? It's my decision. It's only my life. You said you were with me. Are you?"

Matt rocked back on his heels a bit and stretched his neck left and right. It made an audible cracking noise.

"Well shit, Sheriff. You know me. I'll lend you a hand."

"Fine," Tom said.

They led Homer to the back of the building, where Matt lifted up a trapdoor.

"Send my brother home, will you?" Matt said. "Don't send him back here."

"You bet," Tom said.

Homer went out the trapdoor first, moving awkwardly with his hands behind his back. Matt kicked him in the buttocks to speed him on his way. The sheriff went next, and Matt closed the door behind them and waited for the storm.

65

The Winter Family gathered in a dark group in the evening desert, as ill-omened as an unkindness of ravens. They had found the scalpless corpses of the Mexican bounty hunter and Reginald Keller, their faces all loose and baggy, the sand around them starched with blood.

The Mexican had only joined the Family a few months earlier, but Reggie had been with them since the very beginning. He and Winter had been close. Now his body was drenched in molasses and lying on top of a kicked-over anthill. He'd been stripped naked, and his hands were tied behind his back. The ants, big and red with wide pincers, crawled all over him. Dusty was stung while he was retrieving Reggie's body, and he swore and cried out.

"Fucking savages," Foxglove said. "Left him to be eaten alive by ants."

"Ants don't eat people, you idiot," Hugh Mantel said.

"No," Quentin said. "I rather think it was the gunshot that killed him. I'm sure he was stung dreadfully, though."

"You got that right," Dusty muttered while sucking his hand.

Winter poked the body with his polished cane. Ants everywhere. Marching over Reggie's tongue, his eyes, in and out of his ears.

"Shall we bury them?" Dusty asked.

"No," Winter said. "I don't want that slick son of a bitch slipping away on us again, or getting picked up by the army. We ain't but a few hours' ride from Tucson."

"It's dark, Winter," Bill Bread said.

"With this moon, and these tracks?" Winter said. "We ain't going to lose them."

"It's not just that," Bill said. "They could lay another ambush."

To this, Winter did not reply. He just walked back to his horse and pulled himself into the saddle. The other men glanced at one another briefly. Galloping into the dark? Through the desert? After two men had already been killed in an ambush?

Still, they feared the ambush less than they feared Winter.

They rode on.

66

Homer poked his head out from underneath the building into the desert night and then wriggled out on his belly, grinding the dust of the road into his fine suit. Tom followed just behind and hauled Homer up to his feet like a sack. They ran across the street, ducked between houses, and crossed one road after another until they were out in the open desert. Then they sprinted, exposed, toward one of the ancient canals that had been left by the Hohokam a thousand years before.

"Get down," Tom said, as they dropped into the canal. "Get down."

They were silent except for the sound of their breath, coming one gasp at a time. The desert was quiet. No birds, no crickets, nothing. Tom lifted his head above the canal and looked the way they had come, but he didn't see anything.

"Stay low," Tom said. "Go south. Head south."

The canal was ten feet wide and about six feet deep and ran vaguely southeast for almost a mile. Homer had to stoop to keep his head hidden. Except for a little trickle of water between their feet the canal was dry. The ground was baked mud with sparse grass and small cacti. It was hard running among the loose stones and the ground made uneven by ancient movements of water. Above them the sky was turning a dark purple and the stars were starting to light up, one at a time.

Eventually the canal came to an abrupt end as the soil caved in from both sides in a mess of rocks and scrabbling plants. Austin Shakespeare was waiting there, holding three horses.

"I want you to understand something, Mister De Plessey," Tom panted. "You're my prisoner. I'm taking you to Tucson to stand trial."

Homer's face was slick with sweat, but when he spoke he was not in the least out of breath.

"You're doing the right thing, Sheriff. I'm an innocent man. I'd never hurt a soul."

Tom climbed onto one horse and watched as Austin helped Homer mount another. Then Austin passed Tom the reins to Homer's horse.

"Thank you kindly," Tom said.

"I'm coming with you," the boy said.

"No, you're not."

"You need someone to help you watch him."

"I'll be fine."

"You're crazy," Austin said. "He's a murderer and it's a hundred miles to Tucson. You can't possibly watch him the whole time."

Austin jogged toward the other horse, which had wandered off, its neck stretched out, sniffing the ground.

"Go home," Tom said. He put his spurs to the side of his horse and they galloped south, with only the stars and the moon to watch them. He glanced back to make sure Homer was still on his horse, and he saw that Austin was following him.

"Go home!" Tom shouted.

But the boy was probably right anyway. There was nothing to do but ride as hard as they could.

67

Inside Homer De Plessey's general store, Bobby was hitting the furniture with his ax and screaming. He smashed up the glass counter and strewed the candy across the ground and went into Homer's little kitchen in the back and kicked over the pots. He tromped down into the cellar and then came back up again.

Dick watched from across the street with a crowd of people. Some were in chairs. Every now and then Dick would take his hat off and wipe his forehead.

Eventually Bobby came out holding the ax and Dick approached him. Bobby saw him coming, and his eyes narrowed and he pointed at him with the ax.

"There's nothing in there! But if you think . . ."

"Bobby, come on now. You didn't hardly look, you just broke everything up."

"There's nothing in there! I ain't going to let you let him off!"

"No one's going to let him off; he's in the jail, Bobby! And there he'll stay. All right? I promise you. There he'll stay. Now, if you've calmed down some we'll go back and take our time and keep looking till we find something. All right?"

"I'm done looking," Bobby said, his shoulders heaving.

"No, no," Dick said, taking Bobby's arm. "Just come with me, all right? He's not going anywhere."

Bobby jerked his arm free but he watched Dick step through the broken door, and eventually he followed.

It smelled sweet inside. Dick didn't pay much attention to the mess of goods thrown everywhere, other than a brief look at the shattered candy counter. Instead he lit the lamp and flipped through the notebooks and papers.

"What do they say?" Bobby asked.

"Not much," Dick said. "Just appointments and orders."

Homer De Plessey had neat handwriting. His accounts were concise, without notes or commentary. They gave nothing away. Dick examined them as long as he could before Bobby got impatient, and then he put the books down and searched under the counter. Nothing.

"All right," Dick said. "We'll go through those books a little more carefully later."

The back room smelled overwhelmingly of some chemical that made Dick feel light-headed.

"Do you smell that?" he asked Bobby.

"Smell what?" Bobby said.

A shelf of ingredients for sweets and a stove stood at the other side of the room. The strange chemical odor grew stronger as Dick walked in that direction. Glass jars were smashed all over the floor. Essence of peppermint, aromatic oils, orange and rose water, licorice, sacks of cocoa beans and sugar, condensed milk. All of it splattered and mixed together, but that odor, still, hanging in the air, overpowering it all.

"You don't smell that?" Dick asked.

"Smell what?" Bobby asked. "I don't smell so good."

Dick set the lantern on the counter and crouched down to pick through the broken bottles, sniffing deeply, until he felt so dizzy he had to steady himself and accidentally put his hand in a pool of corn syrup. He wiped it off on his pants and picked up a nearby bottle labeled PEPPERMINT EXTRACT. It was larger than the other bottles and had a wide neck and stopper instead of a dropper.

One whiff of it almost knocked him out. When Dick stood he felt like he was on the deck of a ship being tossed in a storm.

"Hold this," Dick said, passing Bobby the broken bottle, "but don't smell it."

"What's it say?"

"It says peppermint," Dick said, "but it smells like the Yankee dodge."

"What's that?"

"Ether."

"Why's he got ether in the peppermint jar?"

"Good question, Bobby," Dick said.

Dick wiped his sticky hand on the counter and looked at the tools. Spoons, ladles, cookie cutters, bowls, cast-iron pots. And knives. He took one out and pressed his thumb against the blade and it cut his skin like it was moving through air.

Finally he got down on his knees next to the stove and poked through the ashes. He raked his fingers back and forth through the soot and burned wood. It might have been his imagination, but he thought there was some faint heat left in the stones.

What temperature did sugar melt at? It was pretty hot. Dick's wife had made some candy in her day. Dick himself preferred pies. They were healthier, it seemed to him, and more flavorful. Candy was too hard or sticky. Bad for your teeth. Too sweet too. And it did something to kids, wound them up. But they'd loved it, and when you lost five in the crib before you got your two you weren't inclined to deny them anything. And so she'd made it, stirring and stirring, saying something about what temperature the sugar was supposed to be before it'd melt. All Dick knew was that it'd been pretty hot.

And then his fingers closed on something cold, and he brought the little piece of metal out and cleaned it off in his hand. It was a locket, warped and twisted by the heat almost out of recognition. Almost.

68

Matt Shakespeare was sitting comfortably with his feet up on the sheriff's desk. His tin of hemp cigarettes was open, the air was fragrant with their smoke, and he was making a series of discordant sounds upon the harmonica. Matt's whole family was or had been musical. His mother had played the piano, and Austin did as well, besides having the voice of an angel at church. Lukas had been a fair hand at the banjo, before he had lost interest in the instrument, and he had been a fine whistler. Matt had no musical talent, but it did not stop him from occasionally playing the harmonica, badly, with the air of someone enormously enjoying a very private joke.

Because of the noise he was making, he did not hear the crowd approaching until they began to pound on the front door.

Matt jerked his feet off the desk and dropped one hand to his revolver.

"Sheriff?" Dick called from outside. "Sheriff, open up."

"Dick?" Matt said.

"Sheriff, open up," Dick repeated.

"Dick, what's going on out there?"

"Where's the sheriff?" Dick said.

"Open the goddamn door!" Matt heard Bobby scream, and then a roar from the crowd.

"What's going on, Dick?" Matt said.

"Where's the sheriff?" Dick asked.

"Are you deaf or stupid?" Matt shouted. "You tell me what the hell is going on out there, Deputy, and why you're leading a goddamn lynch mob . . ."

"We found proof," Dick said.

"What?" Matt said.

"We found proof," Dick said. "He had a pint of ether in a bottle marked 'peppermint extract' and we found things in his oven. A locket, a bit of cloth, something that might have—"

"Sheriff!" Bobby bawled. "You open this goddamn door! You hear me!"

"All right, Bobby," Matt said, his brain scrambling. "All right, you found your proof. Just calm down. Now we'll have a trial and you don't have to worry—"

"Sheriff!" Bobby screamed so loudly that Matt jerked his head away from the door. "I ain't talking to no brother-killing son of a whore! I'm talking to you, god damn it! Open this fucking door! We ain't having no trial."

"Bobby," Matt said, "you know how the sheriff feels about lynchings."

"Sheriff!" Bobby screamed, aggrieved. "Answer me!"

"Oh my god," Dick said, very softly. Which was about right.

"He ain't in there!" someone else cried.

"I been watching the whole time!" Kendron Parkins said. "He's got to be in there!"

And then the ax hit the door with such force the blade went all the way through. Matt thought it might be stuck, but Bobby yanked it back out, tearing away a large chunk of the door with it.

"Do that again and I'll shoot!" Matt cried.

The ax hit the door.

Matt cocked his pistol but then thought better of it. Instead he holstered his gun and raised his hands as Bobby came crashing inside. Bobby took one glance toward the cells, which confirmed what he surely must have already known: there was no one left but Matt Shakespeare. Then he lifted the ax above his head and lunged forward.

But before the ax fell Kendron tackled Big Bobby from behind and drove him into the side wall.

"Let me go!" Bobby screamed. "Let me go!"

"No, no, wait," Kendron said.

"I'm a tired of waiting!" Bobby screamed, weeping now. "That's what you all say! I'm not gonna wait no more! My Jenny! Oh god. Where is he? Where'd you take him?"

"We gotta ask him, Bobby," Kendron said. "We gotta ask him."

"Look what you done," Dick said, stunned.

"You think this was my idea?" Matt said. "That's what you think?"

The mob kept pouring in. Matt backed up to the far wall, his hands still raised in the air.

"Get off me!" Bobby said. "Get the hell off me!"

Kendron let go of Bobby. They both came over to Matt.

"Where is he?" Bobby said.

"What'll you do if I tell you, hmm?" Matt said. "Why don't you just calm down for a second?"

"Matt," Kendron said, shaking his ancient head. "You better just tell us which way the sheriff went."

Eventually, Matt shrugged.

"All right," he said. "He took him up to his sister-in-law's place in Orangedale. Was going to put him in the cellar till the trial. He's safe as safe can be, Bobby. Ain't no one going to turn him loose. Just didn't want him getting lynched in case you guys busted in here. Which, as it happened, you did."

"The sheriff's lost his mind," Dick said. "Lost his damn mind."

"Come on now," Matt said. "I ain't saying I'd have done the same. But he's a law-and-order man. You knew that when you voted him in. You all wanted a law-and-order man. Remember? How things were before? He was the man who changed them."

Bobby didn't bother to reply, only turned to leave, but Kendron caught his arm and then spoke to Matt.

"Matty," Kendron said. "We know it was the sheriff that put you up to this. And there's no one that can say you haven't done your duty."

"Why thank you, Kendron," Matt said. But his heart sank.

"And we're going off to Orangedale now. But if he ain't there, if you lied to us, there'll be hell to pay. And not just for you."

Matt smiled.

"Was that a threat?" he asked. "Me, I don't threaten people. But I'll tell you what. Anyone who hurts my brother is going to die. That's not a threat." He flicked his eyes between Kendron and Bobby and waited. Kendron nodded, just a little.

"He's heading to Tucson," Matt said finally. "Figures to be there by morning. Going to put De Plessey in the jailhouse down there until the trial."

"Hell," Kendron said, wheeling around. Bobby followed. The men started shouting and shoving out the door. Matt made his way back to his desk and sat down and put his feet back up. Then he lifted the harmonica to his lips to play a tune to send the mob on its way.

69

Tom, Homer, and Austin had begun at a gallop, but after fifteen minutes or so they slowed to a brisk trot. A hundred miles was a long way, and there was no telling when or if they could change horses. Overhead the stars were glittering, hard and distant, in the sky.

Every now and then Tom glanced over his shoulder, to check the road behind them and to ensure that Homer De Plessey was still in place. The confectioner sat easy in the saddle, a comfortable rider, relaxed into the jarring rhythm of the trotting horse. Behind them by about ten paces was Austin, crouched forward, wild-eyed and nervous.

They'd been on the road for less than two hours when Tom saw the dust rising on the road behind them, driven high by the hooves of their pursuers and shimmering in the moonlight.

"Hell," he said, pulling up on the reins. "Here they come."

"We should keep going!" Austin said. "We've still got a mile on 'em."

"Yeah," Tom said. "And we've still got eighty miles to go. We needed more of a head start than this. I hope your brother's okay."

"What do we do?" Austin said.

What were they going to do? Tom thought. It was the desert. Yellow sand dotted with cacti and scrub. Tumbleweeds dancing in the night wind. The San Tan Mountain a few miles off to the east, rising up abrupt and rocky, silhouetted against the stars. Everything as dark as you'd like.

"Get off your horse," Tom said, and then dismounted himself.

"What are we doing?" Austin asked.

Tom walked over to De Plessey and helped him get down. He checked to make sure the manacles were tight around De Plessey's wrists and then he gave him a little push southward down the road.

"You got a gun?" Tom asked Austin.

Austin swallowed a little, and his skinny throat bobbed up and down.

"It's all right. Take Mister De Plessey here a little ways down the road and get behind some cover. I don't think he's going to try anything, but shoot him if he gives you a reason. The Lord knows it'd make my life easier."

Austin nodded and took his gun out of his holster. It looked too heavy for him.

Tom turned back to the north. He drew his rifle from where it was secured next to his saddle and then slapped his horse, driving it away. For the next few minutes he stood in the middle of the road with the weapon lowered, alone, cold, blinking against the little sandstorms kicked up by the restless night wind. Somewhere far across the desert a dog howled.

There were only two riders and they were coming hard, real hard. Bobby and Kendron.

Tom raised the rifle to his shoulder and fired. The flash of it was very bright in the darkness and the sound very loud in the silence.

The pursuers pulled their horses to a screeching halt. The horses were foaming and screaming for breath and trembling with exhaustion. Both men drew their pistols.

"Where is he, Sheriff?" Bobby said. "I'm only gonna ask you once."

"He's going to the jail in Tucson," Tom said. "That's all."

"Sheriff," Kendron said. "We found Jenny's locket in the fireplace of his little candy kitchen."

"Is that right?" Tom said. "I'm sorry, Bobby. I truly am."

"Where is he, Sheriff?" Bobby asked.

"Bobby, if what Kendron says is true, and I don't doubt his word for a minute, then you don't have to worry much about the trial. But we have to do it. You understand that, don't you? It's things like trials that stop men like Lukas Shakespeare."

"A bullet stopped Lukas Shakespeare," Kendron said.

"No," Tom said. "Shooting 'em just lets 'em decide how the world works. Makes us live by their rules, or lack thereof. Okay? Matty killing Lukas didn't set us free of him. It's what we do after. It's what we do right now."

Bobby slid off his horse. He still had the pistol in one hand.

"Sheriff," Kendron said, "for god's sake."

"Don't come any closer, Bobby," Tom said. "Please don't."

"That was a nice speech," Bobby said. "But you didn't say anything about my Jenny. She's still dead. Tell that to your laws. Tell them that. Only they won't say anything, they're not real."

"If laws ain't real," Tom said, "then it's men like Lukas Shakespeare who truly understand the way the world works. And I can't accept that. I can't. So get back on your horse, Bobby. Just do it."

A gun fired, from behind Tom, and Kendron's head came apart.

Tom whipped around, his heart pounding in his chest, and raised his rifle. Something smashed into his forehead. Stars blazed in front of his eyes, as if they were exploding, growing a thousand times more brilliant, and then they went out, and all was darkness.

70

The Shakespeare residence was a mile and a half from the sheriff's office, to the north and the west. Matt and Austin had about an acre of land abutting the canal and a small single-story home. The whole place was going to seed. The vegetable gardens were overrun with weeds and the walls sagged inward. Some windows were cracked. The paint peeled. You could smell a faint musty odor in the back of your mind just looking at the place.

Matt felt his throat tighten when he saw that there was no light on inside, no smoke rising from the chimney. Inside the front door he used the jack to pull off his boots, and then he called out, "Austin? Austin?"

There was a lamp on a small table by the front door and he took the matches out of the drawer and lit it.

What would you expect of two young men living together, without a mother to take care of them? It was a mess, with muddy boots scattered around the door, jackets and shirts carelessly thrown over the backs of chairs, and a pile of dirty dishes sitting on the kitchen table. The cupboards were bare and columns of ants trooped boldly across the floor.

"Austin?" Matt called.

He checked their bedroom, shining the lamp around. A set of bunk beds where Matt and Austin slept. Luke's bed was on the other side of the room, neatly made.

Next Matt walked down the hall to his mother's old room, with its large bed and mirror, the glass jars and pots on the vanity, the huge closet of clothes and costumes, and the piano in the corner.

Not here, Matt thought. Did he go back to town?

He returned to the kitchen and set the lamp down on the table and then took a half-empty bottle of whiskey down from the shelf. He drank without using a glass and as his gaze wandered the room it happened to fall upon a framed picture hung just to one side above the fireplace.

It was a charcoal sketch of Lukas that had been done when he was around fifteen. In it, Lukas was wearing a huge hat and a neat new suit. He was grinning hugely, showing off a large gap between his teeth, and resting a hand on a pistol at each hip.

It was the grin that broke your heart. Luke had been a bad seed. Matt had always known it, even if his mother and Austin had tried to pretend they did not. But there was no doubt that the men Lukas had run with had changed him. Luke had always been laughing and smiling about something, even if it was something mean. When he'd returned he'd been different. Hard, unsmiling, bitter, and closed off. That attitude he'd learned from them, for sure. Like laughing was weakness and coldness was strength. For all his talk about starting a gang with his brothers he'd had no patience for them any longer. Especially Austin. Austin never could have become cold like that.

Matt looked at the picture a little longer. The anonymous artist had worked roughly and quickly and not caught much detail. But he had captured some piece of the young Luke's unspoken essence. You could feel his confidence, his wildness, his sense of humor, his capacity for violence.

Matt realized then that his younger brother had run off south with Sheriff Favorite, and a little cold worm of fear wriggled between his ribs and into his heart.

"Shit," Matt said. "Shit, shit."

He jogged back outside, pausing only briefly to snatch up his rifle from the gun rack by the door.

71

The first thing Sheriff Tom Favorite noticed was the smell. How bad it was. As bad as it could get.

His eyes were fluttering, trying to open, trying to see. They felt heavy and sticky. There was a pain, he realized, a terrible pain in his head.

An image started to come into focus. A ghost. A skull. No. No. It was getting clearer all the time, coming together, taking shape.

It was a coyote. A dead one. Rotting. The fur curling up like mold, the flesh bubbling away from the bones. Decomposing eyeballs yellowing and collapsing in on themselves. Flies circling over the body.

And ants. There were ants. Two kinds of ants. Red and black. They were marching all over the dead coyote and . . . were they fighting?

Tom Favorite blinked and saw that they were. The red ants and the black ants were biting one another with their enormous mandibles and struggling back and forth, wrestling over the top of the dead animal.

And then as he moved his head a little, setting off a fresh wave of pain, he thought groggily, What am I doing here?

Laughter. No, not laughter. Giggling. High-pitched and rapid, like a child's. But not a child. He became cognizant of the strong hands that held the collar of his shirt and the back of his belt, and that these hands were holding him over the rotting carcass, and then a mouth pressed into his right ear, and he jerked away, making his head throb in pain again.

"The devil made this world," Homer De Plessey whispered. "And God is dead or sleeping."

Tom struggled. He couldn't move his hands or his legs. He'd been hog-tied.

Homer De Plessey kept giggling, but now he lifted Tom up (effortlessly, it seemed) and threw him across the back of a horse.

Tom tried to turn his head to see where they were going, but it was dark and there was nothing around them but desert. He was still trying to catch his breath and say something when Homer mounted his own horse and cracked the reins and they galloped off into the dark.

72

The moon had come up over the mountain to the east and lit up the desert and made the stars dimmer in comparison. Every now and then a sharp and short breath of wind kicked up the sand.

The men stood around and argued about what to do. They would fall silent, and the silence would drag out, and it would seem obvious that there was nothing to do but swallow the bitter injustice of it and head back to Phoenix. But they couldn't bear it, and someone would say something, to break the spell, and they would start bickering again, blaming one another, proposing theories, discussing plans of action, anything to make it seem like they were in control.

Dick heard the rider and turned to the north, thinking it was one of the stragglers from their group. And then he saw who it was, riding up on them like the avatar of vengeance, and he said, "Oh hell."

The others stopped talking at the sound of his voice and looked too.

"Who is it?" one of them asked.

"It's Shakespeare," Dick said.

"What do we do?" Hank asked. "What'd we do, Deputy?"

Dick spat. "Well, don't make any sudden moves, for starters."

When Matt saw them all standing there, looking at him with their stupid moon faces, some of them holding their hats, backing away from him, opening up a path, that's when he knew. And it was like a bitter taste high up in the back of his throat, a painful sensation, burning, like he was choking on tears waiting to get born. That's how it felt knowing his little brother was dead.

He hauled on the reins and his horse stopped gratefully, instantly, and then trembled and whooped its breath in and out. Matt took up his rifle and dropped to the ground. None of them met his gaze for more than a second. One of them stepped a little farther back, all the way off the road, and Matt saw the bodies at his feet.

Bobby and Kendron had been shot. Kendron in the face, right under his right eye. Bobby in the arm, the leg, dozens of times in the torso. They were both splattered with blood. Farther up the road he could see, in the moonlight, the dark patches where they'd fallen.

Austin hadn't been shot. Instead a dark band of bruises was around his neck, dotted with little spots of unblemished flesh.

"The chain," Matt said. "Choked him with the chain."

He wiped his eyes with the back of his hand, lifting the rifle to do so.

"Where're the sheriff and the confectioner at, Dick?" Matt asked.

Eventually Dick replied, "We don't know."

"What'd you mean you don't know?"

"Well, Bobby and Kendron, they rode ahead. When we caught up, there was just these three."

"I see," Matt said.

Matt's voice was steady but he was crying hard. Tears streaming down his face, nose running. His brother's hair was a mess and he had this urge to lean down and fix it, but that urge was useless now. There was no purpose to feeling like that anymore.

"Well," Matt said. "Nice work, fellas."

"Go to hell," Hank said. "This is all your fault."

"My fault?" Matt said, blinking back tears.

He turned around with his hands on the rifle, keeping the barrel down. All the men flinched back.

"How's it my fault, Hank?"

"Settle down, both of you," Dick said.

"It's your fucking fault," Hank said, emboldened by Matt's tears, by the numerical advantage, and frustrated by the appalling failure the night had become. "You and the fucking sheriff took that—"

The rifle came up and fired once, and Hank's hat flew off his head and up in the air. Matt pumped the rifle and shot the hat again, knocking it higher and farther away, before Hank had time to raise his hands to his head.

It was unnatural, that kind of speed and accuracy. It didn't seem to be skill, but rather prestidigitation, or luck. It was impossible to believe the weapon itself could be so accurate, at any speed, let alone one so quick, no matter who was wielding it.

"Fuck it," Matt said, walking after his startled horse. "Fuck all of it."

"Matt," Dick said, jogging up to him. "Come on now, Matt. We all want the same thing."

"No, we don't."

"Come on, stay with us, help us track this son of a bitch down."

"How's that been going for you so far, Deputy?" Matt said. "Fuck that degenerate and fuck the sheriff. And fuck all you too."

"Come on now," Dick said. "We could use you."

"Oh, I heard that before. And it led me to shooting one of my brothers to save the other."

Matt caught his shying horse by the bit and stepped into the stirrup and vaulted back up into the saddle. He turned south, away from Phoenix, and gave his horse a kick to set it in motion, but when it slowed from a disjointed lope back to a trot and then finally a walk, Matt didn't kick it again. After all, there wasn't any rush to go anywhere, anymore.

73

For someone who'd always seemed rather reserved, the confectioner certainly did love to talk, when you got to know him.

"I couldn't tell you precisely why it is that I love to kill children," Homer said in his musical voice. "I suppose none of us know why we really like anything. Why do you like beer, or chocolate, or music? You just do. If someone asks why, you can make up a reason. But it's as mysterious to you as it is to anyone else."

They were already at the foot of the San Tan Mountain. It loomed over them, craggy and indifferent, as the horses carefully picked their way through the scrub and the cacti. The moon was beaming down with its very white, very pale light, making everything clear and distinct and colorless.

"Do you know why you do the things you do?" Homer asked Tom, glancing over his shoulder to the horse he was pulling behind him. "Do you really? You told a nice story to Bobby, didn't you? About bummers and the Klan and your dead brother. But are you really sure that's where the feeling came from? Or did you just do what felt right?"

Tom, of course, didn't answer. He was thirsty and his head hurt terribly and he could not believe, simply could not believe, that this was happening.

There was the sound, very faint, of one gunshot, and then another. Homer started, his eyes glowing briefly with the moonlight.

"Hmm," Homer said. "I do believe they're still back at the road. I wonder what they're shooting at."

Tom turned his head the way they had come and wondered whether it was worth starting to holler. But they'd been riding for half an hour at least. No one would hear a thing.

His hands and feet were completely numb. The pain was beating in his head like a drum: *thump, thump, thump.*

"Why children, you might ask? Why not grown men? Wouldn't that pose more of a challenge? Wouldn't it be more satisfying? I'm a strong man, and I can use a gun as well as the next fellow. Not very sporting to murder children. All I can say is it's not about sport. It's about that . . . feeling."

The confectioner's voice became a little slower, dreamy.

"The weakness of children, their helplessness, well. It makes you shiver. I think it's because children can still feel just one thing at a time. Once you've grown old your feelings become complicated. But a child can be rendered perfectly happy by the present of something as simple as a licorice whip. And then she can be totally terrified. Completely and utterly. The feeling is so perfect."

Homer glanced back at Tom and their eyes met.

"I'm sure that I can get some sort of amusement out of you, Sheriff Favorite. That's why I'm keeping you around. But if it's any consolation to you, I doubt it will be very much."

Homer laughed, his weird face twisting with his stunted emotions, as they passed a narrow path that wound up the side of the mountain. He did not hear the Apache as they crept up. The first sound they made was when they shot Homer's horse.

74

The shots fired by the Apache carried across the desert: *crack, crack, crack.* The argument stopped, and Dick's head whipped to the east.

"He's heading to the mountains," he said.

Hank ran back to his horse, mounted it while it was shying away from him, and then wheeled it around.

"You sons of bitches can stand around and hold your dicks if you like," he said. "I'm going after them."

With a cry he spurred his horse and raced across the desert.

The rest of the men separated without speaking and hastened to their horses and rode east in a loose group, eyes straining in the darkness, hooves beating out a rapid rhythm over the dry ground as they swerved around cacti.

After about twenty minutes, when they were almost at the foot of the mountain, with its tall dry trees and enormous rocks, split and worn by the hammer of time, Hank yelled, "I see him! He's up ahead!"

Dick drew his pistol. In his heart he was calm. This was it. God would never allow a man who had done the things that Homer De Plessey had done to escape punishment. This was the proof.

He squinted in the darkness and he saw the man running ahead of them. Dick's eyes were not good, but he could tell something was wrong. The person running was too small to be Homer De Plessey, and Dick saw that it wasn't a man at all, but a young woman, an Indian.

The Apache began to shoot. The slopes of the mountain were all lit up with gunfire, blinding, deafening, the sound enormous in the empty and silent wasteland. The first blast blew three men from their horses. Others were left dying in the saddle, or wounded and knocked to the sand.

Dick hauled on his horse's mouth and took off toward the north, listening to the guns fire behind him, not thinking about anything except fleeing as fast as he could. In that moment he was no more intelligent than his horse. Puffs of breath escaped his mouth with little terrified noises.

Just once he risked a glance over his shoulder and he saw a young man galloping after him on a roan pony, with long dark hair streaming out behind him, whooping and firing a pistol. At this sight, Dick began to scream and strike his horse with the reins. Before long he had lost his pursuers, but he kept fleeing as hard as his horse would bear, into the dark.

75

Homer wiped the sweat from his brow with the back of his hand and looked down the slope, back the way they'd come, with the rolling eyes of a spooked horse. The path was steep and narrow, cut between boulders and jagged rocks, almost like a dried riverbed. Pebbles bounced downward in a noisy but gentle avalanche. He had been keeping up a running fight with the Apache as they chased him up the mountain.

Below him he heard the Apache firing their weapons at some new arrivals, but it was too dark to see anything, so Homer resumed his sprint up the path, half carrying and half dragging Tom. The sheriff's face was bruised and bloodied from being clipped against the rocks. All Tom could think was that he had to wait, wait patiently, for his moment to escape.

Eventually the shooting slowed, except for a few isolated pops. Every now and then someone would scream in pain, or one of the Indians would start to whoop and cry, sounding like any other wild thing of the desert, free and deadly.

The path ended in a little plateau, covered in short grass and dotted with large rocks. On one side of the clearing the mountain rose up, as sheer as a cathedral wall. On the other it dropped away steeply. There was no way out other than the way they'd come.

Homer grinned at Tom.

"Well, Sheriff," he said, "looks like we've found a place to make our stand."

The confectioner knelt down and wrapped his arms around a tremendous stone, almost a yard across, and he put his shoulder to it and strained and heaved, so that the tendons on his neck jumped out like the rigging on a ship in the wind, and rolled it to the mouth of the path. Ants and scorpions struggled madly in the spot where the rock had stood unmolested for generations. A rattlesnake gave off its warning buzz from a crevice.

Tom looked at the snake coiling and coiling over itself, the rattle dancing in the air, and thought of all the terrible things you uncovered once you had a mind to change things from the way they'd been.

Homer dropped two pistols and a bowie knife in the dust next to the rock and then pulled a handful of bullets from his pocket.

"How many do you think there were down there? Forty? Sixty?" Homer asked. "We're in a lot of trouble, Sheriff."

Homer stamped down on the rattlesnake, hard, so that its back broke and it thrashed wildly, kicking up sand. Then he grabbed Tom and dragged him over to the rock, leaving him a few feet from the collected weapons, so that Tom could just barely peek over the edge of the plateau.

Tom looked down upon the whole slope of the mountain. A crowd of Indians waited down in the desert, half hidden in the darkness. The shooting was over, but a lot of different voices were yelling in Apache, and he could hear movement, people and horses. Eventually the voices fell silent.

"Go away," Homer whispered. "Go on, get away. Don't come up here."

But after a short time the Apache began to let out war cries, one after another, long and high and almost mournful, and to fire their rifles into the air, and then they charged, one by one, up the path.

"No!" Homer shouted.

He raised the pistol and fired once, twice. The Indians fired back. Bullets whined overhead. Homer kept shooting, and eventually Tom heard an Indian scream.

The Apache melted back into the darkness. All was silent except for the faint sound of someone shouting in Apache. Exhorting, in a deep, hoarse voice, like the mountain itself was speaking to the Indians, driving them up to their deaths.

"Go back!" Homer yelled. "Go away!"

The Apache surged up again, while others fired from cover near the bottom of the mountain. Homer leaned over the top of the rock, but a bullet smashed near his head and he dived back with a squeal of terror.

And then he looked into Tom's eyes and grinned. He picked up the bowie knife and the blade winked in the moonlight.

"Well, Tom," he said. "I suppose it's time."

Tom watched the blade come down toward his back but didn't feel it cut. His hands and legs were suddenly loose, although numb, immobile, and agonized with the rush of blood.

"There's the pistol, Sheriff," Homer said. "Shoot whoever you like."

76

Dick saw the riders coming from the south and he pulled up his horse, planning to bolt. But the riders wore long dusters and proper hats, and so he turned his horse toward them, glancing once over his shoulder to make sure he was not being followed.

"Hey!" Dick cried. "Hey, over here!"

The riders were coming on at a leisurely lope. There were about twenty of them, armed with rifles and pistols.

"Hey!" Dick called.

The riders slowed to a trot and then a walk. They were streaked with dirt and mud, as if they'd been riding a long time, but none of them looked tired. One of them, a little man with fine features, called out to Dick.

"You, sir," he said, "have the air of a man who has just seen a large number of Indians."

"What?" Dick said. "Yeah! There's a whole pack of 'em back there. They shot up my party at the foot of the mountain."

"Dreadful," the little man said. "And you're the sole survivor?"

"I don't know," Dick said. "I guess I am."

"You see an old man with them?" another one of the riders asked. This one's skin was as pale as milk, and his eyes were golden, or so it seemed in the moonlight. He was not wearing a dusty greatcoat, like the others, nor did he have a beard. Instead he wore a linen suit that was surprisingly clean. There was even a withered desert rose in his lapel. "A little one, long gray hair, looks almost like a squaw."

"No," Dick said. "I didn't see any of 'em too closely. Look, I'm not sure there's enough of you boys, there looked to have been—"

And the pale man drew his pistol, slapped its hammer with the palm of his hand, and pulled the trigger, all in one smooth motion. Dick's head blew apart and he fell to the desert as his horse bolted riderless to the east.

One of the riders laughed, a deep, devilish, moronic sound, and then they spurred their horses and rode on.

To the east the sky was lightening with the dawn.

77

Tom slapped his nerveless hand down on the pistol and dragged it toward him. His first thought, his first overwhelming desire, was to blow Homer's head off. But he could not immediately move his stiff fingers, and so he had time to think.

The Indians were rushing up at them. They were divided into two groups, a pack of young men charging and firing wildly, and a group of older men farther back, crouching behind the rocks, firing at Homer's position in order to provide cover.

There were so many of them. There could be no doubt that if they got up here Tom would be killed. He felt better with the gun in his hand.

Three young men had broken away from the pack and were closing on the rock. Homer, cursing, was reloading his pistol with shaky hands.

Tom leaned around the rock and fired one, two, three times. The first two bullets each knocked down an Indian. The third one whistled overhead. The charge was broken and the Indians stumbled backward, knocking into the men behind them.

A bullet kicked up the dirt inches in front of Tom's face and filled his eyes with sand. He took shelter behind the rock and found himself next to the confectioner.

Homer grinned and said nothing. Which was wise. If Tom had heard his voice he wouldn't have been able to keep from shooting him. Instead Homer popped over the top of the rock and squeezed off a few shots. Then he sank back down.

"How many bullets do we have left?" Homer asked. "They're under you."

Tom put his free hand underneath himself and swept up a handful of bullets. Homer took two and cracked his pistol and reloaded and snapped it shut and glanced over his shoulder down the path again.

"God damn," Homer said. "They're coming again. Cover me, and I'll get them."

Tom rolled away, flat on his belly, and aimed the pistol down the side of the mountain. Bullets whined past on all sides. One buzzed by his shoulder and he felt a sharp pain. He took his time and aimed carefully and squeezed off a couple of shots at the Apache providing the covering fire. One of them struck home and a man stumbled back from the rocks and fell down, bleeding, while the women screamed.

Homer came back over the top and started blasting, and once again the charge was broken and the Indians retreated back to relative safety.

"Die, you savages!" Homer howled. "Die!"

Both men reloaded.

"Are there any more bullets under you?" Homer asked.

Tom arched his back and felt underneath him. Homer put his hand down as well and their fingers touched. Tom jerked away and in so doing came out from behind the cover of the stone. Instantly he felt a pain across his forehead and a moment later heard the sound of the bullet. He fell back on Homer's arm.

"Fuck off, get away from me," Tom cried.

"Where are the bullets?" Homer said. "I thought there were more!"

"Well, you thought wrong," Tom said.

"I don't understand," Homer said. "Why don't they leave us alone? Why do they keep trying to get up here? Who do they think we are? What do they think we have?"

Tom was bleeding from two bullet wounds and his legs and arms still felt as if they were being jabbed with needles. His heart was racing and he was out of breath and he hadn't taken the time to stop and ask himself this question. Why *were* the Apache charging up this path, again and again, at people they had never met before?

"They don't care about us," Tom realized. "They're just trying to get up here."

"Why are they trying to get up here?" Homer said. "There's nothing up here at all."

Then they heard the shooting from below.

78

The riders had dismounted a mile off and snuck through the cacti and underbrush, silent and invisible. They came upon the sentries and killed them quietly. And then they were among the sick and the elderly and the young, with their bloody knives out, and those misfortunate souls began to scream and scatter. The riders killed all they could before the bullets began raining down on them. Then they sheathed their knives and took shelter and began to return fire.

"Don't let that red whoreson give us the slip!" the pale rider bellowed. "I ain't going back to Sonora empty-handed again."

The riders were outnumbered but they were hard men, veterans of a thousand gunfights, and they had surprised the Apache, who had sheltered themselves from gunfire from above, not from below. It was not long before the riders slaughtered their way to the path leading up to the plateau and the Apache were trapped.

Homer put his head over the rock. "Rescuers!" he cried. "We're saved!"

Homer pointed his gun at Tom, but Tom was faster. He caught Homer's arm and twisted it into the rock and then bashed his pistol into Homer's face. Homer cried out and struggled, and he was very strong, bucking like a horse, but Tom had him pressed up hard where there was no room to work and kneed him in the body and then finally knocked him to the ground with a heavy blow to the back of his head. Homer's grip on the pistol relaxed and Tom jerked it away and stood.

The riders were making rapid progress up the path. Most of the Apache were dead but a few were desperately fleeing upward toward the plateau. Tom glanced down at Homer, saw that he was curled into a ball and clutching the back of his head, and trained his weapons upon the Apache.

"So close," he whispered to himself, "just do this, and you can set this as right as it can get."

Five Apache were coming up the hill, five survivors out of how many? Fifty? Sixty? Three were young men. The fourth was middle-aged, big and powerful, with broad shoulders, but limping and bleeding. The fifth was a little old man, with gray-black hair cut to about his shoulders, and a wizened, humorless face, as if he'd bitten into something sour. They were all firing at Tom.

Tom shot the three young men quickly, aiming and firing one pistol after another. The big one was shot from behind and dropped on his face without a sound. That left only the old man, who dropped his rifle. Tom didn't shoot him, thinking he was surrendering, thinking that was odd, because there was something about the old man's face that gave you the feeling he wasn't the surrendering type.

The old man dropped to his knees and dug his hands into the sand and threw two fistfuls up the path, shouting out something, loud and unafraid, in Apache.

For a brief, weird moment the little rocky path seemed to be filled with a sandstorm. Tom coughed as the particles got in his mouth, nose, and ears. He was blinded, and his ears seemed full of wind.

The old man barreled into him and knocked him flat on his back, so that his head struck the ground, then kicked the pistols out of his hands. Before Tom could even blink, before he could sneeze and get the sand out of his sinuses, the old man had run past him and jumped off the cliff.

As Tom sat up, coughing, another Indian sprinted past him to the edge of the cliff and raised his rifle and fired three times.

"You fucking shoot him, Billy," another man was bellowing as he charged up the path. "You shoot that cocksucker dead! You hear me?"

As the man ran past Tom their eyes met. The man was heavyset, with a stupid and cruel countenance. Tom could not escape the feeling that they had met somewhere before. The man had joined the Indian at the edge of the cliff. "Son of a bitch," he said.

"I'd say that I might have winged him," the Indian named Billy said. "Only, I didn't wing him."

"Son of a bitch! How the fuck did he get down there without breaking his fool neck?"

"He has his ways, Charlie," Bill said. "He has his ways."

Tom got to his feet and brushed the sand away from his face and mouth. A great deal of it had gone down his shirt. Bill looked even more familiar than this Charlie. And Tom could tell that Bill felt the same way about him. They both stared at each other, waiting for the spark of recognition to catch.

Billy, he thought. Bill. Why does that sound familiar?

And then all of a sudden he knew.

"Oh my god," Tom said.

He dropped to his knees and snatched up one of the revolvers and lifted it and fired.

The hammer came down with a click.

Empty.

Bill had raised his rifle and pointed it at Tom.

"Hello, Captain," Bill said. His voice was very sad. "Small world, ain't it?"

Tom looked down at the other pistol, calculated a second too long, and Charlie swept in and scooped it up.

"Do you recognize him, Billy?" Charlie said. "Damned but he looks familiar."

"Look closely," Bill Bread said.

Charlie's eyes widened and he began to bray with laughter.

"Captain Jackson!" he laughed. "Well I do declare! Fancy meeting you here."

"You've got me mistaken for someone else," Tom whispered. "My name's Tom Favorite."

"Right," Charlie said. "Whyn't you get over there with your friend, Captain. We've got a whole pack of people who'll be tickled to say hello."

Tom didn't move. He asked Bill, "He really jumped over the edge?"

Bill didn't reply. Charlie fired at Tom's feet.

"Get a fucking move on," he said.

Tom turned around. In the dawn light he could see a few of the riders were running after the scattered women and children at the bottom of the mountain. The others were expertly scalping the corpses of the fallen Apache, jerking on the hair, stabbing with their knives, carefully removing all the hair and both the ears, then dropping their gory trophies in burlap sacks that hung from their hips.

Charlie kicked Tom hard in the back of the knees and he stumbled.

"I thought I told you to get!" Charlie Empire snarled.

Charlie threw Tom in the dirt next to Homer and stood over them with his pistol.

"Hey, Quentin!" Charlie shouted down the hill. "Get on up here! There's someone who's looking to meet you."

"Who are these people, Sheriff?" Homer whispered.

Tom looked at the dirt.

"You ever hear people talk about Lukas Shakespeare in town?"

"Some. He was an outlaw, wasn't he?"

"Yeah."

Tom gave a deep shuddering sigh. He was shaking, trembling, like a newborn kitten in the cold. The riders were coming up the hill. The scalped corpses of the Apache looked naked, violated, harvested.

"Well," Tom continued. "These are the boys he used to run with. This is the Winter Family."

79

"My good captain," Quentin Ross said. "What a surprise to see you!"

Quentin wore a heavy oilskin greatcoat and a broad hat and idly twirled a silver revolver on his left index finger. The gun would spin, catching the faint daylight coming in from the east, then it would slap into Quentin's palm and stop. Then it would spin again. Spin, stop. Spin, stop.

Behind him, the riders were putting wads of chewing tobacco in their mouths, lighting pipes and cigars, taking swigs of whiskey, and regarding Tom and Homer, who were kneeling side by side, with varying degrees of interest. All of them were splattered with blood, except for Augustus Winter, who was dressed in a neat suit and leaning on a cane of polished wood.

The sacks of scalps rested at their feet with blood leaking through the burlap and soaking into the greedy earth.

Farther down the mountain, a few men were still reaping their murderous harvest. The faint sound of screaming, begging, and gunshots rose on the air.

Tom could feel Charlie Empire and Bill Bread lurking behind

him and he knew the killing blow could fall at any moment. Still, he kept his eyes on Quentin.

"It's a shame that our reunion has been sullied by the escape of our quarry," Quentin said. "But Geronimo's eluded better men than us. And although it represents a pecuniary loss to our company, I must admit I feel a strange sort of relief. I admire Geronimo. I feel a kinship with him. Just as we, in this company, turned our backs on civilization, so did he. I wish that things could be different, that history had not placed us on opposite sides. But so it has. And at least we won't be going back to Hermosillo completely empty-handed."

Quentin gestured at the bags of scalps.

"For that we have you to thank, Captain Jackson. If the Apache had dug in up here I don't have the faintest clue how we'd have dislodged them. And so, on behalf of our company, I'd like to extend to you our deepest gratitude."

A low, rumbling chuckle rose up from the men.

"Deepest," Quentin said, grinning.

"Well, think nothing of it," Homer piped up.

Quentin, who had given no sign of being aware of Homer's existence, turned his bright eyes upon him. And then he looked back at Tom and said, "May I ask the identity of your traveling companion?"

Tom didn't say anything. He didn't want to give them the satisfaction. Charlie grabbed him by the hair and jabbed the point of his knife into Tom's right ear. Tom said, "He's my prisoner."

"Your prisoner?" Quentin said.

"I'm the sheriff of Phoenix," Tom said.

"You?" Quentin said. "You?"

A few of the riders, the oldest ones, laughed again.

"I was falsely charged," Homer said. "I'm innocent."

"He's guilty as sin," Tom said.

"That's not true," Homer said. "That's not true. In fact, Sheriff Favorite was bringing me down to Tucson to save my life. The townspeople were going to lynch me without the benefit of a trial."

Johnny Empire threw back his massive head and bellowed. Dusty Kingsley slapped his knee. Charlie let go of Tom's hair and laughed as well. Quentin stood grinning, amazed, as if he could not quite believe what he was hearing. Of the riders Tom could see, only two were silent. Fred Johnson, who looked as if he would spit, and Winter, whose expression never changed.

"He was concerned you'd be lynched?" Quentin finally cried, to another gale of laughter. He turned around to face the riders. "No lynching in Phoenix while Tom Jackson is sheriff." And they laughed some more.

Tom looked at his hands. They were shaking. He had a very clear realization that he was now experiencing the worst moment of his life, that there had been some unexpected ruling in a trial he had never known was taking place, that he had been judged by God or the universe and found wanting. And He or it had shattered his dreams and dragged up his past and left him alone, here, on a mountain in the desert at dawn, not just to be killed but to be utterly destroyed.

"Very concerned with legal process, is our sheriff?" Quentin said to Homer. "Hmm?"

Homer looked like he had no idea what was going on or what he should say.

"Well," Homer began, "the sheriff spoke of his experiences and how they'd instilled in him the importance of the rule of law."

"Oh, I see," Quentin said.

"For instance, he'd been in Georgia during Sherman's March to the Sea."

"Indeed!" Quentin said. "As were we. And yet here we are. Isn't it fascinating how men can draw such diametrically opposed conclusions from common experiences?"

"And," Homer continued, "he'd witnessed the excesses of the Ku Klux Klan in Mississippi after the war."

"You fucking son of a bitch," Johnson said.

The riders laughed again.

"Indeed he did witness them," Quentin said, laughing, "from a very, how shall I say this, intimate point of view? His view of those excesses only slightly impeded by the white sheet draped over his own head."

He turned back to the riders, laughing wildly at his own joke, and they laughed too.

Tom could feel all their eyes on him as they laughed.

"My dear Mister . . . ," Quentin began, and then paused. "I don't believe I caught your name?"

"Homer De Plessey, at your service."

"Monsieur De Plessey, your sheriff was once a captain in the Confederate Army. After the defeat of the secessionist cause, he refused to lay down his arms. In those days, your sheriff was entirely unconcerned with due process and murdered those he considered to be carpetbaggers or scalawags. In particular, he harassed, threatened, and killed those Negroes who sought to exercise their newfound political freedoms."

Quentin accepted a silver flask from Dusty and took a drink and handed it back. Then he spoke again, keeping his amused eyes on Tom all the while.

"In his time, he killed dozens, perhaps hundreds of freedmen who sought to vote, to teach, to run for office. However, your sheriff was just a little bit ahead of his times. By 1877 the tide had turned and the Reconstruction came to an inglorious end. But in 1870? Too early, too early. We, as good Union veterans, were employed to put an end to your sheriff's insurrection. And put an end to it we did. His men were butchered from behind as they sought to burn a school for Negroes in Cotton Gin Port, Monroe County, Mississippi. The good captain himself escaped by a hair and was never seen again."

"Is he crying?" Johnny Empire shouted. "Look at him! He's crying!"

"Not long after the skirmish in Monroe County," Quentin continued, "our little company's relationship with the federal government deteriorated sharply. Our methods, while effective, were impolitic. We were forced to fend for ourselves. In subsequent years, we rode with former members of the Klan, and the White League, and the Red Shirts. Never with Captain Jackson, though. At the time I wondered whether he'd died. Seems he'd only had a change of heart."

"He's a hypocrite!" Homer cried. "He's a lying hypocrite!" Homer laughed, the sound of it out of tune, jangling. The riders fell silent. "He's a rotten hypocrite! Who is he to moralize about us? Who is he?"

Tom's head was sunk between his shoulders. The tears were

squeezing out from between his closed eyelids. His hands were dug into the dirt. He tried to tell himself he had nothing to be ashamed of before these men, that Homer was a lunatic and the Winter Family was a thousand times worse than he was. But he was seeing the faces of the ones he'd killed. At the time he'd barely noted their faces at all. Now he could remember every detail: the look in their eyes, that soft look, paralyzed by the horror of those last moments, the profound violation.

Of course he owed them something he couldn't repay. But he'd been trying. He'd been trying so hard. Everything had been for them. Maybe there was only one last thing he could do.

So he lifted his head and looked at Quentin and blinked back tears and said in his trembling voice, "Do your fucking worst, Ross. You go on and have your fun. I'll be judged, maybe for the worse, but not by you. It won't be by you."

"Oh," Quentin said, turning back to wink at his audience, grinning, before looking back to Tom and Homer. "Oh, I don't know about that. I think what we'll do is let each of you give us a little talk on why we should spare you and not the other. And then let one of you live."

At this there was a particular, knowing shout of laughter from the riders.

"What?" Fred Johnson said.

"Oh come now," Quentin said to Johnson. "Let's give them a sporting chance." And he winked again.

Homer was up on his knees with his hands held forward, as if he were praying, with an idiotic look of hope on his face.

"The sheriff and his prisoner," Quentin said. "The lawman and the criminal! Who deserves to live, and who to die? Please be assured that although we are outlaws ourselves we shall give you both a fair hearing. And then we will judge you, Captain Jackson. You and all your works. From Georgia to Mississippi to the Arizona Territory. The good and the bad. The good and the ill."

"This is bullshit," Johnson muttered. He looked at Winter. Winter was staring at Tom with a peculiar and violent intensity.

"Monsieur De Plessey," Quentin said, "why don't you get us started?"

80

Homer smiled broadly. His long black hair was slick with sweat and his nose and mouth were smeared with blood and he was covered in dirt and dust. He started to rise to his feet but Bill Bread hit him from behind and knocked him back to his knees. The smile on his face froze.

"Gentlemen," he said, loudly, but a little unsure. "I stand, or kneel, before you, an innocent man. An innocent man, falsely accused of a terrible crime."

Homer's gaze darted from face to face, looking for some flicker there, but he saw nothing. The smile on his face grew broader and he said again, "An innocent man."

One of the riders spat.

Homer looked down and his shoulders shuddered, heaved. When he looked up again his smile was fixed and unnatural, as if his lips were being pulled apart by wires, and he whispered, "I'm not innocent."

A few of the riders chuckled.

"I killed a little girl for no reason at all, other than I wanted to. I wanted to, with all my heart. It was all I could think about for days. When I finally had my chance, and I did it, it was as sweet a release as you can imagine. It was like my soul was singing. I did it. I did it. I did it!"

This last he screamed out, so the sound of his voice echoed through the hills. A number of the riders laughed. One shouted out, "Yeah!"

"Why? Why? I don't know why. All I know is that it would have been a profound betrayal of who I am if I had resisted that impulse because other men considered it wrong. Do you follow me? Do you understand? But what am I saying? Of course you do. Because you're like me. You are in revolt against the hypocrisy of civilization! You refuse to be bound by the rules of society when they conflict with your nature. You don't listen to what people say, do you? No! You do what you want to do. That is your only law. Isn't it? And how right you are. How right you are! For if I am a monster, is it not God who made me thus? The same God who made the lamb, the sun, this mountain, the sheriff? The scorpions and snakes? Am I not part of his plan? Am I not doing his will?"

Homer stopped and panted while the riders tittered. Someone fired a pistol into the air. Someone else threw a whiskey bottle against a rock.

"Hell yeah!" Johnny cried.

"And so, gentlemen, you should spare my life. You should kill him! Kill this rotten hypocrite, and spare me! And then we'll travel, together or separately, rejoicing in our dark natures, refusing to compromise who we are for anyone!"

Whistles and cheers. Quentin was grinning. He holstered his pistol and applauded.

"Bravo, bravo, Monsieur De Plessey. Powerfully done." He glanced over at Winter, who met his eyes briefly, and then they both looked at Tom.

"Captain Jackson. Your turn."

Tom blinked and wiped his eyes.

"I ain't saying shit," he said.

There was a displeased silence from the riders, and then Quentin spoke.

"Come now, Captain, that simply won't do," Quentin said. "Monsieur De Plessey has delivered an admirable speech in favor of antinomianism, with elements of Augustine and de Sade. Perhaps you could deliver a speech on the necessity of laws, of organized society. Locke or Hobbes. Your choice. Perhaps you could reflect on how men such as us and your former prisoner are dependent on the very laws we constantly violate. How we could not rationally universalize our maxims. These are only suggestions, mind you. Listen to your heart. But you simply must not deny us a little talk."

Tom looked to the east at the rising sun. He was exhausted. His wounds—from where he had been hit in the head, shot, tied, beaten—were throbbing. It had been a very long night.

"Lieutenant Ross," Tom said. "I gave plenty of those speeches yesterday. I'll be damned if I repeat myself for the likes of you and your pack of murderous lunatics."

"This is your life we are dealing with," Quentin said. He had drawn his pistol and was spinning it again.

"You folks already done made up your mind," Tom said.

"I told you, we'll give you a fair chance to plead your—"

"Not against me," Tom said. "Against him."

Quentin's eyebrows shot up and a surprised smile appeared on his lips. He looked like a boy who was halfway through opening his Christmas present and had suddenly realized what it was.

Tom looked Homer straight in the eye. The confectioner looked puzzled.

"On account of the color of his hair," Tom said.

Bill stepped forward, grabbed Homer's hair and jerked his head back, slit his throat and stabbed him in the heart.

How they roared, roared with laughter, delight. Whiskey was spit out, cigars dropped to the earth, men choked on tobacco juice. They'd all known the joke from the beginning, all of them. Quentin was holding his sides, tears pouring down his filthy bloodstained face. The other riders laughed just as hard. Foxglove fell to his knees. He had a hand clapped over his mouth and he was laughing through his hand. His eyes were dancing with laughter. Johnny's voice brayed out above them all. Even Johnson was laughing, a little. He was smiling and his shoulders were gently moving up and down as he watched Homer's body jerk and bleed.

Only Winter was impassive. He just kept looking at Tom, unsurprised and unamused, intent and alert.

Bill Bread knelt on Homer's back while the confectioner's feet twisted and hammered into the dirt. The scalping itself was deft and almost somehow humane, like an experienced butcher cutting the head off a chicken. The whole thing came off, ears and all, and Homer lay dead on the plateau. Tom tried to catch Bill's gaze, but Bill would not look him in the eye. Tom saw that Bill's hands were shaking very badly, and although it was cold, Bill was drenched in sweat.

"Ah ha ha ha," Quentin said, wiping his eyes. "Oh dear. Oh my."

He beamed at Tom.

"Well done, Captain. Of course we would kill Homer before we killed you. Our shared history aside, not even a Mexican would think your scalp came from an Indian. You saw through me! Well done, sir. I don't remember you being so clever. Are you getting wiser with—"

"You think you're different now?" Winter said.

It was amazing how they all fell silent, how they all quit chuckling and spitting and whispering to one another. And looked at Winter. Just looked. Tom hadn't really believed that Winter was their leader. Quentin Ross had developed quite a reputation during the war and the Reconstruction and Tom had always assumed that he was still running things, that the papers had built up Winter on account of his unusual appearance and his flair for the dramatic. But now he knew.

Winter tilted his head back and his eyes glittered underneath his hat.

"That's what you think?" Winter said. "You think you changed?"

Tom said nothing. Winter waited. The silence spun out. Tom remembered one particular night in Mississippi, when he'd burst into the home of a Negro politician with fifteen men, all of them disguised and carrying burning torches, and he couldn't meet Winter's gaze anymore; the pressure from those amber irises was just too much. He looked down at the ground.

"You're less than nothing," Winter said. He made a great show of checking his pocket watch. And then he said, "Quentin, quit playing with your fucking food. We might as well run around the other side of the mountain and see if we can pick up Geronimo's trail before we head back to Mexico."

Winter turned and made his way down the path. The other riders started to leave too. Quentin and Johnson glanced at each other. Quentin shrugged. Johnson spat.

"Maybe we'll see you later," Johnson said. "Sheriff."

"Wonderful to see you're doing well, Captain," Quentin said. *"Adiós."*

Charlie walked past Tom and followed the rest of the riders down the hill. The last to go was Bill, who slapped Homer's scalp on the dusty ground a few times to knock the blood away.

"So long, Captain," Bill said, still without looking Tom in the eye.

Tom lifted his head and watched them go, stepping over the corpses they had left behind, and a feeling grew in him, a powerful feeling that could not be denied. He had nothing to live for and the insult of having his life spared stung him to the quick. So he lumbered to his feet and walked to the edge of the plateau and screamed down.

"Hey, Winter!"

Winter didn't turn around, though several of the riders did.

"Augustus Winter, you look at me when I'm fucking talking to you!"

Johnny Empire laughed.

"What are you gonna do with those scalps, Winter? Eat them? Make 'em into a rug? Hang 'em on your wall? Huh? Or are you going to sell 'em to a civilized man?"

Winter kept walking.

"You think you're rebelling against civilization? You work for civilization, Winter! You think you learned something fancy in the war that regular folks don't know or can't bear to face and now you're at war with civilization? Is that what you think? Look around, you idiot! Does this look like fucking New York City to you?"

Winter stopped, leaned on his cane, and glanced up at Tom with interest.

"I got news for you. The war was civilization. That was it! You ain't fighting civilization, Winter! There's no civilization out here for you to fight. But it's coming. And it's a whole lot bigger and meaner than you, friend. And it's not going to have no use for you when it gets here. So you have a nice fucking ride down to—"

Johnson lifted his rifle to his shoulder and fired. Tom spun and dropped to the ground. There was a roaring sound in his head, like the withdrawing sea.

"Thank you!" Charlie exclaimed.

"I think I just clipped him," Johnson said.

"So fucking what," Charlie said. "The important thing's that he shut up."

"And him saying he wouldn't give us a speech," Dusty said.

"That was a wonderful talk!" Quentin said. "I was quite enjoying it. Although he had, I believe, gotten his main point across. I think Fred did him a favor by cutting him off. Brevity is a virtue. The Gettysburg Address was under three hundred words."

The Winter Family continued down the slope with their harvest. But Winter himself stood for a little while, looking up the mountain, leaning on his cane. The expression on his face maintained its characteristic intensity, but there was something different about it now, in a way that was difficult to explain.

81

Back in Phoenix, the antiquarian breakfasted in his hotel. All the talk in town was of the events of the previous night. None of the men who had set out for Tucson had yet returned and everyone was speculating about what might have happened. Whether or not the sheriff had done the right thing was the subject of lively debate. The antiquarian kept his thoughts to himself. When he had finished his breakfast and his coffee he gathered his equipment and a day's worth of provisions and headed to the ancient canals outside Phoenix. There he spent the day digging with a pickax and carefully sifting through the loose earth. He was so focused on his task that he did not notice the new arrival until he was on top of him.

"Goodness!" the antiquarian cried.

It was Sheriff Tom Favorite, shot in the shoulder, shot in the face, his left ear blown off, his face burned with powder, the back of his head sticky and bleeding from a heavy blow. He was splattered with blood and soaked with sweat and caked with mud.

"Water," Tom said, barely a whisper, and the antiquarian scrambled for his canteen. Tom drank deeply but carefully, not wanting to get sick, and then he collapsed into the shade, leaning his head against the earth wall of the canal and pressing his hand into his sunburned forehead.

"What happened to you, Sheriff?" the antiquarian asked.

"We ran into Geronimo," Tom said, his voice hoarse. "And then the Winter Family."

The antiquarian did not know how to reply. Tom drank again.

"We should get you back to the town right away," the antiquarian said.

"I am not in a hurry," Tom replied.

The antiquarian tried to meet Tom's gaze, but Tom's eyes were downcast.

"Sheriff, are you sure you're all right?"

"I will live," Tom said. "Can we talk about something else? How's your digging going?"

"I suppose it's fine."

"That's good."

It became clear Tom was not going to say anything and he was making no move to get up. The antiquarian spoke to fill the silence. "As I was telling you yesterday, this town is a site of great historical interest. That's why they called the city Phoenix. Rising from the ashes of whatever ancient civilizations made these canals."

Tom did not reply, so the antiquarian continued.

"The Indians called them the Hohokam, but that's just a made-up word. It means 'those who have gone' or 'all used up.' They lived here for almost a thousand years and they built this huge system of canals to irrigate the desert. There were tens of thousands of them, a tremendously developed culture. Something like the Aztecs down in Mexico."

Tom said, "You trying to figure out what happened to them?"

"Certainly," the antiquarian said. "It's an important question. The Hohokam lived here, as I said, for a thousand years. If we wish to avoid their fate, we must make sure we don't make the same mistakes they did, whatever they were. Was it war, or disease, or famine, or revolution?"

The antiquarian looked at the handful of trinkets he'd dug carefully out of the earth.

"We seem to need a dramatic explanation when something terrible happens. Perhaps we need to convince ourselves it couldn't happen to us. My own personal theory, Sheriff, is much more mundane. We are in a desert. People need water. I believe that this land grew so overpopulated the Hohokam couldn't support themselves. Perhaps there was a slight shift in climate or water levels. Perhaps they didn't allow the soil time to recover. In any case, once the process had begun, it was accelerated by societal tensions. Conflict and division. Eventually people just left."

The antiquarian's spectacles winked in the sun.

"Does it seem strange to you, Sheriff, that a civilization so great and ancient could be felled, not by its weakness, but by its own strength?"

And the sheriff said no. No, it didn't seem strange to him at all.

82

The Winter Family came upon a Quechan youth hunting in the desert a few miles to the north of the border with Mexico. He stood still in the desert as they approached, wearing a clean poncho, leaning on an elderly musket, and shading his eyes with his hand. Charlie dismounted swiftly and knocked the boy's weapon away. The young man was startled rather than angry, unable to conceive what was about to happen to him. They learned the location of his village and that there were twenty-seven people in it, along with a white man who had arrived the night before. Then Charlie stabbed the young man hard in the chest, three times, in a punching motion, while the Indian made a surprised and agonized gasping noise. Charlie jerked back on the Indian's hair and scalped him while he still breathed.

"Let's get them all," he said.

A new recruit to the Family, a Mexican named Francisco, expressed some doubt.

"That's a Quechan village. They're not Apache."

"You think those fuckers in Hermosillo can tell the difference?" Charlie said.

"We are close to the border," Francisco said. "We should get across."

"Come on, Auggie," Charlie said. "This is easy money."

Everyone looked at Winter, but something was different about him. It was not that he was unsure, but rather that he was uncaring.

"Auggie?" Charlie said.

Winter leaned back in the saddle and shrugged. He was slightly tanned from all the riding in the desert but otherwise his appearance was pristine.

"It doesn't matter," he said.

An uneasy feeling settled over them. They glanced at one another.

"Let's go," Francisco said.

"No," Quentin said. "Charlie's right. We'll make the detour. It won't take long. Use your knives. There is no need to waste powder or shot. Let's ride now."

Everyone looked to Winter, but he did not even nod. They were disturbed to see him following another man's lead.

The Family rode up hard on the little village and then dismounted. Some men stayed with the horses while the others crept through the scrub toward a few huts clustered around a well, together with a general store and some fenced-off pasture. An old woman pounding on a hanging carpet caught a glimpse of Johnny in the bush. She did not take any time to wonder who he was. She screamed, and the Winter Family sprinted toward her.

At first everything was chaos, as men and women and children ran back and forth, shrieking, while the Family chased them. Then there was the first gunshot.

"Who was that idiot?" Charlie shouted.

A white man had come out of one of the huts. He was tall and thin with red hair, wearing only a pair of trousers with his suspenders hanging down around his knees. A rifle dangled loosely, almost carelessly, in his fingers. But Francisco was lying dead on the ground, with the back of his head a gory mess.

"Who the fuck—" Charlie started, as he reached for his gun. And then he was shot, knocked onto his back and staring up into the sky with a peculiar heaviness in his chest. The bullet had cracked a rib.

The shirtless man's rifle moved from side to side with languid grace. He fired four more shots in four seconds, but there did not seem to be any hurry about it. *Bang. Bang. Bang. Bang.* Four men dropped, unerringly picked off amid all the fleeing Indians, before a single member of the Winter Family could draw a gun. Then the shirtless man grabbed a revolver from a corpse and fell back around a corner.

Charlie sat up, struggling to breathe. Johnny wrapped a thick arm around him and helped him to his feet. Dusty charged past them, his pistol at the ready, heading for the hut that was sheltering the shooter.

And then the shirtless man stepped back out into the road, his left palm hovering over the hammer of the revolver, and he recommenced to shoot.

"Oh!" Dusty cried, knocked back, holding his gut.

"Go, go, go!" Charlie wheezed at Johnny, and the two Empire brothers fled.

The shirtless man emptied his revolver with a kind of preternatural grace the veterans of the Winter Family had seen before. But whereas Lukas Shakespeare had always been exploding with passion, frantic and urgent with his need to kill, Matt was surgical and cold.

The Quechan, heartened by the sight of all the white corpses, were now fighting back. They used what guns they had and even those without guns, even the women and children, were charging forward with knives, axes, hoes, rakes, fists, and teeth. The Family fell back, an undignified retreat, firing their weapons and falling over themselves as they ran.

"Who the shit is that?" Augustus Winter said to Bill Bread. They had hung toward the back and were able to take shelter behind a bush when the shooting began. "He shoots like Lukas Shakespeare."

"It could be Lukas," Bill said. "Wasn't he in Arizona with his brothers?"

"He's too tall to be Lukas," Winter said.

Winter had his rifle out and was peeking through the branches. Matt Shakespeare had picked up a pistol and jammed it in the back of his pants and he had another rifle in his hands. Winter might have been able to shoot him then. But if he missed he would give away his position.

"Let's go," Winter said.

"Not a very profitable sojourn, was it?" Bill said as they jogged away.

"I don't know about that," Winter said. "We don't got to divide up the money into so many shares now."

"What do you think of what the captain said?" Bill asked.

"How do you mean?" Winter said.

"Do you think he's right, Winter?"

"About what?"

Bill thought at first that Winter was being uncharacteristically evasive. But that wasn't it. Winter wanted Bill to say it out loud.

"That when it comes down to it," Bill said, "everyone is just like you."

Winter's golden gaze met Bill's. And then he looked away.

Back in the Quechan village, Matt Shakespeare stood over Dusty Kingsley.

"Oh my god," Dusty said. "I'm going to die."

"Who the hell are you?" Matt said.

"Dusty Kingsley," Dusty said. "Oh my god."

"You're in the Winter Family," Matt said. "That was the god-damn Winter Family. I thought I recognized Charlie."

Dusty lifted his head from the dirt, looked at the blood welling through his fingers, and then leaned his head back and closed his eyes tightly and let out a groan.

"Can I have a drink of water?" Dusty said.

"You can have a bullet between the eyes," Matt said. "Why were you killing Indians?"

"There's a bounty on Apache scalps in Sonora."

"But these aren't Apache," Matt said.

Dusty groaned. Eventually, Matt understood.

"Oh you piece of shit," Matt said, disgusted, and fired his rifle into Dusty's brain. Around him the Indians were coming out of their shock, trembling with fear and weeping for their dead. Two of the men approached Matt, stunned and grateful and slightly awed. When the federal marshals and the Pinkertons, on the trail of the Winter Family, arrived in the village, Matt Shakespeare would be gone. But the Quechan would tell them all about him.

The Winter Family arrived at Hermosillo in the noontime heat, when the air itself seemed to ripple and melt. They made their way through the deserted streets to the Plaza Zaragoza, where they carried their bloody harvest into the State Government Palace, for which they were paid in Mexican gold: the heads of several of Geronimo's lieutenants, packed in salt and still recognizable, as well as scalps of around a hundred souls, including the scalp of a harmless Quechan youth, and of Homer De Plessey, originally of New Orleans, lately of Phoenix.

Every society has at its core an animating myth, a guiding narrative, a shared lens through which to view the world, but Augustus Winter had thought that he was different. That he alone among all men had the courage to face the truth of the world, to live according to the laws of nature, to follow the dictates of pure reason. That he alone gazed upon the face of God. And so it was a double disillusionment for him to discover that this belief itself had been his personal delusion.

When the Winter Family crossed back into the United States, after years of carousing in Mexico, spending their money and wearing out their welcome, they found it much changed. The words of Captain Jackson rang in Winter's ears when Sitting Bull surrendered and the forests melted away and the railroads wormed across the continent, connecting the clusters of men scattered through the wilderness. The new civilization grew like a crystal, as if guided by an invisible hand. Each acre of land was granted to a human owner, who shaped and developed it according to the formless but unrelenting pressure of economics and politics.

After another train robbery, the Pinkerton Detective Agency was engaged to track them down and they acquired a new enemy. It was not like in the old days. There were fewer places to hide and their pursuers were stronger, angrier, more determined. The Winter Family divided, some traveling south to Mexico, others north to Colorado, and still others east to Kansas and Missouri. It did nothing to ease the pressure. Everywhere they went had changed, and everywhere they went they were pursued by the most feared Pinkerton of them all, young and gangly as a colt: Matthew Shakespeare.

The West closed down around them, as fences went up and herds of cattle swarmed over the plains and the Indians vanished. News spread like lightning across the telegraph wires. The Winter Family regrouped; it was all they could do in the face of constant, relentless pressure from their enemy. All around them, pressing from all sides, the people, the people, the people. Soon the only free space left was the Indian Territory, and even that was slowly being subsumed into Oklahoma. The Winter Family was hiding there when it was finally approached by Colin O'Shea.

O'Shea was ten years old when he'd come to America to escape the potato famine. He fought in the War Between the States and used his money to buy land in Georgia that had been devastated by the March to the Sea. Then he spent fifteen years fighting Confederate veterans and the Ku Klux Klan to keep it. In the end, he prevailed.

He had a prosperous farm but it wasn't enough, and his ambitions were blocked in the Redeemed South, where former Confederates had bullied and intimidated their way back into power. In Oklahoma, the land was just opening up and they were practically giving it away. He sold his farm in Georgia for a substantial profit and went to Oklahoma at the head of a small company of men of all races. Instead of waiting for the land runs with the rest of the suckers he crossed into the territory and seized the best land for his own town, to be built according to his personal vision. Bitter men, men who were too slow or too timid, tried to challenge him through the Department of the Interior or otherwise. In the end they were all silenced.

O'Shea invested in the foundation of a town, and the arrival of new settlers drove up the price of land. He lent money to new arrivals or leased them land with an option to buy. He owned the bank and the general store and the post office. He was even in negotiations with the railroad companies.

There was more land, though. There always is. To the east, just across the border into Indian Territory, officially forbidden and out of reach, there was acreage that O'Shea needed to ensure that the railway ran through his town and not some other. However, the Indians who lived on it would not cooperate. O'Shea was not a man to be balked. He discreetly contacted his old friends, Union veterans, to find someone to help him get what he wanted. In 1889, he retained the Winter Family.

The Family's betrayal of him would have destroyed the town, had not Bill Bread, in turn, betrayed the Winter Family. The survivors scattered and fled, to seek refuge in a world that was now without refuge, for it had become too much like them. Winter himself melted into the wilderness, but the wilderness could not hide him much longer.

Oklahoma 1891

83

The sky seemed bigger over the plains. The snow buried jagged edges and hid distinctive features of the landscape, making everything uniform and clean. A bird circling high in the sky, a deer glancing over its shoulder and bounding away. On the earth there were the people. Everything else was gone.

Winter's life was simple, but precarious. If they did not find food they would die. There were no other complications, no politics or social hierarchies. Everyone had to be useful. Everyone put everything he had into the common; everyone took from it whatever he needed. The individual vanished but the people would live forever.

Winter was useful to the people. He could hunt, he could run for hours without tiring, he could make things with his hands, skin a deer, start a fire. He was, of course, a fearsome warrior. And in return he took all the good things in life: women, horses, food, and whiskey. Their language was the language of dreams, and when he sang their songs, it was as if he had sung them all his life.

There was no Winter any longer. He didn't exist. That monstrous ego, that endless hunger, the needs and jealousies and hates and loves, they were all gone. In their place there was not happiness but a healthy emptiness, something calm and pure that filled him as the sky filled up the vacant space on the horizon. Happiness, or what had passed for it, had been a part of the other Winter's life, in the moments of triumph, the pinnacles of ecstasy, and the sweet, numbed aftermath. That life was gone, and no new life had taken its place.

Men say that nature abhors a vacuum. But it is civilization that abhors a vacuum, that cannot bear tranquillity, and so it was civilization that eventually came rushing in.

84

Bill Bread lay flat in the snow and peered over the edge of the hill at the Indian camp about two hundred yards below. The fires flickered dimly through the lean-tos and the smoke was silhouetted against the darker sky. Even the dogs were sleeping. A few horses wandered pointlessly, feed bags strapped over their noses. Past the camp were the trees, and the hills. Other than the wind moving over the snow and his heartbeat thumping in his ears, it was silent.

After a few minutes Bill wormed away from the edge and crept back down the hill to the posse.

"Is he there?" O'Shea asked.

"You call that whispering?" Bill said.

"Well is he?"

"Yes sir."

"Did you see him?"

"No sir."

"Then how do you know?"

"I saw his horse," Bill said.

The men were gathered in a loose crowd, perhaps ten on foot, another six on horseback. A few might have dropped off or joined up since they left the saloon. They had all been drinking but only one or two of them were really drunk.

Not too late to just turn back, Bill thought. Not too late to just let sleeping dogs lie. But it isn't really about being early or late. It's about the way things are going to be, in their own good time, whatever you think about it one way or another.

"Shall I cut around?" the cavalry officer asked from his horse. "Circle around so he can't get to the trees?"

"I think so," Bill said. "We don't want him to slip away on us. He lives through tonight, he's going to kill us all."

"He's just a man," O'Shea said.

Bill looked at O'Shea. Bill Bread was unshaven with a ragged haircut and dressed in clothes that did not seem to fit him even though they did. Colin O'Shea was tall and fleshy and wore a new coat. The rifle in his hands was inlaid with silver.

"Yeah," Bill said. "But you all know what he did to the town two years ago. I rode with some hard fellows over the years, but not one of them held a candle to Augustus Winter. He's the most dangerous man I ever saw. We can't hesitate. Not for one minute. Because he won't. I can guarantee you that. And he won't stop. So we can't either. Once we go over that hill, there's no turning back."

O'Shea made an impatient gesture and the cavalry officer wheeled his horse around. "All the horses, follow me," he said.

Bill felt as if something terrible was going to happen. He knew that what he was about to do would shatter the peace that both he and Winter had found. But there was an inevitable logic to this moment: as tranquil as Winter's new life was, it had always been destined to conflict with his. So he ran up the hill through the snow that was almost up to his knees and swung his rifle into his hands.

One of the drunks let out a whoop and the Indians' dogs woke up and started to bark.

"God damn it," O'Shea said.

Bill sprinted like his life depended on it.

And of course Winter came out of the tent. Of course he did. No amount of whiskey in the world would allow Augustus Winter to sleep through a whoop like that, even out here under nothing but the stars, his past behind him, his self behind him, in a safe place.

"God damn it!" O'Shea shouted.

Bill went down on one knee and brought his rifle up to his shoulder and pulled the trigger. All in one smooth movement. *Crack*. Little flash of light in the darkness. Winter spun around and went down.

"Go!" O'Shea screamed as he charged past Bill. "Kill them all!"

Bill stood up, shaking the snow off his pants, and watched the horses come up on the camp, not from behind it, but from either side. He could feel how wrong it all was. He held his rifle over his head and waded through the deep snow until he came to the first lean-to.

There was screaming now, and the sound of more rifles. Flat and undramatic cracks and pops and people falling bleeding into the snow.

A big Indian came at him, holding a club, winding back for an enormously powerful blow. Bill struck out, straight and short, with the butt of his rifle, and hit him in the throat. The attacker's eyes came out of his head and his club slipped away as he fell to his knees. Bill kept going, the rifle up at his shoulder, and he came to the place where Winter had fallen. The snow was soaked with blood but there was no body.

"Where is he?" O'Shea roared.

The snow was all trampled down and there was blood everywhere but no tracks. Bill ran from the camp, the way Winter would have gone.

"Oh God," Bill said. "You've got to show me where he is. Please God. By everything holy."

And then there was the rumor of thunder in the air, the feeling that there was suddenly more space as the pressure dropped and lightning arced down. Bill saw the blood in the snow and he followed. After a few paces Winter's footsteps separated from the general confusion and became distinct.

"Oh Jesus, please," Bill said.

It was only necessary to look down at the snow from time to time. It was obvious where Winter was going. The trees.

"I need more," Bill said. "I need more lightning."

Instead the thunder retreated. Mocking him and all his endeavors. Like an indifferent god. No, not indifferent. A god of sand and war. The god of Winter.

Behind him the women were screaming and begging in the language of Bill Bread's ancestors. He kept running through the snow, holding his gun over his head so it wouldn't get wet. And finally he saw Winter, just for an instant. Naked white flesh framed by the darkness of the trees. Bill raised his rifle and fired, and then fired again.

Winter disappeared into the trees.

Bill watched the tree line. He smelled the gun smoke from his rifle and felt its heat in his hands. Saw his breath, white and frozen, in front of his face. Then he walked to the edge of the forest and peered into the gloom.

"Winter, it's Bill."

The wind soughed through the trees. Bare branches moving against the dark sky. The rustling of a thousand pine needles.

"Winter," Bill called. "It's me. You've got to come here quick before the others get here. I can give you my gun and a jacket. You can't get far. They winged you and I know you're naked as a jaybird. I know you don't have a gun. Winter, they'll track you. This is new snow and you're bleeding. You've got to trust me, Winter. It's your only chance."

The voice came from somewhere in the trees.

"I've been waiting on you, Bread."

It echoed and seemed to come from everywhere.

"I knew you would come! And when I get my hands on you . . ."

Bill guessed and fired. He must have guessed close because he heard Winter shout. Bill slung the rifle over his back, took the bowie knife from his belt, and sprinted. It was all wrong. Winter could be waiting behind any of these trees with a rock, a branch, his fists and teeth. All manner of things could happen now that they were in the woods.

"It's over, Winter," Bill shouted. "You can't run. You can't."

The trees thinned as they headed uphill. Bill could see Winter ahead, limping and bleeding into the snow, ducking and sprinting from tree to tree. It would take too long to get his rifle out again and so Bill just ran, his grip on the knife so tight that his nails were digging into his palm around it.

Winter saw Bill coming and ran faster, straighter. Even though he was the taller man and the snow was high he was hurt bad and out of breath and Bill was gaining on him.

When he came to the top of the hill Winter jumped off a rocky outcropping. Bill cut around to the left side, wary of Winter lunging out at him. But it wasn't a hill after all. It was a cliff. Winter had jumped into a river that rushed parallel to the cliff for about twenty feet and then turned and dropped away. Bill could see him bobbing and struggling in the freezing white water. He sheathed his bowie knife and took out the rifle again and squeezed off a quick couple of shots. Winter went under the surface and then he went around the corner and was gone.

Bill stood at the top of the cliff for a while, and then he started to tremble with cold and fear and regret and grief. It was so bad that he had to sit down. He closed his eyes and tears pressed out and when he tried to open them again they were frozen shut. After rubbing them open he made his way back to the massacre.

85

Winter's head broke the surface of the water and he bellowed like a bull that had been shot, a deep breathless sound. After the initial shock and agony of the freezing cold something started happening to time.

He was not moving. The water had stopped running and he was suspended in a moment that stretched backward and forward. His arms did not move like he told them to and he went under again and swallowed some water.

There was no pain. He felt as if he were floating. The only trouble was that it was rather difficult to breathe.

A bolt of lightning arced across the sky and he saw it, bright and shimmering, refracted through the river.

And then the devil woke up in Winter, the ego thing, and it wouldn't let him die. He struggled to the surface and breathed deep, exhaled, saw his own breath, the water freezing in his mustache and beard. Won't die. Won't die.

One arm forward and then the next, swimming with the current as his heart skipped unsteadily in his chest. No feeling in his hands or feet.

Will not die.

If they aren't there. If they moved the tent. Then I will.

No. It will be there. I am forcing the tent to be there, Winter thought as he swam, his breath moving through the ice around his mouth. It is there.

The muscles in his legs spasmed but there it was, the big tree, leaning out over the water. It was difficult to steer against the current but he tried to lift his arms out of the water to catch hold of a branch. They betrayed him, stiff and numb, and the current swept him past.

Winter flailed like a madman and turned toward the riverbank. His nerveless feet banged against the rocky bottom of the riverbed and then he was floundering to the shore, the water only to his waist and the wind scalding his upper body.

"Oh God!" he screamed. "Oh Jesus! Ah God."

Now he was in the woods, the snow and ice cutting his bare feet, his arms wrapped around his chest to keep some warmth in him. He stumbled and for a moment he was sure the tent was not there, he looked at the place where it was supposed to be, and it was just not there, but he kept moving forward like an automaton, and eventually he smelled the smoke and saw that the tent was only camouflaged by a layer of snow.

There was no time to find the entrance. Winter dropped to his hands and knees and crawled under the canvas and came up into the oppressive heat and stink. The contrast went to his head and he almost blacked out.

"Help me," he said in the language of the Cherokee. *"Help me."*

Joseph Bird was lying with his old wife at one end of the tent while his children slept at the other. All of them woke up and looked at Winter.

"The fire," Winter said, clenching his teeth so they didn't chatter, stumbling closer toward the fire on his dead hands and his knees. *"Build up the fire. Come close to me."*

"Winter?" Bird asked. *"What has happened?"*

"Come close to me," Winter said to Bird's wife. *"Get close to me, or I'll die."*

She was draping a blanket over him. Winter impatiently threw it away.

"Get down here you stupid hag," Winter said. *"Blankets will only keep the fire away."*

"Lie with him," Bird said. *"Do as he says. Gray, get more wood for the fire."*

The old woman leaned down reluctantly. Winter caught her wrist and pulled her to him.

"Ay ay ay! He's too cold!"

"Shut up," Winter said. He clutched her tight as if he would suck the heat right out of her in his overwhelming desire to live.

One of the boys threw more wood on the fire and it leapt up higher. A young girl lay down behind Winter and rubbed his extremities. He was shaking now, convulsing uncontrollably, but his golden eyes were fixed on the flames and never wavered, never weakened. He was going to live.

"*They killed them, Bird,*" Winter said.

"*They killed who?*"

"*All of them. All of the people.*"

"*Who killed them?*"

Winter shook and as the feeling came back into one of his hands he screamed.

"*Who killed them?*"

"*Men looking for me. They killed them all.*"

Bird's wife began to weep.

"*My sister,*" she wailed.

Bird stood naked next to the fire, fat and calm and almost hairless.

"*All of them?*"

"*They were looking for me.*"

"*Then why did they kill all of them?*"

All of a sudden Winter felt very sick, and he threw up. The old woman he was holding in his arms cried out and struggled free. It felt as if the tent were spinning, the ground rising and falling, everything changing place. Winter dug his fingers into the ground and stared into the fire.

"*For justice.*"

The heat was beating into Winter in waves. I won't die, he thought, but everything was moving around so much, and the pain was so overwhelming, he couldn't stay awake.

86

O'Shea and the other men on horseback rode ahead. Those left behind were mostly hands or the sons of farmers, all charged with the thrill at having fought and lived. They were laughing and talking and passing a bottle back and forth. They knew that Winter had gone naked into the river and they were sure he must be dead.

The sun rose behind them in the east, lighting up the snow, making everything glow.

The party kept losing men to the farms as they made their way to the town. Hearty farewells, waving. Toasts. Bill smiled but did not wave or speak. Just smiled.

The town O'Shea had built with his money was laid out neatly. One road ran straight north and south while the other ran from the west to east and ended a few miles outside of town in token deference to the sovereignty of the Indians. To the north lay a tall dark forest of pines, running next to the road for miles.

The buildings were all so new they smelled of sap. The bank, the general store, the law office. Churches, Methodist and Catholic. Bill lived on the west side of town, just south of the Methodist church.

A few years ago, when O'Shea had arrived with his troop of followers and his sacks of carpetbagger money, before the land runs had even officially begun, there had been nothing here. It was worth remembering. Men like O'Shea made something out of nothing, the same way that men like Winter turned something back into nothing at all. Whatever you thought of O'Shea, his way had to be better in the long run. But the contest between him and men like Winter was, to Bill's mind, still very much in doubt. Maybe it always would be.

Bill opened the door to his little house and then closed it behind him. He hung up his rifle and his knife, pulled his boots off with the jack, and then sat down at the kitchen table and rubbed his eyes. It was very close inside, but scrupulously clean. The windows were small and cloudy, so they only just let the light through. No decoration except for the plain cross over the woodstove. The tub sat in the middle of the kitchen.

Bill wanted to take a bath, but he was far too tired. Instead he went into the bedroom and lay down and slept. After he woke up, he began heating water over the stove for the bath when the knock came at the front door.

Outside O'Shea stood with his hat in his hand. Bill saw that it was snowing and said, "Jesus, don't it ever take a break."

"Hello, Bill," O'Shea said.

"Hello, Mister O'Shea."

"Come take a walk with me."

"All right."

Bill found his coat and followed O'Shea.

"I've got some boys checking the river," O'Shea said.

"That's good."

"They haven't found anything yet."

"Hmm."

"They did come across a hunting camp. Looks like some Indians stayed there the night before. They were gone, though. Snow covered the tracks."

The two of them walked across the muddy road toward the Methodist church. It was a good deal smaller than the Catholic one to the south, but well built. Solid.

"You ever seen a winter like this in Oklahoma?" Bill asked.

O'Shea shook his head.

"I don't suppose you think it means anything."

"Superstition brings bad luck," O'Shea said. "Don't you think Winter's got to be dead?"

Bill shrugged.

"How could he possibly survive getting shot and swimming in a freezing river?"

"I knew a man once that got knocked out by his brother. He woke up and laughed about it. That night he died in his sleep. His brother was near inconsolable. On the other hand I knew a man that had a piece of his head shot off. I mean it. Clean shot off. There was a trench in the man's head. He was fine. Only worried about how it looked. Wouldn't take off his hat indoors. Could Winter have lived? I ain't saying it's likely. He wouldn't have had much time after he hit the water. But if there was a camp somewhere along the river, he could have made it that far. If he got to a fire he could still be alive."

O'Shea rubbed his mustache with a thick index finger.

"There were a lot of times Augustus Winter ought to have died," Bill continued.

"The cavalry let us down," O'Shea said abruptly. "They were supposed to cut off the retreat. They just went in for the kill as soon as they heard the first shot, like they were worried there wouldn't be any left for them. I don't know what I was paying them for."

"Well, I guess they'll make sure the investigation doesn't work its way over to us."

"There's that, isn't there?"

Bill smiled apologetically.

"You don't think we should have gone after him," O'Shea said.

"Well," Bill said. "He wasn't hurting anyone anymore."

"Don't you think he should be brought to justice? For what he did to this town two years ago, if nothing else?"

Bill had the sense not to say that plenty of people ought to be brought to justice for what happened two years ago. Instead he said, "Well, yeah, in a perfect world. I just don't know that it was worth it. I'm not saying he doesn't deserve it. But just because he deserved it doesn't mean we had to go out there and do it to him."

"That's where you and I differ."

"I guess." And then, because Bill couldn't help himself: "And a whole bunch of land has opened up, on account of its previous occupants having died."

"Those weren't even proper Indians," O'Shea said. "You know that most of the Cherokee around here live on farms like civilized people. The Indians Winter was hiding with were nothing but trash."

Bill was getting cold. He thought of the water on his stove for the bath.

"If he lived," O'Shea said. "Then what?"

"If he's alive he's going to get the gang back together," Bill said.

"Do you know where they are?" O'Shea asked.

"Well," Bill said. "Quentin Ross is in federal custody."

"The others?" O'Shea asked.

Bill watched his breath freeze in front of his face. He finally said, "I've got a line on Johnson."

"The Negro?"

"I might be able to talk to him," Bill said.

"And if you can't?" O'Shea asked.

"Don't worry, Mister O'Shea," Bill said. "I'll always do what I've got to do. What about Quentin? If Winter's alive, he's going to try to spring him."

"What are we supposed to do, Bill? Tell the army that an angry gang is going to try to free Quentin, because we shot up a few dozen

Indians? Illegally?" O'Shea regarded Bill coldly. "You should think carefully about our position here. I mean yours and mine. Both of us stand to lose if any of those lunatics start talking about the past."

"Everyone already knows about me," Bill said.

O'Shea took this the wrong way.

"And you think you will just keep living in this town if I'm not here to protect you?" he shouted.

"Mister O'Shea, that's not what I mean. I know how much I owe you."

"Well, don't you forget it," O'Shea said. "I'm beginning to think it was a mistake not to simply bring in the Pinkertons. They handled the James-Younger Gang. Hell, this fellow Shakespeare seems to have killed most of the Winter Family by himself. But you're still a wanted man, and we both know what Shakespeare would do to you if he found you. I trusted that you could handle this!"

"I know, sir," Bill said. "No one is sorrier about this than me."

O'Shea mastered his emotions.

"People remember what Augustus Winter did two years ago. If they think he's coming back it would destroy this town. I won't let that happen. I've done too much. I've put too much of myself into this place to run from him. I won't let him win."

"All right, sir," Bill said.

"Take whatever you need. Men, horses, guns."

"Yes sir," Bill said. "I will."

"He's just a man," O'Shea said. "That's all he is."

"Yeah," Bill said. "That's it."

87

In southeast Colorado the snow was like an untamed thing. It seemed to fall sideways and it was harder, like ice. The town was small but its lights were blazing against the pitch and starless night. Bustling with miners and peddlers and gamblers and whores and thieves and preachers.

Winter's horse was breathing hard from plowing through the deep snow. Its thighs were covered with foam and its flanks were falling in and pressing out shallow and hard. Possibly it would die.

Winter himself did not look much better. He was still bundled in the Indian robes but now they were stained with dirt and ice.

The main street was frozen mud chopped up with hoofprints. Winter led his horse up to the boardwalk in front of the inn and dismounted. The animal stood miserably in the wind. Eventually it knelt down. Winter put his shoulder to the door and pushed it open.

Inside it was uncomfortably warm. An old man, dusty and disheveled, stood behind the counter. A few men were drinking and playing cards around a table. They were carrying guns and they didn't look drunk.

Winter walked up to the counter, his moccasins making no noise on the floorboards.

"Evening," the clerk said.

"I'm looking for two big fellas," Winter said. "Brothers."

"You mean the Empire brothers? You're a bounty hunter, you need to get in line."

"Yeah?"

The clerk motioned to the men drinking not ten yards away. Winter didn't look over at them. "A whole posse come up from Texas."

"Just waiting for them to get drunk, then, are they?"

The clerk looked at Winter, really looked at him. Winter was wearing a hat so the clerk couldn't see his hair, but now he took in his eyes.

"You ain't no bounty hunter," the clerk said.

"Keep your fucking voice down. And don't you look over there."

The clerk's eyes got wider and began to shimmer with tears.

"Mister Winter, I got a family."

"Fuck your family, needle-dick."

Winter never changed his tone of voice.

"Where are they at?" Winter asked.

"Whorehouse."

"Where?"

"Out the door. To your right. Three doors down. Red lamp in the window."

"Do I have to tell you what I'm gonna do if you make so much as a fucking peep?"

"No sir. No you don't."

"Now give me a room key," Winter said. "It don't matter which one. You got a back door, don't you?"

"Yes sir. We do. It's right on through the kitchen."

"Give me the key then."

The clerk turned to get the key and Winter glanced over at the bounty hunters around the table. One of them, a Mexican, lean as a whip, was watching. Winter looked down.

The clerk handed over the key with shaking hands. Winter took it and walked to the stairs at the back of the room. The men sitting at the table glanced up at him but turned back to their cards. Except for the Mexican, who eyed him steadily.

The foot of the stairs was right next to the door to the kitchen. Winter jogged up the stairs, making a fair bit of noise, carefully noting which steps creaked and which didn't. He looked at the number on his key and used it to unlock the door to his room and went inside.

Almost immediately he came back out and quickly and silently made his way down the stairs. The Mexican was talking to the clerk. The other men were watching them speak. No one noticed as Winter slipped through the door to the kitchen. He walked past an old woman frying tortillas and then went out the back door into the snow and the dark.

There was not much time. Winter jogged back to the main street and made his way past drunks swaying like sailors in a storm. A man was waiting outside the whorehouse. One of the bounty hunters.

"Maybe you want to move along, friend," the bounty hunter said. "There's another cathouse just round the way."

"There's going to be some trouble, huh?" Winter said.

"That's right."

"You mind if I get my friends out then?"

"Who are your friends?"

"The fuck do you think?"

The man moved for his gun. Winter let him get it out halfway and then seized the man's wrist and twisted the gun around and pulled the trigger. The sound was not very loud but the man screamed and dropped to his knees. Winter wrenched the gun out of the man's hand and put the barrel up against the man's forehead and fired again.

The madam was waiting just inside the front door. When she saw Winter she was at first puzzled, then horrified. She fell on her knees.

"I didn't know," she said. "They said you were dead."

"The fuck are my boys?"

"The piano room, Mister Winter, Jesus, you have to believe me—"

He hit her once across the mouth with the back of his right hand. The gesture was more bored than anything else. The girls lounging up along the walls and the few customers who remained watched with surprise. A fat whore recognized Winter and started to scream.

"Oh god," she screamed, "oh gaaaaaaaawwwwwd, no, no, oh god."

Winter went up the stairs as fast as he could and walked down the hallway until he came to the door from which the sounds of Charlie banging away on the piano and Johnny bellowing his dumb ox laughter spilled out. That door he opened.

They were both naked of course. The Empire brothers never needed much excuse to take their clothes off. Charlie was sitting at the piano. Johnny was lying on his back on the bed with a bottle of something in his hand and his pants around his ankles, laughing insanely at nothing. The two girls, young, were huddled bruised and weeping in the corner.

"Get the fuck out of here," he said to the women.

The Empire brothers reacted like dogs to the sound of his voice.

"Auggie?" Johnny said.

"Jesus, Winter, is that you?" Charlie said, his fingers dead against the piano keys.

"Get your fucking guns, you fat idiots," Winter said. "The law's on us."

And then to the women: "Didn't I tell you fucking bitches to clear out?"

They went, protecting their throats with their hands, forearms over their naked tiny breasts. Mottled dark blue and yellow around their thighs.

Johnny was pulling up his pants, but Charlie hadn't moved. He was still staring at Winter.

"Jesus," Charlie said. "Look at you. What happened to our dandy?

Look at you. You look like a . . . like a . . . I don't know what you look like. Where have you been? What the fuck happened to your ears? What'd they do to you?"

"Frostbite," Winter said. Indeed, his ears had been mangled down to stumps. "Get dressed, Charlie."

Johnny was pulling his belt tight under his fat stomach. This involved sucking in and then letting it hang over. But Charlie just stood up naked and walked over to Winter, soft wonder spreading over his blunt features, the light from the oil lamps glinting off his bald head.

"Charlie, the fucking law is on us, there's a whole posse in the hotel waiting for you to drink yourself to sleep. They know I'm here. We got to get gone."

"Dandy," Charlie said. "Dandy."

He was grinning.

"It's okay now. It's okay. You're here now."

He wrapped his pale hairy arms around the unresisting Winter and gave him a tight hug. Johnny, now fully dressed, lumbered over grinning like an idiot and did the same.

Winter looked up over all that flesh, and if there had been anyone above him, he would have seen the unbearable rage and hate and sorrow etched in the lines around his eyes.

But when they went downstairs the brothel was deserted. So was the whole town. Whoever the Mexican bounty hunter was, he had been wise enough to see that something big was coming down the pike and to keep his men out of its path.

88

Bill Bread waited a long time at the end of the road that led through the trees to Johnson's farm. Of course there was no one who was more dangerous than Augustus Winter, no one who Bill had known anyway, but that was mostly because of Winter's luck. If you asked who was a better shot, a better boxer, better with a knife, well, that was Fred Johnson. Bill had often reflected that if Johnson had been a white man he might have accomplished just about anything he set his mind to. But since it had never been clear to Bill what was really in Johnson's mind, or his heart, he had always thought that it was probably better for everyone that Johnson had been born a Negro.

"Wait here for me," Bill told the other riders. Then he rode down the lane, passing a small wooden stable on his way to the house. A woman came out and stood on the porch. She had dark hair and eyes and she did not look happy.

"I need to talk to Johnson."

The woman made her hands into fists and then berated Bill in Italian. Bill waited on his horse as patiently as an equine statue until the woman looked behind Bill, toward the stable. Bill knew that Johnson was there before he heard the click of the rifle.

"Hello, Bill," Johnson said.

Bill looked over his shoulder. "Hello, Freddy."

Johnson had his rifle trained on him. But eventually he lowered it and poked the barrel through the snow and leaned on it. He had grown thin with age instead of fat. Ice glinted in his long beard and every time he exhaled a cloud of mist formed around his mouth.

"You're sober," Johnson said.

"Two years," Bill said.

Johnson snorted.

"It's true," Bill said.

"No it ain't," Johnson said. "Winter's back, ain't he?"

"I'm afraid so," Bill said.

"And he's pissed at you, ain't he?"

"Well," Bill said. "You know how the two of us left off. Since then, things have gone downhill."

"I reckon that'd sober you up right quick. Even you could keep dry for a few days or so when you really needed to."

"I'm telling you, Fred," Bill said. "Two years. I've been saved."

"You don't deserve to be saved," Johnson said.

Bill smiled. The pressure of this moment was writ clearly on his face, but when he smiled, he looked younger than he had in years.

"Well, that's what I thought," Bill said. "O'Shea took me into his house and hid me from the federals but it wasn't clear whether I was going to stay. O'Shea wanted me to. He thought I'd be useful, probably, but he was also grateful. I'd saved his grandson. The rest of the town, well, they weren't going to lynch me or nothing, I'd saved a lot of lives by turning on Winter. But they were a little suspicious of my conversion. So I was in O'Shea's house, and I was drinking. As you can imagine, O'Shea was livid. He didn't understand me. Kept saying I was going to throw away my chance over drink. Drink!"

Bill affected an Irish accent. Johnson did not smile.

"Of course I'd heard those kind of talks before."

"It's cold out here, Bread."

"Anyway," Bill continued. "I told him I didn't deserve to be saved. And then O'Shea's grandson laughed. He has this crazy laugh. Sounds like a goose getting fucked. Pardon my language. And then he said to me, the boy, he said, He who despises himself still esteems himself as he who despises."

"Did he make that up, or did he get it from somewhere?" Johnson said.

"I don't know," Bill said. "The boy went to a lot of different schools. Either way it got me thinking. You know, we killed a lot of people, so you could say that we stood in judgment on them. And we had no right to judge them. But before that, before all the sins I committed, what right did I have to stand in judgment of myself? To say that my life was of no worth? Of no import? That I had the right to throw it away? I always thought of myself as weak willed on account of how I couldn't quit drinking. But I started thinking how proud I was. How I thought I always knew best. How strong my will really was. It was just that my will was bent on drink."

"And so you found Jesus."

"O'Shea took me to the Catholic church. They wanted me to go to confession. It didn't take, so I went to the Methodist church. Tried to sit in the back. I was drunk. It was a woman preacher. Abolitionist. Carpetbagger, came down to Alabama in the Reconstruction, moved out west when things heated up. Anyway, she had no intention of letting me off easy. Called me up front. All of them staring at me. Then she started in about what a sinner I was, but how they were all sinners, every one of them. And all we had to do was ask for forgiveness. She asked me if I believed that. And I started to cry. It was a sad sight, Freddy. Me crying in that church. Stinking of whiskey. Crying, and saying no, I didn't think I could ever be forgiven. And she said I could. She said I had to believe it. But I didn't believe it. Of course I didn't. She said if I didn't believe it, I couldn't be saved. So I said, all right, I believe it."

"Did you mean it?" Johnson asked.

Bill waited a long time. A bird called from the trees. The wind swept over the crusted snow.

"I didn't not believe it," Bill said. "That's what it was like, for me to find Jesus. There wasn't no blinding light. I broke. I finally just gave up. I let go of my pride. I surrendered. I didn't ever find God. I just lost myself."

"And you ain't had a drink since then? They should write your story in a pamphlet."

"Well, count no man happy till he dies," Bill said. "My story ain't over yet. That's why I'm here."

Johnson spat into the snow. "You and me go back a long time, Bread. All the way back to the war. But I go back with Winter just as long. Do you honestly think, if I had to choose between the two of you, that I'd pick you over him?"

Bill smiled again, but this smile didn't make him look younger. This was the smile that Johnson remembered: sad and knowing. With an unpleasant jolt, Johnson realized that Bill had never believed that Johnson would join him. Instead Bread had kept him talking, out in the cold, so that his muscles got stiff.

Johnson went for his rifle but Bill was faster. He drew his pistol and slapped the hammer and the gun fired. Johnson bellowed and went down, but he pulled the trigger on his rifle and Bill's horse screamed and Bill was pitched to the ground. The frozen dirt knocked the wind out of him. He struggled to his feet, tried to breathe, and watched his men galloping toward him, past the stable.

"Boss . . ."

"I told you to stay on the road," Bill gasped. "He's behind you!"

And then Johnson came crashing out of the stable at a full gallop and charged up the road, back the way that Bill and the others had come. The horse must have been saddled and bridled, waiting. The hands shouted and turned in pursuit. Bill was left alone, struggling to breathe, bent over double in the snow while Johnson's woman screamed at him in a foreign tongue.

89

When he woke up on the day that he was going to die, Lieutenant Graves could feel some rumor, some tang hanging in the air. Something had been wrong for a while. A few days earlier three strange men arrived in town, tall young hands who looked a little unbolted, drinking every night till they were drunk but never causing any trouble. They were O'Shea's boys, it turned out.

Of course Graves had heard about the massacre in Indian Territory, where Augustus Winter was rumored to have been living. He knew this because Quentin Ross had told him several times.

"Something changed in him all the way back in eighty-one, in Mexico," Quentin had drawled. "Two years ago he left us for good. Shot up a whole town and turned his back on the civilized world to go live with the Indians. There was always something of the savage in him, even if they did call him a dandy. Perhaps it was the war. You know. The March to the Sea. Tecumseh Sherman was a civilized man. Very much so. Rational mind, like a diamond. But all that burning and looting, books and antiques and beautiful houses. If that's the kind of value we place on the fruits of our civilization, no wonder Winter joined the red men!"

Graves did not want to get out of bed, but of course he had to. He shaved himself carefully but quickly using a small silver mirror and a steaming tub of hot water, leaving his sideburns and his long mustache. Then he used the water to wash his face and his armpits, dressed, and walked out to face the day.

The sun was coming up, but it was weak and faint through the clouds. The temperature was close to freezing and the air felt pregnant, as if it would snow. He took the newly shoveled path to headquarters, where the prisoner was waiting in his cell.

"Good morning, Lieutenant," Sergeant Braun said as Graves stamped the snow off his boots.

"How's he been?" Graves asked.

"Quiet. He saves his smart talk for you."

The headquarters was spartan. A desk, a flag, a stove. The cell was in one corner. Two walls of wood and two of iron bars. A cot and a chamber pot. Quentin Ross sat on the cot and watched the lieutenant come in and the sergeant stand up.

"You shouldn't take it from him," Sergeant Braun said. He was older than Graves, hardened and professional, and he knew he had earned the right to speak his mind. "You listen to his shitmouth too much."

"He won't be our problem for much longer."

"Small favors. I'm going to the store. You want me to get you anything?"

"Coffee."

Graves had the can in his hand and it was almost empty.

"You'd run out less if you didn't give him any," Braun said.

"All right, Sergeant," Graves said. "All right."

Braun left. Graves filled the kettle with water from the barrel and put it on the woodstove.

"Did you sleep well?" Quentin asked, a hint of humor in his voice.

Graves didn't reply. He stood with his back to Ross and looked at the kettle. He thought that he didn't have to answer. Then he thought that maybe it was what Ross wanted, to make him uncomfortable, silent. Eventually he lied and said he'd slept well. The words came out sounding awkward, short and forced.

"The sleep of the just," Quentin said. "Quite right. Although I don't think it's the nature of the just to sleep easy. They're always wondering if they should have done more, or less. Hearing again before they sleep the things they've said through the day. Constantly torn by regret and worry. Wondering what might have been. Only true scoundrels never have second thoughts."

"Like you?" Graves said, turning a bit.

Quentin smiled.

Graves sat down at his desk and took up a newspaper he'd already read more than once.

"How long now?" Quentin asked.

"You know how long."

"I suppose my dreams of rescue are getting more and more unlikely by the hour."

"Hope dies last," Graves said.

"I don't suppose your superiors have given any more thought to my offer?"

The kettle was beginning to sing and Graves stood and began preparing the coffee.

"You mean to provide information about O'Shea?" Graves said. "About how he supposedly hired you to kill Indians before you and Winter shot up everyone in his town? Mister Ross, do you know the army still has a file on you from the Rebellion? And the first thing it says is how you repeatedly lied to your commanding officers, about even trivial things? If you'll pardon me for saying so, no one in uniform has given a good goddamn about anything you have to say since the war. And even if they did, nothing you could say about O'Shea would save you from what you've got coming."

The smile on Quentin's face did not budge.

"A shame," Quentin said. "It reminds me of the story of Alexander and the pirates. Surely you know it. Alexander the Great captures a famous pirate and demands to know how he can justify earning his living in such an immoral fashion. The pirate says, 'I rob a few ships and they call me a thief. You rob whole nations and they call you a king.'"

"Well," Graves said. "It's a nice speech. I imagine they fed the pirate to the sharks anyhow."

Quentin accepted a cup of coffee, still smiling that jagged smile.

"I do not remember," Quentin said.

90

A tall fence of uneven logs surrounded the fort. Sergeant Braun emerged from the gate and crossed the road, balancing carefully on a wooden plank set down on top of the mud. Outside the saloon Al was throwing buckets of water on the puke.

"Morning," Al said.

Braun lifted his cap and went into the general store next to the saloon. The clerk Sam smiled his simple smile from behind the counter.

"You got any coffee?" Braun asked.

"Yes sir," Sam said.

Braun saw the coffee on a shelf in the middle of the room with the sugar and the flour and went to pick it up.

"Got a telegram for you too," Sam said.

"For me?"

"For the lieutenant. Came in last night, right before closing. It's from some man named Bread. Don't know where he's from, but it must be pretty far south."

"Oh?" Braun asked, while debating whether to purchase some sugar. "How do you know that?"

"Because if he was from around here, he'd know that winter's been here for a long time."

"Hmm," Braun said. And then: "Excuse me?"

"It's what it says."

"What does it say?"

"Winter is coming."

The tin of coffee fell out of Braun's hands. He walked over to the counter.

"Give it here."

WINTER IS COMING STOP FRED JOHNSON COMING
SEPARATELY STOP I AM COMING WITH HELP STOP TAKE ALL
PRECAUTIONS STOP BILL BREAD

The sound of hoofbeats came through the front door. Braun looked up from the telegram. A black man trotted past the door on the back of a foam-splattered horse. The man and horse both looked exhausted.

Braun realized that he did not have his rifle.

"Sam, give me your gun."

"What?" Sam asked.

"Give me your fucking gun!"

Outside, Johnson slid off the horse's back and went up to his ankles in the freezing mud. He was breathing heavily and blood was encrusted all over his shoulder.

Sam came up from under the counter with the shotgun and handed it to Braun, who was out the door in an instant.

"Don't you fucking move, boy!" Braun said. "I mean it!"

"Sergeant!" Sam called from inside. "You forgot the ammunition! I don't keep it loaded!"

Johnson and Braun looked at each other, frozen in surprise. Then Johnson charged with his head lowered like a bull. Braun was a veteran of the Indian Wars and he struck with the butt of the shotgun, hard enough to crack a skull. Johnson did not avoid the blow; he tucked his head into his shoulders so it glanced off, taking scalp and hair with it. Then he dug his fingers into Braun's eye sockets. Braun let out a dismayed wail that sharpened into a shriek as they toppled over and Johnson got in deeper.

After it was over, Johnson stood, his hands darkened with blood, and picked up the shotgun. Sam fumbled along the back wall, tripping over his things, unable to take his eyes off the horror in front of his store.

"Where the fucking shells at, old man?" Johnson asked.

"Please . . ."

"I said where those fucking shells?"

"There's a box of them under the counter. Jesus, mister, don't hurt me."

Johnson swept everything off the counter with one muscular arm and then reached under it for the shells. The telegram briefly caught his eye as it fluttered to the floor. He broke the shotgun and fed two rounds into the breech and then snapped it shut.

"Get up against the wall," Johnson said. "Turn around."

"Don't hurt me," Sam said, sobbing and shaking. He put his hands up on the wall.

Johnson held the rifle by the barrel and swung the shotgun like a club and smashed the butt end of it into the back of Sam's head. The old man went face-first into the wall and then slid to the right, leaving a streak of blood behind.

Outside the sergeant was still screaming.

"I'm blind! He's here! The Negro from Winter's gang! They're coming! They're all coming!"

Johnson went outside.

"I'm blind!"

He gave the sergeant one barrel in the face. The recoil kicked the shotgun back in his arms.

Two tall men rushed out of the saloon to his left, each of them carrying a pistol, both of them shooting at him. They shot wildly and missed, even at the short range. Johnson leapt back into the general store.

One of the hands came up to the window and Johnson let loose with the other barrel. The buckshot shattered the glass and burrowed into the wood. The hand shouted and dived away.

Through the window Johnson could see soldiers appearing at the gate to the fort. They started shooting too, and Johnson retreated behind a shelf, taking the box of shells with him.

How many were there? Too many. Perhaps ten still in the fort, perhaps three or four in the saloon. How he hated this, the terrible fear, the physical exhaustion and pain. Living on the ragged, bleeding edge. In hindsight it appeared better than it was: simple and clear and exhilarating. When it was happening everything was muddled and uncertain and awful. Why had he done this for so long? He could not remember, and he hated Bill for making him do it again, for driving him back into the blood of things.

"Where are you, Winter?" Johnson said. "You always used to ride in at the last minute."

He tipped over the box of shells, loaded the shotgun, and stuffed the spares into the pocket of his overalls. Tins of chewing tobacco were within easy reach so he opened one and jammed a pinch between his lower lip and his gums. The taste of it numbed his mouth. Nothing to do but wait for them to try to get in here.

91

After the first gunshot, Quentin said, "Now you are down to twelve," and smiled one of his ghastly smiles.

Lieutenant Graves took his boots off his desk and ran out into the cold air. Two of the privates were at the main gate, firing their weapons outside. Graves couldn't tell whether anyone was shooting back.

"Hold your fire!" he shouted.

The other sergeant, a slender bespectacled man named O'Connor, ran over from the barracks. "What's going on?"

"Braun just went out to get some coffee," Graves said. "Is everyone else accounted for?"

"Corporal Shaw went out on patrol with Denton and Williams," O'Connor said. "If Braun is out there too, that leaves nine in the fort."

The privates had not stopped shooting. The lieutenant ran up next to one of them and shouted, "What's going on?"

"I don't know," he said. "There's a Negro in the post office and he's killed Braun."

"Killed him?"

"Yes sir," the private said. "Then O'Shea's boys came out of the saloon and started shooting at the Negro."

A shotgun blast tore into the wood next to the private's head. He flinched and swore.

"Come on out and get some," Johnson bellowed from across the road. "Come and get me!"

The other private climbed up a ladder. At the top, he shouted, "I can see them, Lieutenant!"

"You can see who?"

"Shaw and Denton and Williams. They're coming up the road fast!"

Graves drew his pistol and cocked it.

"Let me know when they're close," he said. "And then I'll lead the charge."

"Yes sir," O'Connor said.

Everything was perfectly silent. No gunshots, or voices, or even birdsong. And then the private at the top of the wall called, "Now!"

Graves bolted through the gate, firing his pistol at the store's shattered window. A flash and a bang came in response and Graves felt something rip into his knee like a swarm of angry bees. He shouted and fell.

O'Shea's two men were crouched under the window of the store. One of them reached up and blindly fired his pistol inside. The rest of the soldiers were sprinting across the road. The shotgun fired again and hit nothing.

"That's both barrels!" Graves shouted. "Get in there before he can reload!"

No one watched the approaching riders, assuming them to be soldiers by their uniforms, and so the Empire brothers got among them before anyone noticed.

"Yeehaw!" Johnny shouted in his moronic child's voice.

He had a Winchester rifle and he was firing and grinning. Charlie had a pistol in each hand. They were both guiding their horses with their knees and wearing the uniforms of murdered soldiers.

One of O'Shea's boys got inside the store, but Johnson knocked him outside with the butt of the shotgun. Then he put his back to the wall and broke open the gun and reloaded as fast as he could. The other hand came inside just as he snapped the shotgun shut. Johnson didn't have time to raise his gun; he just struck out with his tremendous head, old and gray, and smashed the young man in the nose and mouth. The hand fired his pistol into the ceiling.

Outside, Johnny shot like a man too stupid to have any doubts, taking his time as his horse danced around in a panic, pumping the lever and carefully drawing aim. Charlie was blasting everywhere and now he was singing: "In Dublin's fair city, where the girls are so pretty, I first set my eyes on sweet Molly Malone."

Someone shot Johnny's horse and it stumbled, screaming, pitching Johnny face-first into the mud. But then Johnson came out of the store, calm and collected, carefully taking everything into account. One barrel roared and then the other and two men tumbled over. Then he stepped down on the neck of the first of O'Shea's boys and swung the shotgun down like an ax and staved in the boy's skull.

The horse was still screaming and the sound was awful.

It was over now, pretty much. Those left alive were rolling around in the mud or trying to crawl away. One or two had fled. Charlie Empire dismounted and reloaded his pistols and Johnny reloaded his rifle. Then they walked among the survivors, finishing them off.

"God damn," Charlie said, "but it feels good to be back in uniform."

Lieutenant Graves was still alive. He stood up uneasily, his weight on his good leg.

Winter came up on his horse, wearing a corporal's uniform that was smeared with blood.

"Charlie," Winter said. "Get the key from the lieutenant and turn Quentin loose."

Charlie Empire walked over to the lieutenant and held out his hand. Graves didn't do anything, more shocked than defiant. Charlie struck out with his fist and hit the lieutenant in the side of his neck, knocking him over.

"Give me the fucking keys."

Graves felt around in his pocket and held them out. Charlie snatched them and walked into the fort.

Where is everyone? Graves thought. Where are they all?

"What the fuck are you doing here, Johnson?" Winter said.

"Bill Bread," Johnson replied.

"Where is he?"

"I don't know. He was right behind me with a posse. I'm a little surprised he's not here already. I guess he stopped to write a telegram."

Johnny laughed, a lunatic sound.

"Please," Graves said. He was horrified to find himself begging. "Please don't. You don't have to. You don't. I won't . . . I won't. Please."

Graves pulled himself up to his feet just as it began to snow. No blizzard, it was calm and tranquil, fat flakes coming down.

"Please. You don't have to do this, any of this."

Johnny laughed. Then he shot his horse. Pumped the lever and shot again. It finally stopped screaming. The lieutenant realized that it had been screaming all this time.

Winter looked at Graves from atop his horse. The uniform he was wearing fit him like a glove. Graves saw that he was unarmed.

"Please," Graves said.

He started to cry.

"Just don't. Just don't do it."

Behind him came the footsteps of Quentin and Charlie.

"Ah, Augustus," Quentin drawled, "you're a sight for sore eyes."

"I need a drink," Johnson said.

"Please," the lieutenant said.

He turned to look at Quentin.

"I gave you coffee," he said.

Then he looked back at Winter on his horse. Winter's face was impassive.

"Look into my eyes," Winter said.

"What?"

"Look into my eyes and tell me what you see."

"What?"

"What do you see?"

"I don't understand."

"Tell me what you see."

"I don't know what you want me to say."

"I want you to tell me what you see."

"Please," the lieutenant said, sniveling, snot coming out of his nose, "please don't do this."

"I want you to look into my eyes and tell me what you see."

"I don't see anything."

"Exactly."

Winter nodded and then glanced at Quentin.

After Winter and his gang rode out of town, the snow laid a blanket over the corpses.

92

The ride home was long and cold for Bill Bread, with the sight of the young lieutenant's broken body in the snow hanging before his eyes the whole way. The hands called to him in surprise when he rode past O'Shea's house. Bill was beyond caring. When he opened his door and saw the crucifix on the wall, he couldn't help himself. He said, "Why do you love him more than me? You always have."

He lay down on his bed but did not undress. It was less than half an hour before the knock.

Outside an elderly hand was waiting. "He wants to see you," he said.

"I'll bet," Bill said.

Colin O'Shea lived on an enormous farm. Mostly they grew corn, but they also had pigs, and O'Shea owned the distillery. The house was large but uninhabited save for O'Shea and a single servant. The gardens were mostly barren and the furniture was rudimentary.

O'Shea didn't like to spend his money on finery, and since his wife and daughter were both dead and buried (the daughter in childbirth, the wife of influenza) there was no one to push him in that direction.

O'Shea watched through the bay window of the study as Bill and the hand came up the laneway. When they got to the front door, Bill heard a distinctive laugh coming from upstairs, like the croaking of a young frog.

"Is the boy back from school?" Bill asked.

"Got thrown out of another one," the elderly hand said. "Now Mister O'Shea's trying to 'prentice him with the goddamn Pinkertons, if you can believe that."

At the word "Pinkertons," Bill's hand froze on the knob.

"Yeah," the hand said. "Shakespeare's here. He don't look nothing like he does in the papers."

The front door opened from inside, revealing O'Shea. "Why you didn't stop by as soon as you got back?"

"I was tired."

"Tired."

"Yes sir."

"So you didn't think you should tell me what happened?"

"I figured someone else would."

O'Shea shook his head.

"Is Matt Shakespeare here?" Bill asked.

O'Shea's gaze was steady and shameless. He said, "Come in, Bread."

It was a working room, not a library. Only a few books sat on a small shelf beneath the window, and they were works of history and economics, not literature. The rest of the room was dominated by shelves and shelves of paper, logs and accounts. A small desk was tucked in the back corner, and it was at this desk that Matt Shakespeare was eating his dinner. His long red hair was tucked a little behind his ears and he was unshaven. A pair of pistols sat on the desk in front of him. While he ate from a large plate of sweet potatoes and bacon, his eyes never left Bill. Something in that watchfulness, somehow lazy and wired tight at the same time, reminded Bill of Lukas.

"Hello, Bill," Matt said, as he wiped his mouth.

"You don't look like him," Bill said.

"We had different papas."

"You seem like him, though," Bill said. "I knew it when I saw you in Arizona. You have the same . . . I don't know what it is."

Matt pushed his plate away and put a cigarette in the corner of his mouth and lit it. The sweet odor of Indian hemp filled the room.

Bill glanced at O'Shea, who was uncharacteristically quiet, then turned back to Matt.

"What are you going to do to me?" Bill asked. "I know there's a bounty on me."

"Oh, we're all on the same side now," Matt said. "Mister O'Shea has seen to that. Been quite generous to the agency. And to myself. You ought to thank him for that, I suppose. The price on your head wasn't all that much, but it wasn't nothing either."

Bill shifted his weight from foot to foot and again he glanced at O'Shea.

"Of course, he also made sure that the investigation won't turn his way," Matt continued. "Ross did a lot of talking to the federals after he got picked up. About how Mister O'Shea hired the Winter Family to run off some troublesome Indians. Not that he'd be likely to be believed, but it helps tamp down the talk."

"Enough," O'Shea said. "Bill doesn't need to hear any of this. You two are supposed to be making a plan."

"True enough," Matt said, squinting his eyes through the smoke. "Winter's put together a gang of five now?"

"Yes sir," Bill said.

"The Empire brothers, Johnson, Ross, and himself?"

"Yes," Bill said.

Matt nodded. He sucked on of his cigarette, held his breath, and exhaled. "I don't imagine there's anyone else for him to pick up, do you?"

"No," Bill said. "That's all that's left of them."

"So the main thing is, where's he off to next?"

"Oh, they're coming here," Bill said.

"You think so?" Matt said.

"Where else does he have to go?"

"How about anywhere but here?" Matt said. "It'd be suicide to come around this way with only four men to back him up."

"Winter has done a lot of things that people could call suicidal and he's still here," Bill said. After a pause, he added, "But this time I think he knows it's the end. I can feel it too."

"Damn straight," O'Shea said.

"I guess the townsfolk know now?" Bill asked.

"The town has been alerted," O'Shea said.

"They didn't run after all?" Bill asked.

"No," O'Shea said with pride. "They didn't."

"Any other Pinkertons?" Bill asked.

"Just me," Matt said.

"Just you?"

"You want more of them here?" Matt said. "You're the outlaw. Not me."

"You ain't going to be enough," Bill said.

Matt raised an eyebrow.

"I've seen what you can do and I've seen what he can do," Bill said. "I'm telling you."

"Guess we'll see," Matt said, leaning back so that he was mostly hidden in shadow.

"Are you sure they're coming here?" O'Shea said. "That seems mad, even for them."

"I don't think you fully understand the situation," Bill said. "We had a bond like nothing you'll ever know. It was just us alone, outside everything. And I broke it. I chased him down and tried to kill him. They're coming back here for me. And you're not going to stop them, Shakespeare."

Matt looked like he was going to say something witty. Instead he asked O'Shea, "Mind if I talk to Mister Bread in private?"

"Why?" O'Shea asked.

"Well, that's private," Matt said.

O'Shea glowered at them a little but stomped out of the room.

"What have you got to say to me that you can't say in front of him?" Bill asked.

"Sit down, Bill," Matt said. "I ain't going to bite you."

Bill remained standing, lightly spinning his hat in his hands.

"I always heard you were a drinker, Bill Bread."

"I was."

"I guess people can change."

"They can," Bill said. "I know they usually don't. But they can."

"Hmm," Matt said.

"What do you want to talk about?" Bill said.

"Whether you changed or not," Matt said.

"Excuse me?"

"Well, you had the drop on Winter, he got loose. You had the drop on Johnson, he got loose. Now you come back talking all this doom and gloom."

"You wouldn't have said that if you'd been here two years ago," Bill said. "I saved this town. Winter was going to sow salt in the ruins of this place."

"Yeah," Matt said. "But you didn't kill him then, either. You lived happily enough not twenty miles from him. It's only now that O'Shea made you choose."

"I think you know why," Bill said.

"Do you?"

"You killed your brother, didn't you?"

"I did," Matt said.

"Why?"

"To save my other brother."

"I think you just didn't want to live like him."

"No," Matt said. "I could have lived like Lukas. I could have been like you, Bill Bread. Wouldn't have been no trouble at all. When Lukas showed up in Phoenix back in seventy-nine we made a go of it. It was wild back then, just wild, but me and Lukas carved out a place for ourselves. The two of us. The fastest guns in the Arizona Territory. But my little brother. Austin."

Matt shook his head and stared at nothing, his face slack with old grief.

"He'd just. You know. It's like if you tell someone to watch his breathing, to just think about his breathing, it gets all messed up. You know? All of a sudden you can't breathe, because now you're thinking about it."

Matt looked at Bill and Bill nodded.

"Around our place Austin could always hit the target and draw his gun quick and he could spin a pistol on his fingers and toss it in the air, and all that. Then we'd ride out and he'd make these mistakes, every time, forgetting to flip the safety off and missing by yards and getting himself shot. When we got back he'd be shaking. Crying out in his sleep. And Lukas wouldn't let him go his own way. Kept saying that Austin just needed more nerve. Like we had something that he didn't. But I wonder whether it wasn't the other way around. That we were missing something that Austin had. What do you think, Bill Bread?"

"I don't know," Bill said.

"Anyway," Matt said. "I didn't kill Lukas because I didn't want to live like him. I did it for Austin. He wasn't going to make it and I had to choose. I could go with Lukas, and Austin would die, or I could kill Lukas, and Austin would live. So I chose."

"Well," Bill said. "I chose too."

Matt sucked on the cigarette and then said, "After all this time? I'm skeptical, Bill."

"Then be skeptical," Bill said. "You'll see how they feel about me when they get here. They're going to answer all your questions for you."

"Hmm," Matt said, as he stubbed out his cigarette. "We'll see."

"You should have brought more men," Bill said.

"He's just a man," Matt said.

"Yeah," Bill said. "That's all."

93

The forest snaked north of town for miles. Sometimes it was so thin it was no more than a light veil between great white fields. Still it was there, long and unbroken, and it was through this bridge of darkness that the Winter Family came upon the town.

They stayed off the roads and so it took them five days and they had little to eat and drink. The snow was deep and their horses were exhausted and their legs were cut from the crust of ice on the top of the snow. When they finally came out of the forest up onto the road they looked like what they were: a bunch of middle-aged men who would soon be dead.

The Winter Family was, at that time, twenty-seven years old. It had ranged in size from five men to thirty and they had committed every abominable crime under the sun. But their world had steadily shrunk. All of that free land, untamed and wild, that had taken them in every time and hidden them and made them whole. It had melted away, leaving them to the mercy of their many enemies, exhausted and exposed and old. Until it came to this.

It was a clear day, very cold, and the sun was in the middle of the sky to the south. The five horses stood dully in the road. The men checked their weapons one by one.

"Well, boys," Quentin said, "once more unto the breach."

Johnson was crouched up over his horse's neck, almost doubled with pain. He didn't make a sound but it was clear his shoulder was hurting him badly. It had been difficult for him to sleep and he was moving slowly.

Every now and then one of them would be racked with a cough.

Winter leaned back in his saddle, comfortable and clear-eyed. In his hand was Noah Ross's pocket watch, which he had unearthed a few miles back, where he had buried it two years ago when he had left Time behind with all the other trappings of civilization. He remembered Noah's final words. He remembered the warning Captain Jackson had shouted at him on the slopes of the San Tan Mountain. And he watched the second hand move. All that movement just to go round and round. Never actually getting anywhere. Till it wound down and stopped. There was a lesson in it, but whether it was for him, O'Shea, or Bill, he couldn't say. Nor did he care. Parables had always been his father's specialty. He was long past them. The watch tumbled out of his fingers and vanished in the snow.

"Let's go get Bill," he said.

The Empire brothers whooped and spurred their horses to life. Winter's horse jumped to follow. Johnson came next and Quentin brought up the rear, not holding his reins. His rifle was out and he was steering with his knees.

A sentry sat on his horse in the middle of the road. When he saw the five of them galloping toward him at first he couldn't believe it. O'Shea's men were all over the roads and he didn't see how the Family could be here without anyone knowing. He scrambled trying to get the trumpet out of his saddlebag. They were coming so fast. So fast.

Charlie was ahead now, he was the better rider, and he had drawn his pistol, his thumb was on the hammer, and he was closing his left eye to aim. He fired and the bullet hit the sentry, who fell off of his horse.

They came into the town.

"Yeehaw!" Charlie said, leaning back in the saddle and drawing his other pistol.

"Fuck you all, fuck all y'all!" Johnny screamed, drawing his two pistols as well.

Quentin hunched forward and put his rifle to his shoulder and drew a bead on a man standing on the boards in front of the bank in the cold winter sunshine. Pulled the trigger and dropped the man from a hundred feet.

Winter rode in the middle of his men. He had not yet drawn a weapon.

A rush of people came out into the street, and suddenly the Winter Family was outnumbered. The mob was not shooting very well because they were afraid, taking shelter behind barrels and posts and windowsills, but the road quickly turned into a death trap.

"Shit!" Johnny cried, spurring his horse to the side of the road while firing both his pistols. The townspeople scattered. One dropped dead. Johnny dismounted to take cover behind the corner of the inn.

Someone was blowing a trumpet now.

Johnson was following Johnny when his horse was shot and he dropped down in the road. His rifle skittered away and then out of nowhere someone was right up on him, an ordinary-looking man who ran up from between two buildings with a pistol in his hand. Johnson rolled onto his back and produced the shotgun, now sawed off, and gave the man one barrel in the chest. But Johnson had been holding the shotgun in one hand, like a pistol, and the recoil broke his wrist.

"Fuck!" he cried.

Then they were on him, four men, two of them almost boys,

firing their guns again and again, bangs and little puffs of smoke, and holes kept appearing in his body, one after another, until he was crawling in the icy mud, going nowhere in particular. Then one hit him in the head and he stopped.

Quentin fired his rifle and pumped the lever and fired again. He hit two of the men around Johnson. One of them managed to get up and run halfway to cover before Quentin shot him again. Then a bullet whined by and punched a hole in Quentin's hat, and he ducked down and kicked his horse into the alley between the dry goods store and the bank on the right side of the street.

Charlie was on his feet now too, a pistol smoking in each hand, and he ran to where his brother was leaning against the wall of the inn.

"They're in here," Johnny said. "I think most of them are in here."

"You hurt?" Charlie asked.

"Naw. What's the boss doing?"

Winter remained alone in the middle of the street. He saw something to the west and turned his horse by grabbing the reins with his left hand. At the same time he drew his pistol from his holster with his right hand and shot.

"I do believe he's found Mister Bread," Charlie said.

A man leaned around the corner of the building and fired a shot and hit Charlie in the face. Johnny raised his gun and fired back while his brother screamed and bled.

Winter had seen Bread standing on the stoop of his little house with his Winchester rifle in his hands. By the time Bill had lifted it to his shoulder Winter had already drawn, fired, and hit. Bill's hand broke open and the wooden butt of his rifle splintered. Then Winter spurred his horse and he was on top of him.

Bill tried to turn and run back in the house but Winter jumped off his horse and landed on Bill's back, knocking him to the ground.

"No! No, Winter, don't!"

Winter put one boot on Bill's neck and stood up. Two men were riding at him from the west, and the mob was coming from the crossroads. Winter raised his gun and squinted to aim and then he started banging the hammer of his pistol and pulling the trigger. The two men on horseback dropped out of their saddles and their horses came to skidding stops. He only got one of the men to the east but the mob broke.

Bill reached up with his left hand, the one that hadn't been shot, trying to grab Winter's testicles. Winter caught Bill's wrist and twisted the arm so that his elbow was facing up. Then he put his leg over Bill's arm and sat down on Bill's elbow.

"No, Auggie, no, ahh!"

Bill screamed as the arm broke.

Back at the inn, Johnny went around the corner with a pistol in each hand. He kicked the door open and started shooting, using his thumbs to cock the hammers again and again. Seven men were inside. Bullets hummed and zipped through the air. Johnny was screaming. He got hit quite a few times and then he fell down to one side. He kept shooting as well as he could, calmly aiming one gun and shooting and then aiming the other and shooting it too. From his position in the corner of the room he managed to kill four and send the other three scrambling out the door, shooting over their shoulders blind and wild and afraid.

"Fuck all y'all!"

Outside Charlie was kneeling in the mud, touching his face. It felt foreign to him, numb and strange and gushing with blood. Teeth and a chunk of lip came away in his hands. He tried to stop the bleeding by tying his handkerchief around his chin.

On the other side of the street Quentin was grinning and jamming more rounds into his Winchester. Looking left and right and humming, thinking that they would consecrate this ground far above O'Shea's poor power to add or detract.

When Quentin was finished he jogged slowly between the two buildings, away from the main street, until he came out into a field. Two riders were approaching from the west. Quentin fell to one knee and fired a shot. The first rider tumbled out of his saddle.

Out of pure dumb luck, Quentin had shot one of O'Shea's hands instead of Matt Shakespeare.

While Quentin was pumping the lever of his rifle, Matt saw him, drew a pistol, and fired. The bullet caught Quentin right between the eyes and knocked him onto his back. He died instantly. The expression on his face was not surprised or dismayed or frightened or anything like that. He never heard the shot and never knew he was dead.

Matt rode on without stopping, shaking his head, his hands trembling only a little.

Not far away, Winter took a parcel from his horse and then kicked it so it ran off. He grabbed Bill by the hair and dragged him into the house. Since one of Bill's arms was broken at the elbow and the other had a bullet through the hand, he didn't put up much of a fight, just screamed and screamed.

"Are you different, Bill? Did you turn into one of them?"

"Don't do it, Winter, don't do it. Please don't do it."

Charlie had joined Johnny inside the inn. He was still trying to patch his face up with rags. The townsfolk were coming at the inn from all directions now. Charlie fired his pistols through a window and they scattered, but he knew they would be back.

"I'm hurt bad, Charlie," Johnny shouted. "They got me! It hurts real bad!"

"We gotta go, Johnny," Charlie grunted through his ruined mouth. "Get your ass out here."

Inside Bill's house, Winter dragged Bill into the kitchen and threw him into the bathtub.

"Don't, Winter! Don't do it!"

Winter was still holding Bill up by the hair and now he scalped him. Pulled so hard the skin on the top of Bill's head jumped up and then he peeled it right off. Bill screamed and then the muscles of his face relaxed like an old burlap sack, down in the corners of the mouth and the cheeks, and then the blood rushed into his eyes. Blood everywhere.

Winter threw him back in the tub and then shot him through both knees. One and then the other. Bony explosions, little echoes in the tub.

"Ahhh! Ah ha ha ha! Ahhhh! Stop! Stop it! Stop it!"

The gun was empty and Winter smashed it into Bill's face again and again. His own face was twisted with rage, insane and boundless. Winter was crying.

"Fuck you, Bill! Fuck you!"

"I didn't, I didn't do it! I didn't! Stop it."

Winter leaned back, splattered with blood and breathing hard, and closed his eyes.

Charlie and Johnny staggered out into the street, leaning on each other, both holding a gun. Shots came from every direction. The brothers moved quickly, even though they were limping and panting and squirting blood into the frozen mud of the streets.

"Which house is he in?" Johnny panted. "Which one?"

They got to the crossroads. A full posse coming from the west and another from the south. Meanwhile, there was another group in the north, some of whom were circling around to the east.

"Shit," Johnny said. "Fuck, Charlie! They got us!"

Charlie made a grunting noise and pulled his brother toward Bill's house, firing their pistols at the riders coming toward them.

Inside the house, Winter was stabbing Bill. Bill had stopped screaming and was only making little surprised noises and trying to get his hands in the way of the knife. Winter stopped stabbing and stood up and threw the knife away. They were both covered in blood.

"I'm sorry, Bill," Winter said. "I fucked everything up."

Winter swayed a little on his feet as if he were drunk and then he started to take off his clothes.

"It's the end of everything."

One layer of blood-soaked clothes and then another. Winter stood naked.

"Did you change, Bill? Did you change really?"

Winter wiped the blood off of his face and hands and arms as best he could. Some of it was coming off; some of it was just rubbing into his skin, making him look vaguely pink.

The Empire brothers burst in through the front door and slammed it shut behind them.

"Boss!" Johnny called. "We're surrounded, boss!"

Winter glanced at them and then shut the door to the kitchen.

"Auggie!" Johnny shouted. Gunfire began to slam into the walls of the house.

Winter opened the bundle he had brought with him and produced a straight razor with which he began to shave off his long beard.

"I looked at the world, and it was cruel, and I thought that God made it in his image and I thought if I was like Him then God would love me."

Outside O'Shea and Shakespeare were hidden safely behind the fence to the Methodist church.

"How the hell did they get the drop on us?" Matt said. "Do you have any idea how many are dead? It must be over twenty. Good lord. They even almost got me. I do believe poor old Bread was right about these folks. They're in a whole separate category."

"Is Winter in there?" O'Shea said hoarsely. "Are we sure?"

"That's what they said."

"Burn it down!" O'Shea said. "Just burn it down!"

"Bread is still in there," Matt said.

"He is dead. He is dead meat!" O'Shea sounded hysterical. "We have to burn it down!"

Inside Winter was hacking through his fine white beard.

"Do you know why they came after me?" Winter said. "It ain't about what's right, or they wouldn't have killed all the Indians. And it ain't about defending themselves, because I wasn't hurting no one. It ain't about costs and benefits either. They knew if I got loose what I'd do to them was worse than anything they'd get out of killing me. So it's justice. But then what's justice? It's men forcing themselves on the world. You see? I couldn't break the rules and escape. For their rules to be real they have to spread over every inch of the earth. There can't ever be one free space."

The Empire brothers were shooting out the windows.

"Auggie!" Johnny shouted. "We're bleeding pretty bad."

"In order for it to exist it cannot tolerate anything else. You can't be able to step outside of it. It has to be everywhere or else it will die. I thought I was like God, and I guess I was, compared to a civilized man. But I made a mistake. I looked at a civilized man on his own. You can only understand a civilized man as a part of something bigger. They make something when they're all taken together. You take a bunch of nice, civilized men, and put them all together, and you end up with something a lot like you and me. Just meaner. I ain't nothing like this thing they've got now. I never let up for a moment in my life but it wasn't enough. I'm just a man."

Bill shifted a little in the tub. He opened his mouth and blood came out.

Now Winter dressed quickly.

"People don't even really make this thing; it's this thing that makes people. It's as natural as a dream. It's meaner than me, Bill. And it's never going to die."

Winter was dressed. He looked at Bill in the tub.

"Be seeing you," he said, opening the door to the front room and walking out.

Johnny and Charlie were crouched down against opposite walls. When Johnny saw Winter, he smiled.

"Dandy!" Johnny cried. "Dandy man!"

Winter was clean shaven and his long hair was smoothed back on top of his head. He wore a suit with a string tie and leather boots. If he hadn't been missing his ears he would have looked exactly as he had done ten years ago when he had terrorized the west as the Dandy Killer.

Winter held up the pistol and looked at the front door.

"Okay," he said.

In the tub Bill felt a pleasant warmth move through his body, despite the occasional bolt of pain. He shifted a very little from side to side. Small movements. Gentle. He leaned his head back and looked at the crucifix on the wall, and he was hit with a heavy, almost physical feeling of pity for Augustus Winter.

After Bill's house burned down to the embers, and after the embers cooled, Matt Shakespeare strode carefully through the ashes, poking in front of him with the barrel of his rifle to check for traps and holes. Nothing remained of the Winter Family except for a few fragments of bone, charred into formless nubs. And still less remained of the life Bill had tried to build in the past two years. Not a splinter or stitch survived.

Matt Shakespeare kicked the ashes off his feet and rode off, and the people in O'Shea's town were left to grieve and bury their dead, their only consolation that the long and dark and murderous career of the Winter Family had finally been brought to an end, its memory fading like charnel smoke, its last chapter written, except of course for this.

Epilogue:
California 1900

The sun beat down from the cloudless sky. The house was a little bungalow, painted yellow, flat and boxlike and unremarkable, except for the bullet holes in the walls. The detectives crouched against the picket fence were sweating and bored. Inside the house the outlaws shouted, but it was impossible to make out what they were saying. Signal Hill was clearly visible about a mile to the east, bristling with oil derricks like a giant porcupine.

A rider approached, coming down the dusty street at a steady trot. At first he appeared vague and indistinct, almost like a mirage. Then he came into focus, a tall man, middle-aged, with long red hair that was going orange with gray. No mustache and three days' worth of beard. A pistol on each hip.

When the rider got close he drew a pistol, so quickly his hand was a blur, and fired three quick shots toward the house. There was the sound of breaking glass and a scream of pain. The rider dismounted and bent double and hurried over to the fence to speak to the lead agent.

"Is there a burned man in there?" the rider asked.

"I don't know," the lead agent said. "I know that Collins and Randolph are in there."

"What about the burned one?" the rider asked. "They said there was a burned man with them at the bank."

"I don't know, Mister Shakespeare," the lead agent said, a little impatiently. "I know that Collins and Randolph are in there and I know they killed Chas Schumacher. I'm sorry if that ain't enough for you."

"Fine," Matt said. "Let's get this over with."

He cocked his pistol and held it up next to his head and quickly peeked over the top of the fence. Satisfied, he stood up.

"Shout at them," Matt said.

"What's the plan?" the lead agent asked.

Matt laughed, and it made him look much younger. Then he stalked through the gate and down the path to the front door.

"For the last time," the lead agent shouted. "We've got you surrounded. Give yourself up right now!"

The lead agent risked a peek at the house. No one was at either of the windows. Matt Shakespeare had drawn his second pistol and was holding one in each hand, up high next to his ears, with his thumbs on the hammers.

"Any man that gives himself up won't be harmed, you've got my word on that!" the lead agent shouted.

"I said fuck you, you scab fuck!" one of the outlaws screamed, sounding furious. "You can go straight to . . ."

Matt lifted his knee to his chest and kicked the door and it slammed open and he barged inside. The door banged shut behind him. There was an explosion of gunfire, perhaps eight shots in two seconds, then silence, and then another shot.

Someone wailed in pain.

"You shot me!" the person shrieked.

"Put it down!" Matt thundered. "Don't touch it!"

"You shot me!" the person cried again. "Oh my god!"

The Pinkerton agents hurried to the front door and carefully pushed it open.

Inside Matt Shakespeare kicked a rifle away from Randolph, who sat on the ground with his back against the wall and his hands pressed up against the side of his chest.

"Oh my god," Randolph said. "Oh god. It hurts so bad. You've killed me."

On the other side of the room George Collins lay facedown, his head blown apart, blood and bits of bone and other organic matter in a pool around him.

"Ah ha ha ha," Randolph panted. "Oh my god. Oh my god."

"Jumping Jesus," the lead agent said. "You really are a terror, Shakespeare."

Matt holstered his pistols, one at a time.

"I'm going to die," Randolph said. "You shot me."

"You hang on," Matt said. "We've got a doctor coming for you. You ain't hit so bad."

"Don't lie to me," Randolph sobbed. "Don't you lie to me. I'm going to die. I'm going to die."

More agents trooped into the house, their weapons still drawn.

"Fine," Matt said. "I guess you're gonna die."

"Oh no," Randolph cried. "Oh my god. This can't be happening."

"It's all right," Matt said.

"I'm so thirsty," Randolph said. "Can I have a drink of water?"

Matt went into the kitchen and came back with a jug of water. He got down on his knees and tilted it up with both hands and poured some of it down Randolph's throat. Randolph's shoulders shuddered and his Adam's apple bobbed up and down. When Matt took the jug away Randolph gasped.

"I'm so scared."

"Hey," Matt said. "Don't worry about it."

"I'm scared."

"You don't need to be scared."

"What if I go to hell?"

"You won't."

"How do you know?"

"Well, are you sorry for what you've done?"

"Yes. Oh god yes."

"Do you want Jesus to forgive you?"

"Yes."

"Well, then he will. That's his job."

"How do you know?"

"How else could it be?"

"Hold my hand," Randolph said. "Hold my hand."

Randolph lifted one of his sticky, bloody hands away from his side and Matt took it.

"There was a burned man with you when you hit that bank, Billy," Matt said. "Where is the burned man?"

"I'm scared."

"I know you are, we've been through that. Where is the burned man? Hmm?"

Randolph began whispering between deep gasps, and his head drooped forward, so that his chin was resting on his chest. He kept whispering. Matt thought he might be praying.

"Hey," Matt said, shaking Randolph's shoulder. "Hey. Don't die on me yet. Who was the burned man with you when you hit the bank? Where did he go?"

Randolph was still and Matt thought he might be dead. He gave him one more shake but without much hope. As he let go of Randolph's limp hand Randolph began to whisper again.

"You chased him for ten years," Randolph said. "But did you ever talk to him?"

"Who? Winter?"

"Did you?" Randolph whispered.

"No," Matt said. "Is Winter the burned man? Is that what you're saying?"

"If you'd talked to him," Randolph said. "If you'd heard his devil talk. You'd know."

"Where is he?" Matt said. He picked up Randolph's hand and lifted it close to his mouth. "Where is he?"

"It don't matter if it's him or not," Randolph said. "It only matters if he's right about the universe."

"Where did he go?"

"The son of a bitch," Randolph said.

"Where?" Matt said.

He shook Randolph again and Randolph tipped over onto his side. Randolph was dead. Matt stood up and took a handkerchief out of his pocket with his clean hand and wiped the blood from between his fingers.

"Did he give up your man?" the lead agent asked.

"No," Matt said.

He pressed past the Pinkertons back out into the sunshine and made his way toward his horse. A young agent was holding it for him.

"Thank you, son," Matt said.

"No problem, sir," the young agent said. "Thank you. You're just like they said."

"Like who said?" Matt asked.

"In the papers."

"Oh," Matt said. "I ain't like that."

Matt stepped into the stirrup and swung himself up on his horse.

"Do you really think the burned man who hit that bank with Randolph and Collins was Augustus Winter?"

"It ain't very likely," Matt said.

"Is it possible?" the young man said.

Matt leaned back in the saddle and looked up at Signal Hill. All of the derricks rocking back and forth, back and forth, back and forth. Through the day and the night. Never stopping.

"I guess it doesn't matter," Matt said. "Whether he lived or not."

Then he lifted his hat and turned his horse and trotted back to the city.

ACKNOWLEDGMENTS

First and foremost, I would like to thank my agent, Carolyn Forde, and everyone at Westwood Creative Artists (including Jake Babad, who provided an enthusiastic early read) who worked tirelessly to get this book published. My manuscript was the dictionary definition of "unsolicited" but Carolyn took me on as a client anyway and stuck with me for the long haul. I could not have done it without you; thank you so much.

I am also deeply grateful to Melissa Danaczko, my editor at Doubleday, who worked with me in her spare time for almost a year to help me improve this book before Doubleday acquired it, and to Anne Collins, my editor at Random House Canada, for her insightful edits and for providing me with a Canadian publisher when I needed it most.

I would also like to thank Helen Reeves, a freelance editor who assisted me with an early version of this book, and Amy Ryan, my amazing copy editor at Doubleday.

I self-published an early version of *Oklahoma 1891* with the assistance of my good friend Jeremy Panda. Thank you so much, Jeremy. Thanks to Steve Sal Debus for letting us use his store for the launch, to Maggie Prodger, for doing the design, and to all of my friends who came out and supported me during those days. It meant so much to me.

Finally I would like to thank my parents, Tom and Jenny, for supporting me in everything I do, and my sister, Jessica, and her hus-

band, Will (and all of my fans in Uganda) for their kind encourage-
ment, and my wife, Cathy, and our son, Anthony, for everything, but
most of all, for this:

> *Now the house which the Walee had described, in Baghdad,*
> *was the house of that man; therefore when he arrived at his*
> *abode, he dug beneath the fountain, and beheld abundant*
> *wealth. Thus God enriched and sustained him; and this was*
> *a wonderful coincidence.*

ABOUT THE AUTHOR

Clifford Jackman was born in Deep River, Ontario, and grew up in Ottawa. He studied English literature at York University and Queen's University before attending Osgoode Hall Law School and being called to the bar in 2008. He lives in Guelph, Ontario, with his wife, Cathy, and his son, Anthony.